Catching the Tide

JUDITH LENNOX

headline
review

First published in 2011 by HEADLINE REVIEW
An imprint of HEADLINE PUBLISHING GROUP

First published in paperback in 2011 by HEADLINE REVIEW

1

ISBN 978 0 7553 4489 5

Typeset in Joanna MT by Palimpsest Book Production Limited,
Falkirk, Stirlingshire

Printed and bound by CPI Group
(UK) Ltd, Croydon, CR0 4YY

Headline's policy is to use papers that are natural, renewable and recyclable
products and made from wood grown in sustainable forests. The logging
and manufacturing processes are expected to conform to the
environmental regulations of the country of origin.

HEADLINE PUBLISHING GROUP
An Hachette UK Company
338 Euston Road
London NW1 3BH

www.headline.co.uk
www.hachette.co.uk

To Luke and Ethan: welcome.

Prologue

Summer at the Villa Millefiore

1933

At the villa, they were supposed to be resting. Both Mama and Mrs Hamilton believed it good for the constitution to lie down after lunch. Tessa thought resting a waste of time, so she found her sun hat and went outside.

The Villa Millefiore had been built in the early years of the nineteenth century. Its plastered walls had faded to a soft ochre; wisteria and vines rambled along the back of the house. Inside the villa, the marble-floored hallway was dark and cool on the hottest days. The doors leading off from it were always left open in summer to allow the air to flow.

Tessa was seventeen. She, her mother, Christina, and her sister, Frederica, who was twelve years old, had lived at the Villa Millefiore for the past four years, since their father, Gerald Nicolson, had died. It was the longest Tessa and Freddie had lived in any one house. Gerald Nicolson had been an artist, and his search for success and recognition had driven them from place to place. After his death, Mrs Hamilton, who was an old friend of Christina's, had invited the family to the villa. Somehow they had remained there. When they had first arrived, Tessa and Freddie had been so unnerved by the massive dark cupboards and the small barred windows and the owls that hooted from the nearby woodland that they had chosen to share a bedroom.

Mrs Hamilton was an Englishwoman in her mid-sixties. Rumour said that her husband had been forced to leave England after an indiscretion with a handsome footman. The Hamiltons' union had been a *mariage blanc*, an attempt to confer respectability, and the couple had had no children. After Mr Hamilton's death, his widow had remained in her vast, sprawling villa on a hillside overlooking Fiesole, where she gave luncheon parties to the English residents of Florence at which a thin soup was served, followed by a stew of doubtful origins.

The late Mr Hamilton had been a collector, though not, unfortunately for his impoverished widow, a clever one. The villa was full of strange and unsaleable treasures: the marble bust of a man, larger than life-size and missing his nose; a portrait of a boy playing a mandolin decorated with coloured ribbons; and a framed photograph of a parrot on which someone had written in faded spidery ink, 'Darling Bobo, a friend in adversity.' The public rooms displayed a decayed grandeur. The silk-upholstered sofas had faded, the windows were hung with moth-eaten damask and the walls were painted with peeling allegorical frescoes. The high ceilings were now so riven with cracks that sometimes chunks of plaster descended in a puff of powder to the floor. In the outermost reaches of the house, decay had almost completely overcome grandeur. Unused for many years and ignored by the maid, the rooms seemed to have come to terms with the soft blanket of dust that had settled over them.

From the terrace behind the house, Tessa could see the terracotta roofs and domes of Florence, shimmering in a heat haze. Later, in the evening, the chimes of church bells would drift up the hillside to the villa. She ran down the stone steps from the terrace and then headed along a path walled by box and cypress trees. To one side of the garden was the vegetable plot and an orchard; to the other lay ilex woods, banded by laurels. Beyond the garden were vine-yards and olive groves, once the property of the villa but long since sold to pay the bills.

Tessa adored the garden of the Villa Millefiore. Turn a corner, duck beneath an archway, and you might come across something extraordinary: an *allée* lined with tree peonies; a border of huge white lilies, fat bronze moths hovering above them like hummingbirds; or a pond where carp flickered gold and a fountain in the shape of a conch shell flung tassels of water high into the sky. The sound of water was everywhere, falling in a flat curtain in front of the mermaid in her grotto, rushing along narrow chan-nels, finally gathering in a deep circular pool where a stone sea monster coiled its scaly tail as water gushed from its open maw.

Tessa took off her sandals and walked barefoot around the top of the wall that surrounded the pool. A series of statues stood by the perimeter of the wall. They were Muses, perhaps, or nymphs, she could not remember. Scraps of marble clothing slid from their white breasts and plump buttocks. Their fingers grasped ineffectually at the escaping fragments of cloth. She thought their faces bland and stupid-looking.

Beneath her summer dress Tessa was wearing her bathing suit. She pulled the dress over her head and dropped it on the wall. Then she dived into the water.

The pond was deep, twenty feet or so. Mrs Hamilton had told her that in times of drought the household had drunk its water. Tessa hoped they had boiled it, because it was thick with weed. She had always to dive in without thinking, on impulse almost, before she had time to dread the soft, sticky grasp and the way that strands of weed caught like webs between her fingers and toes. Beneath the surface, the water was a dark, clouded green. In its centre was the stone column that supported the statue of the sea monster. When the Zanettis had last visited they had had a competition to see who could swim round the column the most times before returning to the surface for air. Guido had won; Tessa recalled his lithe, dark body flickering beneath the water.

The Zanettis – twenty-two-year-old Guido, his eighteen-year-old-brother Alessandro – Sandro for short – and his sister Faustina, who was fourteen – were friends of the Nicolsons and the Hamiltons. Guido's father, Domenico, was Tessa's mother's lover. Guido had told Tessa this last year, and Tessa had in turn told Freddie. Neither Tessa nor Freddie minded about Mama and Domenico. Domenico made Mama happy, in a way that their father, who had had a short temper and a sharp tongue, had not. Tessa was protective of her mother, whom she loved deeply.

Domenico Zanetti was the owner of a silk-manufacturing workshop in the San Frediano district of Florence. His wife, Olivia, was long-faced and flat-chested. Her brown and cream gowns, though of good quality, did not sit properly on her tall, thin frame – a collar gaped over angular shoulders, a rumpled sleeve fell over knobbly fingers. If asked, Tessa would have recommended a soft coral pink or perhaps sea green, which would have been kinder to Olivia's sallow complexion. Tessa suspected that Guido had told her about her mother and his father to shock her – if so, he hadn't succeeded. Brought up among the shifting population of painters and poets who had fled to Italy to escape the constricting gloom of their native northern countries, little shocked Tessa.

Her lungs were screaming, so she made for the emerald light above her. As her head burst through the surface she gasped for breath. She floated on her back, treading water, her eyes closed. They were to dine with the Zanettis that night. Tessa would wear her new violet silk frock, and Freddie would wear her almond pink. Domenico Zanetti had given Mama the silks, which had been woven in the Zanetti workshops, and Mama and Tessa had made the frocks. Tessa adored nice clothes, devoured fashion magazines whenever she had the chance and was a skilled seamstress. She decided to ask Mama if she might wear the Wakeham garnets tonight. The garnets had belonged to Mama's grandmother and had been one of the few pieces of jewellery to survive Christina's marriage to

7

Gerald Nicolson. They would match her new frock wonderfully.

A voice said, 'You have pondweed in your hair.'

Tessa opened her eyes. Guido Zanetti was standing at the edge of the pond, one foot resting on the wall.

'Your housekeeper told me everyone was asleep,' he said, 'so I thought I'd go for a walk in the garden. Come here, Tessa.'

'Why?'

'So I can get the weed out of your hair.'

There was laughter in his eyes. He looked pleased with himself, Tessa thought. Guido's profile was Roman, his curling hair was black and his eyes were a deep, dark, smouldering brown. He was wearing a light-coloured linen suit with a pale blue shirt beneath. He was a vain man, aware of his good looks – Tessa imagined him tweaking his jacket lapels into place before he left the Zanetti palazzo and smoothing his hair with his hand. He liked to keep himself aloof from the rest of them – they were children, he seemed to imply, and he was a man.

Tessa swam to the edge of the pond. Guido sat down on the wall. The touch of his fingers as he disentangled the length of weed sent a jolt through her. She sensed his awareness of his power as he looked down at her – his looks, his height, his age. She wanted to bring him down a peg, to knock him from his pedestal.

'Come for a swim,' she said.

'I can't, I'm afraid. I don't have my bathing things.'

'I meant,' she said, 'like that.'

'My clothes . . .'

'I dare you.'

She swam away from him, rolling on to her back, kicking the water with her legs. 'I dare you, Guido!' she called out.

He grinned, then took off his shoes and jacket and dived cleanly into the water. Guido swam a fast, powerful crawl. Tessa laughed as he caught up with her.

'There,' he said, spluttering water, 'I've won.' His shirt clung to him, a darker blue now. 'Now I'll have my reward.'

'I'll treat you to an ice at Vivoli.'

'That's not what I want.'

'What would you prefer, Guido?' she asked. The heat in his eyes excited her; she knew what he would say.

'I want a kiss,' he said.

'What if I don't want to give you one?' She was treading water, laughing.

'Then I'll take it anyway.'

She swam away from him as fast as she could, but he was faster, and as he caught her round the waist, she shrieked.

'A kiss,' he said. 'A kiss, my beautiful Tessa.'

His lips brushed against hers. They were face to face, bobbing in the water. Then his arms were around her and their mouths locked together, and as she closed her eyes, they sank beneath the surface.

The dim light, the soft brush of weeds. Dark shapes in the water, like the ruins of a submerged city, and her laughter fading to delight as his mouth explored hers.

She ran out of breath and he steered her to the surface. Gulping air, they both heard the sound of a door slamming as the Villa Millefiore woke up.

'Come on,' he said. 'Quickly.'

He climbed on to the wall and gave her his hand to help her out of the pond. They thrust their feet into their shoes and he scooped up his jacket and her dress. Then they ran, hand in hand, Tessa holding her fingers against her mouth to stifle her laughter, across the gravel to the grove of laurels that grew to one side of the garden. Beneath the dark green canopy, their kisses became urgent, their wet bodies pressing together as the sunlight fractured into diamonds between the leaves.

She was seventeen years old and the summer of their love affair was one of desire and delight. Of his fingers threading through hers as they walked along a path, and his foot stroking her calf beneath the dinner table. Of tiptoeing through the villa at night, between chairs and tables that loomed in the darkness like rocks in a river. A tall, square armoire stood against a wall, like a black gateway to another world; a sound, and Tessa stood motionless, all her senses alert, but it was only a mouse, scurrying to its bolthole in the panelling. When, very quietly, she opened the door to the terrace, she was struck by the warm fragrance of the night. With the light, sure steps of a dreamer, she ran across the terrace and down to the path.

Guido was waiting for her: a crunch of shoe on gravel as he turned to her. They were hidden from the house by the cypresses that stood like sentinels to either side of the path. He did not speak, but took her in his arms and kissed her. His hand stroked her hair and she felt the heat of his skin. They walked to the laurel grove, where they lay down on the soft leaf-mound. His fingers ran along the curve of her calf and the straight, narrow length of her thigh. When he stroked her belly, a fire burned inside her, and she drew him into her, welcoming him.

Afterwards, a cool breeze drifted over them as they lay in the darkness. The splash of the fountain was like distant music. She thought then that they would love each other for ever and that their joy would never end.

Part One

A Kind of Enchantment

1937–1938

Chapter One

There was a pond behind Freddie's school: in cold winters the pupils were sometimes allowed to skate there. That afternoon, when they were in a tea shop in Oxford, Freddie told Tessa about it.

'If you're in the Fifth and Sixth, you're allowed to skate for half an hour before prep. And an hour at weekends.'

'Do you remember,' said Tessa, 'when we were living in Geneva, and we used to go skating on the lake?'

'Mama used to watch,' said Freddie. 'She used to sit in the café, drinking hot chocolate.'

They often talked about their mother; had decided to, mutually and silently, three years ago, the spring after they had left Italy, after they had been told that she had died during an acute asthmatic attack. That was how you kept someone alive.

'We were staying in that funny little *pension*,' said Freddie. 'What was the landlady's name? Madame . . . Madame . . .'

'Madame Depaul.' Tessa smiled. 'We had toasted cheese

for supper every night. Madame Depaul thought that was what English people liked to eat. In the morning, after breakfast, Mama used to put on her fur coat and we'd all go down to the lake.'

Tessa had inherited her mother's fur coat. When it had first arrived from Italy, Christina's scent had lingered. Tessa had put on the coat and closed her eyes and breathed in Mitsouko and had cried, her grief and loneliness soaking the soft fur of the collar. The scent had faded a long time ago, but if Tessa shut her eyes and concentrated, she could still recall it.

'Hot chocolate's never tasted so good as it did in Switzerland,' she said.

'They make it at school but it's watery.' Freddie, who always seemed to be hungry, had wolfed down eggs on toast and since moved on to cakes.

Tessa smiled. 'Slow down, darling, we've plenty of time.'

'Sorry. It's because if you're not quick, you don't get second helpings. Don't you remember?'

Tessa did, now she thought about it. She had remained at Westdown School, where she and Freddie had been sent by their mother in the autumn of 1933, for only six weeks. She had known on the first day it would not do, but had stayed there long enough to be satisfied that Freddie would be all right without her. Now, a little over three years later, her memories of the school were of having to rush everywhere, of doing pointless things at great speed.

Since leaving Westdown, Tessa had lived in London, where she had established a career as a model. To begin with she had taken a room in a lodging house, but then, as her career had flourished, she had rented a series of flats, each one more beautiful than the last. Her current flat, which was in Highbury, was splendid, with an enormous drawing room and a luxurious bathroom. Most of the time Tessa adored London, but every now and then something sparked off a memory and she felt an intense longing for her old life. Now, she recalled skating on the frozen lake in Geneva, gliding along on one blade, her arabesque drawing a thin trace on the ice.

Glancing at the plate, she saw that only the dreary cakes – a currant sponge and a slice of Madeira – were left, so she ordered more. They had a fresh pot of tea, too, and Tessa lit a cigarette.

Freddie was eyeing the chocolate eclair, so Tessa said, 'Go on, have it.'

'It's yours really.'

Tessa shook her head. 'I mustn't. I have to think of my figure. Can't have a fat mannequin.'

'Can I have a cigarette?'

'No, darling. When you're seventeen.'

'Can I drive your car, then?'

'On the country roads, perhaps, if it's not too icy.'

Later, as they were heading back from Oxford, Tessa let Freddie drive her little red MG along the narrow, winding road and up the driveway to Westdown School. Though she sympathized with Freddie's impatience to try everything – to drive, to smoke, to drink champagne, to go to a nightclub – she was very protective of her. After all, they only had each other in the world. Mama's last words to her, when they had left for England, had been 'Look after Freddie for me, darling.'

Like some horribly mawkish Victorian novel, Tessa sometimes thought wryly to herself, but all the same a promise was a promise, and she meant to keep it.

In the school cloakroom, Freddie hung up her coat and hat.

Tessa said, 'If there's anything you need . . .'

'Nothing, thanks.'

'I'll send you some shampoo and talc. I've got masses from the Coty campaign.'

'Smashing.'

'And something from Fortnum's.'

'*Please*, or I'll die of hunger.'

A bell rang. Freddie immediately turned back into her Westdown School self, smoothing down the pleats of her gymslip.

'Prep, I'd better dash.' She hugged Tessa. 'Thanks for coming. Thanks for the tea.'

Freddie's ice skates were in the wire rack beneath her coat peg. Tessa said, 'May I borrow your skates?'

'Course you may. Put them back afterwards, though, or I'll get a black mark.'

They hugged again, and then Tessa watched her younger sister, cool, organized, dark and skinny in her navy-blue uniform and chunky indoor sandals, head out of the cloakroom and down the corridor.

Tessa took the skates out of the rack and walked round to the back of the school. The sky was a dusky mauve and the full moon was haloed by a pale wash of light. The pond lay in a grassy hollow behind the playing fields and tennis courts. A band of trees meant that the school buildings could not be seen from the pond; on its far side the down-land rose up in a frosted grey-green wave.

Tessa sat down on a bench and laced the skates. Then, with stilted steps, she walked to the pond and placed a blade on the ice. It soon came back to her, the glide and balance, how you leaned your weight into each sweep of the skate. A couple of circuits of the ice and her confidence returned.

There was a glorious freedom in being alone in the twilight. She was wearing a close-fitting black woollen jacket, edged in rabbit fur, and a matching calf-length flared skirt – perfect for skating. On her head was a black velvet beret. Her long hair spun out from beneath it as she pirou-etted. Skating, she forgot everything else – her work, her dinner date that evening with Paddy Collison – and was lost in her solitary dance on the ice.

Milo Rycroft preferred to be out of the house when his wife, Rebecca, was preparing for a party. She made him feel in the way, was short with him. And he disliked the dust, and the moving of things.

He decided to take the dog for a long walk across the fields. The day was bright but cold. He liked to walk; he enjoyed the exercise and the changing scenery, and often, if he had had a frustrating morning, a walk released his thoughts and gave him new ideas and inspiration. Some writers gardened; he walked. This was something he had once mentioned in an interview, and the journalist, an unimaginative fellow whom Milo had met a few times at his club, had suggested they take his photograph on the footpath. The photographer had grumbled, hauling tripod and camera up the muddy track, but the image that had accompanied the interview in the *Times Literary Supplement* had been appealing, and ever since, taking the dog over the hills, Milo had sometimes liked to picture himself as he had looked then – long black coat, fairish hair tousled by the wind (though Rebecca nagged him about it, he rarely wore a hat), striding ruggedly through copse and over stile, the spaniel darting ahead.

It was mid-January, and they were in the middle of a cold snap. Milo's route took him alongside ploughed fields that rose in a shallow but steady swell. The thick corduroy ridges of dark brown earth were rimed with frost. Ice, yellow-grey in colour, had formed in the ditches, and each pale stem of reed and grass was fringed with crystals. The spaniel, Julia, had a long, silky chestnut and white coat. Her breath made little puffs of smoke.

Milo, who felt that somewhere inside him was a harsh, muscular poem about Oxfordshire in midwinter, tried to think of a first line as he climbed the path, the field to one side of him and a grove of silver birches to the other. The volume of poetry on which he was working was a new venture; he had so far published only novels. At length, the trees fell away and the path reached the high downland. Pausing, he lit a cigarette as he looked around. This view always raised the spirits. The hills hung high above the blue haze of the valleys, where the spires of the churches gleamed silver. He'd do a six-miler today, he decided. He imagined saying it casually at the party that evening – 'Yes, I dashed off a poem this morning and went for a six-mile walk in the afternoon.' He liked to think of himself as a bit of an all-rounder, a modern Renaissance man – some writers had a tendency to be round-shouldered and rumpled; he had promised himself never to end up like that.

One of his favourite walks took him to the grounds of Meriel's school. Milo was always careful to keep to the footpath and to avoid anywhere where he might encounter Meriel herself. She was a difficult old trout and she could be abrasive. It was hard sometimes to believe that she and Rebecca were sisters. Milo always tried to be kind to Meriel because he could see that she'd been dealt a rough hand – the plain sister, the charmless one. Her fiancé had been killed in the war, scuppering her only chance of marriage. Milo was relieved that Meriel's work meant that she would not be able to come to his birthday party that night.

The high point of this particular stretch of countryside was known as Herne Hill. Milo, who enjoyed rummaging around in odd scraps of mythology, had found nothing to link the area with the Celtic god, but all the same the rounded hilltop had a mysterious air. It always seemed colder here, and on some days a fierce wind rushed round in circles. The opening line of his poem was almost there, just out of reach – *Herne's home: the horned god hovers* . . . No, too much alliteration, like second-rate Gerard Manley Hopkins. But he had a title for his collection: *Winter Voices*. Yes. Milo smiled, then frowned. Or should it be midwinter? He had given the first dozen poems to his secretary, Miss Tyndall, to type up the previous day. Miss Tyndall, who was in her fifties and had bushy eyebrows and a hairy mole,

21

was marvellously efficient. It had been Rebecca who had chosen her from half a dozen applicants.

A few years ago he had suggested they move from the countryside into Oxford, but Rebecca had refused to consider it. She loved their house, which had been converted from an old mill. It was in just the right place, she had pointed out, conveniently near Meriel and not too far from (or near to) her mother. And besides, people enjoyed coming to the Mill House. It wouldn't be the same – they, the Rycrofts, wouldn't be the same – if they moved into Oxford. The Mill House was part of them: people remembered their dinners and parties. *I've been invited to the Mill House*, Milo had once overheard one of his students announcing triumphantly to another. Rebecca was right, he had conceded, they might lose some cachet if they moved into Oxford. And so they had remained where they were.

As it was, he enjoyed working in Oxford once or twice a week, where a friend who lived abroad part of the year allowed him to use his study. In some ways, Milo reminded himself with a stirring of guilt, it was preferable to live out of town. Away from the Mill House, he had more freedom. He had more *leeway*, one might say, with the present arrangement. His thoughts drifted to the half-finished novel at home – stuck, stranded, not a word added for the last three weeks, and yet it was promised to his publisher in only four months' time. Perhaps if he lived in Oxford he would be able to get down to it. Perhaps the constantly changing scenery a town provided would be an inspiration.

Milo had travelled a long way to reach the Mill House. The only progeny of older parents, his beauty and precociousness had delighted and astonished his mother and father. The household had revolved round his needs; his parents had eaten dull food and deprived themselves of amusements and excursions so that they could educate their clever only son privately. The family home had been a small red-brick villa in a lifeless suburb of Reading. Milo's favourite outing had been to the public library a few streets away. Whenever journalists asked him about his background, he edited it somewhat, knowing that it was far too dull to be allowed unimproved into print.

After the end of the war, a scholarship had taken him to Oxford, where he had been socially brilliant and only a little less academically impressive. He had been a post-graduate research student, mired in an obscure aspect of the metaphysical poets, when he had written, in stolen moments, *Penelope's Loom*. When the novel had been published it had been an instant success. The *Times* reviewer had opined that the novel had 'cleverly interwoven myth and modernity – a triumph'. A second, equally successful, novel had followed. By then Milo had been able to abandon his neglected research and had begun to give a series of lectures on modern poetry for the Workers' Educational Association in Oxford, lectures that came to be immensely popular and well attended. He knew he was a good teacher – he never used notes, and often, inspired, the hour's talk branched out in a direction completely different from that which he had originally intended.

Milo still gave a course of lectures twice a year and they were still well attended. He had noticed from the beginning that there was a decidedly female slant to his audience and that his students were by no means all poor shop or office girls hungry for culture. All sorts of people – all sorts of *women* – attended his literary talks. Some were married, as he himself had been by the time the lectures had begun; others were spinsters or widows. Some were students from Somerville or St Hilda's; others were living at home with their parents, waiting for Mr Right to come along. At the end of each lecture they crowded round him, asking questions. A select group then accompanied him for a drink in the Eagle and Child in St Giles'. Rebecca had christened his female students Milo's Maenads, after the wild female devotees of the Greek god Dionysus. When she had first come up with the nickname she had had a certain expression in her eye, so Milo had laughed and said yes, that was about right, his female students were noisy, ill-dressed and not always terribly feminine. And then he had kissed Rebecca before she could say anything else.

Milo strode on across the downs. His path took him along the tops before slowly descending into the woodland that lay to one side of Meriel's school. He liked to loop through the trees before heading back to the Mill House.

Beside the wood was a small, circular pond, which in summer often dried up. Glimpsing a blur of movement through the trees, Milo walked to the edge of the copse and peered through the naked winter branches.

A girl was skating on the pond. She was dressed entirely in black, and from beneath her close-fitting black hat her long fair hair flared out like a banner. Milo stood motionless, watching her. This was not, he found himself thinking, as he gazed at her, entranced, an English scene, or even a contemporary one. The girl was absorbed in her solitary dance on the ice. He thought he detected in her glide and arabesque a rapture – one could only call it that.

He'd thought she hadn't seen him, but then she called out, 'The dog – is it yours?'

'Yes.' Milo walked to the bank. 'She's called Julia.'

'That's a pretty name.'

Her feet together, she glided across the ice towards him, and he saw that she was startlingly lovely. Her complexion was cream and roses, pinkened by the cold, and her eyes were framed by long dark lashes and straight brows.

He said, 'Do you have a dog?'

'I'm afraid not.' She smiled. 'I travel too much, but I should like to one day.' Stooping at the edge of the ice, she patted Julia. 'You are lucky. She's gorgeous.'

'Rather lively, though. She needs a long stretch each day. It's a good thing I like walking. I often come out this way. The footpath goes through the woods, you know.' Milo waved a hand in the vague direction of the Mill House. 'I live in Little Morton, about three miles away.'

'Perhaps you should be going home, then. Won't it be hard to find your way in the dark?'

'Not at all. I know these hills like the back of my hand.'

In the dusk, he could not tell the colour of her eyes. Grey, perhaps, or hazel. He said, 'When I saw you, I thought I'd been transported back in time to old Russia, perhaps, or turn-of-the-century Vienna. I thought for a moment that you were a ghost.'

She laughed. 'I'm no phantom, I'm afraid. I'm utterly real and boringly modern.'

25

He considered her and was once again awed by her beauty. 'When you were skating,' he said, 'you looked as if you were in another world.'

'I do so love skating.'

She seemed about to head back across the ice, so he said quickly, 'I'm afraid I spend far too much time sitting at a typewriter. I'm a writer, you see. My name's Milo Rycroft.'

He held out his hand; she touched it briefly. 'Oh yes, I've heard of you,' she said. And then she moved away, taking small, swaying backward steps. Her retreat was an unexpected arrow to his heart; he felt as if he was losing her.

He cried out, 'What's your name?'

'Tessa Nicolson.' Looking back at him, she smiled. 'Goodbye, Mr Rycroft. I must go and get changed. I have to drive back to London.'

The caterers had sent the wrong sort of cake – fruit instead of lemon, and Milo hated fruit cake – and the wretched vacuum cleaner had stopped working. And where *was* Milo? He could have fixed the vacuum cleaner while she phoned the caterers, and he needed to sort out the drinks.

Rebecca Rycroft picked up the phone and dialled the caterers. A brief conversation ensued – 'Lemon sponge, I particularly asked for lemon sponge,' and, 'So you're telling me it's fruit or nothing?' – and then she put the receiver down with a crash, and the hired maid who was polishing the glasses gave her a nervous glance.

Part of her enjoyed the preparation for a party and part of her loathed it. The part she enjoyed most was making up the guest list. The Rycrofts had a great many friends, and once she and Milo had decided to give a party, Rebecca spent a long time poring over her address book. It was so important to get the mix right. She enjoyed the mingling of people, the wondering whether this person or that person would make the evening go well, lifting it out of the ordinary. Sometimes she made introductions that led to a friendship or even to a love affair. You needed some quieter people too, of course – inviting only show-offs would be disastrous. And you needed new people, interesting people, not just the silly little girls who attended Milo's lectures, though they were useful, Rebecca conceded, in providing glamour.

If the drawing-up of the guest list was fun, the hours leading up to the party were always frightful. No matter how many days in advance she began her preparations there never seemed to be enough time. If she could have done everything herself it might all have worked out perfectly, but she could not. Maids must be hired and food must be got in. And so often the maids the agency sent were lazy or incompetent. This maid was weepy. Say the slightest thing to her and she threatened to burst into tears. Rebecca had ended up polishing the cutlery herself because when she had pointed out a speck of dried food on a fork the girl's lip had trembled.

She had Mrs Hobbs to help her too, thank God. Mrs Hobbs was the Rycrofts' daily. At present, she was briskly sweeping the hall rug with a broom because of the broken vacuum cleaner. After a party, Rebecca and Mrs Hobbs always shared a cigarette and a cup of tea in the kitchen. They were usually too tired to talk much, but Rebecca knew that they were bonded together by a mutual relief that it was over and that everything had gone well.

If it went well. She felt nervous every time, she reminded herself, and yet their parties were always a great success. But this time might be the exception. This time she had reason to worry, as her doubting self pointed out: Milo would fuss about the cake and the maid might have hysterics halfway through the evening, and she wasn't at all sure about the dress she had bought. It was red – not scarlet, but a proper, intense red, her favourite colour. She had bought it from her favourite little shop in Oxford, which was called Chez Zélie. It was made of a fine, fluid wool that moulded to the figure. At thirty-eight, was she too old for a red dress that moulded to the figure?

As she sat on the floor and took the vacuum cleaner apart, Rebecca ran through lists in her head. Cocktails, then champagne, then the men might like a whisky later on. They were to have an informal cold buffet, far simpler than a hot meal, and guests preferred to be able to pick and choose. Cold chicken, ham, vol-au-vents, savoury sandwiches, Russian salad, olives, potato crisps, salted almonds. Music – she must think about music. Milo usually chose the records. Rising, Rebecca tweaked a curtain and looked outside. It was almost dark – where on earth had he got to? With an irritated sigh she went back to the vacuum cleaner, holding up the hose and peering down it. Something seemed to be wedged inside, too far away for her fingers to reach. She could pull it out with a toasting fork, perhaps? No, too short.

She went outside. It was freezing, but a beautiful night

nonetheless, the clear, crisp sky speckled with stars. Frosty grass crunched beneath her feet. She took a lungful of icy air and felt calmer. Another misgiving entered her head as she opened the garden shed to search for a pea stick. January was always a rotten time to give a party – supposing people cried off because of the icy roads? Or if they had a cold or flu? No one had rung to say they wouldn't be able to make it, but then some people, especially Milo's friends, could be lax about these things.

She unearthed a pea stick from the corner of the shed and returned indoors. Delving inside the hose of the vacuum cleaner she dug out one of her stockings, enclosed inside a grey ball of dust and dog hairs. She put the stocking aside for washing, then reassembled the vacuum cleaner and called out to let Mrs Hobbs know that it was fixed. Then she walked from room to room, checking that everything was in place, adjusting a candle here, a lampshade there, tutting when she discovered, behind a chair in the hall, a discarded sweet wrapper. She had a quick peek inside Milo's study to made sure it was tidy, or at least untidy in an attractive way. While she was straightening the books and papers on his desk – just a little tidying; Milo hated anyone to touch his things – she noticed that the typescript of the new novel was still stuck at page 179. Poor Milo, he was always so miserable when his work wasn't going well. She pulled down the blind, and, leaving the room, shut the door behind her.

In the dining room, plates and cutlery were piled up on one end of the table. The sketches she had made that morning were still on the desk of her little bureau, so she gathered them up. She rarely drew nowadays, but that morning, with the glorious winter sunshine pouring through the window and Milo working in his study, she had had a sudden impulse to draw the bunch of snow-drops she had picked the previous day. She leafed through the sketches. She'd throw most of them away, but one wasn't too bad. She put it inside the bureau and crumpled up the failures. Really, she shouldn't have wasted her time.

Glancing at her watch, she saw that it was gone six. The guests would arrive in less than an hour. Rebecca poured herself a gin and lemon, then hurried upstairs to run a bath. Lying in the hot water, sipping her drink, she felt herself relax, and detected the first flickerings of pleasur-able anticipation of the party. It was an effort to get out of the bath and dry herself – she would have liked to have stayed there longer – but she hauled herself out and briskly towelled herself dry. Wrapped up in her bathrobe, she went back to the bedroom. The red dress, on its padded hanger, was draped on the wardrobe door. Rebecca stared at it doubtfully and ran her hands over her hips. A handful of Milo's Maenads were invited to the party. Milo had insisted; 'They come faithfully every week and sit patiently listening to me talking nonsense,' he had said to her. Rebecca had not yet met these particular Maenads, but their predeces-sors had so often been slim, boyish girls. Rebecca herself hadn't been slim or boyish since she was fourteen.

She sat down on the stool at her dressing table and looked into the mirror. With her hair tied up in a scarf to protect it and no make-up on, her face had a peeled, vulnerable look. She pulled at the skin at the corner of her eyes, wondering if it was becoming slacker. Then she raised her chin to inspect her neck. Both Rebecca and her sister Meriel dreaded ending up with a neck like their mother's. On Mrs Fainlight's neck the tendons stood out like taut strings beneath the crêpey skin.

Rebecca's mood sank again and she took a large swig of gin. She and Meriel were to visit their mother tomorrow. The monthly visits, the dreadful routine of them – sitting in the dimly lit detached Edwardian house while their mother prepared for the outing, and Mrs Fainlight's inevitable criticism about her daughter's driving, whichever daughter drove – were lowering to the spirits. She and Meriel might not have much in common, Rebecca had once said to her sister, but they knew that they were both, in their different ways, a disappointment to their mother. Mrs Fainlight would unfailingly be dissatisfied with the restaurant, and afterwards they would return to the house in Abingdon, where the silence, the tension, the creaking footsteps of the elderly maid, and the tea, which always tasted odd even though it was Ceylon, were all utterly oppressive. And at some point in the day, Mrs Fainlight would say, 'As neither of my daughters has seen fit to provide me with a grandchild . . .' a comment that, because of its inevitability, sometimes provoked in Rebecca and Meriel a snort of hysterical laughter that must be hastily suppressed, and yet at the same time had the power to wound.

It was, in every way, a cruel thing to say to poor Meriel. Meriel was two years older than Rebecca and her hopes of motherhood had died in 1916, at the battle of the Somme, along with David Rutherford, her fiancé. Meriel had been

31

one of that generation of women for whom there had simply not been enough men to go round. She had loved only one man since David: Dr Hughes, who attended the girls at Meriel's school. Dr Hughes was married and, as far as Rebecca knew, had no idea of Meriel's feelings for him. Rebecca had met him only once. In his late forties, he was quiet, balding and red in the face, and she had found it hard to understand Meriel's secret passion. She had once, when she had had too many martinis, told Milo about Meriel and Dr Hughes, and had regretted doing so. Milo had thought the whole thing screamingly funny, and Rebecca, who was fond of her sister, had felt ashamed of herself for sharing Meriel's secret. She lived in fear of Milo thinly adapting the situation and putting it into one of his novels.

She and Milo had never wanted children. No, that wasn't entirely true. Milo had never wanted children, wasn't remotely interested in them, but back when she had been in her early twenties and they had first been married, had he said, 'I'd like a family of six,' she might just have gone along with it. She had been so completely in love with him that anything he had said had seemed wise, and it had been important to her that they had always been in perfect agreement.

But really, it had been the right decision. They had been very poor at first, and a child would have meant financial struggle, and then, after Milo had become successful, would there have been room in their lives for a baby? Being Milo and Rebecca Rycroft, the glamorous and envied couple, took up a lot of time and energy. Somewhere along the line they had grown careless about preventing a child, yet still no babies had appeared.

Recently, Rebecca had sometimes found herself regretting that they had not had just one child. She imagined a son, bright and handsome and intelligent like Milo. He would have her green eyes, which had bewitched Milo all those years ago at the Chelsea Arts Ball. He would be called Oscar, perhaps, or Archie, and he would be an independent sort of boy, happy to go off to boarding school at the beginning of each term but equally keen to come home to his parents.

Where *was* Milo? Rebecca glanced at her watch again. Mixed with her irritation was unease. These days she always felt uneasy when she did not know where he was. Early on in their marriage, when she had caught him giving too much attention to another woman, they had had the most tremendous rows. They had yelled and cursed and thrown things – once, she had thrown a butter dish at him and it had caught him on his temple and had left a bruise, and she had felt enormously guilty. Yet there had been something enjoyable about such depth of feeling, something arousing, and during their reconciliations their lovemaking had been at its most passionate, more than making up for her agonies of jealousy, binding him to her.

But that was in the past, and for some time now their quarrels, instead of clearing the air, had left a sour taste. She was afraid that Milo did not want her as much as he once had. In the early years of their marriage, he would have done anything for her. Throughout their first summer together he had given her a red rose every day. They hadn't

33

had any money then, and some of the roses had looked as though they came from someone's garden rather than a florist's shop, but it had been such a romantic gesture.

As the years had passed, their lives had changed. The triumph of *Penelope's Loom* and its successors had enabled them to buy the Mill House. At first, they had planned the house's improvement together, and had done some of the work themselves. Some of Rebecca's happiest memories were of the two of them painting skirting boards and pasting wallpaper.

But as Milo's career had gathered pace, he no longer had time to spare for the house, so it was Rebecca who chose the wallpaper and called the plumber when a pipe sprang a leak. The Mill House had a large garden, almost a third of an acre, and this was also Rebecca's province. These days, a substantial portion of Milo's life went on without her. He went to London lunches and parties to which she was not invited. Newspaper articles were written about him and he was now and then asked to talk on the Home Service. It sometimes seemed to Rebecca that she had not kept up with him.

She knew that on the surface her life looked very enviable. But four years ago, Milo had had an affair with one of his students. He had broken it off as soon as Rebecca had found out, had sworn to her that it had been unimportant, a spur-of-the-moment thing – the girl had thrown herself at him, he'd had a couple of drinks too many, that was all. *All*. Milo's unfaithfulness had rocked her world. Their falling-out had been awful, blistering, scarring. For a month she had hardly spoken to him, and for a long time after that she had been afraid to let him out of her sight. Her confidence in her own powers of attraction had been badly shaken. Though, in time, men's glances and compliments had reassured her that she was still attractive (admiration only, never so much as a kiss, because she had only ever wanted Milo), there remained inside her a vulnerability. If she was shaken so again, she just might break. There had been no talk of divorce, but she had been terrified by the thought that he would leave her. She loved him, adored him, needed him. What would she be without him? She had always known she was not as clever as Milo – nor, obviously, as famous – and if her only assets, her looks and her sexual magnetism, were waning as she grew older, why then should he stay with her?

Somehow they had picked up the pieces and carried on. Milo had been penitent and Rebecca had eventually accepted the genuineness of his contrition. Six months after her discovery of his betrayal, they had taken a long holiday in France, and, in the sunshine and tranquillity of the Lot, had rediscovered some of their former fire. On the surface, they had gone back to being the old Rycrofts – successful, envied, in love. But Rebecca knew that something had changed. And in time Milo's penitence had been replaced by resentment. She kept an eye on him. She was always watchful, though she knew how much he hated it. But she couldn't help herself.

Rebecca made herself concentrate on her make-up. In her twenties, she hadn't bothered with foundation and powder, but she felt she needed them now. She never wore eye make-up, knowing that her curling sooty lashes required no artificial improvement. She took the red dress from the hanger, slipped it over her head, smoothed the fabric over her hips and twitched the shoulder straps into place. A slick of lipstick, and then she untied the scarf and her thick dark hair fell in luxuriant waves to her shoulders.

Downstairs, a door slammed. Milo's voice called out, 'Hello, darling! Where are you?'

Getting ready for our party, which will start in fifteen minutes, she thought furiously.

She heard him bound upstairs. The bedroom door was flung open. He stood on the threshold. Looking at her, his eyes widened.

Where have you *been*? It was on the tip of her tongue to say it, but he beat her, saying instead:

'My God, you look wonderful.'

'Do I? Do you like it?'

'Love it.'

Her doubts about the dress fell away. When he kissed her, she flinched. 'Milo, you're freezing!'

'It's perishing out there.'

'What on earth were you doing?'

'I went for a walk.' He gave a wolfish smile. 'Thought I'd work up an appetite.'

His cold mouth nuzzled her neck. She made a sound between laughter and pleasure. 'My frock . . .' she said, but he had taken her in his arms. He smelled of winter and the outdoors. His hands reached inside the two open halves of her dress and Rebecca gave a contented sigh.

They both heard the doorbell. He went on kissing her, though, until she murmured, 'Darling . . .'

36

'Damn,' he said. 'It'll be Charlie and Glyn. Always early.'

And they exchanged a glance of mutual understanding and amusement, the Rycrofts against the world.

Charlie and Glyn Mason were always the first to arrive and the last to leave. Milo had met Charlie during the war. They had been in the same regiment and had both initially had the same great good fortune in being stationed well behind the lines while the bloodbath of Passchendaele was taking place. The day before their regiment was due to be moved to the front line, Milo had been involved in a car crash. His injuries had led to him being shipped back to England to a hospital and then a convalescent home. He still had the fine white ghost of a scar on his forehead – 'I was injured in the war,' he said, if anyone asked. So it was Charlie who had experienced trench warfare and battle-field combat, and not Milo. Occasionally Milo envied him, but not often.

Now, Charlie owned three car dealerships, one in Oxford and two others in London. Though their paths through life had diverged, the two men had remained friends. Charlie had married Glyn a few years before Milo had married Rebecca; they had been each other's best man. Milo had always thought there was something a little *masculine* about Glyn Mason – the name, shortened by her from the more feminine Glynis, her cropped, curly ash-blond hair, sunburned face and taut, wiry body, which had little in the way of hips or breasts. When she was wearing slacks or tennis shorts (Glyn was a demon tennis player), you might almost have mistaken her for an adolescent boy. Milo had often wondered what it would be like to go to bed with Glyn – fun, he suspected, though not as cushioned and comforting as Rebecca. He had never tried to, of course, because he would never do that to Charlie. The Rycrofts and the Masons frequently had suppers together. The girls were supposed to be friends too, though Milo sensed that they were not really, that Rebecca and Glyn were too different and got along together for convenience's sake. And Rebecca had never been one for female friends.

Milo was beginning to regret having had a last whisky with Charlie after the other guests had left. Whisky gave him a headache. And something Charlie had said during their conversation had bothered him. Charlie had asked Milo if he and Rebecca would come to Sunday lunch to celebrate his elder daughter Margaret's birthday. 'It looks as if we're going to have to ask her boyfriend, too,' he had added. *Boyfriend*, Milo had repeated, before he could stop himself. 'It's hard work getting a sentence out of him,' Charlie had gone on. 'He sits there looking like a frightened rabbit.' *Boyfriend*, Milo had said again, stupidly, and Charlie had given him an amused glance and reminded him that Margaret was seventeen, and that Glyn had been only a year older when they had married.

Milo had recovered himself and had managed a few sensible comments. But it had shocked him that Margaret Mason, whom he still thought of as a little girl, should have a boyfriend. In a year's time, Charlie might give Margaret away in marriage – good God, another year and Charlie could be a grandfather. And as he and Charlie were the same age, the same could have applied to him, had he

38

and Rebecca had children. In two years' time, he would turn forty. Yet he still thought of himself as a young man.

Now, cleaning his teeth in the bathroom at half past one in the morning, he found himself thinking, well, thank God we didn't have children, then. The arrival of the next generation underlined the passing years like nothing else did. Parenthood aged people – he knew he looked younger than Charlie, who was already going grey.

Milo spat toothpaste into the sink and rinsed his mouth. Then he ran the cold tap and scooped up the water, splashing it on to his face. Rebecca always liked to make love after a party, and though a substantial part of him would have preferred to be alone so that he could reflect on the events of the day, he knew that would not do. Rebecca had been a bit funny earlier about him talking to Grace King, though God knows, she had no reason to be; Grace, who sat in the front row during his lectures, had a silly laugh and teeth like a rabbit.

Milo went back into the bedroom. Rebecca was still wearing the red dress. She was sitting at her dressing table, rubbing cold cream into her face. Crossing the room, he squeezed her shoulder. She pressed her cheek against his hand, leaving a small greasy smear.

'Tired?' he asked.

'Mmm. Exhausted. It went well, though, didn't it?'

'One of our best, I thought.'

'I almost had to push them out of the door at the end.'

'Keeps 'em begging for more.'

He eased down the zip at the back of her dress. She stopped tissuing off the cold cream, and gave a soft sigh as she closed her eyes. There was an anxious moment when he wondered if he'd be able to work up enough interest – he was tired, and he had drunk too much – but as he reached inside the front of Rebecca's dress to caress her breasts, an image of the girl skating on the pond came into his mind and he felt the first stirrings of desire.

And then, it was marvellous, a wonderful end to a successful evening. Rebecca had always been a passionate and responsive lover. Fifteen minutes later they lay side by side on the pillows, spent and replete.

When he had got his breath back, he glanced at her. Her eyes were shut; he thought she was sleeping. He climbed quietly out of bed and put on his dressing gown.

As he opened the door, he heard her say, 'Where are you going?'

'I've an idea for my book.'

'The poems?'

'No, no, the novel.'

'Oh. Good.' She curled up on the pillow, closing her eyes.

Milo went downstairs. He ran himself a glass of water in the kitchen, recalling some of the events of the party as he did so. He had had an argument with Godfrey Warburton, who believed that the racial purity of the English was degenerating because of the influx of refugees from Europe. He had reminded Godfrey of the various waves of peoples who had made their home in England over the centuries, and Godfrey had looked at him smugly and said, 'But that's history, dear boy. That's different.' The degenerate race that Godfrey had been referring to had been, of course, the

Jews. Milo would have preferred to have taken Godfrey Warburton off their invitation list – the man was a bigot, and patronizing as well – but unfortunately Warburton was an influential man. He wrote articles in the *Listener* and often spoke on the BBC. It was through Godfrey Warburton that Milo had been asked to take part in talks on the wireless.

Milo took the glass of water into his study and sat down at his desk. Throughout the evening, a part of him had been waiting for this time, when he could at last be free to think through the events of the day. If he could have solidified a single instant in time and kept it frozen like the ice, he would have chosen the moment he had looked out from the trees and seen the girl skating alone on the pond. Something had hurt inside him. She had seemed to point out a lack in his life.

After she had said goodbye to him, she had skated across the pond and walked with careful steps over the grass to a bench, where a pair of fur-trimmed boots had stood. Jamming his hands into his pockets – he had been by then very, very cold – Milo had made his way round the pond to the bench.

'I come up to London quite often,' he had said. 'Would you like to meet up for a drink, perhaps?'

She had been unlacing her skates. Her hair had tumbled over her face and he had been unable to see her expression.

Then: 'Yes,' she had said. 'I'd like that.'

He had felt a rush of triumph and pleasure. 'Where shall I find you?'

She had stood up, tucking the skates under one arm. 'Oh, you'll find me. Do you read *Vogue*, Mr Rycroft?'

'I'm afraid not.'

'Perhaps you should.' Then she had walked away across the frozen grass.

Milo had watched her until she had disappeared out of sight, and then he had whistled for Julia and started the long slog back to the Mill House. Tessa Nicolson had been right: it had been hard to find his way in the dark. He had twisted his ankle in a rabbit hole and become caught up in a thicket of thorns. His hands and feet had been so cold he had begun to worry about frostbite. The prospect of becoming lost in the darkness had been alarming and he had been relieved when eventually he had seen the lighted windows of the Mill House below.

The memory of the girl skating alone on the ice had remained with him throughout the evening: her rapture, her changeable, lovely face, her absorption in her solitary dance. She had looked so beautiful, so alive. A few years ago, holidaying on the west coast of Scotland, he had watched a golden eagle soar over the cliffs. Tessa Nicolson had reminded him of that.

And yet, even now, in a different part of his mind, words were forming, pushing the girl's image aside.

Milo took the top dozen pages from his manuscript, ripped them in half and dropped them in the waste-paper bin. Then, unscrewing the cap of his fountain pen, he began to write.

Tessa had driven from Freddie's school to London at great speed and so had been only three quarters of an hour late for her dinner with Paddy Collison. After dinner, they had

had a drink, and then half a dozen friends had joined them. Then they had all gone on to a Piccadilly nightclub.

Now it was three o'clock in the morning, and because it was hot in the nightclub, Tessa had slipped outside to smoke a cigarette. Others might consider an evening complicated – overcomplicated, perhaps – if two or three of their old lovers were present at the same time, as well as a number of admirers, but Tessa thrived on that sort of thing. She liked her lovers to feel as she did, that love was a delightful and exhilarating game and was not to be taken too seriously.

This was why the men she went to bed with tended to be older than her. Raymond Leavington, for instance, had been thirty-three, fifteen years older than Tessa herself, when they had become lovers. She had met him a few months after she had left Westdown School and had come to live in London. At the same time, she had embarked upon her career as a model.

Tessa's affair with Ray had lasted for six months. Back then, Raymond had been unhappily married to Diana, his second wife. Though Tessa knew that many would condemn her for going to bed with a married man, her conscience was clear. She had never tried to seduce a happily married man. In fact, she never tried to seduce anyone. She never thought of herself as a temptress, she was just Tessa, and though it would have been disingenuous of her to pretend that she did not know that men were attracted to her, and that she did not enjoy their pursuit, she left the chasing to them. She always made it perfectly clear from the outset that she was not looking for anything lasting. She would have hated to have been pinned down. She knew that going to bed with a man involved a certain amount of risk, tried to remember to take precautions, but had had a few pregnancy scares, though luckily they had not come to anything.

Ray was a dear, sweet man, and after their affair had ended, they had continued to be friends. Tessa preferred it that way, found it hard to take seriously what she called to herself 'scenes' – protestations of undying love, declarations that without her, life was not worth living. She liked to remain on good terms with her ex-lovers: it was more civilized that way, she thought. She intended neither to hurt nor to be hurt. Parting from Guido Zanetti had hurt her; that he had not responded to the letters she had written him from England had hurt her more. She had poured out her love for him in those letters, but after a while, receiving no reply, had stopped writing, had hardened herself and begun to see the affair more clearly. Domenico Zanetti's elder son would never have been allowed to marry Domenico's mistress's daughter. Never, ever.

Three and a half years ago, leaving Italy, she and Guido had not even been able to properly say goodbye. The end of the affair had been shockingly quick. Mama had told her and Freddie that they were to go to school in England; at the same time, Domenico had sent Guido away on an extended business trip. Their farewells had had to be made in front of their two families.

It had not taken much insight to work out that Mama and Domenico must have found out that they had fallen in love. Mama had sent her and Freddie away to school in England *because* of Guido. That last Italian summer, absorbed in each other, they had not been careful. Each day they had

44

shared the same single ambition: to be alone together. Five minutes stolen from beneath the watchful gaze of mothers and chaperones had been a delight. Half an hour had been ecstasy. On picnics and family outings they had crept away from the others to kiss and caress in the shelter of a secret valley or the shade of a crumbling Etruscan wall.

By that time, her mother's asthma had been chronic, her struggle for breath visible, so Tessa had not argued with her. And anyway, she could not have allowed Freddie to make the journey to England alone. Leaving Italy, she had felt a dreadful emptiness and a sense of dislocation in being taken away from so much that she held dear. She had hated the school, a place of mist and rain and falling leaves. She had hated being treated like a child, had had nothing in common with the other girls, and silently, at night, in the dormitory she had shared with five other pupils, she had wept for Guido.

And so, to London. She had continued to miss Guido; one reason why she had gone to bed with Raymond Leavington had been because she had thought it might help her to forget. There had been other reasons – Raymond's kindness, his ebullience and love of life, his generosity. After Raymond, there had been André, whom she had met when in Paris for a photo shoot. André had been very rich, good-looking and amusing. He had kept a yacht at Cannes and a racing car at Le Mans. It had been André who had given her the MG, for her nineteenth birthday. They both had busy lives and André was married, so there had been a need for discretion. Their affair had lasted intermittently for eighteen months.

Tessa was very good at being discreet. She disliked gossip, had never seen the need for tittle-tattle. She knew that people talked about her – well, let them talk, she didn't care – but she never discussed her love affairs with anyone, not even Freddie. What happened between lovers was private, she believed. She had become good at keeping the curious guessing.

After she and André had parted, there had been others. She had met Max Fischer a year ago. Max had been a celebrated photographer in Berlin until the rise of the Nazis to power in 1933. He was Jewish, and had not kept his dislike of the new regime to himself, and had been forced to flee Germany in 1935 to avoid imprisonment or worse. Max had quickly become Tessa's favourite photographer. He was intelligent and entertaining and in many ways the ideal lover: considerate, imaginative and just a little detached.

But she had discovered that there was in Max a bedrock of melancholy. Sometimes he drank too much – a lot of men did that, but Max drank alone, locking himself into his flat and emerging days later, white and shaking. His cynicism hid a profound disillusion, and for once Tessa had found herself out of her depth. She had glimpsed a despair in Max that she could not reach, though they continued to be friends and now and then went to bed together, for old times' sake.

A couple of months after she had finished with Max, Tessa had met Julian Lawrence. Divinely handsome and utterly adoring though he was, Tessa had to admit that Jules had been a mistake. He had a habit of sending her ridiculously lavish presents that she knew he could not afford and always returned. All too soon he had wanted an engagement, a wedding, children. He had not even tried to understand when she had turned down his proposal, and their conversation had dissolved into anguished recriminations. Too young and too earnest, he had made an *enormous* scene the night Tessa had ended the affair.

A man like Julian Lawrence would probably think her a hard-faced bitch if she told him the truth – that her career was more important to her than any man – but that was how it was. Tessa loved her work and knew she was good at it. She had always loved clothes, knew that they were important because they gave a woman the confidence to make her own way in the world. She knew how to show a frock to its best advantage and how to switch on that inner light that would illuminate a photograph and make it seize the onlooker's attention. She loved everything about her job; most of all, she loved to travel. She had sailed to New York three times on an ocean liner, and worked in Paris for several months of the year. On her last visit she had flown there in a tiny plane that had landed on the runway of Le Bourget aerodrome, bobbing like thistledown.

Tessa's career had been successful almost from the moment she had signed on at the agency. She had begun by working as a mannequin in department stores and at fashion shows. She had modelled for Chanel, Molyneux and Schiaparelli, and was now much in demand as a photographer's model. She continued to do fashion modelling, but preferred photographic work, which appealed to the theatrical in her. London, Paris and New York *Vogue* had featured her in fashion articles. She appreciated the way in which a clever and creative photographer such as Max Fischer was able to make her into something other than she was.

Her life was glamorous, exciting and varied. She had a good income; the previous year she had earned more than a thousand pounds. Dress designers gave her beautiful gowns, and cosmetic houses offered gifts of scent and lipstick. She spent freely, saved little, saw no reason not to live for the moment. Though she had received many proposals of marriage, she had never been tempted to accept any of her suitors. Why should she want marriage when she had everything she desired and her independence besides? Living with someone else would involve compromise and sacrifice, and she had never been remotely interested in either. She wanted to be successful, rich and famous, to travel and to have lots of lovely clothes, and she believed that marriage would get in the way of all that. Husbands liked telling their wives what to do, she had noticed. Tessa didn't intend ever to let anyone tell her what to do.

Her current lover was called Paddy Collison. They had met at Newmarket racecourse – Paddy loved horse-racing. He was tall and strong-looking, with reddish hair, watchful hazel eyes, a firm jaw and a hard mouth. He had lived abroad for much of his life, managing tea plantations first in India and then in Kenya. He had the confidence that went with his colonial background and an unconventional streak as well.

One of the qualities that had attracted Tessa to Paddy was his fearlessness. He courted danger, thrived on it. It was Paddy who had flown her to Paris. He loved to fly, to ride, to hunt, to sail a boat, to swim in a stormy sea. There was nothing he wouldn't pit himself against.

Tessa recognized a corresponding quality in herself. Other girls complained of butterflies in their stomachs before a fashion show, but she never felt nervous. She had enjoyed driving André's racing car round the track at Le Mans just as much as she had enjoyed the flight to Paris.

Tessa looked up at the stars. She, who was so often surrounded by people, found a delicious liberty in being alone. She let her mind roam back to the pond behind Freddie's school. She had revelled in her solitude, drawing circles in space as the night folded round her and the sky became peppered with stars.

She thought about Milo Rycroft. An attractive man, with his tousled fair hair and hooded eyes. *When I saw you, I thought I'd been transported back in time to old Russia, perhaps, or turn-of-the-century Vienna. I thought for a moment that you were a ghost.* How ridiculous, but at the same time, the image had captivated her.

Tessa dropped her cigarette end on to the paving stones of the tiny courtyard and crushed it beneath the sole of her high-heeled shoe. As she went back into the club, she wondered whether she would see Milo Rycroft again. She couldn't help hoping she would.

Chapter Two

Milo had completed his novel, *The Fractured Rainbow*, in a rush of creativity, in only eight weeks. He always took his manuscripts to his editor, Roger Thoday, in person. He and Roger had a long-established and pleasant routine. Milo caught the train up from Oxford, arriving at Roger's office in Golden Square in the late morning. They had lunch at the Café Royal – champagne to celebrate the delivery of the manuscript, wine with the meal and brandies afterwards.

Milo had told Rebecca that he intended to stay the night in London. He planned to visit a friend who was confined to home following an operation, and there was some research he needed to do at the British Museum.

Both these things had been true. But there was also, rising to the forefront of his mind like a bubble floating to the surface of water, Tessa Nicolson. He had not attempted to contact her since their meeting at the pond. The day after, hung-over and enduring the vague melancholy that for him often followed a party, he had known he must not see her again. The scene at the frozen pond must remain as it was, a fleeting, perfect moment. There had been a poetry about their encounter that in his pensive frame of mind seemed best left alone – to try to extend perfection would be like overworking a stanza of verse. And besides, if Rebecca were to find out, even if nothing at all happened, the consequences would be awful. Milo still shuddered when he recalled her fury following her discovery of his affair with Annette Lyle. Rebecca had a temper and she didn't easily forgive. Milo found her alarming when she was angry. He was used to her admiration of him, and her cold contempt had been hard to bear. Rebecca was a strong woman, and wounding her had been like seeing a lioness brought down, abased. He had had to avert his eyes. Since Annette, he had been careful. Which was not to say that he had always been good.

Do you read Vogue, *Mr Rycroft?* Tessa Nicolson had asked him. His first visit to Oxford after their meeting at the pond, he had bought a copy of the magazine. There had been a photograph of her on the front cover; a paragraph inside had informed him that Miss Nicolson was a mannequin and photographer's model. In the portrait she was sitting at a table in a café, one slender upraised wrist heavy with gold and enamel bracelets. She looked glacially beautiful, almost austere.

Over the ensuing weeks, Milo had written like a fury, emerging from his study only to eat, to go to Oxford one evening a week to give his lecture, and to clear his head for the next burst of writing by walking across the hills.

Though he sometimes walked as far as the pond, Miss Nicolson was never there. As the weeks passed, his initial resolve began to weaken and he became aware that his decision not to contact her was a postponement, not an ending. Almost unconsciously he had made a pact with himself: finish the book and his reward would be to call her. In the elation that accompanied the completion of his novel, he came to believe that he deserved it.

Over lunch, Milo and Roger Thoday talked about the London literary scene, the deteriorating political situation, and Roger's forthcoming holiday, salmon fishing on the Spey. At the end of an excellent meal, they shook hands and Roger headed back to his office. Milo made for a phone booth, where he asked the operator for Tessa Nicolson's number. A wait while he was put through, and then a maid answered. Milo gave her his name. There was a longer wait, during which he heard talk and laughter and music, reduced to a tinny thread by the telephone line. Enclosed in the phone booth, Milo found himself wondering whether Miss Nicolson would remember their brief meeting at the pond.

There was a crackle as the receiver was picked up again. Tessa Nicolson said, 'Mr Rycroft, I thought you'd forgotten me.' Her voice was low and amused. Hearing it again made the hairs stand up on the back of Milo's neck.

'How could I forget you?' he said. 'How are you, Miss Nicolson?'

'I'm very well. And you? Do you still go for walks in the dark?'

He chuckled. 'As a matter of fact, I've just finished my novel. I delivered it to my publisher today.'

'Congratulations. Does that mean you're in London?'

'Yes, I am.' Milo's mouth was dry. 'I wondered whether you had time for that drink we spoke of.'

A silence; his heart pounded. Then she said, 'Yes, why not? Where shall I find you?'

Milo suggested the Savoy. It wasn't the sort of place his friends went to. The people he knew frequented the Café Royal and pubs in Bloomsbury or raffish Fitzrovia. They thought the Savoy overly obvious, the haunt of braying aristocracy and empty-headed actresses. Milo, who had a fondness for glitter and gloss, had always liked the American Bar.

He caught a taxi to the Strand, ordered himself a drink, and waited. And waited. His elation left him and his mood lowered during the hour and a half he sat alone, nursing several martinis, waiting for Miss Nicolson to join him. She had a Highbury phone number – how long could it take a cab to drive from Highbury to the Strand? Had she had second thoughts after putting down the phone? Had she found something more interesting to do?

And then, at last, she arrived. She was wearing a green and white frock and a green jacket and her blond hair was pinned up beneath a green hat. She looked breathtakingly lovely. It had crossed his mind, waiting for her, that seeing her for a second time he might be disappointed, that the moon and the ice might have worked an enchantment on their first encounter. But as he stood up to greet her any reservations fell away, and he felt marvellous, the envy of every other man in the bar.

It went rather downhill from there, though. She seemed to know everyone else in the room. People drifted over to their table, saying, 'Darling Tessa,' and 'How *are* you?' and kissing her on the cheek. It was fascinating at first, watching Tessa Nicolson in action, seeing how she devoted to everyone an equally generous measure of her vitality and charm, never flagging, always effervescent, but soon he began to feel just one of the crowd, and then rather headachy and tired. At six o'clock Tessa had an engagement, and in the end Milo scrubbed his plans of staying on and went home to the Mill House instead. Sitting in the railway carriage, his head pounded and his mouth tasted foul, and he was mortified to realize, as he watched the London suburbs sweep by, that he had hoped – foolishly, he now saw – to be special to her.

Yet at the last moment, as he had taken his leave of her, she had offered him a consolation prize. 'I'm having a party,' she had told him. 'It's to celebrate my birthday. It's on the twenty-sixth, at the 400. If you'd like to come, Milo, please do.'

'Are those new curtains?' asked Mrs Fainlight. 'I thought there were blue curtains in this room.'

'I had these made up for spring, Mummy,' said Rebecca. 'Don't you think they look cheerful?'

'You must have money to burn, Rebecca – new curtains just because it's spring! And I've always disliked yellow.' Mrs Fainlight returned to her roast lamb.

Rebecca, Milo and Meriel were celebrating Mrs Fainlight's birthday on March 21st. After lunch there would be the opening of presents, followed by cake and tea, and then Meriel would drive her mother home. Rebecca had once tried inviting the Masons in the hope of making the day more fun, but it had been a disaster: Mrs Fainlight had taken a dislike to Glyn and had been very rude to her.

Milo said, 'Would anyone like another drink?'

'I never drink wine at lunchtime,' said Mrs Fainlight.

Milo refilled Rebecca's glass. 'Meriel?'

'Yes please.'

Mrs Fainlight said, 'I always remember young Tommy Mackintyre. He was a clever boy and from a good family. He ruined his life through drink.'

'I'm sure none of us intends to end up on Skid Row, Mother,' said Rebecca.

Mrs Fainlight tutted. 'Slang, Rebecca, really . . .' She gave Milo a narrow look, as if holding him responsible.

'Well,' said Meriel heartily, 'you've a lovely day for your birthday, haven't you, Mummy?'

'Have I?' Mrs Fainlight peered towards the window. The weather was fine and bright. On the lawn, the daffodils were coming into bud.

Meriel persevered. 'It's spring at last. We all feel better when the sun's shining.'

'If I had a *grandson* to share my birthday, it might mean more to me. I find it hard to be cheerful when I know the family is going to *die out*.'

Meriel took a handkerchief from her sleeve and blew her nose loudly. The conversation ground to a halt and the four of them ate in silence.

It was Meriel who recovered first. 'Joanna Moore is sickening for German measles, I'm sure of it,' she said. 'She had a rash and a temperature this morning.'

'Oh dear,' said Rebecca. 'That must be a nuisance.'

'The wretched parents don't always tell the truth, I'm afraid. They sign the form and send it back and it's complete nonsense.'

'What form?'

'The quarantine form. Joanna told me that her brother went down with German measles over Easter. Her parents should never have sent her back to school. Of course, Mrs Moore isn't Joanna's real mother. You remember I told you the first Mrs Moore ran off with a lounge-bar crooner.'

'*Meriel*,' said Mrs Fainlight.

'It's all right, Mummy, everyone knows. It was in all the papers.'

Meriel was a dreadful gossip. Rebecca was always cautious about confiding details of her personal life to her sister. She had never, for instance, told Meriel about Milo's affair with Annette Lyle. As this thought crossed her mind, Rebecca's gaze turned back to Milo. It was clear that he had given up taking any part in the conversation. He and her mother had never got on, and Rebecca could have put his preoccupation down to boredom had not his features taken on the expression of dreamy absence that she had noticed more than once during the last few weeks, and which made her suspicious.

Meriel was still talking. 'Apparently they're holidaying in the south of France.'

'Who are?'

'The Moores, of course.'

'Oh, I see,' said Rebecca.

57

'It's a frightful nuisance, what with the house matches coming up. Joanna is one of our best attackers.'

'Oh dear.'

'Anne's are very weak this year but Victoria has some strong players.' Westdown School's four houses were named after English queens. 'I shall probably have to put Imogen Carstairs in the team and she really isn't up to it. Thank goodness for Freddie Nicolson – she played marvellously at the last match.'

Milo's head jerked up. 'Nicolson?'

'Yes, Freddie Nicolson,' said Meriel, adding rather sarcastically, 'I didn't know you were interested in lacrosse, Milo.'

Milo said, 'But a *boy*. I didn't think *boys* played lacrosse.'

Meriel laughed. 'No, no, you've got the wrong end of the stick – oh dear, what a frightful pun! Freddie's a girl. Her name's Frederica, but we always call her Freddie. And lacrosse was of course originally played by men. The Red Indians invented the game, though it has changed considerably since then . . .'

Meriel continued her monologue about the origins of lacrosse. Milo was still staring at her. Catching Rebecca's eye, he gave his most charming smile and said, 'Never understood sport. Don't suppose I ever will.' Then he tipped the remainder of the contents of the wine decanter into his glass and drank it. Rather quickly, Rebecca noticed.

After lunch, while Milo escaped to his study and Mrs Fainlight dozed on the sofa, Rebecca and Meriel walked round the garden.

'How's your cold?' asked Rebecca.

'It's nothing much. I'm sure it's getting better. I thought of crying off, but . . .' Meriel shrugged.

Shorter and stouter than Rebecca, Meriel was wearing a skirt and jacket of scratchy buff-coloured tweed. Beneath the jacket she wore a hand-knitted short-sleeved brown sweater. She never used lipstick or powder and her hair was cut by the same girl who came into the school once a month to trim the pupils' hair. Meriel's eyes were speedwell blue and her complexion was good. Rebecca always felt she did not make the best of herself, and had once suggested they go to Town together to buy clothes, but Meriel had told her that she hated shopping and had no wish to spend her afternoon off tramping round Selfridges.

Now, Meriel's nose was red and peeling. Rebecca thought she looked tired. 'I'm so glad you came, anyway,' she said, and gave her sister a quick hug. 'How's your week been?'

'Pretty frightful. I had a run-in with Miss Lawson yesterday.'

Miss Lawson was the deputy headmistress. Younger than Meriel, she had been recruited to the staff of the school in the previous year.

'What happened?'

Meriel told her story. She had planned to send several chairs from the senior girls' common room for refurbishment, but Miss Lawson had countermanded her order to save the school money. Rebecca sensed that her sister's fury was born of her resentment at Miss Lawson's interference in what Meriel looked upon as her home.

To cheer her up, Rebecca asked after Dr Hughes.

'I'll have missed him this morning,' Meriel said. 'He was going to call to see Joanna.'

'That's a shame.'

'We had a nice little chat on the phone. Apparently Deborah is unwell again. He may have to give up the choir.'

Poor Meriel, thought Rebecca. Her romance, if it could be considered such a thing, had to survive on weekly choir practice at the church (Meriel had a powerful contralto voice and Dr Hughes sang bass) along with occasional cups of tea in Meriel's flat when Dr Hughes called at the school to see a pupil. How awful, Rebecca often thought, to be content with such dribs and drabs.

The sisters' upbringing had been austere. Though the family had not been badly off, economy had been seen as a virtue and had always been practised. Food had been plain, and there had been little heating in the Fainlights' large and draughty home. Rebecca and Meriel had been expected to walk the three miles to and from their day school whatever the weather. There had been an expectation that they do well academically; any failure to do so had been met with disappointment and displeasure. Criticism improves character, Mr and Mrs Fainlight had believed. Though their father had despised religion, he had sent his daughters to an Anglican school. Both Rebecca and Meriel recalled their first few weeks there as an agony of confusion and humiliation – their uniforms, made cheaply by a local seamstress, had been different to those of the other girls, and their ignorance of the Lord's Prayer had been commented on. They had learned to conform – Rebecca, who had always been a pretty girl, had even become popular – but they had known they were different.

At the age of twenty, Rebecca had been accepted to study at art college. Two years later she had met Milo at the Chelsea Arts Club Ball. The following year she and Milo had married. The sisters' father had died in 1927, and afterwards Mrs Fainlight had sold the large house and bought the smaller one in Abingdon. At first Rebecca had hoped that the move, which had brought Mrs Fainlight nearer to her daughters, might coincide with a softening in her mother's character. Yet she remained hard to please. Rebecca and Meriel treated their mother's moods warily. If she was set on being cross and disappointed, then she would find something to be cross and disappointed about. But somehow one kept on trying because there was always the hope that this time it might be different. It was all so exhausting.

They had walked to the river that ran along the bottom of the garden. Rebecca looked back to the window of Milo's study. He was on the phone; she was almost sure – she squinted – that he was on the phone. Who was he calling?

'Monica's invited me to Cleethorpes for half-term,' said Meriel. 'I wasn't going to go because the train fare is a bit steep, but I could do with a few days away. Sea air is always so refreshing, don't you find, and . . .'

Rebecca saw that Milo had put down the phone. He had *rushed* rather to his study after lunch, she thought. Had he done so to make a phone call? Her memory reverted to that odd snippet of conversation at the lunch table. What had Meriel said that had attracted Milo's attention? She had been talking about lacrosse, about a girl in her house, a

61

girl called Freddie Nicolson. Milo had been confused because he had thought that Meriel was talking about a boy. So that was all, nothing to worry about. He had just been muddled.

But she did worry. Running the conversation over and over in her head as Meriel spoke of Cleethorpes and Monica's bungalow, Rebecca remained uneasy. Milo could not possibly be infatuated with this girl, Freddie Nicolson. She was a schoolgirl, for one thing, and his tastes had never lain in that direction, and anyway, he had thought she was a boy, so he couldn't ever have met her. Unless, it occurred to her, that had been a ruse . . .

Rebecca had been looking at Milo when Meriel had mentioned Freddie Nicolson's name. And his expression had not been one of bewilderment. He had looked shocked, Rebecca recalled. Milo had been alarmed.

The 400 Club was in Leicester Square, next to the Alhambra Theatre. Milo went downstairs to the cellar in which the nightclub was housed and gave his coat and hat to the cloakroom attendant.

One of his friends had once remarked that going into the 400 was like returning to the womb. The friend had been a psychotherapist, a Freudian, but Milo could see what he had meant. The walls of the nightclub were covered in dark red silk, the carpet was dark red and so were the curtains. The only lights were the candles on the tables and the small spotlights by which the swing band read their music.

Tessa Nicolson, too, was wearing red. Milo stood at the

perimeter of the room, watching her as she danced. Her evening frock was a deep, dark purplish crimson – the colour, he thought, of the best claret – and she wore a necklace of large dark red stones. Her partner was a tall, tough-looking ginger-haired man. When the foxtrot came to an end, during the ripple of applause, the ginger-haired man kissed Tessa. The kiss lasted until Tessa pulled away.

Milo threaded through the tables. 'Congratulations, Tessa,' he said to her. 'Happy birthday.' Bending his head, he kissed her hand.

'Milo, so old-fashioned.' She smiled at him. 'I'm so pleased to see you. Dance with me, won't you?'

The band struck up 'Night and Day'. Couples squeezed on to the dance floor.

He said, 'Are all these people your friends, Tessa?'

'Yes, most of them.'

'Are you enjoying your party?'

She wrinkled her nose. 'Not much. Paddy's in a foul temper.'

'Paddy?'

'Paddy Collison.' Her gaze flicked to the table where the red-haired man sat, smoking. 'Paddy works for Lipton's,' she explained. 'They've told him they want him to stay in London instead of going back to Kenya. He's furious. We went to dinner earlier, at a friend's house, and he was rude to everyone.' Tessa's eyes, which were flecked green and hazel and gold, were full of laughter. 'Most of the other guests were Cambridge intellectuals. One had long hair and was wearing a spotted bow tie. Paddy hated them. He rather prides himself on his iron masculinity.'

Milo wondered whether Paddy Collison was Tessa's lover. As they danced, he could feel the movement of tendon and muscle through the thin silk sheath of her dress.

He said, 'I have a suspicion that we have a mutual acquaintance, you and I.'

'Who?'

'Meriel Fainlight.'

Tessa's eyes widened. 'Miss Fainlight? You know Miss Fainlight?'

'Meriel's my sister-in-law.'

'Good Lord.' She laughed. 'What a coincidence.'

'Not really. That night we met at the pond, you were visiting your sister, weren't you?'

'Yes, I was. Freddie and I had been out for tea. I couldn't resist borrowing her skates.'

'I'm very glad you did, or we might never have met.'

'I'm rather fond of Miss Fainlight. She seems such a lovely, practical person.'

Milo, who had never in all his years of acquaintance thought of Meriel as lovely, said, 'She was a nurse in the war, did you know that?'

'No, I didn't. I imagine she'd make a very good nurse.' Tessa gave him a close look. 'What? Don't you get on?'

'Meriel can be very brusque.'

'Brusque, Milo . . .' Amused, she studied him. 'Do you mean that Miss Fainlight doesn't respond to your charms?'

'I always think she disapproves of me.'

'You can't assume a woman disapproves of you just because she doesn't fall in love with you.'

He smiled. 'No, I suppose not.'

'And even if she did disapprove just a little, would you really mind?'

'I like to be liked, don't you?'

'Of course, it's unpleasant to be disliked. But I never seek out approval.'

The dance came to an end, and they clapped. Paddy Collison rose from his seat. The band struck up 'Let's Fall in Love' and Collison seized Tessa's hand, saying, 'Come on.' He gave her wrist a little jerk, pulling her on to the dance floor.

Milo felt a rush of anger. He wondered whether to punch Paddy Collison, but Collison was broader and taller than he, and he strongly suspected it would end in humiliation. He made his way back through the tables to the edge of the room, where he lit a cigarette. The skirt of Tessa's dress flared as she danced and the dark red stones of her necklace glittered. She was smiling; perhaps she didn't mind being manhandled by a brute like Collison. As he stood on the margins of the party, Milo's gaze rested on her, his yearning for her mingling with the jealousy and dislike he felt for her partner.

He considered what she had told him. Frederica Nicolson was Tessa's sister, as he had suspected, which meant there was a connection, however tenuous, between Tessa and Rebecca. Which was dangerous. Christ, it had given him a shock when, in the middle of that dire lunch, Meriel had mentioned the name Nicolson.

Tessa was still dancing with Collison. Milo glanced at his watch, then stubbed out his cigarette in a nearby ashtray and left the room. He had given his ticket to the cloakroom attendant when a voice behind him said, 'You're not leaving already, are you, Milo?'

He turned, and found himself face to face with Tessa. 'My last train's in half an hour,' he said. But there was something in her eyes, an openness, an expectation, that made him add, 'Though I could always stay overnight at my club.'

'Good.' Opening a tiny gold bag, she took out a cloak-room ticket.

'What are you doing?'

'I thought we could go for a walk together.'

'That would be delightful. But what about your party?'

She shrugged. 'I'm tired of it.'

'You can't leave your own party.'

'Can't I?'

With a laugh, he said, 'Oh, why not? But what about Collison?'

Another shrug, this time accompanied by a little outbreath of air, signifying, Milo thought triumphantly, *Paddy can wait.*

The attendant passed them their coats: peach-coloured satin with shoulder pleats; black wool for Milo. He said, as they climbed the stairs, 'I wanted to hit him.'

'If only you had, Milo! It would have livened things up.' Tessa slipped her hand through his arm as they emerged into the cool night air. 'But perhaps it's as well you didn't. I'm afraid you'd have come off rather badly. Paddy was a boxing champion when he was younger.'

It was drizzling; he held his umbrella over them. 'Where would you like to go?' he asked.

'Anywhere. I love London at night, don't you?'

They headed along Charing Cross Road. A taxi drew up by the kerb and a man in evening dress and a girl in a cloud of pale green tulle climbed into it. A woman wrapped in layers of frayed knitting and a ragged overcoat slept in a doorway; Milo dropped a coin into the chipped teacup beside her.

As they reached Shaftesbury Avenue, he said, 'I'm rather fond of Soho, but perhaps you'd rather go somewhere else. We could take a taxi to the Savoy if you like.'

'I often shop in Soho,' said Tessa. 'There's such lovely Italian food.'

'It's different at night.'

'I *love* the night.'

They turned into Romilly Street. Away from the glitter of the theatre district, the streets were enclosed and dark, and had a sense of mystery – and menace, perhaps. Although Milo was familiar with Soho by day, at night the criss-cross of narrow streets seemed to belong to a foreign land. In a small shop window, differently coloured Chinese ginger jars lined up on a shelf, dragons breathing fire on their bulbous ceramic bellies. A couple, arm in arm, disappeared into a narrow doorway, and there was an echo, something between a laugh and a scream. From an upper storey came the wail of a saxophone.

As they walked along Greek Street, a dozen sailors, shouting to each other in some Eastern European language – Polish, perhaps – ran down the road towards them. Milo steered Tessa into the shelter of a doorway as the sailors passed them, drunk, roaring, laughing. Her scent mingled with the flat scent of the rain, and he was close enough to her to see, in the flicker of the streetlights, the fine grain of her skin.

He bent and brushed his lips against hers. She linked her arms round the back of his neck and they kissed. Beneath the peach-coloured coat his hands rested on her hips, and he felt the warmth of her flesh and the smooth musculature of her narrow body.

She shivered. 'You're cold,' he said. 'We should head on.'

In the aftermath of their kiss, a tremor ran down his own spine. He put his arm round her, drawing her to him as they walked along the empty street. The rain sheened the tarmac to black satin. She fitted into the crook of his arm, and the weight of her head, resting against his shoulder, gave him such pleasure he would have liked to go on walking for ever.

They went to an all-night café in Soho Square. Inside, Tessa gave herself a little shake, as if the brighter light had startled her. A handful of people were sitting at the half-dozen tables. Milo fetched tea from the counter, then sat down beside Tessa.

'I've a birthday present for you,' he said.

'Milo! How exciting.' She smiled brilliantly.

He took a manila envelope out of his coat pocket and offered it to her. 'Happy birthday, Tessa.'

She opened the envelope and drew out the folded pages of foolscap inside. She read out the title typed on the top page.

'*Midwinter Voices* by Milo Rycroft. Is this yours, Milo? How wonderful!'

'It's the manuscript of my poems. I'm wondering whether it's horribly conceited of me to inflict them on you. Perhaps you hate poetry.'

'No, not at all.'

'Or you may simply not think much of mine. In which case you may use them to light the fire or chuck them in the bin. Whatever suits.'

'I'm very touched.' Beneath the table she squeezed his hand.

'You'll be the first person to read them. Not even my editor has seen them. They're a new venture. I've only written novels before.'

'Am I a new venture, Milo?'

'What do you mean?'

Her expression was serious. 'You're married, aren't you?'

'Yes.' Shame and confusion; he dropped his head. 'I should have told you,' he muttered. 'There hasn't seemed to be the right moment. I'm sorry. I didn't set out to deceive you.'

'I didn't think you did, darling. But I bought one of your books, you see.'

He couldn't help asking, 'Which one?'

'*The Dark and Distant Hills*. Because of Tuscany. I was brought up there.'

'Were you? How marvellous. We spent a summer there, while I was writing the book. I loved it. I wouldn't have minded staying for ever, but Rebecca wanted to go home.'

'It said on the dust jacket that you were married. But I'd guessed that anyway.'

'How?'

'You look married, Milo.'

Surprised, he let out a roar of laughter. 'What do you mean?'

'You look well cared for. Bachelors have frayed sleeves and grimy collars.'

'Do they?'

'Perhaps not the rich ones, with valets.'

'I've no valet, I'm afraid.' He felt relieved that they were moving away from a dangerous subject.

'I adored your book. So beautiful, so magical.'

'Thank you. Were you born in Italy, Tessa?'

'Near Siena. We moved around a lot. My father was always hoping to make his fortune. He was an artist, a rather unsuccessful one; not a bad one, actually, but he drank too much, and he had a temper. I expect he quarrelled with too many gallery owners and patrons. One time, we stayed in the south of France, in the hills. The scent of lavender always makes me think of that house. Once, we came to England, when my father had hopes of inheriting from a cousin. I remember that it was very cold and it rained all the time. Our cottage was beside a riverbank. Freddie and I used to play there – Freddie was always falling in the river and I was always fishing her out.'

As she spoke, he felt himself falling in love with her. The angle of her jawline, and the way that now and then she carelessly swept back the shining fall of honey-coloured hair from her face: all these were snares for him. Sometimes they touched, as he lifted his teacup or she took her lighter out of her gold bag. He had once, travelling in Sicily, felt an earth tremor. Being with Tessa reminded him of that:

70

he was knocked off balance, and the normal, everyday run of things had become unreliable.

'And then?' he prompted.

'After my father died, we went back to Florence. When I was seventeen, my mother sent Freddie and me to school in England.'

'Did you like it? Were you happy?'

'Not at first.' She looked down, stirring her tea. 'There was someone I was rather fond of, back in Italy, and I missed him.'

Fond of, she thought. She had loved Guido Zanetti. It had taken her rather a long time to forget him.

She asked Milo about his family. 'My father died six months after he retired,' he said. 'I've always thought, what a bloody awful, dull life. He worked for the local council. Nothing important or interesting, just filling in forms. We went to the same guest house in the same seaside resort every summer. My father bought a new hat every other year, a new overcoat every five years. He couldn't afford to drive a car on his wages, so whenever I think of him, he's riding a bike and he's wearing cycle clips round his turnups. So bloody depressing.'

'Poor Milo.'

'No, poor Dad. I escaped. I was at Oxford when he died. My mother lived for another six years. She knew about Penelope's success. She was so pleased for me.'

'And proud of you, I'm sure.'

'Yes, that too.'

'You must miss her.'

He didn't, enormously, having as a very young man found

his mother's breathless awe at his achievements – school scholarship, Oxford, publication – irritating and embarrassing, but he said, 'Yes, of course.' Then he found himself adding, 'What you want when you're eighteen or twenty-two isn't necessarily the same as what you want when you're thirty-eight. These decisions we make when we're young – we don't realize at the time how important they are.'

A wave of unhappiness washed over him. Lately, he had been unable to shake off a dissatisfaction that hung around him like a swarm of flies, black and poisonous.

'I've always tried,' Tessa said, 'not to become trapped. Obligations, responsibilities – I've never wanted that. My mother was trapped. Her marriage trapped her.'

'Do you think marriage is always a trap?'

'For women, yes. For women, it can be a sort of slavery. For men – I don't know.'

He said, 'I thought of marriage as an adventure.'

'And was it?'

'Yes, to begin with. We thought we were living in a new way, Rebecca and I. We were going to do better than our parents. We were setting out on an exciting journey, hand in hand.'

'Do you have any children?'

'We didn't want them. They would have limited us. I've always thought that children, rather than marriage, would be the hindrance.'

'A woman will stay in a bad marriage for the sake of her children. There's an ownership, a possession implied in marriage that I dislike. And I've seen too many lousy marriages – not just my parents', but here in London, too, couples who stay together for money, or for form's sake, because they can't face the disgrace of a divorce. That's not love, Milo, it's a legal contract, and a rotten one at that. I believe that marriage kills love.'

Had he stayed with Rebecca out of love or out of habit? These days, she was so restless. Everything had to be perfect. The house, the garden – sometimes he wondered whether one day she would take a look at him, decide he was a bit of a mess and tidy him away too. When had that happened? When had she turned from the adoring, vibrantly sexual girl with whom he had fallen in love into a woman who minded an ill-placed cushion, a muddy footprint on the hall tiles? After *Penelope's Loom*, he thought, but before Annette. Sometime in the years between, the years of his success as a writer and their social success as a couple.

'I'm sorry, Milo.' Tessa gave him a sympathetic look. She put her hand on his arm. 'I don't mean to make you unhappy.'

'I'm not. I don't think I've ever been happier.'

She looked out of the window. 'It's stopped raining. Shall we go?'

They left the café. Milo offered to hail a taxi but Tessa told him she would rather walk.

'What about love?' he said, as they headed down Charing Cross Road. 'Is love a trap?'

'Oh no.' She linked arms with him. 'Love's the most important thing in the world. But it's a mistake to try to force it into a mould. If you do, you distort and destroy it. Love lasts as long as it lasts, that's what I believe. And when it dies, you walk away from it.'

Had he himself tried to hold on to love, long after the best of it had died? Did that account for his feeling of dissatisfaction? There was hardly a soul on the streets and few cars on the road. It seemed to Milo that the great city had emptied itself out just for them, so that they could walk and talk and kiss undisturbed.

'I wouldn't want to hurt anyone,' Tessa said.

'No, of course not.'

'You must do what you think is right. And I'll do the same.'

She was biting her lip; she seemed, just then, he thought, very young. A rush of excitement rose inside him, and he knew that he was on the brink of something wonderful, something life-changing. He raised her hand to his face, pressing his cheek against her fingers.

They reached the Embankment and looked out over the river. Then Tessa glanced at her watch. 'It's late. It isn't my birthday any more.'

'Have you enjoyed it?'

'It's been one of the best.' Standing face to face with him, she threaded her hands beneath his coat. 'You should go home, Milo,' she murmured.

'I don't want to. Anyway, I can't – I've missed my last train.' He stroked her face with his thumb. He said quietly, 'I don't think I can go back.'

'Then your club . . .'

'That's not what I meant.' He kissed her. 'This feels too important. Don't you feel that too, Tessa?'

'Yes.' A whisper.

'Sometimes it seems preposterous to me how much we're

bound by convention, by proprieties. Why should it be wrong of me to talk to someone, to spend time with someone?'

'Talking . . . spending time . . . Is that what you want?'

'If it's all that's on offer, then I'll take it, and gladly. But I want more, Tessa, you must know I want more.'

And he buried his hands in her hair and kissed her again. You could talk these things to death, he thought, but in the end the need to touch, to hold, to consume, to lose yourself in another person was inescapable. Touching, they seemed to draw the essence from each other. The river flowed, unceasing and timeless, as they kissed.

And so it began.

She had left the party with Milo Rycroft to annoy Paddy, but then, somewhere in a word, a gesture, a kiss, desire had flickered into life, a spark to begin with, but soon glowing, burning. She liked the curve of his jaw, the hollow of his upper lip, and the way that his eyes, which were the pale grey of ice on shallow ponds and might so easily have looked cold, came alive as soon as he saw her. And she loved him for his mind, which was clever and original and had a touch of magic.

She had been attracted to him the first time they had met. He had come out of the woodland by the frozen pond, a creature of frost and darkness. A glimpse, that night, of what it was that charmed, his capacity to see the extra-ordinary, his talent for making a story from the hiss of a skate on the ice and the swirl of a skirt hem in the night. *When I saw you, I thought I'd been transported back in time to old Russia, perhaps, or turn-of-the-century Vienna. I thought for a moment that you were a ghost.* He painted pictures with words, as Max framed them through a camera lens, and the pictures he made beguiled her.

She hadn't meant to fall in love with him. They would be occasional lovers, she had thought. He would be her *cinq à sept*, to amuse her in the dead hours of the early evening. She would be careful, she wouldn't let this love affair get out of hand. He was married, it said so on the dust flap of his book: *Milo Rycroft is married and lives in Oxfordshire.* Eight words that told her to be careful and should have warned her off. They would make love, oh, once a month or so, when he came up to London, and afterwards he would go back to his beautiful wife in the countryside. Mrs Rycroft must be beautiful, because Milo liked to surround himself with beautiful things. A Mont Blanc pen, a Burberry overcoat, and a lovely wife, chosen many years ago, before he got bored. Occasional lovers, and then he would go home to Rebecca, and no harm done.

She reasoned to herself, trying to rub out the ripples in her conscience. *If not me, then someone else. Better to be me, because I won't want to own him. I'll share him for a while, that's all. All* – how patronizing, she came to see as time passed, and how cruel. Take the seeds and leave the husks for his wife. She would have hated that, had she been Rebecca Rycroft.

Their affair took on a particular choreography. Meetings in the British Museum, that haunt of illicit lovers, their fingers threading together and then drifting apart as they walked between a monumental stone hand, plucked from the desert, and the sarcophagus of an Egyptian queen. Coffees and suppers in ordinary cafés in ordinary streets, well away from the haunts of his friends or hers. Phone calls from public call boxes or from his office in Oxford, conversations that went on as the afternoon turned into evening because neither of them could bear to be the one who put the phone down. They made love in an Oxfordshire water meadow where the air was perfumed by may blossom. This so-called part-time love affair, which she had meant to keep to reasonable hours, seeped into every part of her day.

'I remember hot, small rooms in hot, small Italian towns,' she told him, one afternoon when they were in bed together in her flat. 'My parents always seemed to quarrel in the evening. My mother would put Freddie and me to bed and then she'd go downstairs to serve my father his supper, and then it would start. First, he'd be sarcastic. Sometimes I could hear the words he said; at other times only the tone of his voice. To begin with, my mother would try to appease him. Now, when I think back, I expect that made him angrier. He'd shout and call her names. Then she'd cry. Then, sometimes, he'd break things. Plates, glasses, whatever was to hand. I don't know whether he hit her. I went downstairs once because I thought he was hurting her, but my mother screamed at me to go back to my bedroom. I've always regretted doing as I was told.'

'Poor little girl,' he said.

She curled up into his arms. 'My mother had run away with my father and her family didn't speak to her any more. She had two small daughters and no money of her own.

I'll never make that mistake. I'll never be dependent. The only marriage I've seen at close quarters was a battleground, not a friendship. My father almost destroyed my mother and he certainly destroyed himself. People assume that children forget such things, but they don't.'

You could concentrate so hard on avoiding other people's mistakes that you failed to notice the traps of your own making. She should have put an end to it. She should have written him a note, made a phone call, flirted with another man while he watched from the sidelines. She should have made him hate her. She should have told him face to face that it had to stop. She should have, but she didn't, because by then she was in love with him.

Then the tiredness began, and she had never felt tired in her life before, had brushed off the late nights and the early starts as mere inconveniences. She experienced a nausea that for some weeks she put down to her irregular hours and rushed and infrequent meals. A bug that wouldn't clear up, or exhaustion after the spring fashion shows.

Stupid of her, really. The first time it occurred to her that she might be pregnant was at a party in a country house in Hertfordshire. She was in the bedroom they had put aside for the ladies, and she was sitting at the mirror, touching up her make-up. A girl was lying on the bed, talking to her friend. 'So bloody tired and I throw up every morning. I didn't realize having a baby made you feel so utterly ghastly.' Tessa stared at her reflection in the mirror as the pieces of a pattern slotted into place.

A friend, another model called Stella Bishop, scribbled

the name of a Dr Pomeroy on a scrap of paper for her, along with a Harley Street address. *He's a creep,* Stella had added, *but needs must* . . . A little shrug.

Dr Pomeroy wore a black tailcoat. The buttons of his grey-striped waistcoat gaped over his rounded belly. His vowel sounds were aristocratic and his long upper lip and Neville Chamberlain moustache failed to hide the blackened holes in his front teeth. With a flick of rubber gloves he examined Tessa and told her that she was around fourteen or fifteen weeks pregnant. She should have come to him earlier; she was a silly girl to have got herself into such a condition. He took it that there was no husband in the offing? He should be able to help her, but it would cost her fifty pounds. She must not delay. She must ring this number and his secretary would book her into his clinic. All this said while she was lying on the couch, the leather cold against her back, her legs splayed out like a frog's.

Over the next few days, Tessa thought about Dr Pomeroy. About the gleam in his eyes, and the touch of his fat rubber hands probing inside her. She wasn't afraid of much, but hospitals repelled and frightened her. A sort of paralysis crept over her. If she didn't think about it, perhaps it wouldn't happen.

A few days after the consultation, she travelled to Paris. She stayed there for a fortnight. When she returned to London, she could feel, when she lay down, the small, hard swell of her womb. She had lost the notepaper on which Dr Pomeroy had written the telephone number of the clinic. A couple more weeks passed, and then, one morning, lying in bed, she felt a strange mothlike fluttering inside her. She put her palm on her belly and thought, if you are a girl, I shall call you Christina.

Inactivity made her decision for her – a coward's way, she knew, and foolish, too. The child must have been conceived during the first rapturous weeks of her affair with Milo Rycroft. There must have been a time when she had forgotten the wretched thing – this was the term Tessa used to herself for her Dutch cap. Perhaps it had been the afternoon she had driven to Oxford and they had made love by the river. Or perhaps, on one of their evenings at her flat, she might have thought she had put the thing in, but had forgotten.

She must tell Milo, Tessa thought. It troubled her to realize she was afraid to.

Chapter Three

On the afternoon of the last day of the summer term, Freddie caught the train from Oxford to London. She had assured Miss Fainlight that her sister would meet her at Paddington station, but when Tessa wasn't waiting on the platform, Freddie wasn't at all surprised and so plunged alone into the fuggy darkness of the tube.

She caught the Hammersmith and City line to Moorgate, then changed to the Great Northern and City Railway. On the journey to Highbury and Tessa's flat, she sat with her small suitcase at her feet, taking pleasure in the rattling and squawking of the carriage, in being in her home clothes instead of her school uniform, and in having no school for the next six weeks.

Freddie liked London. She liked its solidity, its purposefulness, and the impression it gave of interesting and involved lives going on behind the grimy façades of the buildings. She enjoyed the contrast between her London life and her school life. At school, every moment of the day was divided up and allotted to some particular task. Her London days were formless and unpredictable, often taking her in unexpected directions. The two lives suited different parts of her and she kept them firmly separate.

Alighting from the train, Freddie walked along Highbury Place until she reached the red-brick block of mansion flats in which Tessa lived. The porter greeted her as she entered the building and offered to carry her suitcase upstairs. Freddie smiled and said no thank you, it wasn't heavy at all, so the porter held the lift door open and she stepped inside.

On the second floor, she let herself into the flat. She knew immediately that Tessa wasn't there. You always knew when Tessa was at home; Freddie wondered whether she somehow made the air vibrate. She put her suitcase down in the hall and looked round. The flat was tidy, which meant that the maid must have cleaned that morning. Her own room was just as it had been when she had left it to go back to school at the beginning of term. Tessa had promised her when she had taken the flat that no one else would ever be allowed to use her room.

Searching through the kitchen, Freddie found a loaf of bread and a pot of strawberry jam and made herself a sandwich. Tessa hardly ate anything, just nibbled throughout the day on crackers and grapes and slivers of cheese, but there was always food in the larder for friends, thank goodness. Tessa had an eighteen-inch waist. Freddie's waist was only an inch wider, which wasn't bad, she thought, considering she ate anything she could get her hands on. She had grown a lot taller recently and she wondered whether her increased height somehow accommodated all the suet pudding they were fed at school.

Careful not to drop blobs of jam on the white carpet, Freddie wandered round the flat, becoming reacquainted with it. There were some new photographs on the drawing-room walls, of Tessa in a series of elegant frocks and extraordinary hats. In one of the photos she was standing in a pond, and in another she was wearing a black and white frock and stroking the neck of a zebra. Some words were scrawled on the bottom right-hand corner of the zebra photo: 'In homage to the serene Tessa, Max Fischer.' There were several picture postcards on the mantelpiece, which Freddie turned over and read too. 'Paris isn't the same without you.' 'Frightful place, it's bucketing with rain and the hotel's foul.' And, mysteriously, 'I've found the chessboard.'

Tessa's bedroom was spacious, with a bay window that looked down over a street lined with London planes. Freddie threw herself on to the wide double bed, which had a headboard shaped like a scallop shell, and gave a sigh of pleasure. So much of her life seemed to be taken up with longing for things she couldn't have: delicious food, lovely clothes, champagne, cigarettes, a ride in a sports car. She had other longings, which she couldn't even put into words, but which every now and then a phrase from a song or a passage in a novel seemed to sum up for her.

Her eye was caught by a small parcel on the dressing table, and she slithered off the bed. Beside the parcel, a gold powder compact held in place a five-pound note and a folded piece of paper with 'Freddie' written on it. Unfolding the paper, Freddie read Tessa's note.

Would you be a darling and deliver this for me? 'This' must mean the package, Freddie assumed. *Here's some money for a taxi. You must give it to Julian in person.* The last two words were underlined several times. *Then come and join us for tea at the Ritz. Can't wait* – again underlined many times – *to see you.*

The parcel was addressed to Julian Lawrence. When Freddie shook it, she heard a faint rattling sound.

Opening Tessa's wardrobe, Freddie began to scan through the long rail of hangers. Tessa wouldn't mind – she always lent her clothes. Freddie settled on a fitted dress and jacket made of black cotton sateen with a cream silk ribbon trim. She took off her yellow and white gingham frock and put the dress and jacket on over her navy-blue knickers, white bra and vest. Then a pair of silk stockings and some beautiful high-heeled Italian shoes. She sat down at the dressing table. Her straight dark hair was cut in a bob and parted to one side, her eyes were deep brown and her skin was clear and pale. Carefully she put on red lipstick and face powder. She studied her reflection. She had a way of jutting her jaw and frowning when she was thinking hard; she was doing that now. She erased the frown, pouted and lowered her eyelids. That was better. The schoolgirl had gone and she looked older, more polished. Was she pretty? Yes, she thought she might be.

She tucked the parcel and the five-pound note inside a patent-leather handbag, found an umbrella because it was raining, and left the flat. Downstairs, the porter hailed her a taxi and gave the driver the Kensington address from the label of the parcel.

Freddie asked the cab driver to wait while she delivered

the parcel. A huge buddleia, its purple spears dripping with rain, filled the small front garden. Beside the front door of the house were four bells; Freddie rang the one with 'Lawrence' printed next to it.

The door opened. Julian Lawrence was young, dark, handsome and sleepy-looking. He was wearing grey trousers, and a white shirt with no tie, and his black hair was untidy.

'I'm Frederica Nicolson,' said Freddie. 'We met once, in the tea room at Fortnum and Mason's.' She held out the parcel to him. 'Tessa asked me to give you this.'

His expression suddenly suspicious, Julian ripped open the brown paper and drew out a string of pearls. 'Christ,' he said angrily. 'I won't take them. Here, have them back.' He thrust the pearls at Freddie, who took a step backwards.

'You must keep them, Mr Lawrence. Tessa wants you to.'

Furiously he hurled the pearls and the crumpled brown paper into the buddleia. Then he sat down on the doorstep, groaning, his head in his hands.

'How could she do this to me? Do you know where she is? I've been trying to speak to her for days.'

'I'm on my way to the Ritz to meet her.'

'Is that your taxi?'

Freddie nodded. Julian Lawrence rose from the step. 'Right then,' he said. 'I'm coming with you. Don't budge an inch. I'll be back in a mo.'

He headed back into the house, returning a few minutes later wearing a jacket and with a tie clutched in his hand.

'The pearls . . .' Freddie said as he marched down the path.

'Damn the pearls.' He flung open the cab door and they

drove away, leaving the necklace suspended like drops of rain from the branches of the buddleia.

As they made their way towards Mayfair, Julian talked about Tessa. Where and when they had met, their courtship, her beauty, her cruelty. Freddie thought of trying to explain that Tessa had no intention of being cruel, that she showed whichever aspect she chose to the world but kept her private self hidden from almost everyone – but then that was Tessa's business, and besides, listening to Julian, she guessed there would be no point. So she asked him instead about his family and his job and found out that he came from Kent and was working as a private secretary to an industrialist, but in his spare time was learning to fly.

'It's the most marvellous fun,' he said, his face lightening. Then he asked her what she did and she had to tell him that she was still at school, and he said, 'Good Lord, are you really? I should have thought you were at least twenty.' Which was very gratifying.

At the Ritz, Freddie and Julian were shown to Tessa's table. Miss Nicolson had not yet arrived, the waiter confided, but some of her friends were already there. Two men and a woman were sitting at the table. Freddie recognized both men. One was Raymond Leavington, and the other was a Spanish poet called Antonio, who had fled his country when the civil war had broken out. She said hello to them.

'Hello, darling girl. Released you from prison, have they?' Standing up, Raymond hugged her. 'You're looking very pretty, Freddie.'

Raymond was tall, broad-shouldered and thickset. He had a ruddy face and sandy hair that was turning white at the temples. His moustache tickled Freddie's cheek when he kissed her. Raymond bought and sold property – he had found Tessa her flat in Highbury. He was a very cheerful person, except when talking about his wives. He had two ex-wives, the first called Harriet, the second Diana.

Raymond introduced Freddie and Julian to the young woman, who was called Bee. Bee was a dancer. She was dark and tiny, with the sort of face, Freddie thought, that might have been ugly, but was not, because it was so vivid and intelligent.

'Where's Tessa?' asked Julian.

'She said she might be late.' Raymond slid the three-tiered sandwich plate towards Freddie. 'Help yourself. Champagne?'

'Please.' She would be seventeen on July 20th, in just a few days' time, and Tessa was not there to say no.

Freddie ate sandwiches and drank champagne and talked to Raymond about his business while Antonio and Bee flirted and Julian Lawrence glared at the hotel entrance in a cross and hungry way. Then Raymond ordered more sandwiches and cakes and another bottle of champagne to celebrate the end of Freddie's term. The champagne was delicious; Freddie imagined being rich, like Tessa, and drinking champagne with her afternoon tea every day.

'How's school?' Raymond asked her.

'Much as it always is. I think that's the thing I like best about it, that it's always the same.' Freddie glanced at the clock. 'If it was term time I'd have just finished afternoon lessons and I'd be eating bread and margarine in the butler's pantry in my House.'

Raymond grinned. 'Bread and marge – at my school it was bread and dripping. Have a cake, Freddie.' His face changed. 'Oh God, Diana.'

Dressed in an emerald-green skirt and jacket, Raymond's second wife was bearing down through the tea room in their direction. She had, Freddie thought, a mean look in her eye. Diana sat down beside Raymond and they proceeded to have a tetchy, muttering conversation, so Freddie listened to the pianist, who was playing 'Let's Face the Music and Dance', and watched the woman on the next table feed her tiny pug dog morsels of sandwich.

Eventually Diana stalked off and Raymond mopped his forehead. Then he smiled and said, 'Here's the girl, here she is,' and looking up, Freddie saw Tessa walking towards them.

She was wearing a white dress and bolero jacket. Her dark blond hair was parted at the centre and pinned into shapes that Freddie thought resembled cream horns. Her tiny white hat, perched to one side of her head, was decorated with an orchid.

'Darlings,' she said, smiling brilliantly. 'I'm so sorry I'm late.' Though she didn't sound it a bit; Tessa was always late and never at all sorry.

Julian rose, saying, 'Tessa, I must speak to you,' and Tessa made a little raise of the eyebrows in Freddie's direction, complicity and greeting all at once. To begin with, Julian waved his arms around and said things like 'I can't bear it any longer' and 'You don't seem to realize what you're doing to me, Tessa', but by the end of their dialogue he had calmed down and Tessa was holding his hands and giving him soothing little smiles. Freddie watched, always intrigued to observe how Tessa managed her complicated love life.

More tea, more sandwiches. Tessa nibbled at a slice of cucumber. Half an hour later, the sisters dashed back to the flat to change into their evening clothes. In the taxi, Freddie told Tessa about tennis matches and her School Certificate exams, and Tessa described her recent week in New York. When they reached the flat, they took turns to have a bath while they chatted. As Freddie cleaned her teeth, Tessa gave a very funny imitation of modelling for a difficult customer at Selfridges, alternately being herself and the customer. Freddie laughed so much she had to clamp a hand over her mouth to stop herself spitting toothpaste.

But there was, in fleeting moments, a preoccupation in Tessa's eyes, a tiredness and a retreat into the self. It seemed to Freddie that in the six weeks that had passed since they had last seen each other, something had changed. Freddie didn't ask, because she knew Tessa would only tell her what was troubling her when she felt like it. Or she wouldn't. Asking, persuading never made any difference with Tessa.

None of Freddie's evening frocks fitted her any more, so Tessa lent her the most adorable froth of coffee-coloured tulle over a slender tube of cream satin. Tessa's frock was of bronze silk. Powdered and lipsticked and wearing evening capes, the sisters went out again.

Ten of them dined together at the Mirabelle that night. The party at the Ritz had been joined by Paddy Collison and a friend of his called Desmond Fitzgerald. Desmond brought with him his two younger sisters, both fair-haired like himself. Halfway through dinner, the photographer Max Fischer arrived. Max was thin and wiry, with dark hair and a hollow, interesting face.

Julian Lawrence said furiously, 'Max!' and stood up so quickly he knocked over his chair.

A waiter darted across to pick it up. Julian, after throwing down his napkin dramatically, marched up to Max and hissed, 'What do you think you're doing here?'

'I've come to see my friends, naturally. What else?'

Julian raised his fist. Tessa said gently, 'Jules,' and after a moment he lowered his bunched hands to his sides, whispered, 'Damn you all to hell, then,' and strode out of the restaurant.

'Oh dear, young love, so affecting,' murmured Raymond.

Max walked round the table, greeting everyone, kissing the women's hands – a more lingering kiss for Tessa – and shaking hands with the men. When he reached Freddie, he said, 'My dear Miss Nicolson. Enchanté,' and bent over her hand. He raised his head and Freddie saw that his small black eyes were glittering and amused. 'The Nicolson sisters dining at the Mirabelle,' he said. 'It sounds like a John Singer Sargent portrait, doesn't it?'

Freddie remembered the photographs in Tessa's flat. 'Why did you take Tessa's picture with a zebra, Max?'

'Because I'm a surrealist and that's the sort of thing sur-realists do.' He sat down next to her, in Julian Lawrence's chair.

For the next half-hour, Max and Freddie discussed the difficulties entailed in a photo shoot involving a zebra and a python. Then they talked about the plays on in the West

End. 'They are all banal and silly and not worth wasting a couple of hours of your life,' said Max dismissively. 'I'll send you tickets for something a friend of mine is putting on in a pub in Whitechapel. It's rather remarkable.'

After they had finished their coffee, Tessa said, 'I don't know about everyone else, but I'm longing to dance.'

They collected their coats and umbrellas and went outside. The doorman hailed them taxis. Sitting in the back seat beside Bee and Max, Freddie looked out of the window. It was dark now, and the drips of rain on the glass made the bright lights of Piccadilly shine and multiply. Half a dozen girls wearing mackintoshes and high heels laughed as they ran for a bus, all shimmering and liquid in the night.

The nightclub was in Shaftesbury Avenue. Coats dewed with raindrops were handed in to the cloakroom and make-up was checked and reapplied. The music – the raucous clarion call of a trumpet and the silvery arpeggio of a piano – drew them inside. The walls were lacquered in shiny black stuff, and a huge chandelier, its fluted trumpets made of gilt glass, was suspended from the ceiling. A spotlight played on the band and there were candles on the tables.

Heads turned as Tessa entered the room; they were her entourage, thought Freddie, and Tessa was their queen.

The night became punctured by the moan of the saxophone, a flare of bronze silk and a peal of laughter as Tessa danced the quickstep.

'I wish I was older,' Freddie told Max, some time in the early hours of the morning. 'I wish I was properly part of this instead of always feeling on the edge.' She could not have precisely said what 'this' was – Tessa's friends, London, the adult world, perhaps. She was a little drunk, she supposed.

Later, dancing the tango with Antonio, her movements were as fluid as water and her steps matched the beat perfectly. The music, both sensual and exciting, seeped into her body. When the dance ended, Antonio gave her a wicked smile, then bent his head and kissed her. His moustache scratched her upper lip – but the glory of it, Freddie thought, to have drunk champagne and been kissed for the first time, in the same evening.

Soon afterwards, they headed home. The rain had cleared. Dawn light gleamed on the wet pavements, and a milkman's dray stopped and started along the kerb. Images flickered through Freddie's mind as the taxi drove through quiet streets: the nightclub singer caressing the microphone; the beggar in the shop doorway; the pearls strung on the buddleia. She wondered whether they were still there.

The taxi reached Tessa's flat. In the lift, they yawned, gave each other blurred smiles, and said, 'My *feet*,' as they wriggled off their shoes.

Tessa unlocked the door to the flat. 'You enjoyed yourself, didn't you, darling?'

'Enormously.' Freddie yawned again.

'Do you want anything? Cocoa . . . hot milk . . .'

'No thanks.'

'You should get to bed, then.'

'What about you?'

Tessa had taken a cigarette out of her case. She lit it, closing her eyes as she inhaled. 'I might stay up a while.'

'Tessa, what's wrong?'

92

'Nothing's wrong, nothing at all.' Tessa was looking out of the window, smoking.

Freddie sat down on the sofa, one foot tucked beneath her. 'I'm not a child,' she said.

'I didn't mean . . .' Tessa made a regretful, fluttering movement of her hand.

'Aren't you feeling well? What is it? Have you a headache? Is it the curse?'

'I wish it was.' Tessa gave a short laugh.

Freddie stared at her. 'Oh.' Suddenly she felt wide awake. 'Oh, *Tessa!*'

Tessa pursed her lips. 'I hoped it was a scare. I've had one or two scares before and it was always all right.'

'But it isn't this time?'

Tessa shook her head. 'No, I'm afraid not.' She stared at her cigarette. 'Foul habit. I keep meaning to stop.' She crushed it in an ashtray. 'I thought of doing something about it – the baby, I mean. I got the name of someone from a friend – I knew my doctor would never help, he's far too stuffy – but then . . .'

Freddie almost said, *Do something about it? What do you mean, do something about it?* Then she understood. It was a lot to learn in one night, she thought; rather too much, in fact – the taste of champagne, the touch of a man's lips on yours, and the news that your sister had considered getting rid of her unborn baby.

'Poor old Tess,' she said.

'Oh, don't feel sorry for me. The wages of sin, I suppose. I do try to remember to be careful, but I obviously wasn't careful enough.'

'What will you do?'

A croak of laughter. 'I'll have a baby in five months' time, that's what I'll do.' Tessa bit her lip, frowning. 'I can't imagine it. It doesn't seem real.'

Freddie said, 'Is it Paddy's?' She hoped it wasn't.

Tessa did not answer. Her shoulders were hunched, her back was to Freddie.

'Tessa.'

Tessa looked back. 'I'm not going to tell anyone who the father is. Not even you, Freddie.'

'Have you told him?'

'The baby's father? No.'

'Tessa, you must.'

'I don't want to. I don't know what to say.'

It disconcerted Freddie to see Tessa so at a loss. She said, 'Are you going to marry him?'

'Certainly not. I can't even consider it.' A closing-off in Tessa's eyes; she turned away. 'I'll manage by myself. I don't need anyone else.'

'You don't have to manage by yourself. You've got me. I'll help you. I'll leave school and help you with the baby.'

'No,' said Tessa sharply. 'I don't want that. But thank you for offering, darling, it's kind of you.' She seemed to gather herself together. 'It'll be all right, I know it will. It might even be fun.'

There was a streak of impracticality in Tessa that sometimes alarmed Freddie. She said, 'Tessa, even if you don't tell anyone else, you really do have to tell the baby's father.'

'Do I? Oh dear.' Tessa sighed. 'He'll hate this, I know he

will.' She knotted her hands together. 'He doesn't want a baby, never wanted a baby, didn't bargain for a baby.'

'Neither did you.'

'It's different for women, isn't it? At the back of our minds we always know we're taking a chance. And if we can't bear to take that chance, then we're good girls, aren't we, and we save ourselves till marriage. I've never been a good girl. You know that.'

Freddie felt rather sick. The food at the Mirabelle, she supposed, or the champagne. Perhaps the evening had been too rich for her, too indigestible.

She asked curiously, 'Do you love him?'

'Rather a lot.' Tessa sounded tired. 'And I'm afraid . . .'

'What?'

'That this will get in the way.'

'Are you feeling awful?'

'Better now. I've been hideously sick in the mornings.' Tessa reached up and took the pins out of her hair, and the cream horns uncoiled ash blond to her shoulders.

Freddie didn't know much about pregnancy. At school, they only did rabbits, and even that had been rather rushed through.

'When will it show?'

Tessa glanced down at herself. 'So practical, darling, but I suppose I must think about such things. A friend told me she managed to hide it till she was six months gone. And there are always foundation garments, aren't there?'

They sat for a while in silence. Freddie's gaze drifted round the room, settling briefly on the black and white tiled fireplace, the photographs on the walls, and the clock, whose square, elegant face told her that it was almost seven in the morning.

Tessa said, 'You should go to bed, darling. It's very late.'

In her room, Freddie took off the coffee-coloured dress and hung it on a hanger. In bed, she tried to read but could not concentrate. Switching off the lamp, she lay back on the pillows. *It'll be all right, I know it will.* It was hard, she found herself thinking, to see how that could possibly be true.

The summer followed its usual pattern. At the beginning of August, the Rycrofts left for France. They always stayed in the same place, in a small stone house in the Lot that belonged to an Oxford friend of Milo's. This year, Milo seemed restless. He was in the middle of a new novel, he had grumbled before they left England; he did not want to interrupt his flow. In his demeanour there was the suggestion, which Rebecca found irritating, that he had come on holiday to please her. She suggested he work in the mornings – she would go out so that he wasn't disturbed, and his secretary, Miss Tyndall, could type up everything when they returned to England. The next day, Rebecca drove off in the rusty Citroën that Milo's friend let them use and spent an enjoyable hour buying cheese and charcuterie from a village market. The day was warm and humid; afterwards she parked the car beneath tall trees, changed into her costume and swam in the lazy green waters of the Dordogne. When she returned to the house, Milo was sitting in the garden, drinking a glass of wine. It was too hot to work, he said, too hot to think.

In the end, they returned to the Mill House a week early. Rebecca didn't mind, because they were to give a party at the beginning of September to celebrate the publication of Milo's latest novel, *The Fractured Rainbow*, and she was worried about the garden. But it was on the Channel ferry, as they stood side by side, watching the white cliffs emerge like a bleached linen frill from the blue-green sea, that the fears she had been nursing for months crystallized. *Suspicion*: such a quiet, whispery word, which did not seem to her to convey the pain it inflicted. But something in Milo's eyes told her, a gleam of expectation and excitement, preening and self-satisfied and secretive, like a peacock about to fan out its tail, an expression that he blanked out as soon as he saw her looking at him. In that instant, a great deal fell into place – his mood earlier that year, which had lurched between elation and distraction, his reluctance to go on holiday and his impatience to return home. He was seeing someone; she was sure of it.

Except that she wasn't. Often her certainty slipped away, like dry sand between her fingers. The lurch and swoop, the corrosiveness of suspicion and relief, wore at her, making her tired and jumpy. The evidence, when she examined it closely, seemed insubstantial. Look too hard and it frayed, disintegrating into nothing.

The garden party to celebrate the publication of *The Fractured Rainbow* took place in the second week of September. The rain held off and a string quartet played in the dining room, the music pouring like honey out of the open French doors. Guests clustered on the Mill House's lawn and on the terrace. Rebecca wore a frock of white linen strewn with huge blue poppies, bought at Zélie's shop in Oxford. Only a tall woman could wear such a pattern, Zélie had told her.

Toby Meade, one of the few friends from Rebecca's year at art college with whom she had kept in touch, arrived late. Toby was short, dark-haired and broad-shouldered. He lived a louche, hand-to-mouth existence in a rented Chelsea studio flat. When he kissed her, she didn't mind that at the same time his hand stroked her bottom: his lechery had always had an undemanding quality.

She told him that Milo's latest book was doing awfully well, and he said rudely, 'Bugger Milo. I trailed all the way down here for you, not Milo.' Which she appreciated. Then they talked about Toby's work and his next exhibition. 'I'm sharing the gallery with that halfwit Michael Turner,' said Toby. 'But I suppose it's better than nothing. You'll come, won't you, Becky? You look like you could do with a break.'

Rebecca put her hands to her face. 'Oh God, Toby – do I look frightful?'

He reassured her. She was as beautiful as ever, but she seemed . . . worried. Preoccupied. Did she want to share it with Uncle Toby?

No, she did not. She diverted him – parties were always such hard work, and she and Meriel were going to lunch with their mother tomorrow and she was dreading it. Years ago, Toby had met her mother, so he was sympathetic. Then she introduced him to some people, made her excuses, and hurried off. On the way to the kitchen she paused in front of the hall mirror and studied her reflection. Did it show in her face, the unease, the weight of it, the ache?

Stepping out on to the terrace after taking the musicians a drink, she saw them together: Milo and that girl, Grace King. They were standing in the shadow of the copper beech. Miss King was vehement, passionate; Rebecca could tell so by the whirl of her hands. Milo reached out, one hand cupping the crook of Miss King's elbow. The wind-mill movement of Miss King's arms abated, and she tilted towards him, her pale hair falling over her face. Another guest crossed the lawn to join them and Milo and Miss King drew apart.

Rebecca's imagination provided the script: *I have to see you – you know how much I love you. Look out, someone's coming.* She turned away. It hurt to breathe. He had taken her heart in his hand and was squeezing it hard; blood leaked between his fingers.

Milo had always been good at the little gestures, the red rose, the ring wrapped in tissue paper and left on the pillow, the fleeting, caressing touch. Rebecca wanted to run her fingernails down Grace King's smooth, pale cheek and watch the scratches redden.

Monday: Milo was late coming home from Oxford. Some bore he knew had hailed him as he was walking to his car, he said, and had kept him talking for ages. Rebecca slammed his congealed dinner on to the table in front of him and left him to eat on his own.

Wednesday evening: he took a long time walking the dog. Rebecca wondered whether he had stopped at the phone box to call Grace King. When he came home, she asked him where he had been.

'Herne Hill.' And then, looking at her, 'Where did you think I'd been?'

'I don't know. How should I know?'

'Oh for Christ's sake.' He flung Julia's lead on to a peg and went upstairs.

On Saturday evening they had supper with Charlie and Glyn. Afterwards, they played a hand of bridge. Milo was at his best – amusing, clever, charming. She wondered whether he knew that she knew, whether he had noticed that she was watching him and was putting on an act.

That night, she woke in the early hours, desperately unhappy, hating herself. This was what it had come to, then, her marriage to a man whom she had never, in all their years together, doubted was the love of her life: that she should see treachery in the turn of a card, duplicity in a smile.

Her wretched mood lingered into the next day. She was headachy and tired; she had drunk too much at the Masons'. Sundays were Mrs Hobbs's day off, so in the evenings Rebecca and Milo always had a scratch supper, eaten in the sitting room while reading the newspaper and listening to records.

The phone rang while Milo was winding up the gramophone. He went to answer it. Rebecca heard him pick up the receiver and say his name, and then his voice dropped. She rose and left the room. The receiver had been replaced in its cradle on the hall table. Standing outside Milo's study, she heard the low rumble of his voice. He had transferred the call to the extension. She strained to make out his words, but could not.

She tapped on the door. 'Would you like a coffee, Milo?'

He opened the door. She saw that he had put the phone down. 'Please,' he said.

'Who was that?'

'One of my students.' He went back into his study; she saw him bend over his desk and scribble something on a sheet of paper.

In the kitchen, Rebecca put the kettle on the stove. Then she stood at the sink. She saw that outside the weather was turning, the air chilling, raindrops falling in dark blots on the garden path. So: Milo had answered the phone in the hall and had then gone to his study to take the call on the extension, closing the door behind him. I know you, she thought. I know you're lying to me.

Mornings weren't Milo's best time, so Rebecca always rose first and brought them tea in bed. That Monday, when she went back upstairs with the tray, he was already in the bathroom. She could hear the taps running.

She poured out the tea, put a cup and saucer on his bedside table. After a while, he came back into the room.

'You're up early,' she said.

'Have to catch the train.' He was towelling his hair.

'Where are you going?'

'London. Didn't I tell you? Lunch with Roger. He wants to talk about the poems.'

Rebecca felt as alert as a gun dog. Her skin prickled. 'I thought all that was decided.'

'Not quite.' He had taken off his dressing gown and was looking through his wardrobe. 'There are still some problems. Layout . . . a few questions about the text. It's a bore, but if we can clear up everything today, it'll be worth the effort. I'm afraid I'll need the car to get to the railway station. You don't mind, do you?'

'Of course not.' She thought her voice sounded false. 'I was going to play tennis, but I'm sure Glyn could pick me up.'

'It's not really tennis weather.'

'Perhaps I won't bother, then.'

Rebecca drank her tea while Milo dressed. Grey Savile Row suit, white shirt from T. M. Lewin, blue silk tie. He looked neither happy nor expectant – rather, on edge. Perhaps he was telling the truth.

He peered in the mirror, running a hand through his damp blond curls.

'Will I do?'

She said sweetly, 'Perfectly, Milo.'

In the end, the rain cleared, and Glyn drove over and picked her up and they played a game of tennis. Back at the Mill House by midday, Rebecca washed and changed.

Mrs Hobbs had gone home to make her husband's lunch, so Rebecca had the house to herself. She went into Milo's study. Running her eyes over the desk, opening drawers, she was unable to find his address book. Perhaps he had taken it with him.

She flexed her hands, took a deep breath. As she picked up the telephone, her feeling was almost one of relief. Soon she would know for certain. She dialled the operator and asked to be put through to Milo's publisher.

* * *

Later that day, Milo caught the 4.10 train back to Oxford. In the restaurant car, he ordered a whisky. The blackened brick houses that backed on to the railway line blurred through the rainswept window. By the time he had finished the first whisky and ordered a second, the houses had been replaced by villages and shaven, mustard-coloured stubble fields.

Tessa had phoned him yesterday evening – at his *home*, for God's sake – to tell him that she needed to talk to him. She had refused to say what she wanted to talk about, had insisted he come to London, and then he had had to end the call because of Rebecca. Wretched, worried, and imagining all sorts of awful scenarios, he had slept badly.

Over lunch in a tiny Soho restaurant, she had told him that she was expecting a baby. They had had only an hour – she was working all day – and there had been an argument going on in the kitchen, and he had thought he had misheard her. 'A *baby?*' he had repeated, and she had said, 'Yes, Milo, I'm going to have a baby. Your baby.' *Are you sure?* he had asked her, and her expression had stiffened, and then she had said calmly, 'Sure that I'm pregnant or sure that it's yours? I'm certain of both, actually.' He had taken her hands and held them while the waiter had served their soup, and when the fellow had gone had said, 'I didn't mean that. You know I didn't mean that.'

'Yes. Sorry.' Tears had glittered in her eyes.

Then he had lit cigarettes for both of them. 'How long have you known?'

'A month or two.'

A month or two. Did that mean – he was unsure about

103

these things – that she was too far gone for anything to be done about it? His mouth dry, he asked her when the baby was due.

'Some time in December, I think – or perhaps it's January.'

He had always found her carelessness charming, but just then her lack of certainty about something so important had infuriated him. But then he had noticed the expression in her eyes and had said, 'Poor darling.' He had never seen Tessa look frightened before.

Neither of them had been able to eat much. When the hour was over he had walked her back to the photography studio and they had kissed goodbye in the street, holding each other tightly, their bodies pressed against each other, her fingers dug into his hair, as if they were drowning.

Milo had gone to the library in the British Museum in the hope that the familiar silence, the muted footsteps and the smell of books would comfort him. But instead, as his situation sank in, his alarm had increased. A *baby*. He had never wanted children, had not minded at all that Rebecca had never conceived. An unexpected feeling of pride that he was capable of fatherhood was quickly extinguished by his conviction that Rebecca was suspicious already. A big thing to hide, a baby. And he would have to go on hiding it for a long, long time, in all likelihood for the rest of his life.

An instinct that he might need a way to save his skin made him leave the library and take a taxi over to Hatton Garden. Afterwards, he had felt sufficiently composed to head home – in fact, he longed to go home. Not that he didn't love Tessa – he did, desperately. There had been a moment during their conversation when it had occurred to him that she might want him to divorce Rebecca and marry her. Tentatively, he had voiced the possibility.

A peal of laughter, and then she had said, 'Oh goodness me, Milo, you don't have to do that.'

An odd mixture of emotions: hurt that she should find the idea of marriage to him so risible, and relief that he would not have to tell Rebecca. 'You must let me help,' he had said, squeezing her hand.

She had shaken her head. 'This isn't your problem, Milo, it's mine. I didn't want to tell you at first. I was afraid you might be cross. Thank you, darling, for not making a fuss.'

Yet though he had said all the right things, and although they had parted on good terms, along with shock and sympathy for her, he felt resentment. He disliked complications. Of course, one could say that a love affair was a substantial complication in itself, but he had not bargained for this. And it wasn't as if he had *forgotten* about contraception. The first time he and Tessa had made love, he had asked her whether it would be all right and she had told him that it was. He would have taken precautions had there been any doubt, but, not unreasonably, he had felt reassured that Tessa, who was, after all, an experienced woman, was taking care of that side of things. 'I suppose I must have forgotten,' she had said to him that lunchtime, wrinkling up her nose as if she was talking of an umbrella left behind in a taxi.

Milo welcomed intensity, but disliked upheaval. He knew himself well enough to know that he needed a calm, steady background in order to write. His new book had hit a sticky patch and he had an uneasy feeling that his stab at poetry might have been a mistake. He knew that he felt far more deeply for Tessa than he had for Annette Lyle or any of the others, but for the first time he found himself questioning his involvement with her. He was out of his depth. He did not know what to do. He had lost control of events; they were flying out of his grasp. Should he tell Rebecca the truth, even though he shrank from it? It would be an awful thing to do to her – cruel, in fact – and what would be the point when Tessa seemed utterly set against marriage?

What a mess, he thought as, eventually, the train drew into Oxford station, what an absolute bloody mess. He found himself longing for the comfort and familiarity of the Mill House, longing to pour himself a whisky, to retreat into his study and lose himself in a book. As he drove home through the rain, he made himself compose a conversation with Roger in his head. Roger fussing about details, as usual . . . important that the layout was just right . . . and a menu (consommé, Dover sole, jam omelette) for their lunch.

At the Mill House, Rebecca came downstairs as he was taking off his mackintosh.

'How was your lunch, Milo?'

'Fine,' he said.

'How was Roger?'

'Fine.'

Her tone of voice alerted him; he glanced at her. She was standing at the foot of the stairs. The colour had drained from her face and her skin was the hue of raw pastry.

'Actually,' she said, 'Roger's in Edinburgh.'

'What?' He stared at her. His imagined lunch remained vivid.

'Roger's in Edinburgh. I phoned Miss Gaskin and she told me.'

Oh Christ. 'You phoned my publisher?'

'Yes.' She bared her teeth.

'You were checking up on me?' It was unreasonable, Milo knew, to feel angry, but he did.

Rebecca took a step towards him; instinctively he backed away. 'Where have you been? Where were you? Were you in Oxford?' Her questions fired like bullets. 'Perhaps you and Grace King went on a nice little jaunt. Was that why you wanted the car, Milo?'

Grace King? He said blankly, 'I don't know what the hell you're talking about.'

'Liar!' The word rose in pitch, a fishwife screech. 'I know you're seeing her!'

The penny dropped: Rebecca thought he was having an affair with boring, rabbit-toothed Grace King. 'Oh for God's sake,' he said furiously, pushing past her into the drawing room. 'I can't go through this all over again!'

As he opened the sideboard, his head pounded and he felt very tired. She screamed, 'You can't go through it again! You can't! What about *me*? How do you think I feel?'

In the moments it took him to take out and unstopper the whisky decanter, he struggled to gather his thoughts. He began to see that unwittingly she might have provided him with a way out. Along with annoyance that she should accuse him of something so ludicrous, he felt a rush of

107

relief. So much easier to be able to tell the truth – or, at least, a part of the truth.

'For your information,' he said, turning to her, 'I haven't seen Grace King for weeks.'

'I don't believe you.' She spat the words out.

'Believe what you like.'

'I saw you at the party, Milo.' Her voice was low, hissing and taut. 'I saw you with *her*.'

He dragged his mind back. 'I *talked* to Miss King,' he said. 'Of course I talked to her. She was one of our guests.'

'I *saw* you!' Her screech hurt his head, making him wince. 'You *touched* her! You *held* her!'

Had he? He couldn't remember. He took a mouthful of whisky. He felt angry and guilty both at the same time.

He sat down in an armchair. 'Miss King's mother is dying of cancer,' he said coldly. 'She told me about it a few months ago. I've tried to be kind to her. I've given her a shoulder to cry on, I suppose.' And God, he thought, how Grace King could cry. Buckets of tears had been sobbed in the Eagle and Child.

'You're lying.' Her lip curled and there was hatred in her eyes.

He found himself disliking her intensely. 'For pity's sake, Rebecca, the girl's only nineteen years old. It wouldn't cross her mind to think of me as a lover.'

Hypocritical bastard. Tessa was only a few years older than Miss King. But then Tessa always seemed far older than her years. Tessa Nicolson, he sensed, had stopped being a child a long time ago.

'Annette Lyle was only twenty-three,' said Rebecca.

'Not now,' he said sharply. 'Give me a break, Rebecca, not now.'

'You betrayed me!' Her face was contorted and ugly. 'How can you talk about it like that – as if it were just some piece of . . . of *tactlessness*! You broke my heart, can't you see that?'

'Does it make you feel any better, to go over all that again? Does it?'

She was twisting her hands together. 'That's not the *point*!' she cried.

'I told you how sorry I was. I thought we'd come through it. I thought . . .' he leaned forward, fixing her in the eye, 'that we'd learned to trust each other.'

Rebecca gave a sob and covered her face with her hands. 'How can I trust you when you lie to me?' Her words were muffled by her fingers.

He could tell by the tone of her voice that she was starting to doubt her own conclusions. 'Let's be logical,' he said. 'You say you saw me comforting Miss King at the party. Grace's father died when she was a child. I think she's come to look on me as a sort of father figure. As I told you, her mother's dying, so she's going through a rough time. Surely you wouldn't begrudge her a little human kindness?'

A dying mother – cancer – he was laying it on thick. Perhaps he should tell her the truth. Bite the bullet, get it over and done with, do it now. What if he said, *It's not Grace King, it's someone else, and I've fallen in love with her and she's expecting my child?* Would that be a better, more honest thing to do?

But she muttered, 'I don't know. I don't know what to think any more,' and the moment passed.

'Miss King isn't even in Oxford just now,' he said, following up his advantage. 'She didn't come to my last lecture. One of her friends told me that Mrs King is near death, so Grace has had to go home.'

'Oh.' The word was tremulous, wondering. She looked up at him. Her face was blotched and shiny with tears. She said tiredly, 'But the phone call last night – and Roger. You lied to me, Milo.'

'I told you before, the phone call was from a student. I took it in my study because I had to check some notes.'

Rebecca sat down at last, slumping into a corner of the sofa. 'But – *Roger*.'

'I can't believe you phoned my publisher!' His anger was unfeigned. 'What will they think? My jealous wife, checking up on me – I'll be a laughing stock!'

'No, no,' she said quickly. 'It's all right, I'm sure they'll think nothing of it. I only asked Miss Gaskin if I could speak to Roger, and she told me he was away. I'm sure it'll be all right.' She dug her fingers into her hair, pushing it back from her face, so that it stuck up in dark, witchy coils. 'And you still haven't told me where you were.'

'It was supposed to be a surprise.'

She snuffled, wiping her eyes with the back of her hand. 'I don't understand.'

'I know I haven't been good company recently.' Milo went to sit down beside her. 'I know I messed up our holiday. The truth is, I've been having such a battle with the novel.'

Rebecca screwed up her face, frowning. 'You didn't *say*.'

'I didn't want to admit it.' Which was true: he was always superstitious about discussing any problems with his work. His talent seemed such an ephemeral thing; if he spoke of his difficulties he might never shake them off.

'If only you'd told me.' Rebecca's tone was bleak and exhausted. 'If only you'd let me help. You used to let me help.'

Milo took from his jacket pocket a small package. 'I went to London to buy this.'

She stared suspiciously at the package. 'What is it?'

'It's for you. Open it.'

'For me?'

'I wanted to make up for being such an old grouch. I wanted it to be a surprise. I told you I was seeing Roger because I didn't want you to wonder why I was going to London. I didn't know you'd take it the wrong way. Go on, open it.'

Rebecca unfolded the tissue paper and raised the lid of the white leather box. 'Oh!' She pressed her hands to her mouth. 'Oh, this is so awful!'

Inside the box was a pair of ruby drop earrings, bought from a jeweller in Hatton Garden. 'Don't you like them?' he said.

'They're beautiful! But I feel dreadful. I'm so sorry!' She was crying again. 'Forgive me, Milo.'

'Forget it,' he said magnanimously. 'Let's not talk about it any more.'

Noble Milo, generous Milo. He patted her back as she cried. He could almost taste his self-disgust, but really, he thought, what else could he have done?

Later, after they had dined, and after they had gone to bed and made love, and as she slept, he went to his study, hoping to find consolation in the familiar peaceful focus of writing.

He couldn't work, though. He kept thinking, a *baby*. After a while he put his pen down and stared out of the window into the darkness. My God, a *baby*. Into his mind leapt unwanted the thought that something might happen, but he wiped it quickly away, seized by foreboding, a horror at the wickedness of hoping that there might not, somehow, be a baby.

Chapter Four

A photo shoot on a shingle beach on the Suffolk coast: Max Fischer was fighting the wind to take pictures of spring frocks for *Harper's Bazaar*. As he packed away his camera and tripod he said, 'You could marry me, Tessa, if it would help. It might not be what you had in mind, of course, marriage to a forty-one-year-old German Jewish refugee, but it would make me very happy.'

Tessa hadn't told anyone except Milo and Freddie that she was pregnant. She had thought she was hiding it rather well. She said so, and Max said, 'Oh Tessa, everyone knows. Didn't you realize?' She managed to produce a gracious refusal of his proposal but had to hide her sense of humiliation as they piled into the car and drove away from the beach.

Shortly afterwards, she seemed to balloon. Max thought of all sorts of clever ways of using her – coats and capes, a carefully placed pot plant – but soon she knew that the most she could hope for until after the baby was born was the occasional portrait shot. And the reality of pregnancy was grim: the heartburn, the exhaustion, the aching legs and back. When you considered how many women had babies, you might think it would be easy, but it wasn't at all.

Some of her girlfriends were sympathetic; some confided to her stories of false alarms and botched abortions. One or two of the more Bohemian admired her, seeing her condition as a statement of conviction, a rejection of the conventional. Others – her doctor's receptionist and the manageress of the women's fashion department at Selfridges – did not trouble to disguise their distaste.

She discovered that she was no longer welcome in certain circles. Her telephone calls were not returned, her letters not answered, her invitations declined. Walking along Regent Street one morning, she caught sight of an acquaintance, a society hostess, and she smiled and said good day. Only a certain hardening of the woman's eyes as she passed told Tessa that she had not suddenly become invisible and inaudible. Tessa repeated her greeting. The woman paused. Blue-veined patrician eyelids lowered and thin lips stretched in the coldest of smiles. A voice murmured, 'Do understand that we no longer know each other, Miss Nicolson. I'm sure you would prefer not to embarrass either of us.' Though she later made fun of the incident, Tessa was wounded perhaps not so much by the ostracism itself, but by the discovery that she minded. Her acceptance had always been conditional on her good behaviour, she supposed; those people had always known that she was not like them.

But for every cold shoulder, another was generously

offered to cry on. 'At times like this you find out who your real friends are,' Tessa said mockingly to Freddie in her East End charlady voice, but it was true. Paddy Collison said, 'Christ, Tessa, you've got yourself in a pretty bloody mess, haven't you?' and then offered her the cash to sort things out, as he put it. Julian Lawrence offered to marry her.

If Max and Julian's proposals touched her deeply, Ray's made her cry. One evening, they dined at Quaglino's and then went back to the flat. Tessa put a record on the gramophone; when she turned round, Ray was lowering his bulky frame to one knee.

'I wondered,' he said, 'whether you would do me the enormous honour of marrying me, Tessa.'

'Oh Ray,' she said. 'It would be lovely, but . . .' She took his hands and he lumbered back to his feet.

'I take it that's a no.'

She hugged him. 'You don't mind, do you, darling? I'd make you a lousy wife.'

'Rot. You'd make me a wonderful wife. You'd make every day an adventure.'

'I can't believe you really want a third wife, Ray.'

'I wish you'd think about it. I know you're not in love with me, Tessa, but I believe you're fond of me. And I love you, I always have. No . . .' he raised his hand, stopping her speaking, 'let me finish. I'm afraid you don't realize how difficult this will be for you. I'm afraid you don't understand how small-minded people can be. Women carry the can and men get away with it. It isn't fair, but that's how it is.'

115

'I'll be all right, Ray. My friends – my *best* friends – have been so kind.'

'What I'm trying to tell you is that this will change everything.'

'I won't let it. Only a few months' time and I won't look like an elephant any more, and then I'll go back to work.'

'What will you do with the baby once it's born? Will you have it adopted?'

'I don't know. I hadn't thought.'

'Tessa . . .' He sounded exasperated.

She tried to explain. 'What I mean is, how can I decide what to do with it before I've even seen it? I might detest it or I might love it. I don't know, I can't tell. I never *planned* to have a baby. I'll make up my mind after it's born.'

'It might be better to decide on the practical matters beforehand,' he said gently. 'Women have a way of falling in love with babies.'

'If that happens, then I'll hire a nursemaid and she can look after him while I go to work.' Tessa looked Ray in the eye. 'I won't be stuck at home. You know I'd hate that. And wouldn't you hate it, wouldn't you *really*, having to pretend another man's child was your own?'

'I don't think so. A baby's a baby. You have an instinct to protect them. I'm not sure I believe in all this guff about flesh and blood. And I have thought about it.' He took something out of his pocket. 'I've thought about it a great deal. I'm perfectly serious, Tessa. I want you to marry me.'

He opened his hand and she saw the diamond ring lying on his palm. 'Oh, *Ray*,' she said. Tears stung her eyes; she couldn't speak.

After a while, he put the ring back in his pocket. 'Oh well. Thought I'd try. Nothing ventured and all that. If you change your mind, let me know. The offer stands.'

'Dear Ray.' She kissed his cheek.

'What about the father? Can't you marry him?'

Tessa shook her head.

'Why not? Is he married already? If he is, the bastard should get a divorce. I'll send someone round to have a word with him, if you like.' Ray's business employed a lot of large men on building sites.

'No, darling.'

'Why won't you tell me who he is? You shouldn't have to go through this on your own.'

'I'm not on my own. I've got you, haven't I, darling?'

'What about money? Are you all right?'

'Everything's fine.'

Though it wasn't. Only a couple of weeks ago she had bought three pairs of shoes at Rayne's in Bond Street to cheer herself up. A stern letter from her bank manager a couple of days later had made her realize she must economize. She was out of the habit, though, had become unused to worrying about money. Milo had insisted on paying her doctor's bills and, when the time came, for the nursing home. It's the least I can do, he had said. Because by then she had been six months pregnant and her modelling work had dried up, she had accepted his offer. An all-in-one girdle could only achieve so much.

'I might nip up to London tomorrow.' Milo was unknotting his tie. 'There are a few things I need to do.'

'I could come with you.' Rebecca stepped out of her dress and hung it on the hanger.

When she turned round, she saw that his eyes had narrowed. 'What?' he said. 'Don't you trust me?'

'Milo!'

'Still checking up on me, aren't you?'

The bedroom door slammed. A clunk as the bolt on the bathroom door was slid home and then the hiss of running water.

When he came back into the room, she said quietly, 'I wasn't checking up on you, honestly, Milo. I thought it would be nice to go up to Town together, that's all. It seems ages since we have. I could do some shopping while you're working in the library, and we could stay overnight, perhaps take in a show.' She went to stand behind him, resting her head against his shoulder. 'It would be fun, wouldn't it?'

It wasn't, though. In the past, they had stayed at the Savoy, but this time Milo didn't want to. All the good hotels were full, so they took a room in a rather dreary place in Marylebone Street. And though Rebecca dutifully shopped in Oxford Street while Milo went to see Roger Thoday, she did not enjoy it as much as she had expected to. She had become used to buying her clothes at Zélie's, and found the large array in Selfridges rather exhausting. On the train from Oxford in the morning, Milo had insisted she treat herself, so she ended up buying two costumes, one cherry red and the other a speckled brown tweed. When she returned to the hotel and tried them on again, she saw that the cherry red pulled across the bust and she was horribly afraid the brown was a mistake — it was so draining to a pale skin. She wore the red for lunch, then wished she hadn't. The other women in the restaurant were dressed in black or dove grey or navy, trimmed with touches of white. She felt conspicuous. She had become out of touch, she realized. The fashions in Oxford were not the same as the fashions in London.

In the evening, they went to see French Without Tears at the Criterion, which Rebecca enjoyed until she glanced across at Milo. He looked, she thought, bored. 'Don't you like it, darling?' she whispered, and he started, and whispered back, 'Oh yes, it's marvellous,' and then a woman in the row behind shushed them. Rebecca apologized and looked back at the stage. No, not bored, she found herself thinking. Unhappy.

It was her fault, of course. When she recalled their quarrel – her anger, and the way she had jumped far too easily to conclusions – she was ashamed. She knew that a distance persisted between them. On the train back to Oxford the following morning, sitting in the First Class carriage with Milo, a lady in a dogtooth check and a clergyman, it saddened her to think how far their lives had diverged. Almost without noticing it, they had drifted apart. Once, they would have whispered together, making up stories about their fellow passengers. Childish and impolite, no doubt, and she supposed one had to grow out of such nonsense, but there was something she could not imme-diately find a name for that just then she missed deeply, wretchedly. A closeness, a shared life. When had they stopped sharing? When had they begun to live their lives in parallel, rather than together?

* * *

119

Tessa thanked the porter for carrying her shopping upstairs and let herself into the flat. It was raining outside, a cold, spiteful November rain, and she had taken the bus instead of a taxi to save money. She hung her mackintosh on the hook on the bathroom door, where it dripped sullenly. In the bedroom, she peeled off her damp stockings. It was extraordinary, she thought, how pregnancy changed all of you. At seven and a half months, her ankles no longer looked like her own ankles; instead, thickened and shapeless, they seemed to have been borrowed from the stout, weary woman she had sat next to on the bus.

She went to the kitchen to unpack the bags. Because Milo worried about being seen in restaurants, she had offered to cook dinner for him in the flat. She had chosen the menu with great care: cream cheese and pineapple salad, beef olives (always so delicious) and *gâteau de pommes*. It was almost three weeks since they had seen each other and she was missing him dreadfully. Something always seemed to get in the way of his coming to London, and though she had offered to drive to Oxford, Milo hadn't been keen. What if something happened, he had said, what if the baby came early?

There was a horrible moment when, crouching down to get a dish from a low shelf, she was afraid she might not be able to get up again, but she managed to haul herself upright, using the cupboard handles for support. She would make the salad first, she decided. You had to mix the cream cheese with salad dressing, and then, the recipe instructed, 'roll it on a wet board with a wet knife'. Then you placed the ball of cream cheese in the centre of a pineapple ring.

She wasn't sure whether the board was too wet or perhaps not wet enough, but the cheese stuck to the knife, the board and her hands, and, in the end, she had to scrape it up with a spoon and push it into the middle of the pineapple rings with her fingers. Then she started to make the beef olives. The telephone rang as she was frying the onions, so she dashed to answer it, thinking it must be Milo, who had promised to phone before he left Oxford. But it wasn't Milo, it was Antonio, telling her that Bee had agreed to marry him, and would Tessa like to come to The Lamb in Lamb's Conduit Street to celebrate? Tessa congratulated Antonio, explained that she had a previous engagement, and then, smelling burning, ended the call as soon as she decently could.

The kitchen was filled with smoke and the onions were blackened. She was too tired to start slicing again, so she fished out the least charred ones, put them in the dish with the beef olives, made up some Bisto, poured it over them, and put the dish in the oven. Then she made herself a cup of tea and sat down on the sofa. She should tidy up, she thought, as she surveyed the clutter of books, magazines and teacups on the coffee table. She had reduced the maid's hours to two days a week to save money and now the flat always seemed to be a mess. I'll do it in a minute, she thought, and lay flat on the sofa, closing her eyes. She rested her hands on the dome of her womb and felt the baby make its slow, swimming, deep-sea movements.

When she woke up, it was a quarter to seven. Milo must have had to hurry for a train, and had not had time to phone. Bleary with sleep, Tessa went to the kitchen. She opened the oven door and poked a knife in the beef olives. They looked unpleasant: the stuffing had oozed out of the meat rolls and was bobbing pinkish-grey in the gravy.

She hadn't yet started the *gâteau de pommes*. As she peeled and cored apples at the sink, her back and head ached. Only six more weeks, she told herself. Six more weeks and it would be over. She hadn't yet decided what to do. It would be sensible, she knew, to have the baby adopted. Just as it would have been sensible to accept Ray's proposal of marriage.

When the sliced apples were in a saucepan, she poured water over them, put them on the hob and turned on the gas. She read the next part of the recipe: 'Put the sugar and water into a saucepan and boil until it becomes sugar again.' She frowned, mystified. Why? What on earth did that mean? Why bother to go to all that trouble if the sugar was only to revert to its original state?

She read on. 'Pour the apple mixture into a mould and when it is quite cold turn it out.' How long did boiled apples take to go cold? Half an hour – an hour? She did not know. She glanced at her watch. Quarter past seven. Milo was due at half past and she hadn't even changed.

The apples had turned to a frothy mass, so Tessa drained them into a colander, mixed in some sugar, poured the lot into a blancmange mould and put it in the fridge. Dirty crockery and utensils covered every surface, and the soles of her shoes stuck to the splatters of boiled apple on the floor.

No time for a bath, so in the bathroom, she filled the washbasin. Her reflection looked back at her from the glass, hollow-eyed and pallid, a black smear across one cheek. After she had washed, she went to the bedroom. In her wardrobe hung the slinky bias-cut little frocks that she had once, in another life, worn for a night out. Seeing them, she felt as if she was mourning old friends. She put on a dark green wrap dress she had made herself because the maternity clothes in the shops were so frightful, and anyway, she had always enjoyed sewing. Then she did her face, covering up the dark circles beneath her eyes, rubbing a little rouge on her cheeks.

Ten to eight. Milo was late. The traffic must be bad – it was often hard to find a taxi in the rain. A quick dab of Guerlain's Véga behind the ears and then she checked the seams of her stockings and went back into the sitting room.

As she tidied away the magazines and put the dirty teacups in the sink, a flicker of intuition told her that he would not come. This small certainty she at first dismissed, but it grew as the moments passed. Though she laid the table and lit the candles, she noticed that she did these things now with a lack of conviction.

She sat down on the sofa again, tucking her feet under her, waiting. There might have been an accident, she thought. Restless, she turned on the wireless, and a chorus from a comic opera filled the room. No news flashes interrupted the music to tell of train crashes or sudden storms or floods, and after a while she switched the set off.

She longed to hear Milo's voice. Perhaps he had missed his train and was waiting at the friend's office he borrowed when he was in Oxford. On that line they often talked for hours. She dialled the operator and asked to be put through to the Oxford number. No one answered. Tessa thanked the operator and put down the receiver. She thought of phoning his home, knew she should not. He would be here soon. At this moment he was probably sitting in a taxi, a bunch of flowers in his hand, a bottle of wine in his overcoat pocket, on his way to Highbury. When he arrived at the flats, he would pay the driver and hurry into the building. He never took the lift, always bounded up the stairs two at a time. When she answered the door, he would put the flowers on a chair, or they would crush the bouquet between them as they embraced, his hands sliding around her as they kissed hungrily.

She went to stand at the window, drawing the curtain aside as she looked out. A taxi headed along the street; she willed it to stop. But it did not, and the rear lights shimmered in the rain as the vehicle disappeared round the corner.

In the kitchen, she took the apple mould out of the fridge and dipped a fingertip into it. It was still liquid, so she put it back in the fridge. She sat down again, lit a cigarette, then stubbed it out. She should take up knitting, she thought. All this silence, all this waiting – she would feel better if she had something to do.

The phone rang. She hurried to it, short of breath, afraid it would stop ringing before she reached it.

She snatched up the receiver. 'Milo?'

'Tessa?'

'Oh, Milo!' A flood of relief; her heart lifted. 'I thought something had happened! Where are you?'

'I'm still at home, I'm afraid.'

'But our dinner . . .'

'I know, I know. I'm furious about it.'

'What's happened, darling?'

'Something's gone wrong with the blasted car. Rebecca was driving it back from Abingdon and it started to make a noise. It's had to go into the garage. Then I thought I'd take a taxi to the station but old Fred Holland was fetching someone from the Radcliffe. And then I thought a bus – but I never take buses and Rebecca was giving me funny looks anyway, so I didn't dare suggest that. It's bloody difficult – she watches me like a hawk.' He sounded annoyed.

'Poor darling.'

'I've been desperate to get to a phone. I didn't want you wearing yourself out with all that cooking.'

'You mustn't worry about that.' Tessa laughed. 'You've probably had a narrow escape. I'm a pretty awful cook.'

'No, no, I'm sure it would have been wonderful. I was looking forward to it so much. I'm so sorry, darling. I'll make it up to you, I promise.'

'Where are you?'

'The phone box in Little Morton. I took Julia for a walk. It's pouring with rain here.'

'And here. I wish it was summer.'

'How are you, my love?'

'I'm fine. Rather tired. My feet ache.' She laughed again. 'I sound like an old lady.'

'Poor little thing. I wish I was there. I could rub your feet for you.'

'Tomorrow?'

'Tomorrow's no good, I'm afraid. We've some people

125

coming. Tell you what, I'm in town next week. I have to do something at the BBC.'

'I miss you,' she said. 'I love you.'

'I love you too. So much.'

He ended the call shortly afterwards – there was a queue of people outside the phone box, he told her, and he did not dare stay away from home too long.

In the kitchen, Tessa took the beef olives out of the oven and the salad and the apple mould from the fridge. They looked messy and unpalatable. As she scraped the food into the bin, she thought savagely, well, what did you expect? You are not part of his life, you live only in the intervals between it. You have no right to him; he belongs to someone else. He belongs to his wife, to Rebecca. He always did.

She saw his faults – his egotism, his vanity – and yet, and here was the thing, they didn't stop her loving him. She hadn't often, she realized, loved before. She had thought she had, but she hadn't, not really. She had been in love with Guido Zanetti when she was seventeen, and now she loved Milo. Her other men, those men in between, she had liked and appreciated and been attracted to. But she had not loved them.

In the kitchen, she piled the dirty dishes into the sink. A whoosh of water as she turned on the tap, and she found herself thinking of Rebecca, whom she had never met. Did Milo love Rebecca? A discontent, a deterioration between them was implied but rarely spoken of. Had they loved each other once? Yes, she thought so, Milo would not have married without love. Milo needed love. And he feared

126

Rebecca's jealousy. Did jealousy feed off love or ownership? Once, she would have been sure of her answer. Love that depended on possession, on exclusiveness, she would have said, was not worth having. It was a distortion of love, love's ugly sister. Dependency, jealousy, guilt: these were emotions she despised, and which had never before been a part for her of the map of love.

She had made her choice. If the restrictions of marriage were not for her, then she, in turn, had no right to be his jailer. Love lasted as long as it lasted, she remembered saying to Milo on the evening of her birthday party. When it died, you walked away from it.

Leaving the dishes to soak, Tessa switched off the kitchen light and blew out the candles on the dining table. She went to the window and looked out, as she had done earlier, waiting for him. The rain had stopped. You could go out, she reminded herself. You could take a taxi and go to Antonio's engagement party. You could phone someone.

Instead, she went to her bedroom and undressed. Naked, her abdomen had the smoothly belling curve of a ripe pear. Sitting on the edge of the bed, she covered her face with her hands, pressing them against the bones of her eye sockets to stem the tears. Love lasted as long as it lasted, yet this relationship could not be walked away from. Through his child, Milo Rycroft would always be a part of her. Oh Tessa, she thought wearily, what have you done?

Tessa went into labour early on the morning of December 27th. Freddie went with her in the taxi to the nursing home in Bayswater. Afterwards, feeling rather at a loose end, she took the tube to Julian Lawrence's rooms in South Kensington.

When he answered the doorbell, she said, 'Tessa's having her baby,' and he said, 'Oh,' and then, 'How long will it take, d'you think?'

'At the nursing home they said probably not till tomorrow morning.'

'Good Lord.'

'They wouldn't let me stay with her. It's a fearsome place and the nurses are dragons. I feel so useless. I wish I could do something.'

'If I can help . . .'

'You can take me out to breakfast if you like, Jules. We didn't eat before we left the flat because Tessa felt sick.'

Julian dashed upstairs to get his jacket and wallet. Then they walked along Pembroke Road to Earls Court Road. It was very cold and a sprinkling of snow frosted the tops of the privet hedges and the smoke-blackened walls.

In the café, workmen in navy-blue overalls drank mugs of tea and ate thick wads of bread. Julian asked Freddie what she wanted.

'Toast, I think.' She, too, felt rather sick, thinking of Tessa, all alone in that horrible place.

Julian went to the counter. When he came back to their table he was carrying mugs of tea. 'Chin up, old thing.'

'I'm trying not to think about women having babies in books. You know, like David Copperfield's mother.'

'Tessa's not some wilting Victorian heroine. She'll be fine.'

'At the nursing home they kept calling her Mrs Nicolson,

128

as if that made it more respectable. I wonder if I should phone anyone? Or should I wait till the baby's born?'

'What about the father?' Julian stirred sugar in his tea. 'Should you call him?'

'I would if I could but Tessa won't tell me who he is. I've asked her lots of times.' Freddie looked Julian in the eye. He had nice eyes, long-lashed and as dark a brown as her own. 'It isn't yours, is it, Jules?'

He shook his head. 'Not a chance. Tessa finished with me over a year ago.'

'You're the only person I've asked outright. It's a bit of a nerve, isn't it, but I thought you wouldn't be offended.'

'I'm not. I expect it's that heel Max Fischer.'

She asked curiously, 'Why don't you like Max?'

Julian scowled. 'Probably because Tessa likes him better than me and I can't see why. Max is older than me, poorer than me, and I think he's uglier than me. It's all right, I don't mind any more.'

Though his tone was light, Freddie saw that he did mind, a lot. 'You're terribly handsome, Jules,' she said comfortingly. 'I did consider falling in love with you myself, but then I decided not to.'

'Why not?'

'There's a girl at school who's fallen in love with a boy at home and she talks about him all the time. It's so tedious.'

A crack of laughter. 'Just wait till it happens to you, Freddie.'

The girl at the counter called to them that their breakfasts were ready. Julian went to collect them. Returning, he put a plate of toast in front of Freddie. 'Or it could be

Paddy Collison,' he said. 'They were together at about the right time.'

'I hope not. He once made a pass at me, did I tell you? I went to his flat to take him a note from Tessa and he made me a martini and then tried to kiss me. I was only sixteen.'

'The old goat.' Julian looked shocked. 'Did you tell Tessa?'

'Of course not.' Freddie cut her toast into four. 'Then there's Ray, though I don't think it's him, or that man in Paris . . .'

'André.'

'Yes. And there was an awful man, a Lord Something she met at Ascot racecourse. I think he was married. It could be him. I only met him once.'

A procession of Tessa's men at parties and nightclubs: which one? I can't marry him, Tessa had said, that night she had told Freddie she was pregnant. Freddie regretted not having pressed her then, not having asked her to explain what she meant. I can't marry him – had that been because he, the baby's father, was married already, or because, in spite of everything, in spite of the baby, Tessa's rejection of marriage remained absolute?

'It makes me angry,' she said.

'That he's getting away with it while Tessa's having such a rotten time?'

'Yes, that's about it. Tessa doesn't seem to feel the same, though.'

'Cheer up, Freddie. The thing I eventually realized with Tessa – she's so beautiful, you think she's made of glass. But really, she's pretty tough.'

Freddie spread marmalade on her toast. 'Perhaps I'll know who it is when I see the baby. Perhaps it'll look like its father.'

'A ginger moustache if it's Ray's?'

She giggled. 'How are you, Jules? How was Christmas?'

'Terrific.' He leaned forward, eyes shining. 'Actually, I've some marvellous news. I've been accepted for pilot training. I'm going to join the RAF.'

'Oh, Jules.' She beamed at him. 'Congratulations. Well done.'

'I had my interview with the selection board a few weeks ago. Thought I'd made a frightful hash of it, but then they told me I was through. Then there was the medical. And then, on Christmas Eve, I got the letter saying I'm to report to the training school at the end of April.'

'Are your parents pleased?'

'My father is. My mother's not so keen. She thinks there'll be a war.'

'Don't you?'

'Yes, I expect so. But that's the point, isn't it? If there is a war, then I've got to be in the RAF. What about you, Freddie? How much longer do you have at school?'

'A year, at least.'

'What will you do when you leave?'

'Miss Fainlight, my housemistress, thinks I should go to university.'

'Would you like to?'

'Yes, I think so.' University had for some time been a part of her plan. 'Though it depends,' she added.

Most of all, it depended on money. Coming home from

school at the end of the Christmas term, Freddie had read the bank manager's letters that Tessa had stuffed behind the clock on the mantelpiece. Once more she had offered to leave school and get a job, but Tessa had said forcefully no, certainly not, one of them had to be clever and do well. Freddie had pointed out that Tessa herself had done very well indeed, and Tessa, with a flick of the fingers, had said, 'Modelling . . . it isn't what I want for you, darling.' Because Tessa had looked tired and pale, Freddie had not argued.

She checked her watch. Half past nine, only an hour and a half since she and Tessa had arrived at the nursing home. 'We don't expect baby to arrive before tomorrow morning,' the dragon nurse had told her, and yet Tessa's face had been contorted with pain during the taxi journey from the flat.

Chin up, old thing. Freddie had some time ago acquired the knack of putting on a calm and confident face to the world. What you pretended to be, you eventually became.

She said to Julian, 'Tell me about the RAF. Tell me about the planes. I want to know everything.'

They had sent Freddie away, though Tessa had asked if she could stay. 'Certainly not, Mrs Nicolson,' the nurse snapped, as if she had suggested something indecent. Then, after all sorts of awful things were done to her, Tessa was tucked up in bed and the nurse went away. It was a perfectly nice room, which looked out on to a scrap of winter-brown garden, but she felt forlorn, trapped beneath starched sheets and woollen blankets. It hurt dreadfully — she had asked the nurse whether they could give her something for the pain, but they had told her she wasn't far enough on.

The hours passed slowly. Every now and then someone came to the room to take her temperature and pulse and then went away again, flat shoes clattering on the lino floor. At one o'clock a nurse brought her a tray of food she could not eat. A tea tray at five. A nurse in a dark blue uniform came into the room and said, 'You must have your tea, Mrs Nicolson. You need to keep your strength up,' so Tessa ate a sandwich, then vomited it over the starched white sheets. Two nurses came and changed them, rather crossly.

A long time passed during which she was left alone. She wanted Milo; she wanted Freddie. She wanted to die, and she screamed very loudly and three nurses came running at once. One scolded her, so Tessa swore at her, and the girl looked shocked. Then the sister in the dark blue uniform examined her and told the nurses to take her to the delivery room. After an unspeakable journey along linoed corridors in a rattling wheelchair, she was helped on to a high couch in a brightly lit room. They gave her gas and air and told her to push and a nice nurse held her hand and told her she was doing awfully well. An hour later, with a final fierce contraction and a squirm and a cry, her son was born. They weighed him – six and a half pounds – and then the nice nurse wrapped him in a blanket and gave him to Tessa. The sister came back into the room and hissed, 'What are you doing, Dawkins? Take him away from her. The baby is to be adopted.'

'No he isn't,' Tessa said. 'I'm keeping him.'

And there, her decision made, so easy in the end. Her son's face was crumpled, as if he had been folded up like a handkerchief inside her, and he had a tuft of fair hair, and dark eyes that opened briefly, quizzically, to glance at the world. She knew that it would have torn her heart along the seams to give him to a stranger.

The next day, at visiting hour, they all came to see her: her friends and Freddie, two at a time, because patients were only allowed two visitors in the room at once. They filled the room with flowers and chocolates and magazines, and afterwards the nurses were nicer to her, because among her visitors were a famous musical-comedy actress and a breathtakingly handsome polar explorer.

That evening, after everyone had gone, Tessa climbed cautiously out of bed, careful of the pain between her legs, and found notepaper and an envelope, and wrote to Milo. The nice nurse, Dawkins, posted the letter for her.

He heard the mail clatter through the letter box while Rebecca was in the bathroom. He hurried downstairs; these days he always tried to get to the post first. And the phone.

Recognizing Tessa's handwriting, he put the other letters on the hall table and ripped open the envelope.

'What's that?'

He looked up. Rebecca was standing at the top of the stairs.

'Just another fan letter,' he said, pretending to read the note. 'Loved *The Fractured Rainbow* but *Penelope's Loom*'s still her favourite. Funny how they always think it's a compliment when they say that.'

She said, 'Ah. Scrambled eggs or kippers?'

'Kippers,' he said automatically.

Rebecca went into the kitchen. Milo made for his study,

where he shut the door and sat down at his desk. There was a film of sweat on his forehead. He read Tessa's letter.

Darling Milo, it said, *I have a little boy! He was born very early on Thursday morning and he is the most adorable little thing imaginable.*

Such a conflict of emotions – shock, pride, anxiety, and relief that she had survived the ordeal of childbirth – that he had to sit down, his heart pounding. He read on.

I'm going to call him Angelo Frederick. Angelo because he has golden hair and blue eyes and he looks like an angel, and Frederick after Freddie, of course.

Milo frowned. *I'm going to call him Angelo Frederick . . .*

Quickly he read the rest of Tessa's letter. They had talked about the possibility of adoption: no, not quite true – he had several times tentatively attempted to raise the subject, like a horse shying at a high fence, knowing that, though it might seem to him blindingly obvious that adoption was the best and most sensible course, he had no right to impose his opinion on Tessa. But she had a way of sensing when he was on the verge of bringing up a difficult subject, and deflecting him. She was so rarely serious; it was one of the things he loved about her, yet at the same time it was frustrating. Once, when they had been in bed together, he had understood with untypical clarity that there was nothing he wanted more than to be with her for the rest of his life, and be damned to the difficulties, and had started to speak, but she had pressed her forefinger against his lips, silencing him. 'No, Milo,' she said softly. 'Don't say anything. It's perfect as it is.'

But he had hoped she would have the baby adopted. He had counted on her having the baby adopted. It was in every way the wisest solution. Better for Tessa herself, and better for the child, surely. A boy needed a father.

Milo stared out of the window. Snow was falling, puffy white flakes, the sort that settled. He thought, *a son*, and had a beguiling vision of getting to know the boy, the two of them enriching each other's lives. The boy would call him uncle, of course, and he would have to persuade Tessa not to land him with the name Angelo, which would make it harder for him to fit in and would see him ribbed at school.

The vision dissolved; he saw the cold truth. He remembered a fellow pupil at his prep school. The boy had been illegitimate, and throughout his school years a sense of disgrace had clung to him, a moral greyness that had made Milo both pity him and feel repelled by him. Again he scanned the letter. There was no mention of adoption; every word Tessa had written told him that she meant to keep the child.

And if she did, what were the implications for him? A lifetime's prolongation of the anxiety and suspense he had suffered for the last six months, and a perpetual fear of discovery. He had been walking a tightrope, and the thought that there might be no end to it appalled him. Tessa might believe they could continue to be lovers while keeping the baby's parentage hidden, but Milo suspected that that would prove impossible. Sooner or later they would be seen together, sooner or later people would ask questions. They both had a public face: hers looked out from the cover of a magazine, his from the flap of a book jacket. The scandal would destroy him.

Milo picked up his pen and began to write. *Darling Tessa,*

I was so pleased to hear your news. Stared at the sentence, tore the sheet of paper into tiny pieces and took out another. *Darling Tessa, I was so relieved and delighted to hear your news . . .*

Disappointingly, the baby didn't look like anyone. He didn't even, Freddie thought, look much like Tessa. Angelo looked – this was not an opinion she shared with Tessa – like a little creature who had arrived from outer space, other-worldly, not quite human. Tessa thought him very beautiful, but then Tessa would. He had a surprisingly large nose and surprisingly large hands and feet, a pursed crimson mouth, and very dark blue eyes that seemed sometimes to operate independently, one eye remaining closed while the other peered about, or both eyes not quite shut, narrowed to dark blue slits when he was, to all intents and purposes, asleep. He was very dear, though, and his funny mewing cry when he was hungry and his habit of snuggling up into a little bundle on her chest and falling asleep enchanted her.

When, after ten days, Tessa came back to the flat from the nursing home, Freddie watched carefully the reactions of the various male visitors to Angelo. She studied them, looking for . . . what? Guilt? Paternal affection? She supposed it wasn't very nice of her to be so curious about the baby's parentage, but she couldn't help it. It had occurred to her that Tessa herself might not know who Angelo's father was, or that she might, at least, be unsure. Freddie couldn't help feeling a certain amount of yearning for the sort of life when one might become confused between one lover and the next.

When Freddie offered Angelo to Tessa's men friends,

asking them whether they would like to hold him, some shrank away, muttering that they might drop him, while others picked him up with a practised hand, dandling him against their shoulders and patting his back. Some arrived at the flat with huge bouquets of flowers and enormous boxes of Swiss chocolates, while others presented Tessa with a bunch of snowdrops wrapped in newspaper or a bag of iced buns. By mid-January, when Freddie went back to school, she was none the wiser about Angelo's parentage. As always, Tessa hid her secrets well.

When he cried, his sobs were tearless. Tessa's own tears were copious, prompted by anything – a thumb pricked by a nappy pin, regret that her mother had died without knowing her grandson, the pain of her stitches and aching breasts. The sight of his naked little body in the bath, and the weight of him when he fell asleep, lying across her body, filled her with such an intense and precarious happiness that she wondered whether, giving birth, she had lost a protective layer of skin.

At night, wrapped in her dressing gown and padding into the kitchen to warm up his bottle, she and Angelo seemed to inhabit their own private world. Sound was reduced to the rise and fall of his breath and the murmur of the songs she sang to him. Her lids drooped, feeding him; she bit her lip and sat upright to keep herself awake. Horrors darted into her mind – an infant smothered by his sleeping mother, another who had choked as his mother had dozed. Though, after the first weeks, her breasts stopped weeping milk and her crumpled, swollen stomach shrank, and her figure began to snap back into something like its former shape, she knew she had been changed by the birth. She had lost her blitheness, her confidence in the happy outcome of events. The responsibilities that she had discarded so thankfully when she had first come to London had been thrust back on her a hundredfold. She was vigilant, making sure she did not do anything dreadful through lack of sleep or carelessness – leave the baby, sleeping in his basket, in the back of a taxi, or discover in the middle of the night that she had forgotten to buy him his milk. There were days when she didn't manage to get bathed and dressed until the afternoon. Her first expedition to the shops with the pram, a huge, shiny coach-built Silver Cross that Ray had bought for her, took hours of preparation.

Milo first saw his son when Angelo was three weeks old. He waited until Freddie went back to school, just to be safe, because of Freddie's connection with Miss Fainlight. Tessa felt sorry for him, missing those first weeks. Angelo changed daily, like a flower unfurling. Milo arrived at the flat bearing gifts for her and the baby as well as food he had bought in Fortnum's. He insisted on making their lunch himself. She mustn't do a thing; she must have a rest and he would lay the table, serve the food, wash up. Which was good of him, because the maid hadn't been and there were dirty dishes and baby things – bottles, nappies, little night-gowns drying – everywhere. Milo tidied up, washed dishes, made tea. He cradled Angelo gently, diffidently, and after lunch, when she was tired, they lay on the bed, the baby sleeping between them.

* * *

Sometimes Rebecca was afraid she was going mad. She had begun to think of her suspicion as a thing, a creature, an ugly, grey, misshapen gargoyle that followed her round or perched on her shoulder, a gloating grin on its face as it reminded her that Milo was late home from Oxford, a mocking whisper in her ear when he dashed downstairs before breakfast to collect the post.

She wondered whether she should talk to the doctor. *I have these ideas, these imaginings; I try every day not to think them but they always come.* But the thought of sitting in Dr Hunter's consulting room, with its smell of antiseptic and floor polish, and listening to the condescension in his voice as he suggested she sign up for an evening class or take a day trip to London – *a change of scenery, Mrs Rycroft, so beneficial* – was off-putting.

Perhaps her imaginary Dr Hunter was right. Perhaps she needed more to occupy her. The months after Christmas were always miserable – not much you could do in the garden, and going out for a drive held little appeal. She would establish a new regime, she decided. She would take Julia for a long walk each morning and make sure to talk to someone every day, Meriel or Glyn or one of her friends in the village. She would volunteer to run old ladies to the Radcliffe Infirmary on the days when Milo didn't need the car. She would learn to cook new dinner party recipes, to extend her repertoire. They would have a party at the end of March, to celebrate the publication of *Midwinter Voices*.

Rebecca turned out the cupboards in the Mill House, gave unwanted clothes and books to a charity, and put boxes of clutter they hadn't used for years away in the attic. There, she found a bundle of letters and cards: as she went through them, she knew that a part of her was searching for evidence – a love letter, a postcard, *Darling Milo . . . love and kisses*: who? Not Grace King; she felt certain Milo had told her the truth about that. But the letters she discovered were old, and many were addressed to her – rambling epistles from school friends with whom she had long lost touch, invitations to parties and weddings and christenings, kept for sentimental reasons. Would it have been different, she wondered, if they had had a child? She supposed it would: a child would have kept her busy, and she would not have focused all her love and passion on Milo. But would it have been *better*? Now that was another question. Her ghost child, Archie or Oscar, with his friendly, open face, his independence and his intuitive understanding of her moods – would Milo have minded if she had given some of her love to him?

She took out her easel and pencils. As she sketched a bowl of catkins, her mind wandered, mapping out scenarios. Say he had a crush on some girl. Say she lived in Oxford, as Annette Lyle had done. Easy enough for them to meet up – an afternoon tryst or an hour in the evening, exhilarated by the success of his lecture. But surely he would be frightened of being seen, as he had been eventually, with Miss Lyle. The affair had been exposed when an acquaintance had spotted them together in a hotel bar on the outskirts of Oxford. Not Oxford, then: London. Milo's lover would address her letters to the office he borrowed at the university; he would phone her rather than the other way round. He would call her when he was alone in the house or from the phone box in the village. Easy, really.

He's twitchier than usual. He jumps when the phone rings or the postman knocks at the door. He takes the dog for a long walk each night, when he used to skimp if the weather was bad. He doesn't look happy – surely if he was besotted with some girl he would look happy?

She followed him one evening, muffled up in coat and hat. There were no street lamps, and through the thin mist she could see only the bobbing white circle of his torchlight. Reaching the village, Milo walked on, past the empty phone box. He didn't even glance at it. Feeling foolish and utterly ashamed of herself, Rebecca headed home.

It was harder to go back to work than Tessa had anticipated. For a start, there was her figure, that annoying two inches that refused to budge from her waist. Then, the disapproval she had encountered during her pregnancy persisted: the big department stores gave her the brush-off, telling her they had already engaged their models for the spring season. She persisted, because she needed the money, for Angelo now, as well as for herself and Freddie. She called in favours and rang the contacts in her address book, and eventually, when Angelo was seven weeks old, she secured two days' work modelling hats for *Vogue*.

She engaged a girl from an agency to come in and look after the baby during the day. The evening before, she made sure there were plenty of clean nappies, nightgowns, sheets and towels, as well as sterilized bottles and teats. She rose at half past five in the morning to bathe, feed and dress Angelo, dress herself and do her hair and make-up. She stayed long enough to show the nanny, who was costing her a fortune, where everything was, then she kissed her son, collected her bag and hurried out. In the lift, she thought, well, she seems nice enough, but what if she forgets to warm his bottle? What if she sits and reads magazines while he cries for hours? What if she's not who she says she is, and she kidnaps him and takes him away and I never see him again?

They survived, both of them. This was what she was aiming for, these days: survival. She hadn't realized how hard it would be to travel round London with a baby. Taxis were expensive and she was trying to save money, and the pram wouldn't fit on the bus or the tube. She acquired a routine of sorts, a way of getting through the day. Sometimes, when Angelo slept and she had managed the ordinary things of life – eating, sleeping, getting out, seeing a friend – she thought it was all right. Other days, when no work came in and Angelo cried all night and her hair needed washing and no one had called, she, like the baby, cried herself to sleep.

She learned never to mention Angelo while she was working. At work she must be serene, glittering, beautiful Tessa Nicolson, unchanged, as if the whole experience of pregnancy and giving birth to a son could be filed away and forgotten, like a holiday, or toothache. When a photographer wanted her to work late, she must say, *I have to catch the boat train*, or, *I'm meeting someone* – anything but *I have to get home to my baby because I'm so tired I can't think straight, and if you ask me to stand still a moment longer I shall fall asleep on my feet.*

She saw things differently now. She tried to be good with money – easier now that she had no time to shop – and she tried to keep the flat clean, even on the maid's days off, because she was worried about Angelo catching germs. Time had become precious. She learned how to rush round on a work morning, Angelo tucked into one arm, while she collected her purse, keys, lipstick and address book. She learned how to manoeuvre the pram smoothly in and out of the lift, and how to fit the Moses basket into the MG. Angelo loved being driven in the car. In the early weeks, when it was late at night and he wouldn't go to sleep, she put him in the car and drove till he dropped off. She felt at peace as his cries faded first to whimpers and then to silence as the dark, empty streets flickered by. When, at half-term at the end of February, she drove all the way to Freddie's school in Oxford, and Angelo slept in his basket the entire time, she couldn't have felt more proud of herself if she had climbed Mount Everest.

There were things Tessa minded. She minded when people saw her with the pram and said, 'But I thought you were having him adopted.' Or when they looked at Angelo as if he shouldn't exist, as if he was dirty, contaminated, as if the transgression had been his rather than hers. Though in public she remained stony-faced, in private she wept bitter tears.

But she minded most about Milo. The first time Milo saw his son, Tessa was touched by the expression of wonder in his eyes. As time passed, she began to think that it hadn't been wonder, but bewilderment. She had assumed that although Milo was unable publicly to acknowledge his son, he would have a singular tenderness for him. She had imagined a unique relationship: if he could not be a conventional father to Angelo, he would be something other, something equally wonderful.

What had been exciting during the early months of their affair – the secrecy, the unpredictability, the snatched moments together – was not any more. Motherhood had hardened her, had made her less forgiving. Was he cooling off their affair? Was it possible? No, she would not believe that of him. Yet she found herself adding up the number of times he had been unable to keep a rendezvous or had ended a telephone call, and felt a sort of despair because in doing so she was breaking her own rules. Rules for love – how foolish of her to have believed herself exempt from the everyday contract and payment of the heart!

Chapter Five

'The party went very well,' said Rebecca. 'It was a shame you couldn't come.'

It was a Sunday morning in early March and the sisters were driving to Abingdon for lunch with their mother. The Rycrofts' party to celebrate the publication of Midwinter Voices had been held at the Mill House the previous night.

'I don't much like parties,' said Meriel. 'All that standing around. Why it's thought a good idea to eat a meal standing up, balancing a plate and cutlery, I have no earthly idea.'

Meriel always said that and Rebecca always felt irritated. The Rycrofts' parties were famous – people begged for invitations. It shouldn't be too much to ask, should it, she thought, that her only sister be a little less dismissive?

'We had a marvellous time,' she said stiffly. 'It went on till past one o'clock.'

'I like to be in my bed by ten.'

Meriel's tactlessness and the apprehension Rebecca always

felt before visiting her mother made her press her lips together to stop herself snapping. She was tired; she could have done with an extra hour in bed. She changed gear noisily and made herself concentrate on the road.

'Anyway,' said Meriel, after a while, 'I always go completely deaf at parties. I can never hear a word anyone is saying. I'll give Milo a ring and congratulate him.'

Rebecca recognized this as an olive branch. Meriel hardly ever phoned Milo. 'I'm sure he'd love that,' she said. Then she confided, 'He's rather browned off, actually. Some woman gave the book a bad review in The Times.'

Perhaps the kindest thing that can be said about Mr Rycroft's poetry, the reviewer had written, *is that he should concentrate on writing novels.* The comment had visibly stung Milo. Even the party hadn't cheered him up; in fact he had got very drunk, which was unusual for Milo, and Charlie Mason had had to help her get him upstairs to bed.

'Oh dear,' said Meriel. 'Still, the poems were just for fun, weren't they?'

'He worked very hard on them,' said Rebecca touchily.

'Perhaps it's a bit much to expect to be wonderfully successful at two things. How marvellous to be really good even at one.'

'Yes, I suppose so.' Rebecca braked for a crossroads, looked left and right, and drove on. 'How's Dr Hughes?'

The corners of Meriel's mouth turned down. 'Deborah's trying to persuade him to move to Cornwall.'

'Cornwall?'

'Yes. For her health. Apparently she's always loved Cornwall.'

148

'What about his work?'

'Yes, I know, it's awful, isn't it? He's been Westdown's doctor for ages.'

'Awful for *you*.'

'Yes.' Meriel looked aside, out of the window. 'I should miss him a great deal if he left.'

'Does he want to go?'

'No, not at all.'

Poor Meriel, thought Rebecca. How dreadful to be so utterly wretched about the possibility of someone going away, when that same someone didn't even know you cared for them.

'I shouldn't worry,' she said comfortingly. 'I expect dreary old Deborah will change her mind. Hasn't she come up with this sort of idea before?'

'Oh yes. Often.' Meriel sighed. 'But she does seem particularly keen on Cornwall.' Then she said, 'What about you, Becky? How are you?'

'Me? I'm fine.'

'You've seemed a bit down recently.'

'Have I?' Rebecca tried to laugh. 'I expect it was the party. It's such a lot of work. I'm fine. Everything's wonderful.'

'It doesn't always have to be, you know.'

'What?'

'It doesn't always have to be fine,' said Meriel. 'It doesn't always have to be wonderful.'

The expression in her sister's eyes was disconcerting. Rebecca felt she had let herself down. How humiliating to discover that her anxiety must have been obvious to onlookers.

'I'm perfectly all right,' she said firmly. 'It's just that I hate this time of year, you know that.' She changed the subject. 'What are you buying Mummy for her birthday?'

'Bath salts and talc. Dull, I know, but I can't think of anything else. What about you?'

'I thought about gloves, but I'm sure I gave her gloves last year. Slippers, perhaps.'

'I wondered whether to buy her a really nice box of chocs, but she'd only say she couldn't manage them with her teeth.'

'Even the strawberry creams . . .'

'You can suck a strawberry cream.'

Both sisters giggled. The car headed into the outskirts of Abingdon.

Then Meriel said, 'Oh! I simply *must* tell you! The most *shocking* thing.'

'What?'

'Freddie Nicolson's sister has had a baby.'

'Has she?' said Rebecca vaguely. She signalled to overtake a pair of cyclists.

'*Becky*. She isn't *married*.'

'Oh! That is rather awful.'

Like a warning bell, something seemed to prick in her consciousness. Something troubling, but she was unable just then to dredge it to the surface.

'Whose sister?' She frowned. 'Who did you say?'

'Freddie Nicolson's sister, Tessa. She's a model.'

'A model?'

'She's frightfully famous, apparently. Freddie showed me her picture in *Vogue*.'

'Freddie . . .'

'Freddie Nicolson, yes, I told you about her. Frederica, but we all call her Freddie. Delightful girl. She did awfully well in her School Cert., and she's vice-captain of the First Eleven. I do feel for her, with her family. There are some things that can't be swept under the carpet, aren't there? Anyway, Miss Nicolson hadn't been to Westdown for ages and she was always so good about visiting Freddie. And that must have been why! She was having a baby!'

Frederica, but we all call her Freddie. The memory crystallized. Almost a year ago: the Mill House, her mother's birthday. Daffodils on the lawn and her mother complaining of the cost of curtains. *Thank goodness for Freddie Nicolson,* Meriel had said, *she played marvellously at the last match.* And Milo had looked up and had said, *Nicolson?* And she, Rebecca, who knew him so well, had seen that he was frightened.

'The baby,' she said. 'How old is it?'

'Two months . . . three. I'm not sure. Miss Nicolson showed him to me. Dear little thing, but I was so taken aback I hardly knew what to say.'

Then Meriel touched her arm. 'Rebecca?' she said. 'That was our turning. You've missed our turning. Rebecca?'

First, the certainty that Milo was having an affair with that woman, Tessa Nicolson. It would explain why he had started so at the dinner table, why the mention of the name, Nicolson, had alarmed him. It would explain his elation last spring and summer, the phone calls taken on the study extension, his absences. Push the pieces around and they fitted. If Tessa Nicolson worked as a model, she must be young and beautiful. Westdown School was only six miles from the Mill House. Milo could have come across her on one of his walks – perhaps her car had had a puncture, and Milo, the knight in shining armour, had changed the tyre for her. Or perhaps she had stopped to ask directions, or, if she was the sort of woman who would drink alone in a pub, he, calling in for a pint, might have struck up a conversation with her.

Next, and equally convincingly, the doubt. Her imagination was running away with her again. Her conjectures were ludicrous. Meriel had spoken to her of the mother of an illegitimate child, and within a few moments there she was, assuming Milo to be the father of that child. Worse than ludicrous – insane. She was losing her grip, she was cracking up.

Monday morning: Milo's day for working in Oxford. She couldn't wait until he had left the house; waking at seven after a disturbed and restless sleep, she brought him his tea, then bathed and dressed. While he was in the bathroom, she went downstairs.

Light shone through the stained-glass window in the front door, pouring streaks of sapphire and ruby on to the hall floor. The house looked beautiful and expectant, as if waiting for the events of the day. In Milo's study, Rebecca pulled up the blind, sat down at the desk, opened a drawer and took out his address book. She ran a finger down the cut-away edges of the pages until she came to the letter N. Nash, Neale, Nesbit . . . there was no Nicolson. Then she turned to the Ts. Tattersall, Taylor, Thorne . . . The name 'Tessa' was not listed. She closed her eyes, dropping her head, and heard the rush of her outward breath.

Something made her turn the page. She saw that a little apart from the list of names, Milo had written a letter T. A phone number, Highbury 259, was scrawled beside the initial.

Using the extension, Rebecca dialled the operator, and asked to be put through to the Highbury number.

A pause, noises on the line, and then a woman's voice said, 'Miss Nicolson's residence. Can I help you?'

Rebecca dropped the receiver as if it had stung her, cutting off the connection. Pressing her fists against her mouth, she looked out of the window. The low winter sunlight was turning the dew on the grass into stars. Such a beautiful day. From the recesses of the house she heard a door close and Mrs Hobbs call out good morning. There was the clunk of the kettle as it was placed on the hob, a clatter as vacuum cleaner, bucket and broom were taken out of the cupboard.

She left the study and went upstairs. Milo was still in the bathroom. Her gaze ran round the room, settling first on a pair of stockings folded over the back of a chair, then on her perfume bottles on the dressing table, and then on Milo's jacket, hanging on the wardrobe door. All had taken on a strange and unfamiliar significance, as if she was seeing them properly for the first time.

She sat down on the edge of the bed. Shock coursed through her like electricity, leaving her weak, burned out.

Milo came into the room. At first he did not seem to see her. As he hummed a tune and towelled his hair, he went to the wardrobe and began to dress. He must have caught sight of her then, sitting on the bed, because he turned.

'What is it?'

'Tessa Nicolson.'

He stilled. 'What?'

'Her phone number's in your address book.'

He said quickly, 'She's someone I met at a party in London, that's all.'

She considered him, faintly ridiculous now in underpants and damp hair sticking up in tufts. 'I don't believe you,' she said.

He pulled on his trousers. 'Let's not have a row, Rebecca, please.'

'The only thing I want to know is whether you've been having an affair with this woman. And, if so, whether you're the father of her child.'

He gave a little laugh. 'Rebecca, for God's sake . . .' He crossed the room, took her limp hands in his. 'Of course I'm not having an affair with her. Of course not.'

She pulled away. 'I'll phone her, then. I'll ask her myself.' She stood up.

With sudden speed, he intercepted her, standing in front of the door. 'Rebecca,' he said. 'Please.'

Something inside her shrivelled and died; she realized that she had still hoped she was mistaken. She whispered, 'Shall I phone her, Milo?'

For a moment he seemed frozen. Then he shook his head.

Stumbling away from him, she sank back on to the bed, closing her eyes. A voice – her voice – said, 'How long?' and when he did not answer, she screamed the question at him.

'I said, how long?'

'A year. About a year.'

'Don't you even know?'

'Mrs Hobbs,' he hissed; trembling, she heard the alternate roar and clunk of the vacuum cleaner as Mrs Hobbs hoovered the stairs. Milo muttered, 'I met her last January, but we didn't – there was nothing – till later.' His voice dropped.

'*January.*' Rebecca wiped the perspiration from her forehead with the flat of her hand.

'Meriel,' she said. 'You met her through Meriel.'

'No.'

'But Meriel *knows* this woman.' Another awful thought: did Meriel know that Milo was Tessa Nicolson's lover? Was that why she had made that peculiar remark in the car? *It doesn't always have to be fine. It doesn't always have to be wonderful.*

'No,' he said again. 'I was out for a walk. Tessa was at the pond – the pond at the school. She was skating. It was nothing to do with Meriel.'

Tessa. The easy way he said her name tore a scar across her heart. Her eyes were blinded with tears. She turned to scrabble in the bedside table for a handkerchief, blew her nose and scrubbed her eyes.

'And the child?' she murmured.

When he did not reply, she forced herself to look at him. His guilt was written in his eyes. She whispered, 'It's yours?'

He nodded, then dropped his head. 'I'm so sorry.'

He took a step towards her. If she let him, he would reach out and touch her.

'I want you to go away.' She sounded calm. 'I want you to leave me alone.'

'Rebecca, please . . .'

She screamed, 'Go away! Go to bloody Oxford! Or go to London, go to her, if that's what you want! I don't care!'

Then she curled up on the bed, sobbing. She heard the bedroom door close as he left the room.

Monday evening. She had a pulsing headache. She took a handful of aspirin, made herself a strong coffee. She sat in the back room, smoking and drinking the coffee.

She jumped when she heard the front door open. Milo looked into rooms until he found her.

'I didn't think you'd come back,' she said.

He sat down on a low stool by the window. 'I didn't know if you'd want me to.'

She shrugged. 'You told me you met her last January.'

He dropped his head. 'Yes.'

'At Meriel's school.'

'Yes.'

'And then?'

A silence. Then, 'A couple of months later I ran into her in London.'

'Don't lie to me, Milo.'

A quick outward breath. 'I phoned her.'

'And then you went to bed with her.' She stood up. 'She must be a slut,' she said contemptuously. 'Does she go to bed with every man she meets? Did you have to wait in a queue, Milo?'

Then she left the room, slamming the door. She had eaten nothing all day; she realized that she was very hungry. In the kitchen, she sawed a couple of slices of bread off the loaf, and slammed a chunk of ham between them. Then she went into the sitting room, turned up the wireless very loud to warn him off, and ate her sandwich.

That night, he slept in the spare room. Waking in the early hours of the morning, her bravado dissipated. Too scoured out to cry any more, she lay awake, wondering how she would survive when he left her. Because he would leave her, she saw that now. Why should he stay with her when he could have this beautiful girl, Tessa Nicolson?

She knew that she would be nothing without him. In spite of his faults, in spite of his betrayals, she still loved him. The first day she had met him, she had known that she wanted to spend the rest of her life with him. No one else made her laugh like Milo did. No one else made her feel wanted and beautiful and amusing. A part of her, even now, longed to go to the spare room and climb into bed with him and for him to wrap his arms around her and tell her that it was all going to be all right, that he still loved her, and always would.

Tuesday: she hated him. The way he moved, the way he spoke, the weakness of character she saw written in his face: she loathed every part of him.

She nurtured her rage till the afternoon, when Mrs Hobbs had gone. They conducted the disintegration of their marriage, she thought with grim amusement, according to the hours of their cleaner.

'I want to know everything,' she said. 'You're to tell me

everything. Is she beautiful? What does she look like? Is she young?'

They were at the dining table, eating the lunch that Mrs Hobbs had left for them. Or rather, pushing the lunch Mrs Hobbs had left for them round their plates.

He said heavily, 'I can't see this will help.'

'It's not supposed to help, Milo. Why should I want to help? Actually, I want to make you suffer.' She put down her cutlery. 'How old is she? That's a simple enough question, isn't it? Surely you can answer that?'

'Twenty-two,' he said.

'Twenty-two. 'Good God. You'll be seducing schoolgirls next.' She lit a cigarette. 'What does she look like?'

A jerk of the hand. 'I don't know.'

'Of course you do, Milo. You've been to bed with her, haven't you? Or don't you look at her face?'

He flushed. 'There's no need to be coarse.'

'Isn't there? Blonde, redhead, brunette – you must have noticed.'

'Between blonde and brunette. Honey-coloured.'

'Honey-coloured,' she repeated sarcastically. 'How poetic. What about her eyes?'

'Green,' he muttered. 'They're greenish-hazel.'

'Is she beautiful?'

A silence, then he said flatly, 'Yes. Very.' He raised his head, looking her in the eyes. 'I don't know why you're doing this. I don't know why you *want* to do this.'

'I don't,' she said, her voice cracking. 'But I have to know.'

Then she clattered the plates together and carried them into the kitchen. She began to scrape the uneaten food into the bin. *Honey-coloured. Greenish-hazel.* A handful of carrots escaped the bin and slid on to the floor. She hurled the plates hard down on to the quarry tiles and watched them explode into fragments.

Wednesday morning: she took the dog out for a walk. She walked for a long time, heading up to the hills because she did not want to meet anyone she knew. Her shoes slipped in the mud as she climbed to the wind-blown tops. She remembered walking here with Milo when they had first bought the Mill House, how he had run ahead, waving his arms triumphantly as he reached the summit of the hill. How he had noticed on the map the name 'Herne Hill', and they had walked on, searching for it. She had known that he was trying to read the ancient stories written beneath the grass and harebells.

Now she walked blindly, without a map. The swell and curve of the hills had no meaning for her. The villages in the valleys seemed to float above the earth, unreal, unrooted. It came to her as she walked that it was her own life that was pathetic, not Meriel's. *Poor Meriel:* poor Meriel, whose fiancé had died in the war, who had never been to bed with a man, and who treasured a hopeless calf love for the school doctor. At least these things were honest. Instead, it was poor Rebecca, poor, stupid Rebecca, who had imagined herself to be fortunate, blessed, and yet was living a lie.

At length, growing cold, she walked back down to the main road. Standing on the verge, she lit a cigarette, cupping her fingers round the flame. A baby, she thought, and he had never wanted to have a baby with her. Tears brimmed in her eyes. Milo had a son and she did not. Her ghost child, Archie or Oscar, would never exist. The thought pulled at the fissure in her heart, tearing it in two.

A car, a green Humber, drew up by the verge. The driver's door opened; a voice said, 'Excuse me, is this the Oxford road?'

Rebecca exhaled smoke. 'No, I think you must have taken a wrong turning.'

'These little country lanes all look the same. I say, you couldn't set me right, could you?'

'Of course.' She gave him directions.

'It seems frightfully complicated,' he said. 'You aren't heading the same way, are you, by any chance?'

'I live in Little Morton. It's a couple of miles away.'

'I could give you a lift, if you like.'

'Well, I suppose . . . but the dog . . .'

'The more the merrier. I love dogs.'

He leaned across and opened the passenger door for her. She dropped her cigarette end on to the verge and climbed into the car. The spaniel scampered on to her lap.

He said, 'What's her name?'

'Julia.'

'That's nice.' He had started up the car; he said, 'My name's Edward Robinson, but my friends call me Ned.'

He had a lean, handsome face, black hair smoothed back from his forehead, brown eyes and a thin red mouth. Coils of black hair sprouted on the backs of his hands. If she gave him the right signals, he would ask her to dinner, take her to his bed. Would that be sufficient vengeance?

she wondered. Would it hurt Milo as much as he had hurt her?

But she was cold and tired, and the effort of conversation, let alone of pretending passion, was beyond her.

She said, 'My name's Mrs Rycroft. If you turn right at this T-junction, you'll soon reach my house. I can show you a very easy route to the Oxford road from there.'

'Ah.' He gave a regretful little smile. 'Thank you.'

At the Mill House, the car drew up by the verge. 'There you are,' he said. 'Home and dry.'

She thanked him, and standing at the roadside, watched the Humber drive away. Then she walked round to the back of the house. In the scullery, she took off Julia's lead and wiped her muddy paws with an old towel. She went into the kitchen. There was a stew bubbling on the hob and the tea cloths were neatly folded on the rail. Mrs Hobbs must have left, she realized; she had not thought so many hours had passed.

She walked through the house. The door to Milo's empty study stood open. She caught sight of him in the dining room, standing at the French windows.

'I suppose,' she said, 'you want to leave me and marry her.'

He turned. 'No.'

'Milo, you have a child by her.'

'She doesn't want to marry me.'

'I find that hard to believe.'

Today he looked as tired and strung out as she felt. He made a sweeping motion of the hand. 'It's true.'

'Did you plan to have the child?'

His eyes widened. 'Of course not! Rebecca, it was a mistake – an awful mistake!'

'Are you sure?'

'How can you imagine that I wanted a child?'

'I don't mean you, I meant *her*. Are you sure she didn't get pregnant to make you marry her?'

'No.' He shook his head vigorously. 'No. You don't understand.' He sat down on the sofa. There was a glass on the occasional table – whisky, she thought. He gulped a mouthful. 'Tessa has no intention of marrying me or anyone else. She made that clear from the outset. She's very independent and unconventional. Adventurous.'

'Does she have a lot of lovers?'

He squeezed his eyes shut. 'I don't know.' A pause. 'Yes.'

She said crisply, 'I expect you've got it all wrong, Milo. I expect none of her lovers *wants* to marry her because they know the sort of woman she is. No decent man wants used goods. She'll have got herself pregnant to trap you, to make you marry her.'

He looked up. 'No, that's not so. I told you, Tessa doesn't want to marry me.'

And the hurt she saw in his eyes made her step back, her composure crumbling. 'Do you love her?' she whispered.

A longer pause, this time. 'I don't know,' he said.

Thursday: they had been invited to lunch in the rooms of a Fellow of Merton College. The room looked out over a grassy courtyard and the walls were covered with dark wood panelling. The room smelled of beeswax and old books. I wish I'd done better at school, Rebecca thought.

I wish I'd been a bluestocking. I wish I had facts, figures, landscapes in my head that would stop me thinking about this. I wish I was a nun and lived in a cloister. I wish I was young and beautiful and my photograph was on the front cover of *Vogue*.

'What was she to you?' she screamed. They were at home now; she had drunk too much port at the Fellow's lunch and her head was pounding again. 'Another of your bloody conquests? Or your *muse*? Is that what they are, these girls? Do you put them in your books, Milo? Your soppy, wilting heroines – are they your inspiration, those tarts? Is that what they are to you – a thrill, a bit of excitement, so that you can scribble your mushy little books?'

They were in the hall; he had taken off his scarf and hung it on the peg. Now he crossed the space to her, putting the flats of his hands on the wall to either side of her, trapping her.

'No,' he said venomously. 'I'll tell you what they are. They're my escape. They're my escape from you, Rebecca. Shall I tell you why I need to escape from you? Because you've become unbearable to live with. Your jealousy, your histrionics, your nagging and fussing – they've driven me away. It takes two to wreck a marriage, didn't you know that? You've changed; you're not the woman I married. Everything's got to be perfect for you, hasn't it? The house, the garden, me. Well, I'm not perfect. What I did was wrong. But you're not so bloody perfect either, don't think for a minute you are.'

'Bastard,' she said. Raising her hand, she slapped his face.

'You bastard.' Then she ran past him, through the house, out of the French doors and into the garden, across the terrace and down the lawn, beyond the cedar tree, to the millstream that marked the boundary of their land.

Coloured lights flickered around the periphery of her vision, flecking the broad stream with golds and pinks and purples. *Everything's got to be perfect for you.* Was Milo right? Hadn't Meriel suggested much the same thing? Was that the person she had become, a tiresome perfectionist whose unreasonable demands had alienated her husband?

She heard footsteps behind her. She turned and saw him, crossing the lawn to her. His left cheek was reddened where she had struck him.

'I'm sorry I hit you,' she whispered.

'I'm to blame,' he said. 'I'm the only one who's to blame. I won't see her again, I promise.'

She shut her eyes, trying to extinguish the dancing lights, but they were still there, imprisoned beneath her lids.

'And the child?' she said.

He shook his head. His expression was empty, desolate.

She realized that she did not know the child's name. Better that way, she thought. Better that it should remain nameless, the nasty, misbegotten thing.

Her migraine lasted for two days, forcing them to reach if not a truce, at least a stalemate. Milo brought her glasses of water and aspirin, drew the bedroom curtains for her, made sure that the house was quiet. When eventually she stopped being sick, he made her tea and toast.

He sat on the edge of the bed while she lay propped up on pillows, tearing pieces from the toast, trying to swallow them.

'I never wanted the baby,' he said. 'I was horrified when Tessa told me she was pregnant. I didn't know what to do. She thinks I should love the baby, but I don't, I can't. I can see she's expecting me to love it, and I can see she's disappointed in me, that she thinks I'm letting her down.' He pressed his hands against his face. 'I'll have to pay the boy's school fees, of course, that's only fair. I'm not asking you to forgive me, Rebecca. I know I've no right to ask that. But please – I can't bear it when you're so angry with me.'

He had reached out his hand, so that his fingertips touched hers. She did not move her hand away. She saw how it must have happened. That woman, that man-eater Tessa Nicolson, had taken advantage of Milo's weakness. She had baited her hook and he, poor fool, had taken the bait. Milo must have been a trophy for her. Good-looking, charming and famous, he would have been a significant conquest. *I never wanted the baby. She thinks I should love the baby, but I don't.* She felt, for the first time in that long, dreadful week, a measure of triumph.

On Monday morning, Rebecca had an appointment for a fitting at Chez Zélie in Oxford. Light-headed in the aftermath of her migraine, she let Milo drive her into town. Milo would work while she went for her fitting and did some shopping. Afterwards, he suggested, they could have lunch together. He would book a table at her favourite restaurant. He was trying hard.

165

The rain began as they drove into Oxford. It thickened as the morning went on. A brown stream, laced with cigarette ends and sweet wrappers, ran through the gutters. There was relief in going through the motions of an ordinary day, in her life taking on once more at least a simulacrum of normality. She looked at fabrics in Chez Zélie, walked round the shops, bought herself a coffee. In the newsagent's, her gaze drifted along the racks of magazines, alighting on *Vogue*. Was that her, on the cover? No, the girl in the cover sketch was dark-haired, blue-eyed.

At twenty to twelve she headed down St Michael's Street to meet Milo. The pavements were crowded, umbrellas like black mushrooms bobbing in the rain. Skirting a queue of people at a newsvendor's stand, she caught sight of Milo at the corner of the street, where it met the Cornmarket.

He was talking to a girl. Rebecca froze. As the girl turned away, she caught a glimpse of fair hair and pale skin and recognized Grace King. They had not kissed goodbye, she pointed out to herself; they had not touched. Miss King had crossed the road and was walking up Ship Street. Milo wasn't even looking at her.

But if not her, then another. If not Tessa Nicolson or Annette Lyle or Grace King, then someone else. She would never be safe. Her rage, which was powerful and destructive, simmered to the surface once more, splashing over.

Turning on her heel, she walked back in the direction she had just come. Reaching a phone box, she collapsed her umbrella and went inside. She picked up the receiver and asked the operator to put her through to Highbury 259.

Whirrs and clicks, and then a voice said, 'Hello, Tessa Nicolson speaking.'

In the background, a baby was crying. Rebecca said, 'I believe you know my husband, Milo Rycroft. I expect he's told you he won't be seeing you any more. Or perhaps he hasn't – he always was a coward.'

A second's silence, then the voice said, 'Mrs Rycroft?'

'I'm phoning because I thought you should know that he's moved on. He's found someone else. Some little trollop in Oxford.'

Tessa Nicolson said, 'I don't believe you.'

'Don't you? Are you sure? Her name's Grace King. She lives in Woodstock Road. Go and ask her yourself if you don't believe me.' Rebecca laughed. 'You must realize, Miss Nicolson, that Milo is the sort of man who'll always have his slut on the side. It's in his nature.'

Tessa put down the phone. Its ring had woken Angelo, who had a cold. She took him out of his basket and held him against her, feeling the birdlike rise and fall of his chest against the fast beating of her own heart.

She sat down on the sofa. She was trembling and she felt cold, her skin iced by shock. Rebecca Rycroft knew. How long had she known? Tessa tried to think back. It was almost a month since she had seen Milo. And a long time – a week, perhaps ten days – since he had written or phoned. What had happened? When had his wife found out? Why hadn't he told her?

Angelo had quietened, so Tessa tucked him back into his basket. In the hall, the telephone crouched on the side table like a black toad. It was Monday, Milo's day for working in Oxford. Tessa gave the operator the Oxford number. The phone rang out.

I expect he's told you he won't be seeing you any more. Or perhaps he hasn't – he always was a coward. Was he sitting at his desk, afraid to answer the phone, waiting for the ringing to stop? Had he promised his wife not to call her – had he meekly, obediently, returned to his marriage, the good husband once more, as if their affair had never happened?

After a dozen rings, Tessa thanked the operator and replaced the receiver. She went to the window and lit a cigarette. Rain streaked down the windowpane and the view was a blur of greys and browns. She felt a sudden longing for an Italian spring, for greens and blues and a light that sparkled like champagne. There were so many ways of ending a love affair. A quarrel, a letter, a silence. Many – most – would say she had no right to feel such hurt. She looked away from the window, pressing her knuckles against her mouth as her gaze drifted to the baby sleeping in the basket.

So. Milo's wife knew about the love affair. What else had she said? That Milo had found someone else. Another mistress, another – what had the phrase been? *Another slut on the side.* Had she lied, with the intention of wounding, or could it possibly be true?

Tessa did not know. Miserable, that, to realize she did not trust him. *He's moved on. He's found someone else. Some little trollop in Oxford. Her name's Grace King. She lives in Woodstock Road.* Had she then, simply been *available*?

Grow tired of me, Milo Rycroft, if you must, but not of

your son. Her fury made her sweep through the flat, gathering up raincoat, umbrella, keys, bottles and nappies. She had to know. How dare he hide away from her! How dare he lack the decency, the courage, to tell her to her face. She wouldn't be left dangling on the end of a telephone line, like a fish on a hook. Other love affairs she could have walked away from, but not this one. One day she would have to tell Angelo about his father. What would she say to him? That his father had had so little interest in him, so little feeling for him, that he had turned his back on him before he was even three months old?

Tessa picked up the Moses basket and left the flat. She took the lift to the ground floor; outside, she held the umbrella over the basket as she ran to the MG. She put the basket on the passenger seat, then started up the car and drove away from the flats, heading south-west, for the Harrow road. Beside her, Angelo slept in the basket. Driving, she felt calmer. The motion of the steering wheel, the movement of foot on accelerator and brake, and the rhythm of the windscreen wipers, beating away the rain, became hypnotic. She had always liked to travel. She needed movement, a journey, a destination.

At Harrow on the Hill, she stopped at a garage to buy petrol and cigarettes. Waiting for a gap in the traffic, she thought of turning round and going back to the flat – the futility of this journey, when she had already lost him! – but she knew that to do so would be only a postponement. Better to face it now. She drove on. Pedestrians, bundled in raincoats and sheltered beneath umbrellas, huddled at crossings and bus stops. She was driving through suburbia, stopping and starting in a long queue of traffic through a ribbon of undistinguished housing, stuccoed and Tudor-beamed, a black Austin or Morris in the driveway, dripping laurels and privets demarcating the boundaries of the front gardens. I was not made for this country, she thought. When Freddie is twenty-one, I shall go back to Italy.

The traffic thinned, and Tessa glimpsed to either side of her fields and copses. At Rickmansworth, she turned south, heading for the road that would take her through Beaconsfield and over the Chiltern hills to Oxford. Angelo was stirring. On the outskirts of High Wycombe she stopped at a café and ordered tea for herself and asked for a jug of water to warm Angelo's bottle. The waitress, sixteen or so, whose permed curls stuck out from beneath an unflattering cap, admired Angelo as Tessa fed him. 'He's so sweet. How old is he? When I get married, I'm going to have four little boys. I don't want girls – they're more trouble, my mum says.' She stroked Angelo's cheek. 'Your daddy must be ever so proud of you.'

Angelo dozed off halfway through his bottle. Tessa tucked him back into his basket and stirred her tea. A memory like a shard of ice: Milo kissing her, on the day she had told him she was pregnant. That awful lunch, when the sight of food had made her queasy, and the shock in his eyes as she had told him about the baby. And yet, after he had walked her back to the photographer's studio, he had drawn her to him as they stood on the pavement, his hands reaching beneath her coat, his fingers gripping her waist. They had held each other so tightly, as if they had been trying to root themselves into the earth, to make themselves permanent. The body did not lie: she knew he had loved her then.

She left a threepence for the waitress, picked up the Moses basket and left the café. Inside the car, she sat for a moment, exhausted. She wished she were not alone. She wished Freddie or Ray or Max were with her.

She drove on, through the Chilterns. A lorry overtook her, wheels sending up curls of brown water and drenching the windscreen so that for several seconds she was unable to see out. In his basket, Angelo began to whimper. 'Hush,' she murmured, 'not long now.' As they climbed the hill, the lorry slowed, leaving the MG crawling along in its wake. When the lorry stopped at a crossroads, Tessa too had to stop, and Angelo's cries became louder. The lorry started up again. Tessa hung back, looking for a straight stretch of road where she might overtake. A patch of blue and orange, glimpsed through the rain, formed into a sign advertising Lyons' Tea, flapping in the wind. A cyclist in a yellow oilskin freewheeled down the hill towards them, the single star of his headlamp smudging, multiplying. How much further? Angelo's hands were clenched and he was screaming. 'Soon, darling,' she murmured. 'We'll be there soon, I promise you.' Her heart was pounding; reaching across, she stroked his face, trying to comfort him. Rain drummed on the thin roof of the car. The lorry slowed to take a corner and Tessa, like Angelo, could have screamed with frustration. Then, as they rounded the corner, she saw that the road peeled out in front of her, clear of traffic, so she stamped her foot hard on the accelerator and pulled out on to the wrong side of the carriageway.

She saw through the blur of rain a horse and cart coming out of the field opening ahead. Her hand darted to the horn — a fraction of a moment's indecision: would the noise startle the horse? She thought she had enough room to get back on to the right side of the road before reaching the opening, and wrenched at the steering wheel.

The car lost traction, its wheels skating, spinning on the wet road. Though she fought to control the skid, the MG was pulled horizontally across the carriageway. Tessa heard herself cry out. And then everything that was familiar was torn into fragments — the baby's cries, the squeal of brakes, the hammering of the rain, and the verge and the hedgerow whirling up in front of her, a green and brown wall that filled the windscreen.

The ditch and the hedgerow broke the MG's skid. The impetus slammed Tessa against the steering wheel, then back against the seat, and then into the steering wheel once more.

It was as if a wave had broken over her. Light fractured, and there was the sparkle of breaking glass.

Then she was plunging into the depths, into the darkness and the cold. And then, silence.

Phoning Tessa Nicolson had lifted a weight from her shoulders. Rebecca felt that she had evened things up. Now, Miss Nicolson too knew what it felt like to be betrayed.

They treated each other warily over the next few days, she and Milo. So much had been done and said that hurt; they seemed to limp around the house, their wounds open and raw. Waking in the night, she was sure she would lose him. Her fears resurfaced whenever he left the house. She was afraid he might not come back.

Late on Thursday afternoon, Rebecca was laying the dining table when the phone rang.

She answered it. 'Hello, Mrs Rycroft speaking.'

'Mrs Rycroft,' a girl's voice, 'you don't know me, but my name's Frederica Nicolson.'

Rebecca stiffened. Frederica Nicolson went on, 'I found Mr Rycroft's phone number in my sister's address book. I'm phoning all Tessa's friends. I hope you don't mind me calling you, but there's been an accident, and I thought I should let everyone know.'

'An accident?'

'My sister's been injured in a car crash.'

'Oh.' And then, stiffly, 'I'm sorry.'

'It was three days ago. The car went into a ditch. They said the road was very wet.'

'Three days ago?' Rebecca tried to calculate but could not.

'Yes, Monday afternoon. Tessa's very ill. She's in the Radcliffe Infirmary. They won't let anyone else see her. Just me.'

The succession of short phrases seemed to run out and there was a silence, during which neither of them spoke. Tessa Nicolson – an accident – the Radcliffe Infirmary. Rebecca could not absorb it.

Then the voice on the other end of the phone said, 'The baby died, you see. Angelo died. That's why I'm calling, in case Mr Rycroft would like to come to the funeral. Tessa won't be well enough, but I thought her friends . . .' Again the voice petered out.

Rebecca said, 'The baby's *dead?*'

'Yes, I'm afraid so. He was thrown out of the car. They said he must have died instantly.'

A long silence, this time, during which Rebecca could hear, on the other end of the phone, shaking breaths. Then Tessa Nicolson's sister said quickly, 'I'm sorry, I have to go. I'll let you know about the funeral.' The phone line went dead.

The most awful thing, in a long succession of awful things, was packing away the baby's clothes. In Tessa's flat, Freddie sat on the floor of the bedroom folding tiny cardigans and nightgowns, bonnets and bootees, putting them into the case that Ray had given her. Ray had offered to keep the case at his house, and then, if . . .

Then, if. If Tessa recovered. If she asked to see Angelo's things. If she could ever bear to look at them again. Ray had also offered to pack the case for her, but Freddie had declined. She wanted to do this for him, for Angelo, who had curled up on her chest and fallen asleep, and who had once seemed to mistake her cheek for a breast and had sucked so furiously he had left a small red mark, like a kiss.

She folded the last nightgown and put it in the case. She hunched her knees to her chin and scooped the tears from her face with her thumbs. Then she clasped the lid of the suitcase shut.

The curtains round Tessa's bed were drawn, but beyond them Freddie could hear the muted murmur of the other patients' visitors' voices and the clank of a trolley. Tessa had broken her leg, arm and collarbone and had cracked three ribs, and the force of the crash had thrown her through the windscreen, concussing her. The nurses had cut off the front part of her hair and there was a bandage round her forehead, covering the gash left by the broken glass of the windscreen. The skin around her eyes was bruised to the colour of flint.

The first two days, while Tessa was unconscious, Freddie sat by the bed, willing her to live. *You can't go, you can't leave me all alone, I won't let you.* When, at the end of visiting hour, the nurse put her head round the curtains and told her that it was time to leave, Freddie wanted to scream at her. She was afraid Tessa might ebb away in the night if there was no one to call her back.

On the third day, Tessa's eyes opened and she began to drift in and out of awareness. Sometimes she asked for Angelo, and Freddie squeezed her hand and said gently, 'Hush, go to sleep.' Then Tessa closed her eyes and drifted off again. It was as if, Freddie thought, she were sailing a boat that kept trying to come into port but never quite made it.

There was an afternoon when a nurse drew Freddie aside as she arrived at the ward and told her that they had informed Tessa about the baby. 'Poor little thing,' the nurse added, and Freddie was unsure whether she was referring to Tessa or Angelo. That afternoon, Tessa didn't cry, didn't say a word, in fact. The next visit, she wept and wept until a nurse came and gave her an injection. The day after that, she lay still, her face as white as the pillowcase, the bruises

175

round her eyes turning to crimson and yellow. She asked questions; there was a long gap between each one, as Tessa tried to take in Freddie's reply. Sometimes she asked the same question twice.

The funeral was held at Christ Church in Highbury, nine days after the accident. Before the service, the mourners drifted into the churchyard. There were Tessa's fellow models, elegant in black suits and veiled hats, and there were owners of delicatessens and ice-cream parlours from the Italian community in Soho, and musicians and artists and writers, and Tessa's smart friends, from Mayfair and Belgravia. So many people. Freddie shook hands and said good morning and thank you for coming. And she remembered: she had a good memory.

A tall, dark-haired woman came up and introduced herself as Rebecca Rycroft.

'I'm afraid my husband's unwell,' said Mrs Rycroft. 'He sends his apologies and his condolences. I thought I would come . . .' she seemed to search for a phrase, 'to represent him. I hope you don't mind.'

'It's very kind of you,' said Freddie. 'I appreciate it. I'm sure Tessa will be touched.'

That was a lie: Tessa wouldn't be touched, because Tessa didn't care about anything any more. She lay in her hospital bed, said little, did as she was told. She had turned into a poor imitation of her former self, someone who looked a little like the old Tessa, sounded a little like the old Tessa, but was in fact completely different.

Mrs Rycroft asked after Tessa, and Freddie repeated the formula she had already used many times that morning.

'The doctor says she's improving.'

'You said on the phone that your sister is in the Radcliffe Infirmary. But I thought she lived in London.'

'The crash was on the Oxford road,' Freddie explained. 'The Radcliffe was the nearest hospital. I don't know why she was driving to Oxford. I suppose she must have been coming to see me, but she hadn't said anything, and she never usually visits on a Monday afternoon. But Tessa's like that. She often does things on the spur of the moment.'

'Can't she remember?'

'Not at all. She's hurt her head. And it doesn't matter, does it, why she was there, and it's really just as well she can't remember anything.' The thought of Tessa remembering her last journey with Angelo was too horrible to contemplate.

Mrs Rycroft was looking upset. Her hands opened and closed as if she was grasping words out of the cold air. Eventually she said, 'Is there anything I can do?'

'Thank you, but there's nothing. There's to be a buffet lunch at the flat after the funeral. You're welcome to join us.'

'No thank you. It's kind of you, but I'm afraid I can't. I'm so sorry.' Mrs Rycroft pressed her lips together. 'The poor little baby. I'm so very sorry.' Then she turned away, and her black coat was swallowed up in the sea of black.

They had begun to file into the church: Max, Paddy Collison, Antonio, Julian Lawrence. Tessa's French lover, André, had taken the boat train over from Paris the night before. So many men, Freddie thought. Which one of you was Angelo's father?

If you're married, she vowed to herself silently as, taking Ray's arm, they walked into the church, then I shall tell your wife. If you value your reputation, I shall destroy it. If other people look up to you, I'll make sure they do so no longer. The force of her anger almost blinded her, and she stumbled and would have fallen had it not been for Ray's hand on her arm, supporting her.

Part Two

Rebecca's Angel

1938–1939

Chapter Six

Rebecca left Milo three months later. Early one July morning, while he was still asleep, she phoned Meriel at Westdown School. Meriel – dear Meriel – said, after Rebecca told her that she needed somewhere to stay, 'Yes, of course. I'm free between half past one and two, so that would be a good time for you to arrive. Come straight up to the flat.'

Milo left for Oxford at ten, by taxi, because Rebecca had told him she needed the car to take an elderly neighbour for a hospital appointment. If Milo was keeping the Mill House, she was damned well having the Riley. She spent the rest of the morning packing and sorting out the house, which was ridiculous: what did it matter whether the Mill House was tidy or not, when she would not be living there any more? She wrote a short note to Milo and left it on his study desk, and then went for a walk round the garden, both to calm her nerves and because she would miss the garden. Then, once Mrs Hobbs had gone home, she put her suitcases in the boot of the car and drove away. She had wondered whether she might feel regretful, but a neighbour's dog was wandering across the road and by the time she had negotiated her way round it, the Mill House was out of sight and she had not even looked back.

Meriel's flat was in a whitewashed villa some way apart from the main school building. Meriel herself answered the doorbell and took one of the suitcases. Her broad navy-blue-clad bottom swayed ahead of Rebecca as they made their way up several staircases. 'I've put up the camp bed for you,' she said, over her shoulder. 'It's quite comfortable. I always use it when I'm camping with the Guides.'

They were both red-faced and puffing by the time they reached the flat. Meriel made tea and offered Rebecca a sandwich, which she declined. Then Meriel said, 'I'll have to dash, I'm afraid. I've the Remove for maths. Hopeless lot, they can't even add up.' She peered at Rebecca. 'Are you going to be all right? There are lots of books to read, or you could go for a walk in the grounds.'

'I'll be fine, thanks. You head off.'

'I've managed to wangle it so I can eat here tonight instead of with the girls.' Meriel gave Rebecca a clumsy hug.

'Thanks,' said Rebecca again. 'So sweet of you. I do appreciate it, you know.'

When Meriel was gone, Rebecca wandered round the flat. Though it was small – sitting room, bedroom, bathroom and a tiny kitchenette – it was pleasant, with views over playing fields bordered by horse chestnuts. On one of the fields, girls were playing a game of hockey. Rebecca, who as a schoolgirl had enjoyed hockey, felt a pang of yearning for those uncomplicated days. Except, she reminded herself, they hadn't been uncomplicated at all; the fierce friendships and jealousies of school had been, in their way, as painful a morass as marriage, and she had always lived a double life, the oddness of her home and parents kept firmly hidden away. Which was perhaps where she had acquired the habit of concealment. Though never, ever had she kept a secret as dreadful as she did now.

She chose a book from the bookcase and sat down on the sofa to read it. But she felt unexpectedly sleepy – relief at leaving the Mill House, perhaps – and after a while she put aside the book and curled up on the sofa and drifted off.

They had supper – scrambled eggs on toast followed by fruit salad – at half past six. Then Meriel had to supervise prep and hobbies. At half past eight she returned to the flat, sighed and exchanged her shoes for tartan slippers. 'Matron and the prefects can cope with the rest,' she said. 'I could do with a drink, couldn't you?'

Meriel made gin fizzes. A brief conversation about her day, and then Meriel, who had sat down in the armchair, said, 'Well?' and looked at Rebecca.

'I've left Milo,' said Rebecca.

'Yes, you said. Do you want to talk about it?'

She had thought she didn't, but it seemed unfair to impose herself on Meriel and not even offer an explanation. She said, 'I know you've never liked him.'

'I wouldn't say that. Milo's clever and amusing and

charming and he's always been very kind to me, and I know I'm not the sort of woman he'd normally bother with.'

Rebecca drank her gin quickly. 'What do you mean?'

'Milo likes pretty women. He thinks the rest of us are a waste of time. Make yourself another, won't you?'

'You?'

'Please.' She handed Rebecca her glass.

Rebecca mixed gin, soda water, sugar and lemon juice. 'You are pretty, Meriel,' she said. 'You have lovely eyes.'

'Rot. I'm as plain as a pikestaff. It's all right, I don't mind, I'm used to it. And I think it's easier for a woman to make something of her life if she isn't distracted by men and marriage, all that.'

Rebecca wasn't sure whether she cared for Meriel's implication, but she said, 'The trouble is, Milo's awfully fond of pretty women.' She couldn't help sounding bitter.

Meriel first looked blank, then shocked. 'Oh. I'm sorry, I didn't realize.'

'Honestly?' Rebecca glared at her.

'Honestly. If you want the truth, I've always thought he was madly in love with you.'

'He was. He says he still is. But he falls madly in love with other women as well. And I can't bear it any longer.' For the first time that day, she felt close to tears.

'Oh dear, how awful. The cad.'

'The thing is, I don't care for him any more. I did for years and now I don't. I thought I still did, after the last time, but it's just gone. Actually, I despise him.'

'And you don't think . . . if you talked, perhaps?'

'I can hardly bear to look at him, let alone talk to him. The last three months have been awful. I've sometimes thought I was going mad.'

'What will you do?'

'I'll get a divorce, I suppose.' Rebecca had sat back down on the sofa; she took a gulp of gin. 'I wouldn't bother – I shall never marry again – but I can't imagine Milo staying single for long.' She laughed. 'That's the funny thing. He likes being married even though he's so bad at it.'

'Did you tell him you were leaving?'

Rebecca shook her head. 'I left a note. I couldn't face the scene. Was that feeble of me? I felt too tired.'

Meriel patted her shoulder. 'You can stay here as long as you want, you know.'

'That's so kind of you, but I've decided I shall go to London.' She had made no such decision: the thought had just popped into her head, surprising her. Yet it seemed a good idea. 'When I was at art college,' she said, 'I loved living in London. And it'll be a change, being in a city. But thank you so much for having me here. I needed a breathing space.'

'Will you be all right for money? I'm sorry to be so blunt, but I've some savings put by.'

'Sweet of you, but Milo can pay for my board and lodging,' said Rebecca bitterly. 'He's not short of cash. He's done very nicely these last few years. And, after all, he owes me.'

'A divorce . . .'

'Yes, I know, Mummy will be furious.' Rebecca swallowed her gin. 'I ought to go and see her and tell her face to face.'

'I wouldn't. Write her a letter. Then she might have got used to the idea by the time you next visit.'

'It'll be high on our list of failures, don't you think, the first divorce in the family?'

They each had another gin and then they got ready for bed, taking turns to use the bathroom. Meriel fell asleep quickly – only a few feet away, on the narrow camp bed, Rebecca could hear her sister's light snores – but as she searched for a comfortable position, the gin seemed to be keeping her awake, rather than sending her to sleep as she had hoped.

All the thoughts she had tried to avoid during the day resurfaced. She hadn't had to worry about running into Freddie Nicolson at Westdown because Meriel had told her some time ago that Freddie had left school to look after her sister. Mixed with her grief and resentment at the ending of her marriage was horror at what she had done. *Tessa can't remember the accident because she's hurt her head*, Freddie had told her at the funeral. *She can't remember why she was driving to Oxford.* Perhaps on that day Rebecca had thought for a fleeting moment that Tessa Nicolson's memory loss had let her off the hook, but if so, she had been mistaken. As the weeks had passed, she had come to realize that she had been caught, pinioned, and might never escape.

Should she have told Miss Nicolson the truth at the funeral? Should she have said, 'I know why your sister was driving to Oxford that afternoon. It was because of my phone call'? Because that had been her inescapable conclusion: that her telephone call had prompted Tessa to come to Oxford to confront Milo. She hadn't told Freddie Nicolson

186

about her phone call because she hadn't had the nerve. And if she had had the guts to tell the truth, would that have been the right thing to do? Or would it have relieved her of the burden of secrecy while doing nothing at all to lessen the Nicolson sisters' grief?

She had told Milo nothing of her own role in the events that had led up to Tessa's accident. She had reasoned to herself that she did not know for certain that her phone call had prompted Tessa's decision to drive out of London that day. There might have been a dozen other explanations for her having been on the Oxford road that rainy afternoon. She might not even have been driving to Oxford itself – it was perfectly possible that she had been rushing into the arms of some other lover, somewhere en route. And besides, thought Rebecca, hadn't she had every justification for making that phone call? Hadn't Tessa Nicolson done an unforgivably wicked thing in going to bed with another woman's husband? She had put up with Milo's philandering for years – hadn't she the right to fight back? And it wasn't her fault, was it, that the car had skidded on the wet road.

Yet her mind returned with dreary inevitability to the knowledge that had haunted her ever since Freddie Nicolson had told her about the accident. That she had wanted to hurt Tessa. That she had hated her. That telephoning Tessa that rainy afternoon and counterfeiting a tale of Milo's affair with another woman had been an act of vengeance, and of spite.

Milo had refused to attend the baby's funeral. 'But he was your *son*!' she had shouted at him, and he had flinched

187

and muttered, 'I can't do it. I just can't do it. You may think what you like of me, Rebecca, but I can't bear it.' In the weeks that had followed, he had remained at the Mill House, cancelling his evening lectures in Oxford, pleading illness, leaving the house only to walk on the downs.

But as time passed, his former bounce had begun to return. An American publisher had bought the rights to three of his novels, and Milo had opened a bottle of champagne to celebrate. He had accepted a speaking engagement on the radio. He never mentioned the baby, never spoke of Tessa.

Rebecca flicked on the torch Meriel had lent her to look at her watch. Almost one in the morning. She was coming to know such nights well. The stomach-churning guilt and regret, the slide into a broken sleep not long before dawn, the exhaustion the next day. London, she thought. I shall think about London. There's nothing I can do about the past, so I must think instead of the future. I shall find some-where to stay, somewhere nice. A new start, a new life: that's what I need. She willed her eyes to become heavy, the pounding of her heart to slow.

Rebecca stayed with Meriel for a week. Milo phoned several times but she refused to speak to him. Dr Hughes called to see one of the pupils, who was unwell; Rebecca tact-fully invented an errand while he had a cup of tea at Meriel's flat. The flat was too small for two to live in comfortably. Rebecca sensed that if she and Meriel were not quarrelling now, they might soon do so – and besides, that bloody camp bed.

Meriel recommended a hotel in which she herself some-times stayed when in London, so Rebecca phoned ahead and booked herself a room. She did not know the proced-ure; she had never booked into a hotel before. Milo had always taken care of all that.

The hotel, which was called the Wentworth, was in Elgin Crescent in Notting Hill. The porter carried her suitcases up to her room and Rebecca fumbled in her purse for a tip. The porter left, closing the door behind him. She was unsure whether she had given him too much or too little.

In the room there was a wardrobe, a chest of drawers, a bedside table and a washbasin. The sight of the single bed depressed her. She ran a fingertip along the mantel-piece – the room seemed clean, at least. She sat down, tired by the long drive, and eased off her shoes. She felt a lowering of the spirits that had become familiar to her, the start of a descent down a slide. A plan: she must make a plan. There were so many wonderful things to do in London. She could go shopping or visit an art gallery or walk in a park. When she had been a student, she had loved walking in London's parks.

She checked her face in the mirror, and left the hotel. En route to Kensington Gardens, she bought herself a sand-wich and an apple. It was a fine, bright summer day and her certainty that she had made the right decision in coming to London returned. She ate her lunch sitting on a bench in the Italian Garden and afterwards walked to Knightsbridge, where she wandered round Harvey Nichols, looking at clothes. How nice, she told herself, to be able to window-shop without having to worry about Milo being bored.

After she left the department store, buoyed up by the success of her expedition, she went into a phone box and dialled Toby Meade's number.

'Yes?' It was more of a grunt than a word.

'Toby, is that you?'

'No, this is Harrison.'

'May I speak to Toby Meade?'

'No, you may not.'

How rude, thought Rebecca. She could hear voices in the background. She said, 'This is Toby's flat, isn't it?'

'Toby's out. Something to do with a gallery.' Harrison's voice had a northern lilt.

'Could you give him a message?'

'I expect so.' A rustling. 'Christ, you'd think there'd be a bloody pencil. Right. Who are you?'

'Rebecca Rycroft.' She was beginning to feel irritated. 'Could you please tell Toby that I called. Please tell him I'm in London.' She realized that she did not know the phone number of her hotel. 'I'm staying at the Wentworth, in Elgin Crescent. If he could give me a ring . . .'

'Okay.'

'Thank you.'

Then Harrison said, 'I'll give him the message. By the way, you have a lovely voice, Rebecca.'

'Oh!' she said, startled. But he had put the phone down.

Her solitary meal in the hotel dining room that evening was interrupted by the waiter telling her there was a phone call for her. She went to reception to take the call. Toby Meade was on the line. A quick conversation – she was restricted in what she could say by the fact that the receptionist, a fierce-looking girl with a heavy fringe and thick black eyebrows, was only a few feet away – and then Toby said, 'I've a few people here, we're having a bit of a get-together. Are you free to pop over for a drink?'

Rebecca accepted the invitation and rang off. She did not return to the dining room and her half-eaten apple pie, but went upstairs to her room. It felt odd, getting ready to go out without Milo. All her social life had been conducted with him; he might have gone to his London parties without her, but it had been sixteen years since she had been to a party without him. Would it be awful, being on her own? But then she and Toby had always been such friends – it would be fine, she told herself. She ran a comb through her hair and reapplied her lipstick. A last check in the mirror – the green silk blouse she was wearing suited her, she knew it did – and then she left the room.

She took a taxi to Toby's studio in Chelsea. The lights were on in the upper storeys of the house. No one answered her knock at the door, so she gave it a cautious push. It opened, and she went inside. Toby lived at number nine. As she climbed the stairs, the noise – music and a low roar of voices and laughter – became louder. She had to step around people sitting on the treads.

A number 9 was painted on a flat piece of bone – a jawbone, from the teeth on it – that hung from a hook beside an open door. People spilled out of the door into the corridor. The buzz of conversation and laughter rose and fell, muffling the music of a piano.

Rebecca squeezed herself through the crowds, looking

for Toby. Mauve crêpe paper had been wrapped round the light bulbs and guests sat on sofas and chairs or stood beside a trestle table, on which there were plates of food. The music came from an upright piano. The pianist's fair hair was long enough to touch his collar and he was wearing an overcoat.

Toby was on the far side of the room, talking to a girl. She was short and slightly built but buxom, and she had pale, freckled skin. Her long red hair tumbled in Pre-Raphaelite curls down her back. She was wearing a peasant blouse and a long dark skirt, beneath the hem of which could be seen bare, sandalled feet.

Rebecca said, 'Hello, Toby,' and he turned.

'Becky, *sweetheart*.' He hugged her. 'How are you?'

'Very well, thank you.'

'So good to see you.' Toby glanced over her shoulder. 'Too Bohemian for Milo, then?'

'He isn't with me. I came to London on my own.'

He gave her a curious look, but said, 'I'm delighted you did. This is Artemis Taylor.' The girl in the peasant top smiled. 'Artemis, this is my old friend Rebecca Rycroft. We were at college together.'

The girl said, 'What sort of thing do you do?'

It took a moment for the question to make sense, then Rebecca laughed. 'Nothing now, I'm afraid. I haven't painted for years. Are you an artist, Miss Taylor?'

'A sculptor. I'm using driftwood just now. We went to Aldeburgh at the weekend. We found some marvellous pieces on the beach.'

'We carried them back on the train,' said Toby. 'I think

the other passengers thought we were mad.' His arm was around Artemis's shoulders; with sudden intuition, Rebecca knew that they were lovers, and felt, unreasonably, a wash of disappointment. Once, a long time ago, before Milo, Toby had thought himself in love with her − of course his life had long since moved on.

Toby asked her what she would like to drink. Rebecca opted for beer, which arrived in an enamel mug. They talked for a while about Toby's work, but then more guests arrived and Rebecca found herself squeezed to the outer edges of the circle. Her mug was empty, so she went to the table in search of another drink. The plates bore the remains of a red jelly and crumbled pieces of cake and a few sandwiches, curled up at the corners.

A voice behind her said, 'You must be Rebecca.' Turning, she saw the pianist.

'I'm Harrison Grey,' he said. 'We spoke on the phone.'

This, then, was the impolite man who had taken her call. The man who had said *You have a lovely voice.*

She said coolly, 'Good evening, Mr Grey.'

'Good evening, Miss Rycroft.' There was a touch of mockery in his eyes, which were light and translucent. His face was gaunt, with hollowed cheekbones, and he had a long, thin nose and a small mouth.

'It's Mrs, actually,' she said.

'I beg your pardon, Mrs Rycroft.' He spoke in a slow, amused drawl. She suspected he was laughing at her.

Insufferable man, Rebecca thought. 'If you'll excuse me . . .'

'You're not going to leave me all alone, are you?'

193

'You're hardly alone.'

'But I detest parties. What about you, Mrs Rycroft? I shouldn't have thought this was your sort of evening.'

'Why do you say that? You don't know anything about me.'

'No, but I can guess. You have such a lovely plummy voice. Do you sing, Mrs Rycroft?'

'Only at church, I'm afraid.'

'You go to church?'

'Sometimes. Not often.'

He made a hissing sort of laugh. 'You're too good to be true. Which are you − RC to cope with the middle-class guilt, or Anglican because you like the words and music?'

'Anglican,' she said crossly. 'And yes, I do like the words and music. Is that so dreadful?'

'I believe all religion is the opiate of the masses, but we can argue that another day. And in my time, I've loved a good hymn.' He made an apologetic gesture. 'I haven't been sleeping well recently. It makes me bad-tempered.'

She felt some sympathy towards him. 'Everything seems to irritate after a bad night, doesn't it?'

'Ah, you too.'

He was flirting with her − in a peculiar, annoying way, but it was flirting nevertheless, and the realization lifted her spirits.

He asked, 'What are you drinking?'

'Beer.'

'I've something better.'

He took from the pocket of his overcoat a half-bottle of

gin and poured a measure into her mug. 'I'm afraid I've no ice or lemon. Is that too uncivilized for you, Mrs Rycroft?'

'I'll cope, thank you. How do you know Toby?'

'Ah, cocktail party opening gambit number three – have we skipped origins and occupation?'

'Not if it bothers you. You don't come from London, do you?'

'I was born in Leeds. And you?'

'Oxfordshire.'

'Very Home Counties. I work for an engineering company. They call me a manager but I'm really just a glorified sales rep. It's loathsome, but it pays the rent. I met Toby in a pub. I was playing the piano and Toby asked for a tune. What about you, Mrs Rycroft?' He put on an upper-class accent. 'How long have you known our host?'

'Since art college. Eighteen years.'

A little more than the span of her marriage to Milo. Such a long time, and yet now the years seemed to contract and disappear, as if nothing significant had happened in them. Her small bubble of happiness burst and she could have cried.

'Your husband,' said Harrison Grey. 'The lucky Mr Rycroft. Is he here?'

'No.'

'Well, I can't say I miss him.'

'Neither do I.'

He smiled, then clinked his glass against hers. 'Cheers, then.'

'How could you tell it was me?' she asked. 'How did you know I was the person you'd talked to on the phone?'

'Wasn't difficult. You hardly look like an habituée of Bohemia.'

Artemis Taylor's outfit, Rebecca had noticed, was far more typical of those of the other female party-goers than her own tweed skirt, silk blouse and heels.

'And I asked Toby whether you were coming,' he added. 'I've been looking out for you. I had high hopes of you.'

'Then I'm sorry I've disappointed you.'

'Disappointed?'

'My plummy voice . . . my churchgoing.'

'Actually, you're not a disappointment at all.' A wolfish smile. 'You're quite perfect, in fact.'

Sometime that night, a length of purple crêpe caught fire and there was a great deal of shrieking and foot-stamping and the smell of smoke. Later, Rebecca found herself standing at the piano as she and Harrison Grey sang 'I've Got You Under My Skin'. Afterwards, they danced. Harrison still wore his overcoat. He was tall and gangly and, in truth, not a very good dancer, but he held her close and when the music ended he raised her hand and kissed it.

'I have to go now,' he said. 'I've enjoyed meeting you, Mrs Rycroft. I might give you a ring sometime.'

He seemed to expect a response, but the pleasure she had felt, dancing, was draining away, so she managed only, 'Yes, do, if you like.'

Shortly after Harrison left, the partygoers began to drift off, and eventually there were only three of them, Rebecca herself, Toby and Artemis. This was when she began to cry. Great blubbering tears billowed over her lids and poured down her face, like a saucepan boiling over. Toby said, 'Oh Rebecca,' and 'Don't cry, darling girl,' and 'It's Milo, isn't it?' but still she cried. She was vaguely aware of Miss Taylor tactfully leaving the studio, and of Toby making tea for her and giving her aspirins. She managed to gulp a mouthful of tea and swallow the tablets, and then he said gently, 'Tell Uncle Toby.'

So she did. Not everything, of course, not about Tessa Nicolson and the baby and the phone call, because these were things she would never tell anyone. But she told him about Milo's unfaithfulness, and he said, 'The bastard,' and, 'You're better off without him,' which for some reason did not cheer her at all.

She crushed Toby's handkerchief into a wet ball. Her marriage was over, and she could not understand what she was supposed to do with the rest of her life. She felt pointless without Milo — yes, that was the word, pointless. She did not know how to spend her days. She hated being all alone in that beastly hotel. She hated the way the receptionist looked at her and she hated that the waiter, seeing she was a woman on her own, gave her the smallest table in the dingiest corner of the dining room.

She stopped crying. She was beginning to sober up.

Toby said, 'Do you want to go back to Milo?'

'No.' They were sitting side by side on the sofa. The debris of the party lay scattered around them, cups and glasses and blackened flakes of crêpe paper. 'I can see now that it was over years ago,' she said miserably, 'but I was too stupid to realize. But I don't know what to do.'

'I don't see that you have to do anything, Becky,' said Toby. 'You don't have to get a job, do you?'

'Thank goodness, no. Milo's always been very good about money. For all his faults, he's never been stingy.' They shared a joint bank account; it occurred to her that this was hardly an arrangement that could continue if they were to divorce – yet another dreary adjustment she must make.

'Then why not just live? Why not wait and see what life turns up? Why not have some fun?' Toby smiled. 'I've never been much of a planner. I've always pottered along from day to day. It's not so bad.'

'I'm not sure I'm capable of that.'

'Give it a go. I'll be always around if you need a shoulder to cry on.'

'Dear Toby. I feel so ashamed, making such a scene.'

He hugged her. 'Nonsense. What are friends for?'

'I'll try,' said Rebecca, with resolve. 'I'll do as you say, I'll let things happen. Who knows, I might even enjoy it.'

Toby made more tea and told her she could sleep on the sofa if she liked. After she had drunk the tea, she curled up under a blanket and, to her great relief, fell asleep.

The next morning, her head ached with crying. She rubbed the smudged mascara from under her eyes in the grim shared bathroom, then thanked Toby and caught a bus back to Elgin Crescent. Walking into the hotel, wearing the clothes in which she had gone out the night before, she felt grubby and dishevelled. As she collected her key, the receptionist gave her a knowing stare. Rebecca stared back; the girl dropped her gaze.

The poky little bedroom seemed oddly welcoming.

Rebecca drank several glasses of water, put up the 'Do Not Disturb' sign, climbed into bed, pulled the eiderdown over her and went back to sleep.

She tried, she really did. *Why not just live? Why not have some fun?* She went to the National Gallery and the Tate and to afternoon recitals at the Wigmore Hall. She went for a walk whenever the weather was fine, to one of the Royal Parks or along the Embankment. She went on a shopping expedition and returned to the hotel with carrier bags of new clothes.

Eating in the hotel dining room was a twice-daily ordeal. Was she imagining the derision of the waiters and the curiosity of the other guests? She could not be sure. And though she considered calling up friends, she did not do so. Those friends had come to parties at the Mill House; they had known her as part of Rebecca and Milo, that enviable, glamorous couple. They might disapprove of her leaving Milo. Worse, they might pity her.

Harrison Grey didn't write or phone. She had thought he might, but he didn't. He probably flirted with every stray single woman he met. *You have a lovely voice, Rebecca*: she suspected that had been — what had he called it? — his *opening gambit*.

She moved to another hotel, on Ladbroke Grove. This hotel, the Cavendish, lacked the pretensions of the first. The room was small — one had to turn sideways to pass between her suitcases and the bed — but it suited her, was more anonymous, and just now she chose to be anonymous. The bar was populated by travelling salesmen and company representatives. Sometimes, in the evening, she had a drink with them. She became adept at inventing a fictional family, a story to explain her solitary stay in London, to ward off the hand on her knee, the offer of a nightcap in their room.

Milo wrote to her; she tore up his letters without reading them. Returning to the hotel one morning, she found him waiting for her in reception. They needed to talk, he said, he couldn't go on like this. So they had an awful lunch at the Lyons at Marble Arch, and then an even more awful walk in Hyde Park, quarrelling in low, hissing voices so that passers-by did not hear. 'I can't think why you would choose this,' he said to her. 'Living in that hotel, away from your home and your friends. I know what I did was wrong, I know that I've hurt you, and I'll say I'm sorry a hundred times more if that will make you come back to me. I was a fool, and I promise you I'll never look at another woman again, never.'

'The thing is,' she said, 'I don't love you any more. I don't even hate you. I feel nothing at all for you.' Milo's face seemed to fold in on itself, his buoyancy punctured. They parted; he went to catch his train.

That night she went to bed with a salesman from Bolton, whom she met in the hotel bar. He was younger than her, mid-twenties, she guessed, not much more than a boy. He had a handsome, friendly face, all neatly sculpted lips and soft grey-blue eyes, and a skinny body so white it seemed to have a greenish tinge. In the morning, abashed, presumably, at finding himself in bed with a woman, he put on his overcoat over his naked body, bundled up his clothes in his arms and went along the corridor to the bathroom to dress. His name was Len and he gave her his address and asked her to write to him, but she never did.

She knew that she was falling, sinking, fighting for air. Not long, and she might drown.

There was a day when she didn't leave her hotel room. She woke early in the morning with tears in her eyes. She couldn't face the walk to the bathroom – she could hear other guests shuffling along the corridor. A paralysis crept over her. She shrank from the thought of going down to the dining room, where the salesmen and reps each morning looked up from their eggs and bacon and stared at her.

The next morning she wrote out a plan in her diary. Breakfast in a nearby café would get her out of the hotel and spare her the ordeal of the dining room. She would buy a sandwich for lunch and eat it in the park every fine day; lunch in a Lyons if the weather was bad. She would make an appointment to get her hair cut and she would do her nails. She would go to the cinema on Tuesdays and to a concert on Friday afternoons. She would buy a sketchbook and start drawing again instead of moping around. She would consider Toby's suggestion that she rent a flat instead of living in a hotel, though there was a permanence in the idea that she found herself shrinking from. She would keep rigidly to her plan, because the alternative, the lethargy that had kept her lying in bed all day, frightened her. She sensed that she was trying to hold on to something, but was not sure what.

One afternoon there was a letter waiting for her when she came back to the hotel. It was from Harrison Grey, asking her whether she would like to have supper with him. She would; it was arranged that he would call for her at the hotel at eight o'clock on Friday evening.

As they walked from the hotel to the tube station, Harrison said, 'Toby told me you'd moved hotel. I wondered whether you'd forgotten me. The blasted firm sent me to blasted Birmingham for a month.' They went into the station; he bought tickets. On the escalator, standing behind her, he murmured into her ear, 'Whenever I'm in Birmingham, I think I've died and gone to hell. I'm sure they only do it to punish me.'

'"They"?' she asked. 'And why would they want to punish you?'

'The directors. They doubt whether my entire soul is devoted to the best interests of Saxby and Clarke.'

She laughed. 'Is it?'

'Certainly not.'

There was a train at the platform; they hurried to catch it. There were no free seats so they stood by the doors.

She said, 'Do you prefer London to Birmingham?'

'I loathe all cities, actually.'

'Where would you like to live?'

'I like to picture myself on a sunny beach . . . every now and then I'd have a dip in the sea or wander off to a café and get something to eat. Or I could live in the country-side. I've always fancied being self-sufficient. It would be so much more *real*, so much more *honest*.'

Growing their own vegetables at the Mill House hadn't made her or Milo honest or real, Rebecca reflected.

'Last Sunday,' she said, 'I took Toby and Artemis to the Suffolk coast.'

'When you say "took", do you mean you own a car?'

'Yes, a Riley. I park it on a side street round the corner from the hotel.'

They changed trains at King's Cross, then left the underground at Piccadilly Circus. Lights glittered and Rebecca's spirits lifted and she began to feel alive again, part of the excitement of London at night. They found a table in a restaurant in a narrow street off the Haymarket. Their first courses – prawns Marie Rose for her, whitebait for him – had been served when he said:

'So. Mr Rebecca Rycroft. Where is he, then?'

'In Oxfordshire, I expect. At our home.' She said it without a pang: she was forgetting Milo, she thought proudly, she was making a new and interesting life for herself.

'And you're here, in London.'

'As you see.'

He gestured with his fork, on which were speared half a dozen whitebait. 'What did he do?'

'He was unfaithful.' Her lip curled. 'Congenitally unfaithful. I expect that even if he were married to Greta Garbo, Milo would still be unfaithful.'

'So you walked out on him. Good for you. Do you miss him?'

'Not at all.' She raised her glass, chinked the rim against his.

She anticipated more questions – details of Milo's betrayal, her plans for the future – but instead he said, 'I always regret ordering whitebait. It sounds appealing but then there's something off-putting about it.'

'We could swap, if you like.'

'Could we? You don't mind?'

'Not at all.' They exchanged plates. She said, 'Are you back in London for long, Harrison, or will you have to go to Birmingham again?'

'God, I hope not.' He smiled, his light eyes settling on her. 'I really hope not.'

He liked to tease her about the way she spoke – 'plummy' – and her background – 'achingly middle class'. His grandfather had been a miner; a tough childhood was implied, battles fought and won. Sometimes she went with him to clubs and pubs, where he played the piano. He had wanted to be a musician, he told her, but he had been unlucky – a bout of bronchitis when he was on the verge of landing a regular spot on the wireless, and later, a jealous colleague had cheated him out of a contract with a swing band.

She felt sorry for him; she knew about crushed hopes, missed chances. Harrison was undemanding and, if you didn't mind his teasing, good company. She was attracted by the languorous, catlike way he moved and his elegant hands, and how, when he smiled, his small mouth pursed up and his pale eyes narrowed. He never lost his temper, never shouted. At the weekend, they went for jaunts in her car, to Box Hill or Whitstable. She noticed that though he said he loved the countryside, Harrison didn't seem to care for walking – a short stroll and then they headed for a pub. He was incurious about her former life, which was sensitive of him and a relief to her.

He tried to teach her to sing – the breathing, the phrasing, how to shape a note. He told her she had a lovely, gravelly voice, but it was a pity she sometimes sang out of key. She thought this summed her up: a few limited natural gifts that she nevertheless managed to negate. She sang 'Brother Can You Spare a Dime' in a pub in Fitzrovia while he thumped out the melody to keep her in tune. People clapped and she felt elated, and later that night, they kissed for the first time.

He went away again, this time for a fortnight. He didn't write or phone while he was gone. She shouldn't mind, she told herself; it was a bad habit of hers to be possessive, one that had helped destroy her marriage.

In August, Meriel came up to town for the day and they had supper together. Meriel talked about this and that — her camping holiday in Scotland with a friend, and Dr Hughes's return to Oxfordshire after a fortnight in the West Country. Deborah had decided she didn't want to live in Cornwall after all, which was a blessing. Mummy was fine, Meriel added, and Rebecca, feeling very guilty, promised to visit her mother soon. She wrote to her regularly, but had neither phoned nor visited since she had left Milo.

'It's all right, I can cope with Mummy,' said Meriel.

'I know, but miserable for you, and so cowardly of me.'

'You don't look well,' said Meriel bluntly. 'You look awfully thin. Are you sure you're all right?'

She was absolutely fine, Rebecca told her. She made promises to visit, and then they parted, Meriel to take the tube to Paddington station, Rebecca to go back to the hotel.

Harrison returned to London. They went to a show, and afterwards, buoyed up by a bottle of wine and cheerful music, to bed. Harrison's lovemaking was like his kissing:

slow, hesitant, and just a little half-hearted. A spring breeze, she told herself, rather than the thunderstorms of Milo's passion. It was a relief to know that she was able to respond, that she was not utterly dead inside.

They were invited to dinner by a friend of Harrison's, a Mrs Simone Campbell, who lived in a red-brick house in Stoke Newington. The house was very untidy, heaps of books and clothes everywhere and too much furniture crammed into the rooms. Simone Campbell was fiftyish, with a round, pleasant face and curly grey-brown hair. Shorter than Rebecca, she had a substantial bosom and hips, and a series of undulations between. She was wearing a plum-coloured floral frock beneath a shapeless black jacket. The clothes did not sit tidily on her; they ruckled and clung.

Simone was a widow, Harrison had told Rebecca on the drive over. 'Her husband was killed in the war,' he said. 'Some battle or other.' There were two children, a boy and a girl.

Another couple and two single women joined them for supper – 'Here come Simone's lesbians,' Harrison murmured to Rebecca, not very sotto voce, before they were introduced. The food was delicious, a rich lamb stew and a lemon tart, served in a dining room that looked out over a nicely overgrown back garden. The discussion over the supper table turned quickly to politics: the bloodless takeover of Austria by Nazi Germany earlier in the year, and the increasing tension generated by Germany's claims to a part of Czechoslovakia, the Sudetenland, were talked over and worried about. Rebecca was not ignorant – events in Europe had frequently been dissected over the Mill House's dinner table, and she sympathized absolutely with the plight of the Jews: how awful to have home, occupation and country taken from you! – but it was as if a wall had been raised between her and the others, a wall that only she could see. She made sure to speak now and then, so that the other guests did not think her odd, and she drank several glasses of wine in the hope that it would lift her mood. But her sense of not belonging was powerful. It was as if some cruelly playful god had picked her up and deposited her here at random, in this house, with these strangers.

After supper, Simone asked Rebecca to help her with the coffee. The kitchen was even untidier than the rest of the house, the sink full of unwashed dishes; photos and reminders and crumpled recipes, torn out of magazines, overlapping each other on a pinboard.

Simone looked round despairingly. 'I love cooking but I hate the cleaning and tidying part of it.'

'Can I help?'

'Certainly not. I didn't invite you to my house to spend the evening washing up.'

'I'm not sure you invited me at all, Mrs Campbell. I have a suspicion that Harrison foisted me on you. I'd be glad to help. I like to be useful.' And there was the crux of it, Rebecca thought: she was no use to anyone now, and if she disappeared in a puff of smoke, then who would care?

She turned away, pressing her nails into her palms to stop the tears welling to her eyes. She ran her gaze over the pinboard. The reminder notes said things like 'Call Dorothy', 'Biscuits for book club', 'Pot up seedlings'.

'I'm delighted you came,' said Simone. 'You are an

ornament to my supper table, Mrs Rycroft. I'm always so impressed by women who succeed in matching their shoes to their handbags.'

She had controlled her tears. 'Oh, that's nothing. Anyone can do it.'

'No, that's not true. To look attractive and well turned out takes a great deal of effort. I go into a clothes shop and I buy the first frock I can get into because I find the whole thing such an ordeal. My daughter tells me off.' Simone filled the kettle and put it on the hob. 'May I ask . . . are you widowed?'

'Separated.'

'That must be hard. People tend to assume that it's worse to be widowed, but I can't help thinking there must be a particular anguish in knowing that one of you *chose* to end the marriage, or that love simply died.' Simone smiled. 'You must forgive me for being so nosy. Are you fond of gardening?'

'Very.' Rebecca felt a pang of longing for the Mill House's garden. Right now, the leaves would be on the turn – she could almost smell the bonfire smoke.

'May I show you my garden?'

'I'd love you to.'

They went outside. It was mid-September and the evening light was dying. In Simone Campbell's garden, an air of stillness and of mystery had been achieved by the careful placing of trees, trellises and paths. They discussed pruning and ways of dealing with black spot until Mrs Campbell sighed and said, 'We'd better go inside, I suppose. My guests will be gasping for their coffee.'

In the kitchen, Rebecca arranged cups and saucers on a tray.

Simone said, 'You haven't known Harrison long, have you?'

'A few months.'

'He's perfectly pleasant, but he's lazy – a sort of spiritual laziness, I always think. But I'm sure you'll have noticed that yourself.' Simone poured boiling water into the coffee jug. Then she scribbled on a notepad, tore off the leaf, and gave it to Rebecca. 'Here's my phone number. Do come and see me, if you have time. I always enjoy the company of intelligent women.'

Half an hour later, Rebecca and Harrison took their leave. Rebecca felt tired. She had drunk too much, and for some reason she could not pinpoint, her conversation with Simone Campbell had upset her.

She was pulling out of a side street on to the main road when she failed to notice a cyclist without lights. She had to jam the brakes on hard to avoid hitting the cyclist, who wobbled and then rode on.

Rebecca watched her hands shake as they gripped the steering wheel. A voice in her head said, *You nearly killed someone else.*

'I'm too tired,' she said. 'I can't concentrate. Could you drive?'

'I can't.' Harrison looked aghast. 'I mean, I don't. Not at all.'

So she took a deep breath and inched the car out on to the road, and they drove all the way back to his flat in Earls Court at twenty miles an hour.

* * *

The evenings were the worst part. At first, she tried to fill them — she would dine out, she would go to see Toby and his friends, she would read a book or do a crossword in the hotel lounge. But more and more she retreated to her room, had a sandwich and a drink sent up by room service and then another drink to send her to sleep. She was not made for living alone, she often thought. Perhaps she should go back to Milo. Perhaps a bad marriage, any marriage, was better than this.

Her dates with Harrison were her lifeline. They would have supper somewhere and then go back to his flat, where he would make love to her in his slow, lazy fashion. She liked him and felt safe with him because he was everything Milo was not. He lacked Milo's energy, drive and ambition — and thank God for that, she thought.

They were in bed when Harrison told her about the cottage. A friend of his, Gregory Armitage, had a place in Derbyshire. Miles from anywhere, on a hilltop, not another soul around. Harrison rolled on to his side, looking up at her. Greg had told him he could borrow the cottage. Wouldn't it be great to get away for a few weeks? She would come with him, wouldn't she?

In her imagination, Rebecca saw a charming little house in a meadow speckled with flowers. 'Oh *yes*,' she said.

Three days later, she picked Harrison up from his flat. He loaded a rucksack, a Harrods bag and a music case into the boot of the Riley. Then they set off for Derbyshire.

Harrison's friend's cottage was in the Peak District, midway between Sheffield and Manchester. You had to drive off the

Manchester road down a narrow single-track lane, which petered out into a grassy track lined with hawthorns heavy with dark crimson fruit. The track became a footpath and Harrison sulked when Rebecca parked the car and told him she couldn't drive any further. She must have taken a wrong turning, he said. She spread the map out over the steering wheel. She was sure they were in the right place. They would leave the car here and walk the rest of the way to the cottage.

Grumbling, Harrison shouldered the rucksack and picked up the Harrods bag. Rebecca carried her suitcase and they headed off along the footpath. Soon they found themselves among gently rising meadowland. Rebecca's spirits rose. It was a fine day, and to one side of them lay the valley, where farmhouses and barns sheltered in a lavender haze; to the other rose the hillside, sunlight gleaming on the blades of grass.

After half an hour, with several stops for Harrison to rest, they reached the top of the hill. The summit was flat, as if it had been sliced off with a knife. Paths threaded between tussocks of dark green, spiky grass.

Rebecca caught sight of a solitary house in the middle of the moor. 'That must be it,' she said.

They walked over the moor to the house. Though it was small, its square stone solidity lent it grandeur. Putting her suitcase down on the front doorstep and waiting for Harrison, who had the key, to catch up, Rebecca looked up at the fanciful armorial shield that had been carved in the granite over the front door.

Harrison unlocked the door and they went inside. As he

slid the rucksack on to a large rectangular table with a sigh of relief, a cloud of dust rose into the air.

They were in a kitchen: shapes loomed out of the darkness and there was a musty smell. 'It's rather gloomy,' Harrison said.

Rebecca drew the curtains and wrestled with a window latch. 'There, that's better, isn't it?'

Sunlight slid on to the flagstone floor. A handful of mismatched chairs surrounded the table and a wooden rocker stood beside a black iron stove. Against the far wall was a piano. Beneath the window was a sink, with a dresser to one side of it. There was no electric light, Rebecca noticed, and dust greyed the glass bowls of the oil lamps.

Harrison opened the piano and played a few chords. 'It's out of tune.'

'Shall we explore?'

He complained about his sore feet, but she disregarded him and went upstairs. In the sitting room, she drew curtains and opened windows. The furnishings were old and dusty, the rug by the fire grimed with coal dust. Another flight of stone steps led to the topmost storey of the house. Rebecca leaned out of the window. The moors and hills seemed to sparkle and the sky was crystalline. She filled her lungs with cool, sweet air, and for the first time in months, some knotted piece of her, as taut as a piano string, relaxed.

She called downstairs, 'What's for lunch?' Harrison had offered to bring the food.

'Have you any plasters, Rebecca? I've blisters all over my feet.'

She went down to the kitchen. He was sitting in the

212

rocking chair and had taken off his shoes and socks. She opened her suitcase and found plasters, cotton wool and TCP.

He flinched as she dabbed the blisters with TCP. 'Don't be a baby,' she said. 'Where's the food?'

'In the Harrods bag. I thought I'd treat us.'

Inside the carrier bag were Bath Olivers, tins of artichokes, olives and sardines, a jar of bottled peaches, a bar of Cadbury's chocolate, two bottles of wine and a half-bottle of whisky. Where's the tea, the sugar, the milk, the bread? Rebecca thought, but said, 'Shall I see if I can find us a nice place to eat outside? This room needs a good clean and it seems a shame to waste such glorious sunshine.'

A garden, bounded by a dry-stone wall, surrounded the house. There were currant bushes and an apple tree, its branches distorted by the wind. A climbing rose, scattered with late blooms, grew in a sheltered spot.

Rebecca could not find a tablecloth but had thought to bring tea towels, so she spread them out on the grass. After they had eaten, Harrison lay on the grass, his eyes closed. Greg had told him they could have the cottage for three weeks. He didn't think Greg used the place often; perhaps they should ask him if they could rent it for a year. They could make something of the place, grow vegetables, keep a pig.

When he fell asleep, Rebecca went indoors to clean the kitchen and make a list. How lovely to have her own kitchen again. She had been so sick of the hotel. That was all that was wrong with her: the hotel and London. She wrote on a scrap of paper, *milk, tea, coal*. And she must buy a torch so that at night she did not have to stumble downstairs by candlelight to reach the outside lavatory. She sat in the fall of sunlight from the open window, chewing her pencil.

They sunbathed, read novels and picked up provisions from the nearest shop. The fine weather lasted for four days. On the fifth day, Rebecca woke up with a sore throat. She made tea and took a couple of aspirins. After breakfast, they walked over the moorland and down the hill to the car and then drove to the village. She gave her list to the assistant in the local store. 'Coal,' repeated Harrison with a squawk: she wasn't expecting him to carry a sack of coal up that bloody hill, was she? 'If he wanted to eat,' she said. He muttered about deliveries, and she said briskly, 'Don't be silly, Harrison.'

They stopped at a pub for lunch and afterwards made a detour to a farmhouse to buy milk, eggs and a chicken for roasting. Puffy white clouds masked the face of the sun, casting shadows on the flagged courtyard. The first drops of rain fell as they ferried their provisions from the car to the house. Rebecca carried the rucksack and Harrison trailed after her with the sack of coal. Her throat felt worse, and Harrison's complaints mingled with the pattering of the rain.

At the house, she laid a fire in the stove while Harrison went upstairs for a rest. She rediscovered the satisfaction of lighting a fire: the crumpling of newspaper, the careful laying of kindling and coal, the feeling of triumph as the scraps of wood caught light. She prepared the chicken, peeled potatoes and scraped carrots, then took more aspirins

214

and sat down in the rocking chair. Later, they ate the roast chicken to the drum of the rain on the windows and a flare of heat from the stove. Afterwards, Harrison played the piano and she sang, but not for long because her throat was too sore.

She woke several times in the night. It was painful to swallow, so she sipped cautiously at a glass of water and listened to the rain. In the morning, they rose to a grey and brown world. The greens and golds of the moorland had been muted by the weather and the sky had jammed itself over the hills like an iron lid.

It rained all day. Puddles formed on the front path and on the tracks across the moor. They played rummy and German whist and ate cold chicken. Rebecca read *Gone With the Wind*, sitting in the rocking chair, because when she lay down, she coughed.

The next day there was no coal left and Harrison picked the chicken carcass for breakfast. He would have to go to the shop, she told him.

He looked out of the window. 'It's pouring.'

'Is it? I hadn't noticed.' Her sarcasm cost her; it hurt to speak.

'Jesus. Look at it.'

'I don't feel well. I might go back to bed. If you could just manage a bit of coal and some bread and milk.'

Turning, he stared at her. 'I can't go by myself.'

'Harrison,' she said. 'I'm ill.'

'It's only a cold. You've got to come. You need to drive the car.'

'Can't you drive *at all*?'

'No. I tried once but it was too complicated.'

'If I explained to you . . .'

'Don't be ridiculous.'

'*Me*, ridiculous?' The words came out as a rasping gasp. 'How can you have reached the age of thirty-nine without being able to drive? *That's* ridiculous!'

Coughing, she began angrily to button her mackintosh and pull on her wellington boots. She grabbed her handbag, shoved the rucksack at him, put up her hood and went outside. They did not speak as they started across the flat expanse of moorland. The rain had turned the paths and grassy clumps into a bog, and from behind her she could hear Harrison, who had forgotten to bring boots, muttering curses as his shoes let in water.

She sat in the car while he bought coal, lamp oil, sausages and aspirin from the shop. She ached all over – perhaps she had flu. A lull in the rain on their return journey across the hills brought about a partial truce between them. Back at the house, she realized they had forgotten to buy a newspaper. There didn't seem to be a scrap of paper in the entire building, so Harrison tore up the first few chapters of *Gone With the Wind* and used that to light the fire. Burning books, she thought – what next?

The next morning she woke coughing. Her pillow was wet. Looking up, she saw a stalactite of water forming on the ceiling above her. A drop loosed itself and plunged to the bed.

She woke Harrison. The roof was leaking; he had to do something.

'What?'

'You have to fix the roof. Perhaps a tile has come loose.'

He blinked. 'Christ, Rebecca . . .'

'I saw some stepladders in the outside lav. You'll have to go out and take a look at it.'

'Go out?'

'Out of the trapdoor,' she said furiously. 'The bloody trapdoor, Harrison.'

She went downstairs to fetch a bucket and cloth. Her head felt peculiar, as if someone had filled it with straw, and her chest hurt. When she returned to the bedroom, Harrison had put the stepladders up beneath the trapdoor.

'I'll get vertigo,' he said.

'Don't be so feeble.'

'I hate heights.'

'We can't sleep here with rain pouring on to our heads. We'll die of pneumonia.'

'Perhaps we should go back to London.'

'London?' She stared at him.

'I'll tell Greg the weather broke.'

'I don't want to go back to London. I like it here.'

'It's uncivilized,' he muttered.

'What did you imagine?' she said scornfully. 'All mod cons? Just fix the roof, Harrison.'

'Fix it yourself,' he said, and went downstairs.

So she climbed the ladder, released the catch on the trapdoor and pushed at it with her shoulder. It opened with the rank smell of cobwebs. The roof sloped gently and she saw that a corner of one of the stone flags had cracked. Standing on tiptoes, she pushed the crumbling pieces back into place. She ducked back inside the house and closed the trapdoor, then descended the ladder. With an effort, she moved the bed so that it was no longer beneath the drip. She was shivering; she lay down on the bed for a long time, coughing, trying to get warm.

When she went downstairs, he was standing by the stove, drinking a mug of tea. He poured one for her. 'Sorry,' he said. 'It's just that I can't stand heights.'

'It doesn't matter, I've done it.' She sat in the rocking chair, wrapping her hands round the mug.

'We should go back to London. I didn't think it would be like this.'

'No,' she said obstinately. 'You promised, Harrison. Three weeks. The rain can't last for ever.'

He toasted bread and boiled eggs. Rebecca couldn't eat hers so he finished it for her.

After breakfast he said, 'We're running out of stuff.'

The business with the roof and the bed had exhausted her. 'You'll have to go yourself this time,' she said. 'I don't feel well enough to drive.'

Harrison rinsed the crockery, then put on his coat and hat, shouldered the rucksack and left the house. From her seat by the fire, she could see his figure growing smaller and smaller as he made his way across the moor.

She took some aspirins and went back to the bedroom. She curled up on Harrison's side of the bed, the dry side, and dozed off. Eventually she woke, shivering and coughing. She looked at her watch. It was past three o'clock. She had slept for five hours.

She put a cardigan on over her jersey and went downstairs. Harrison was not there. His mackintosh was not on the peg and there was no sign of the rucksack. Perhaps he had stopped at the pub for lunch. Another hour passed, then two, and she knew in her heart that he had left her, that he had gone back to London without her.

What the hell, she thought. She was better off without him. She would just stay here. Why return to London when there was nothing there for her? It didn't look as if Harrison's friend used the house much. She might find out whether she could stay on through the winter.

Milo would have climbed the ladder and tried to fix the roof. Harrison was soft and spineless. She had liked him because he was different from Milo and she had thought him sensitive in not asking her questions about her past, but she had since realized that he simply wasn't interested, that he avoided complication and confrontation. She had thought that was what she wanted, after Milo, but it wasn't. Quarrelling with Harrison was like quarrelling with a wet rag.

She made herself a scratch supper out of leftovers, but found she wasn't hungry, so covered it with a plate and put it on the windowsill to keep cool. It was a relief not to have to make the effort of conversation, when she was feeling so unwell.

She sent herself to sleep that night with three aspirins and the remains of the whisky, but woke in the early hours of the morning, coughing. Now, there was no pleasure in being alone. She knew herself to be worthless and rotten, and it seemed to her that Harrison's abandonment of her was justified. Her mind reeled back over the months. Her first phone call, when she had discovered that Milo was having the affair with Tessa Nicolson. Her grief and wretchedness and rage, and the consequences of that rage. *The baby died, you see. He was thrown out of the car. They said he must have died instantly.* Her horror was as vivid and overpowering now as it had been seven months ago, on the day Freddie Nicolson had telephoned the Mill House. Her responsibility lay on her like a heavy weight, making it hard to breathe.

She spent the next two days in bed. She couldn't see the point in getting up. There was no one to talk to, nothing to do. Now she felt lonely; she wanted someone, anyone. She wished she had taken the dog with her when she left Milo – Julia would have been company. She dried out the damp pillow on the stove, and propped herself up in bed on the two pillows and a folded jacket, trying not to cough. Making a cup of tea in the kitchen, she saw in the distance two figures moving slowly across the moorland – hikers, presumably, from the heavy outline of the rucksacks on their backs. The rain made a barrier between herself and the hikers. She hadn't spoken to anyone for more than two days. If she tried to talk, the words would come out in a rusty croak.

That night, she dreamed that Tessa's baby was lying on the roof, crying, and she was trying to reach it. She was standing on tiptoe on top of the stepladders and she had outstretched her arms till they hurt. But the infant was always just out of reach.

She was weeping when she woke, the baby's cries still in her ears. A part of her knew that she was having a break-down, and so, though she continued to weep and to cough, some instinct of self-preservation made her force herself

220

out of bed and bundle on some clothes. Her legs felt weak and shaky, and she put the flat of her hand against the wall to steady herself as she went downstairs. In the kitchen, she saw that she had run out of water, so she went outside to the hand pump and filled the enamel jug. The rain had stopped and the brightness of the sun made her blink. Back in the house, she placed the last few pieces of coal on top of the pink embers in the stove, slopped some water into the kettle and put it on to boil. She should go to the shop, she thought, and buy a bottle of cough mixture.

It was warmer outside than in the house, so she dragged out a chair to sit on the front step. The marshy land shimmered like shot silk. Sunlight gleamed on the pools, streams and stones. The landscape before her looked washed clean and new and beautiful. She thought of the poor little baby who would never see such loveliness and she began to cry. The waste of it, she thought, the utter, stupid, unforgivable waste.

Looking up, wiping her eyes, she caught sight of a figure, a hiker, not far away, crossing the moor, approaching the house along the narrow footpath through the heather. She thought for a moment it was Harrison, come back to see how she was, but soon saw that the hiker was shorter and older than Harrison.

At the dry-stone wall, he paused, taking off his cloth cap. 'Good morning. It's a splendid day, isn't it?' His hair was silver and his face was tanned and lined. He carried a knapsack on his back.

'Splendid,' she echoed.

'Could you could spare me a drink of water?'

'Of course.' Rebecca went inside the kitchen and filled a mug. She gave it to him and he drank deeply.

'Have you been walking for a long time?'

'Many days,' he said, with a smile.

'Through all that rain?'

He nodded. 'I don't mind the rain.' He had blue eyes, with a web of laughter lines around them. 'You get wet, and then you dry out again, don't you?'

His smile was infectious; she found herself responding. 'I suppose so.'

'When I first saw you,' he said, 'I thought you were crying.'

She looked away, embarrassed. 'It's nothing.' But she found herself adding after a few moments, 'No, that's not true. But there's nothing to be done about it.'

She saw that his cup was empty. 'May I get you more water?' she asked. 'Or perhaps you'd like a cup of tea? I'm just making some.'

'If it's no trouble, tea would be smashing.'

She opened the gate to let him into the garden, then made the tea and poured out two cups. She noticed, as she handed him the cup and saucer, that the cuffs of his jacket were frayed, the elbows shiny through wear. His accent was local – he had once worked in a factory in Manchester or Sheffield, she guessed, and had been laid off in the slump and now passed the time hiking.

She put out a chair for him and he sat down. 'Oh, that feels good,' he sighed. He put his walking stick and cap on the grass and loosened the laces of his boots.

Rebecca took careful sips of her tea. 'Where are you going?'

'Bakewell, mebbe. Or I'll see if I can make it to Dovedale.'

'Don't you plan?'

'These days I go where my feet take me. Plans don't always work out, don't you find?'

'Every plan I make seems to go wrong,' she said bitterly.

'Why's that, duck?'

'I don't know. Bad luck, I suppose.'

'My mother always used to say we make our own luck.'

'Then perhaps I've made my own bad luck.' And she found herself saying to him, 'Do you think that if something you do makes something terrible happen, it's your fault, even if you didn't mean it at all?'

He considered. 'Hard to say.'

'It *feels* as if it was my fault.'

'What did you want to happen?'

'Not *that*.' Honesty made her add, 'But I wanted to hurt.' More tears; they blurred the stranger's face and the landscape. 'I wish I could change the past,' she said softly. 'I wish I could rub it clean, make it different. I wish I could think what to do, where to go.' Then she gave an embarrassed laugh. 'I'm so sorry, I don't know why I'm telling you this. Please forgive me.'

'Perhaps you need someone to talk to.' His smile was remarkably sweet and gentle.

'Perhaps.' By way of explanation she added, 'I haven't been very well, you see.'

'You don't look too bright. And this is a lonely spot.'

'I'm only borrowing the cottage.'

'I like to be alone, out in the hills, but it's always good

223

to go back to family and friends. Too much time on your own and you end up imagining things.'

Had he said that or had she? She was unsure. His voice seemed to echo inside her head. The shimmer of light on the moors was unreal and piercing.

They sat for a while, drinking their tea. When he had finished, he said, 'You make a good cup of tea. Thank you. I'd best be getting on. Should make the most of the fine weather, shouldn't I?'

'Could you use something to eat? I'm returning home today and the food will only go to waste.'

'That would be kind,' he said.

As she gathered up their cups and saucers, he spoke to her again.

'You told me you didn't know where to go. I'd say, a doctor first. That's a nasty cough.' He stood up. 'And then perhaps you should think about stepping outside.'

Stepping outside? They *were* outside. What on earth was he talking about? Still, he was probably right about the doctor.

'Yes. Thank you,' she said politely. 'I'll go and find you some biscuits and things.'

In the kitchen, Rebecca wrapped Bath Olivers, cheese and other odds and ends of food in greaseproof paper. She thought about what he had said to her. *It's always good to go back to family and friends.* But she didn't seem to have many *good* friends, and she didn't get on with her mother, and Meriel hadn't room for her. And her husband had broken her heart. She almost cried again, but stopped herself.

She went outside. The sunlight blinded her; she closed her eyes. When she opened them, she saw that the hiker had gone. The chair was empty and his walking stick and knapsack were no longer there. Puzzled, she went to the gate to look for him. She could not see him. She walked all the way round the dry-stone wall that surrounded the house, trying to spot him. The moorland was flat and open. She could see for miles. There was no sign of him.

Perhaps she had taken longer than she had thought to fetch the food and he had got fed up waiting. She went back to the front porch. It was then that, looking across to the gate, she realized that she could not see his footprints on the mud between the gate and the house. She could see her own footprints, but not his.

Inside the kitchen, she sat down at the table, trying to make sense of her strange experience. A hiker stopped at her house, chatted for a while, and then disappeared into thin air, leaving not so much as a footprint behind him. Had she imagined him? Was she so very ill? Had she been hallucinating?

Yet what he had said to her remained with her, and in the absence of anything better, she decided to do as he suggested. She began to pack, folding her clothes and putting them into her suitcase. Doctor first, and then – what had he told her to do? *Step outside.* Complete nonsense; she must have dreamed him.

She remembered the evening she had spent at Simone Campbell's house. Mrs Campbell had asked her to come and see her. *I always enjoy the company of intelligent women.* Rebecca had put the scrap of paper on which Simone had written her phone number in her purse – was it still there? Yes, there it was, folded up in a corner.

She had been running away for a long time, but she had reached a point when she couldn't run any more. She felt far too ill to manage the long walk to the car and the much longer drive back to London, but she knew she had to try. She had survived worse, she reminded herself – a childhood lacking in love, and marriage to a man the depth of whose love had never matched her own. She would stop at the phone box in the village, she decided, and call Simone and ask if she could put her up for a day or two. If not, she would have to think of something else, but remembering Simone, and their easy rapport as they had walked round the garden, it seemed to her that she might find a temporary sanctuary, at least.

As she left the house and set off on her long journey, she thought once more, *step outside?* What *had* he meant? And what a strange thing to tell her to do.

And yet it occurred to her that here she was, in the sun, putting one foot in front of her, and then another, surrounded by the honeyed scent of the heather, stopping every now and then to rest, but carrying on towards some unknown destination, step by step by step.

Chapter Seven

Tessa's recovery was slow. From the beginning she blamed herself for Angelo's death. If she had been a better mother, if she had been a better driver, if she had not been so stupid and negligent. She veered between outbreaks of crying that lasted for hours and a withdrawn silence that frightened Freddie more than the tears. Often, in the months after the accident, Tessa curled up on her bed, her eyes closed, not speaking to anyone. Once so outgoing, she disliked leaving the flat. Her moods were erratic, never the same from day to day.

Always slim, she had become painfully thin. She cut short her long fair hair and wore it in a fringed bob to hide the jagged red scar on her forehead. Though her physical health slowly improved, the alterations to her personality remained. She was quieter, less gregarious, and far more self-contained. She rarely spoke of Angelo or of her life before the accident. When friends came to the flat, she might wear a smile, but her eyes were always haunted.

Freddie had left school at the end of the spring term, her plan of going to university forgotten. To begin with, she took part-time evening jobs that left her free to spend the day with Tessa, while Tessa's friends organized a rota to keep her company in the evenings. Then Miss Fainlight, with whom Freddie had occasionally corresponded since leaving school, put her in touch with a Miss Parrish, who lived in Endsleigh Gardens, near Russell Square. Miss Parrish engaged Freddie as her assistant, working on a magazine called *The Business Girl*, which contained articles and practical advice aimed at the single working woman.

Doctors' bills had long since swallowed up Tessa's remaining cash, and jewellery had had to be sold. Every penny Freddie earned counted. Stockings must be darned, shoes repaired, and she walked whenever she could to save the fare. She had given up the lease on the Highbury flat while Tessa was still in hospital, knowing they would not be able to afford the rent, and afraid that the associations of Tessa's old home might upset her. Ray had offered her one of his flats, rent free, but she had politely refused. They would manage; they would live within their means. She saw that it was going to be like this for the foreseeable future, so they may as well get used to it now. Tessa would never return to her modelling career; it was possible that she would never work again. Freddie had, however, agreed to let Ray help her look for a new home, and he had found them the place in South Kensington. The new flat, on the second floor of a large Georgian building, was much smaller than the Highbury one, only two rooms, with a shared bathroom, but it was clean and sunny and had a pleasant outlook over gardens.

At the end of August, Ray took Tessa away for a holiday in the south of France. Postcards arrived, from overnight stops on their leisurely drive through France. It seemed to Freddie that the further south the town or city on the front of the card, the more flashes of the old Tessa were revealed. A glimpse of humour in Tessa's description of an American couple encountered in Lyon, and from Marseille, a cartoon of a smart Frenchwoman with a toy poodle in her handbag. On the back of a card from Nice was another little sketch, of Ray, fast asleep in a deckchair on the beach, a straw hat tipped over his face.

For the first time in more than six months, Freddie allowed herself to hope. Her optimism persisted in spite of the deteriorating political situation, through the alarm of the Munich crisis as Europe teetered on the brink of war. She clung on to that hope as trenches were dug in the London parks and anti-aircraft guns perched like crows on the tops of tall buildings, and as, at the end of September, Neville Chamberlain flew back from Germany to Croydon airport, triumphantly flourishing the piece of paper that, he claimed, guaranteed 'peace in our time'.

The first of the autumn fogs fell soft and grey on the city in early November. Leaving work, Freddie caught the tube train to South Kensington, then walked the rest of her way home, now and then reaching out to touch a wall or railings, as if to reassure herself that behind the veil, the buildings still existed.

She had taken her keys out of her bag when she heard

a car door close behind her. Looking round, she saw Ray walking towards her out of the fog.

'You're back! Oh, Ray! How are you?' Freddie squinted. 'Where's Tessa?'

'In Italy,' he said.

'Italy?'

'I'm afraid so. May I come in?'

'Yes, of course.'

She let them into the building. Heading upstairs, she thought, *Italy*, but said to Ray, 'Had you been waiting long?'

'Half an hour.' He shivered. 'It's bloody freezing.'

In the flat, Freddie put on the fire and filled the kettle. While it was boiling, she said to Ray, 'Do you mean that Tessa's visiting someone in Italy? I thought she was going to travel back with you. How will she get home? When is she coming back?'

'I think,' he was unbuttoning his coat, 'she means to stay there.'

'Oh.' Clumsily, she made tea, splashing water on to the floor and mopping it up with her handkerchief.

She stirred two sugars into Ray's cup and handed it to him. Then she said, 'I don't understand, Ray. What happened?'

He swallowed a mouthful of tea. 'These last few weeks we were staying in Menton. I found a decent hotel near the seafront. We didn't go out much, just the occasional drive in the countryside. Most of the time we sat on the beach, if it was warm enough, or maybe went for a swim or a walk. I thought Tessa was all right. She seemed better, less on edge. You know she's always loved the sun. She *looked* better, Freddie, she honestly did. I suppose I was an idiot to think that a few weeks in the south of France and I'd get the old Tessa back again, but you can't help hoping, can you? And then, one day, we were having lunch and she asked me how far away Italy was. I told her it was a few miles to the east. I remember she went very quiet. I asked her whether anything was wrong and she said nothing, she was just tired. We went back to the hotel and she spent the afternoon in her room. In the evening, when we met in the bar, she told me she had decided to go back to Italy. I thought she meant for a short holiday so I said okay, I'd see whether it was possible to pop over the border for a couple of days. And she said no, that wasn't what she'd meant, she'd meant that she wanted to live there again.'

Freddie stared at him. 'Oh, *Ray*.'

'I tried to talk her out of it. She told me she didn't think she'd ever fitted in in England. Thought she had for a while but realized she'd been wrong. She told me there were people she'd thought were her friends who hadn't spoken to her since she became pregnant, and that there were others who hadn't spoken to her since the baby died. Well, you know how people can be. They don't know what to say so they end up saying nothing. But she does have friends, Freddie, true friends. She has people who love her.' Ray blew his nose. 'I tried to talk her out of it. She told me she needed to go away somewhere where nobody knew her – where no one knew about Angelo. She said she needed to start again. I pointed out to her all the difficulties – how would she support herself, where would she live, that sort of thing. And Italian politics, of course – Mussolini isn't exactly a fan of the English, and I've heard that some Englishmen who've stayed on there have had a pretty rough time. In the end, she promised me she'd think about it. She promised me she wouldn't do anything rash, damn her. The next morning she'd gone. Got up at five, caught the first train out of Menton. She left a letter for me. You can read it if you like, Freddie.'

Freddie scanned the letter quickly. Tessa thanked Ray for his patience, kindness and generosity and asked him to forgive her. 'I know I'm doing the right thing,' she had written. 'There's nothing I've wanted for a long time – except to turn the clock back, of course – but I find I do want this: I want to go home.' At the foot of the note Tessa had written, 'Please tell Freddie not to worry and that I shall write to her very soon.'

Freddie folded up the letter and gave it back to Ray. 'It wasn't your fault,' she said. 'You know Tessa. She does what she wants to do and no one can make her change her mind. What did you do?'

'I went to the railway station. A chap at the ticket office remembered her.' He gave a grim smile. 'That's Tessa, isn't it? Everyone remembers her. He told me she'd bought a ticket to Genoa, so I decided to go after her, have a look for her in Genoa, try to make her see sense.'

'And did you? Did you find her in Genoa, Ray?'

'No. Never reached the damned place.' Ray looked furious. 'The bloody guard was so damnably rude at the border post I almost lost my temper and thumped him. The fellow made out there was something wrong with my passport – absolute rot, nothing wrong with it at all, they were just throwing

232

their weight around. So I went back to the hotel in Menton. The concierge was a decent chap and he phoned round half a dozen hotels in Genoa for me. Nothing. She could be anywhere, Freddie.' He frowned, then said, 'She didn't want me to find her. I've thought about it and I know she didn't want me to find her. I was going to ask her to marry me again. What a fool. What an utter bally fool.'

Ray left shortly afterwards. *I find I do want this*, Tessa had written. *I want to go home.* For how long had she been thinking of returning to Italy? Freddie wondered. Had it been a spur-of-the-moment decision, or had she been considering it for some time?

A sudden idea, a suspicion, and Freddie went into the bedroom and opened the drawer in which Tessa kept her jewellery. There, beneath the bangles and cocktail rings, was the leather box that contained their mother's garnets. With a sinking feeling, Freddie opened the lid. The garnets lay inside, dark red, gleaming and mysterious. Oh Tessa, she thought. Of all her jewellery, Tessa had loved the garnets best. Other necklaces had been sold, to pay the rent and doctors' bills, but not their mother's garnets. Tessa would not have *forgotten* to take them. Had she left them for *her*, as a sort of consolation prize? Or as a promise, perhaps, that one day she would return?

As she cooked herself supper, Freddie thought about Tessa's letter to Ray. *I want to go home*, she had written. But where was Freddie's home? Which one of the numerous places in which she had lived since she was born could she truly call home?

*   *   *

233

Rebecca went to live at Mayfield Farm at the end of November. The farm, a sprawling collection of red-brick, red-tiled buildings, stood on a ridge in the High Weald, south of London, five miles from Tunbridge Wells. It was owned by David and Carlotta Mickleborough. David's landscape paintings adorned the walls of the farmhouse. He had been living in Spain when the civil war had broken out, and had fought in the International Brigades. After being wounded in 1937, he and his wife and their two young sons, Jamie and Felix, had returned to England, where they had bought the farm.

David Mickleborough was a friend of Simone Campbell's. Rebecca had stayed with Simone for more than a month, while she recovered from bronchitis. Once she had felt well again, she had known she must find somewhere more permanent to stay, and it had been Simone who had suggested Mayfield. 'Most of the people who live there are artists,' she had told her. 'They help on the farm in return for renting a studio. Everyone mucks in – they eat their meals together and lend a hand to do whatever needs doing. It's all rather rough and ready, but it's in a lovely part of the countryside and it would give you a breathing space.'

Rebecca had thought it sounded ghastly, but had not said so, out of politeness. And besides, what alternative did she have? 'I'll give it a go,' she had said. And then, afraid she had sounded grudging, 'Thank you, Simone. You've been so very kind.'

In the days before she left for Mayfield Farm, Rebecca had given Simone's house a thorough clean and tidy, as a way of saying thank you. On the morning of her departure,

Simone had said to her sternly, 'You must look after yourself properly this time. No more letting yourself fall ill, and no more throwing in your lot with hopeless men like Harrison Grey. You're to promise me, Rebecca.'

Meekly, she had promised, and had also promised to write to Simone and to visit when she was in London. Then she had loaded her belongings into her car and driven out of the capital. Negotiating ever narrower rural roads as she neared her destination, the map balanced on her knees, she had felt neither excitement nor anticipation, but had resolved to make the best of what the farm had to offer. However much she hated it, she would stay for a year. Anything less, and she would feel disappointed in herself. Another failure would be chalked up to add to her already oppressive sense of guilt and inadequacy.

But to her surprise, she didn't hate it. It *was* rough and ready – the walls of her bedroom were of unfinished plasterwork, and the floor was covered with bricks laid in a herringbone pattern. There was only a cold tap in the bathroom and if you wanted hot you boiled a kettle. The farm had its own electricity generator, which failed now and then, and Carlotta cooked on an old-fashioned iron range and did the washing in a copper. But the house had a solidity and a rootedness that appealed to Rebecca. There was a part of her that welcomed simplicity now, and that welcomed also the hard physical work of the farm.

Ten people lived at Mayfield Farm. As well as the four Mickleboroughs and Rebecca, there was Noel Wainwright, who, like David Mickleborough, was a landscape painter, and his wife, Olwen, who made fabric collages. John Pollen and his sister, Romaine, were both in their fifties, quiet and serious and gently spoken. John was a potter; his bowls and plates were coloured the earthy red-browns, creams and soft greys of the Sussex landscape. Romaine, who limped following a childhood attack of polio, made stained glass, using her brother's kiln.

Though she was on good terms with everyone at the farm, Rebecca avoided closeness. Intimacy would have meant explanations and self-examination, and she shrank from both. So much of her felt raw, and there was much of which she was ashamed. She worked on the vegetable plot, wrestling with the half-acre of windswept sticky clay, and helped with the renovation of the farmhouse. Her old skills, acquired while doing up the Mill House with Milo, became useful again. She rubbed down flaking paintwork and repainted doors and windowsills. One day, David showed her how to lay bricks, and she spent the morning kneeling in the dirt, mixing mortar and placing bricks along the line delineated by a taut length of string. In the evenings, after supper, she went to her bedroom, where she read or wrote letters.

The farm's tenth tenant lived in a barn some way from the main buildings. Connor Byrne was an Irishman and a sculptor. Tall, broad-shouldered, black-haired and blue-eyed, with a craggy, weatherbeaten face, he dressed in dusty, worn corduroy trousers and a flannel shirt. Connor smiled little and spoke less. The first day Rebecca arrived at the farm, he glanced at her, nodded his head, and then returned to eating his supper. Rebecca wondered whether he resented the arrival of a newcomer. He emerged from the barn only at mealtimes or to help David Mickleborough with the heavy work. He could be silent through an entire supper. When he did smile, though, she noticed that there was kindness, as well as a spark of humour, in his eyes.

Walking past the barn on her way to the vegetable plot, Rebecca heard the chink of chisel on stone. In the New Year, a truck arrived at the farm with a block of granite roped to its open trailer. She watched as Connor and David improvised levers and pulleys to transport the block into Connor's studio.

One morning, passing the barn, she looked up at a window and caught sight of a pale face in the darkness. She paused, trying to make it out.

Connor's voice called out to her. 'Would you like to see him?'

Rebecca opened the door a few inches. 'May I?'

'Come in.'

She went inside the barn. It was high-ceilinged and very cold, scarcely warmer than outside. Tools lay on rough wooden benches. The block of granite was supported on trestles. A grey stone face, harsh-featured and monumental, peered down at her. The thought crossed her mind that the stone was coming alive, that the being Connor was creating was finding his way out of it.

'Who is he?' she asked.

'Manannan mac Lir, the sea god of the Manx. He gave to King Cormac of Ireland a magic cup and branch.'

'He looks stern.'

'The gods should be stern, wouldn't you say, or what would be the point of them?' Connor gave her one of his rare smiles and then picked up the hammer and chisel –

a clear message, she thought, that he wanted to go back to work, so she left him to it. But most days after that, she stopped in at the barn on her way to the fields, to bring a cup for tea for Connor and to watch the stone god emerge from the granite. Connor was the antithesis of Milo, Rebecca thought, dark, scruffy and silent where Milo had been neat, fair and talkative. She felt at ease in his company, and liked to pause for a while, watching him as he worked. He and his stone god had something in common: a presence, a quietness that nevertheless spoke to her.

She went to London only once, at the end of February 1939, to meet Milo at the lawyer's office. Applying make-up and putting on a smart skirt and coat had by then become unfamiliar to her. These days, she wore trousers and jerseys and tied back her hair with a scarf. As she put on her lipstick, she stared at her reflection in the mirror. She was changing, she thought, but she did not yet know what she was changing into.

Milo had agreed to admit to being the guilty party in the divorce. At the meeting, documents were drawn up and decisions about money made. This was the official dismemberment of their marriage, Rebecca found herself thinking, this polite conversation about property and alimony. Every now and then Milo glanced at his watch – she wondered whether he was meeting someone.

After they had left the solicitor's office, they spoke to each other outside, on the pavement. Milo had agreed to give her half of the proceeds of the sale of the Mill House – Rebecca sensed he considered himself generous. She should leave that farm, he told her, and buy herself somewhere decent to live. I like the farm, she heard herself saying, in the same obstinate tone with which she had the previous autumn said to Harrison Grey of the Derbyshire cottage, I like it here. Milo shrugged. There were books, items of her clothing – what did she want him to do with them? 'Send me my paints and my sketchbooks,' she told him. 'The rest can go into storage.'

When they parted, Rebecca drove back to the farm. In her room, she lay on the bed, letting the events of the day trickle through her mind. Then it was time to feed the hens, so she changed and put on her wellies and a mack-intosh and went outside. Was she angry with Milo? Did she hate him or did she still love him? She thought of the poor Mill House, uncared for, soon to be passed over to a stranger, and her belongings. She had asked Milo to put them into storage because to see them would remind her of him. There was still a part of her that loved him, then. All she had been through and yet a part of her still loved.

A week later a parcel containing her sketchbooks and art equipment arrived at the farm. She began to draw again, mostly because that was what people did at Mayfield Farm, even David and Carlotta's boys: they drew and painted and sculpted and made pots. Rebecca drew whatever was in front of her. She drew the view through her bedroom window, the pattern of field and hedge and rolling hills, and the alder trees in the dusk, bending their heads to the wind. She drew a pile of books, a clock and a tangle of stockings put aside for washing. While she was working in the vegetable plot, she found herself planning what she would draw that evening.

In the middle of March, she drove in to Tunbridge Wells to return her library books. She was walking back from the library to her car when she noticed the headline on a news-stand. She bought a newspaper and read it sitting in the car. The German army had occupied the remaining, defenceless part of Czechoslovakia. The Munich Agreement, extracted from Hitler the previous September and intended as a guarantee of peace, had been torn up. As for Czechoslovakia, it had ceased to exist.

One sunny Saturday afternoon, Freddie and Max sat in deckchairs in St James's Park, listening to the band and eating ices.

'Every time I write to Tessa,' said Freddie, 'I ask her when she's coming home.'

Max peeled aside the wrapping of his ice and sandwiched it between two wafers. 'What does she say?'

'Most of the time, nothing. She doesn't say anything at all. That's the trouble with letters: you can ignore whatever the other person's written.'

'Where is she now? Still in Bologna?'

Freddie shook her head. 'She's in Florence now. She expects to stay there for the summer at least. She's working in a dress shop.'

'Tessa always had an obstinate streak. If she doesn't want to come back to England, then she won't. I would say leave her to her own devices, let her live her life in her own way, but . . .'

'What, Max?'

'It's infuriated me, these past few years, how the British

appear to believe that war will start at their convenience. But people seem to be waking up at last. Mr Chamberlain seems to have abandoned the illusion that Hitler and Mussolini will behave themselves if they are spoken to nicely. I'm afraid that Tessa may not have much time left if she means to return to England before the outbreak of war.'

Freddie felt depressed. 'I've said all that to her. I wrote that it might be dangerous for her to stay in Italy, and that she couldn't just pretend it wasn't happening. She said that she'd rather be unsafe in Italy than safe in England, and anyway, if there was to be a war, she might be better off in Florence than I would be in London. Because of bombs, you see. She could be right.'

'If Germany were to declare war and if Italy were to declare war on Germany's side, then Tessa would be an enemy alien in a hostile country. *That's* what concerns me.'

Freddie looked at him closely. 'Are you worried about that too, Max?'

Max picked up his camera and focused on an old couple sitting across the grass. The woman was wearing a straw hat and the man had fashioned himself a sun hat by tying knots in the corners of his handkerchief.

The shutter clicked. 'It crosses my mind now and then,' he said. 'My worst nightmare would be to be sent back to Germany. This is what we ask each other, we foreigners, we aliens, when we are alone together. If there's a war, will the British send us back to Germany?'

'If they try to, Max, I'll hide you in a cupboard in my flat.'

'Thank you, Freddie.' The band began to play a Sousa

march. 'I would prefer something a little less martial,' said Max, with a frown. 'What troubles me most is that I'm not sure that Tessa really cares whether she lives or dies.'

In spite of the sun, Freddie shivered. 'You mustn't say things like that. I care. And if Tessa won't come home, then I'll go and fetch her.'

'Will you?' Max smiled. 'Good for you, but don't leave it too long.'

He pointed his Leica at her and adjusted the viewfinder. 'You have ice cream on your nose. No, don't wipe it off, it looks very fetching.'

If Tessa won't come home, then I'll go and fetch her. Freddie's remark, made not on the spur of the moment, exactly, but nevertheless only the vague beginnings of a plan, became a firm intention. Her sister needed to come home. Tessa dismissed any written pleas to return to England, and so she, Freddie, must go to Florence and make her.

First, she must save up enough money. She economized ruthlessly and drew up a schedule of repayment, which she showed to her employer, Miss Parrish. If Miss Parrish would be so kind as to advance some of her wages, then this was how she would pay her back. Did Freddie realize that such an undertaking might be difficult? Miss Parrish asked her. Did she understand that though the Italian people themselves might not be hostile to the British, officialdom might well be? She would be careful, Freddie said, she would be sensible, but she was used to travelling, had spent much of her early life in Europe, and had since been abroad several times with her sister in the school holidays. She was spending her evenings brushing up her rusty Italian and she was studying railway and shipping timetables. Miss Parrish gave her a hard look, and then said, 'I should travel by train. Far more pleasant and no risk of sickness.'

On May 22nd, during a visit to Berlin, Benito Mussolini, the Italian leader, signed an alliance with Hitler. The alliance, nicknamed the Pact of Steel, committed Italy and Germany to military cooperation and mutual support in the event of war.

The next day, Freddie spoke to Miss Parrish again. Miss Parrish agreed to allow her a week off work. A week – four days, travelling, so just three days in which to persuade Tessa to come home. Freddie bought her ticket from Thomas Cook and Son, packed a suitcase, and on the last day of May left England.

The boat train, the Channel crossing, and then another train from Dieppe to Paris. Freddie crossed Paris on the Métro and then made the long overnight journey through the heart of France and over the Alps to Turin, where, taut with a mixture of tiredness and anticipation, she alighted from the carriage and bought fruit and coffee from a stall on the station. An hour later, she caught a slower train that chugged across the plains of northern Italy, through Bologna and on to Florence.

She arrived in the city in the late afternoon. Santa Maria Novella station, a huge new brick and glass edifice, was crowded. As she walked out of the station, the bright sunlight made her squint. She felt suddenly apprehensive. She had not warned Tessa of her decision to travel to

243

Florence; instinct had told her not to. What if Tessa had already left the city?

But as she walked through the piazza and towards the river, her fears fell away. Every step encapsulated a memory. On that pavement she had fallen and grazed her knee and Mama had bound it up with her handkerchief. Along that narrow street had been the bakery where they had bought the croissants filled with custard that she and Tessa had loved to eat. When she reached the bank of the Arno, she leaned her elbows on the wall and looked out across the water. The sun was setting and the soft evening light gilded the terracotta roof tiles of the buildings and turned the river to a sheet of silk, so that it seemed that the air itself was powdered with gold.

Just a little longer and she would be with the one person in the world who shared her memories and experiences, who had known her her entire life, who was her companion and protector, who laughed at the same things, and who understood without question her need to edit her past, to shape it into a form acceptable to outsiders. And if, in the past year, their roles had been reversed, and it had been she who had protected Tessa, then why not? It had been her turn, surely.

On the south side of the river, she checked her map as she made her way through a criss-cross of roads and alleyways. Massive iron-bound doors, surrounded by stone arches, were set into the impenetrable walls of the buildings, and political slogans were daubed on the walls. The cobwebbed windows of the lower storeys were guarded with iron bars. A stone escutcheon was set above a doorway, and a statue of the Virgin Mary peered out from a niche. A vast palazzo, its frontage covered in ornate black and silver paintings, looked haughtily down, and from a shop window, the evening sun flashed coloured lights on the facets of a chandelier.

Freddie turned off the Via Maggio into an alleyway that was only a few yards wide. Here, the high walls of the building blocked off the sun and the heat. There was someone at the far end of the alley, blackly silhouetted, walking towards her. Freddie strained to see clearly. The woman was tall and slim and she was carrying shopping bags.

Putting the bags down, Tessa called out, 'Freddie? Oh, Freddie, is that really you?'

Tessa's rooms were above a second-hand bookshop. In the smaller of the two rooms there was a single bed and a chest of drawers. The window looked out over a courtyard in which dustbins, empty wine bottles and a child's rusty tricycle stood shoulder to shoulder. In the larger room, which was at the front of the house, there was a fireplace, a sofa and a chair and a small table. In the corner was an oil stove and the cupboard in which Tessa kept food and crockery. The light from the window, which faced on to the alley, stained the room the colour of ochre.

Tessa prepared dinner. While she cooked, she asked questions. Why hadn't Freddie told her she was coming? Had she travelled alone? *How* had she travelled? Third Class, sitting up all night? Oh Freddie, you poor thing, I shall pour you a glass of wine and you'll soon feel much better. How was everyone at home? How were Max and Ray and Julian?

In describing her journey to Tessa, it became an adventure instead of the exhausting and occasionally alarming experience it had seemed at the time. The few stops she had travelled on the Paris Métro from the Gare du Nord, where a man sitting across the carriage had stared at her and chased up the station steps after her when she had left the train at the Gare de Bercy, seemed funny rather than menacing, and her broken night's sleep, sitting between a fat farmer who snored and a woman who muttered as she ran her rosary beads through her fingers, became comical rather than tiresome. At the border, the Italian police had walked through the train demanding to see identification; she had made herself look as young as possible, she told Tessa: no lipstick or powder and a ribbon in her hair, for heaven's sake. When the guard had glared at her passport she had pretended that she was about to cry, and he had patted her head and moved on to the next passenger.

'Tessa,' she said, and Tessa must have recognized her tone of voice because she said, 'I know why you're here. You want me to come back to England with you, don't you? We won't talk about it now. We'll talk about it tomorrow, when you're not so tired.'

As she sat on the sofa after supper, Freddie's eyes refused to focus, her lids dragged shut by tiredness. Memories of her journey flicked through her consciousness like film stills. It was no use – Tessa was tucking a blanket over her – she curled up and fell asleep.

She had three days to make Tessa see that she must come home.

They had lunch, panzanella and a plate of salami, in a small trattoria near the shop where Tessa worked. On the wall was a faded fresco of clouds and cherubs. Half a dozen businessmen in navy striped suits talked and laughed at a table by the stairs. Now and then their gazes slid across the room to where Freddie and Tessa were sitting.

'I'm sorry I just *went*,' said Tessa. 'But if I'd told you, you would have tried to talk me out of it, wouldn't you?'

'You could hardly have expected me not to.' Freddie speared a slice of tomato. 'You *planned* to go, didn't you?'

'Not exactly *planned*. I knew I might, though. And when I reached Menton, I was sure.'

Tessa was wearing a charcoal-grey cotton dress with a white piqué collar and cuffs. It was the sort of cheap frock, thought Freddie, that Tessa the mannequin would never have worn. But here she made it look elegant.

'I felt bad about Ray,' said Tessa. 'Was he dreadfully cut up?'

'Dreadfully. But he's seeing a woman who works for the Home Service. She has a terribly posh voice and she says things like, "And now a concert of Wagner and Brahms by the BBC Symphony Orchestra." So you're not irreplace-able, Tessa.'

Tessa smiled. 'I never thought I was.'

'You left the garnets on purpose, didn't you?'

'I left them for you. I thought you'd look after them better than me. I don't always look after things well.' Tessa's smile had gone; looking Freddie in the eye, she said, 'I had to go. You do see that, don't you?'

'I wondered whether London reminded you too much of Angelo.' There, the first time either of them had said his

247

name, a bridge that must be crossed, even if in doing so she upset Tessa.

'Angelo's here, in my heart. He always will be.' Tessa put her fist to her ribs. Then she said, 'I didn't leave London because of Angelo. I left because of his father. He didn't call me or write to me once after Angelo died. Not once, Freddie. I couldn't bear to think I might see him again, that I might turn the corner of a street, and there he'd be and we wouldn't know what to say to each other. Or he would say something tactful and clever and it would break my heart. You do understand, don't you, Freddie?'

'I understand that what he did has divided us. And I hate him for that. I wish you'd tell me who he is.'

'Why? So you'd know who to hate?'

Yes, thought Freddie, and why not? She said, 'I'd like to make him understand the hurt he's caused.'

'Revenge, you mean.'

Was that what she wanted? She said, 'I'd call it justice.'

'What would be the point?'

'If it wasn't for him, all this would never have happened. If it wasn't for him, you wouldn't be here.'

'But I'm better here, Freddie.' Tessa leaned forward and took Freddie's hand. 'I wouldn't say I was happy, but I know I'm better. I knew I had to start again from scratch and I knew I couldn't do that in London. In London, I was Tessa Nicolson, who used to be beautiful, or Tessa Nicolson, who'd had a baby out of wedlock. Or I was poor Tessa, whose baby had died.'

The businessmen roared with laughter. One of them, catching Freddie's eye, raised his glass.

Tessa said softly, 'Here, no one knows about Angelo or the accident. I haven't told anyone and perhaps I never will. I have somewhere to live and I have work and I'm getting by, Freddie, so please don't be angry with me.'

'I'm not angry with you.' She looked away, because she was afraid she might cry. 'I just miss you.'

'And I miss you too. I miss you all the time.' Tessa smiled at Freddie. 'You could always stay here with me. Think about it.'

'Max says that if there's a war, you'll be an enemy alien.'

This, a conversation that must take place in Tessa's rooms. Freddie had noticed, walking through the city in the afternoon while Tessa worked at the shop, that there was a watchfulness in Florence's streets, and an air of oppression. At midday, the sun beat down and you could almost see old memories, old rivalries imprisoned in the blue-black shadows of loggia and alleyway.

'My Italian's fluent,' said Tessa. 'I can pass for Italian quite easily.'

'Your passport . . .'

'I'll manage, Freddie. You mustn't worry.'

'I do worry. I worry that you don't realize how difficult things might become, that you don't understand . . .' She broke off, seeing Tessa's expression.

Tessa was making an alteration to one of the dresses from the shop where she worked. She snipped a stitch, wound a length of thread round a bobbin. Then she said, 'Tell me, Freddie, how can anything that might happen to me in the future possibly be worse than what's happened already?'

'I didn't mean . . .'

'Yes you did. You're afraid I won't be able to look after myself. You're afraid that I came here on a whim, that I haven't thought it through. Aren't you?'

'No.' Freddie spread out her hands, looked down at them. She thought of what Max had said to her, that day in the park. She said softly, 'I'm afraid you don't care any more.'

Tessa put aside her needle and thread. 'I didn't, for a long time, it's true. I wished I'd died in the accident with Angelo.'

Freddie was afraid to ask the question. 'And now?'

'Every now and then, something pleases me. I sit in the piazza and feel the sun on my face. I listen to the people talking in the marketplace and just for a while, I'm glad to be a part of it. I've made a life for myself here. It's a small life, and it's not at all the sort I once thought I wanted, but it suits me. I have friends, Italian friends, who would help me if I needed it. If I can't stay here, then I shall go to the countryside. There are hills and valleys where I could lose myself, if I had to.'

Freddie was too hot in the small room: sweat trickled down the back of her neck, and her shoulders hurt where she had burned them, walking too long in the sun. She said, 'If you stay here, then I shall worry all the time. If war breaks out I shall be afraid for you. I expect I'll be afraid every single day.'

'Then I'm sorry for that,' said Tessa gently. 'I'm truly sorry for that.'

* * *

250

They took a bus to Fiesole. The road wound up the hillside; to either side bougainvillea and oleander smothered the high walls that surrounded the elegant villas of the wealthy. Leaving the bus in the main piazza, they walked out of the small town to the Villa Millefiore, where they had lived with Mrs Hamilton.

The doors of the villa were locked and the windows were shuttered. To one side of the house a narrow, sloping path, overrun with nettles and bindweed, ran downhill, beside the garden. They walked in single file, Tessa ahead, knocking back the vegetation with a stick.

The trees to the sides of the path fell away, letting in the full blaze of the sun. Squeezing through a gap in the iron railings, they entered a thicket of laurels. The shrubs rose above them, their dark, leathery leaves forming a roof. Pinpoints of light flashed overhead and the sharp scent of the laurels mingled with the dusty smell of the dry earth. Tiny grey moths, like fragments of cobweb, rose from the branches.

Here, in the laurel grove, remembered Freddie, Faustina Zanetti had buried her doll and, try as they might, they had never been able to find her again. Did she still lie here, china-blue eyes eternally shut, yellow hair blackened by the earth? Beyond the laurels was an ilex wood. Frilled brown leaves carpeted the ground and the spiky branches reached out to grab a sleeve or a hem.

They emerged from the woodland into the garden. Freddie blinked at the blaze of the sun. The gravel paths were overgrown with weeds and grass. Resting her forearms on the wall that encircled the pool, she looked down into the deep, dark bowl. There was a rotten smell, and flies darted on the thick green water far below. The sea monster, festooned in khaki skeins of blanket weed, glared at them, marooned on his island.

'I used to love swimming here,' Freddie said. 'We used to see who could hold their breath longest. Do you remember?'

'Guido. It was always Guido.' Tessa lay on her back on the wall, her eyes shaded by her dark glasses, soaking up the sun.

A memory came to Freddie of an afternoon at the pool: the sun, the heat, and the Zanetti boys, Guido and Sandro, swimming, their brown arms scything through the water, Guido's dark head sleek and dripping.

She dropped a pebble into the pool. 'I wonder whether Mama minded living here. After all, it wasn't her house.'

'I don't think she minded after Domenico.'

Another pebble – a plop, an echo. 'I liked Domenico,' said Freddie. 'He was a lot nicer than Mama's other lovers.'

'A lot nicer than Father,' said Tessa.

'I don't remember him much. Sometimes he used to read me a story at night.'

'I remember him throwing a chair through a window. And Mama cutting her hand when she picked up the broken glass.' Tessa's face was tilted to the sun, and when she swept her hair back from her forehead, Freddie saw the jagged scar. 'When they quarrelled, I used to think it was my fault, that I hadn't been good enough.'

'Mama once told me that the first time she saw Father, she thought he looked like a pirate.' Freddie dropped another stone into the pond. 'I asked her, why would you marry someone who looked like a pirate?'

Tessa said slowly, 'The first time I met Angelo's father he was interesting and the second time he was amusing. It was the third time that I fell in love with him.' The twin black discs of her sunglasses turned towards Freddie. 'You don't have a choice, Freddie. It just happens.'

Freddie didn't believe that. She suspected that to fall in love you had, at least in part, to want to fall in love, that it wasn't something that just happened to you, like tripping over a kerbstone – and even that, after all, you could avoid if you looked out.

You could always stay here with me. Think about it. If Tessa wouldn't come back to London, then she would stay in Florence with Tessa. They would live together in the rooms over the second-hand bookshop, and she would find a job in a shop or an office, perhaps, as soon as her Italian was fluent enough. In the evenings, they would eat supper in Tessa's ochre-washed room. She would become used to it, and after a while her skin wouldn't redden and burn in the sun.

It didn't sit, somehow. No matter how she imagined this and that, it didn't convince.

The walls of the English Tea Rooms had been daubed with slogans, and Florence's hotels, its Edens and Bristols and Britannias, had been given other names, Italian names. Most of the English colony had fled the city, no longer welcomed, flattered or cultivated, as they once had been. Some of them had lived in Florence for decades.

Freddie found it hard to tell how much Florence had altered, because she didn't remember the city well enough. Flashes mostly, discontinuous vignettes. She had been a child when she had lived there with Tessa and Mama and Mrs Hamilton, and she had noticed the things a child notices. And that, perhaps, was the crux of it. She was a child no longer. She had a home and friends and work that she would miss if she remained in Florence with Tessa. She needed to belong somewhere; she was not like Tessa, had never liked to flit about, and had long ago acquired the knack of making herself fit in to any group of people. She had never sought out attention and had never been able particularly to understand why some people went out of their way to make themselves different. She felt sympathy and some fellow feeling towards those who couldn't help but be different – the girl at school whose leg had been lamed by an attack of polio, for instance, and some of Miss Parrish's correspondents on the magazine, women who had been squeezed to the margins of society because they had been unfortunate enough to reach adulthood as the war had scythed its way through the men who should have been their fiancés and husbands. But why try deliberately to cultivate difference? She couldn't see the point of it. You could retain independence of spirit and mind while seeming, on the outside, to be much the same as everyone else.

Mama had been different, and look where it had got her. Tessa couldn't help but be different – it was integral to her – and because of that she had suffered. Tessa might be able to fit into this city – she had always been cosmopolitan, restless, as exotic as a migrating bird – but Freddie could not. Her pale skin, unlike Tessa's golden one, burned in the sun, and the heat made her head ache.

She *was* English, had somehow without noticing it during her years at school and in London become English, and because of that, whatever she thought of it, for better or worse and with or without Tessa, she would go home. This was what she had discovered during her stay in Florence: that England was her home, just as Italy was Tessa's, and whatever she said, and whatever she did, Tessa would remain here.

Outside the entrance to Santa Maria Novella station, cars were drawing up, disgorging officials in uniform and businessmen in black suits and hats. Men with the arched noses and thin lips of Medici princes stood, brushing flecks of dust from their jackets as their chauffeurs and secretaries gathered up their luggage. Crowds squeezed into the ticket hall, soldiers and schoolchildren and nuns and mothers ferrying their infants across the polished black marble floor.

Driven by Freddie's dislike of being late, they had arrived at the station far too early.

'Let me change your seat for one in a sleeping car,' offered Tessa. 'You can't possibly sit up all the way to Paris.'

'No thanks,' said Freddie. 'I don't mind. Good of you to offer, but honestly, I'll be fine.'

'A magazine for the journey, then – do you have a magazine?'

'I don't want one, I've a book. And they'll all be in Italian anyway. I don't need anything.'

'No.' Tessa smiled at her. 'Of course you don't.'

'I do need *you*,' Freddie said carefully.

Tessa nodded. 'I know, darling.'

'You should go.' Freddie looked at the clock. 'The shop . . .'

'Damn the shop, I'll be late.'

'No, Tessa. Go, please.' Freddie tried to smile. 'Or I'll cry.'

Tessa gave a quick nod. Then they hugged, holding each other tightly.

Tessa said, 'You'll be all right?'

'You know I will.'

'Write to me, Freddie.'

'I promise. And you're to write to me often too, Tessa,' she said fiercely.

Tessa walked away. The soldiers and the rich men with their entourages stepped aside for her. For several minutes Freddie stood frozen, and then a sudden impulse to see every last glimpse of her sister made her push through the crowds to the entrance and out on to the station forecourt. There was Tessa walking along the pavement, and there was Tessa briskly crossing the street. And there, locked in her memory for ever, was a final image of Tessa in her leaf-green dress. Then she turned a corner and was gone.

Chapter Eight

Freddie moved away from the fuss of cars and taxis in front of the station building and found a quiet spot, where she put down her case, wrapped her arms round herself and took a deep breath.

Suddenly someone swept up her case, saying in a well-bred English voice, 'Let me help you with that,' and headed, with her suitcase, away from the station.

She ran after him. 'Put that down!'

He gave a quick look over his shoulder to somewhere beyond her. 'If you like.' He put down her suitcase on the pavement. And then, without warning, he pulled her to him and kissed her.

Freddie squawked and stamped on his foot.

'*Ouch*,' he said. 'That hurts. I'm doing this for King and Country. Where's your patriotism?'

He kissed her again, hard on the mouth, his arms around her, locking her to him. He kissed very well, so that for a second or two she almost forgot she was being kissed by a complete stranger. When he let her go she was at first speechless with shock, then she opened her mouth to scream for help, but he said in a low voice, 'Please don't yell. I'm not going to hurt you, I promise, but there's some gentlemen over there I'm trying to avoid.' He picked up her case again and flung his free arm round her shoulders, steering her forcefully away from the station entrance. 'They're looking for one person, not two, so with a bit of luck they won't even look at two lovers leaving the station and we'll be able to get away without them noticing us.'

He was hauling her across the Piazza Adua. 'I don't want to leave the station!' Freddie cried furiously. 'I've a train to catch!'

'This area's no good for me. The *carabinieri* are just over there' — a nod of the head — 'and soon they'll be all over the place. The thing is, I'm bleeding like a stuck pig and I'm afraid I'm leaving a trail. So I need to get away from here, Miss . . .'

Habit made her supply, 'Nicolson.'

'My name's Jack Ransome.'

'I don't care what you're called. I just want to catch my train!' She made a grab for her case but he was holding it fast.

'As you wish, Miss Nicolson. But I'd have thought some conversation might lighten our journey.'

He propelled her along the Via Fiume. Large, important-looking buildings rose to either side of the street.

'Journey?' Her voice rose in pitch. 'What do you mean, *journey*?'

'I need you to drive me out of the city. I've been shot, you see.'

'Oh, for heaven's sake!' she cried. 'I've no time to play silly games!'

'Nor I. I can't say I fancy spending the war in an Italian prison. And that would be the better option.' His arm slipped from her shoulder at last and he tugged at his trouser turn-up. His ankle was dark with blood. Freddie gasped.

'It's nothing much, only a flesh wound,' he said. 'But as I said, I'm leaving a trail.'

Freddie looked behind her. Drops of blood, like crimson rain, spotted the pavement.

'Come on,' he said.

'No.'

His gaze fixed on her. His eyes were a cool, clear blue.

She said, as steadily as she was able, 'I'm sorry you're hurt, but I don't know what you're involved in and I've no wish to know. But if I don't go back to the station now I shall miss my train. Please give me back my suitcase and let me go.'

'I can't. And anyway, it's too late. If OVRA catches up with us, they'll assume you are my accomplice, whatever we say.'

Now she was frightened. OVRA were the Italian secret military police. Looking back, she saw three figures silhouetted against the sunlight. Her gaze flicked quickly back to Jack Ransome. He might be a criminal or he might be a madman. Or he might be neither.

She pulled off her silk scarf and gave it to him. 'Tie that round your ankle.'

He knotted her scarf around the wound; she saw him wince. Then he took her arm again and they headed on, up the Via Nazionale. He was limping, every alternate step pulling at her arm. Behind them she thought she heard footsteps.

They turned into a narrow street. Tall stone walls soared to either side of them, the windows barred by iron grilles. There was the scent of roasting coffee and a whiff of drains. Jack looked back over his shoulder; when Freddie did likewise, she saw that the three men were still there. The echo of their footsteps on the paving stones seemed to fill the alleyway.

'Damn,' murmured her captor. 'I hoped we'd lost them.' Taking Freddie's hand, he began to run, weaving round cyclists and a truck unloading bags of sand, and overtaking a pair of priests who were disputing earnestly.

The alley opened out into a marketplace. Porters carrying baskets on their heads threaded up and down the paths. Gleaming pyramids of tomatoes and fat cream-coloured rounds of cheese were arranged on the stalls. Great bunches of herbs wilted in the sun. Short, square men bawled out the prices of their wares and black-clad women sat behind tables displaying embroidered linen.

Jack Ransome gave a charming, apologetic smile to one of the stallkeepers, a woman in a hessian apron, and then spoke to her in Italian. The woman beckoned them behind the stall, pulled aside a length of cloth and gestured to them to hide beneath the trestle table.

The stall belonged to a fishmonger; an open barrel of salted cod stood close by. Freddie breathed in the oily smell of fish.

'What did you say to her?' she hissed.

'I appealed to her romantic nature. We've fallen in love and your father and uncles are trying to stop us marrying. Shhh.' He put a finger to his lips.

Freddie saw, only a few feet away, on the path between the market stalls, three pairs of polished black shoes and navy trouser turn-ups. Her heart pounded. Should she call out, take a chance that the police would believe her story and allow her to catch her train?

She remained silent. The black shoes headed on, into the crowds. She closed her eyes, let out a long breath.

Jack murmured, 'We should go,' and they clambered out from under the table. He thanked the stallkeeper and then they hurried on, out of the square, along a series of roads, turning corners, threading through the crowds, and waiting while a crocodile of schoolchildren walking hand in hand crossed the street at a busy intersection.

'We need a car,' he said.

'A car?' Freddie stared at him blankly.

'Yes. I told you, I need you to help me get out of the city.'

He was still carrying her suitcase. His other hand was clamped round hers. She should have run away while she had the chance. She should have called out to the police in the marketplace. *I need you to help me get out of the city*, she thought. And then what?

'Miss Nicolson,' he said sharply. 'We must hurry.'

She felt the curious glances of passers-by. They didn't blend in: his limp, the foreign cut of their clothes, their English conversation and their air of haste – all these must

261

pick them out from the crowds. She began to walk again. She thought she could hear the footsteps of their pursuers, but, looking over her shoulder, she realized the pounding beat was the drum of her own heart.

Every so often, they passed a parked car. To a gleaming Mercedes Jack said, 'No, too noticeable.' To a battered van parked beside a row of shops he shook his head. 'Too many people around. It might take me a minute or two.'

For King and Country; I've been shot; the military police. It was all ridiculous and probably a pack of lies. A handsome face and an upper-class voice were no guarantee of honesty: he could be anything – a conman, a thief, a murderer. Freddie thought with longing of her train and her carefully organized journey, the books she had meant to read, the letters she had planned to write.

They had reached the Piazza San Marco. Cars were parked around its perimeter. They circled the square as Jack checked one vehicle after another. A rusty black Fiat was parked in a quiet corner of the square. Jack looked to left and right. Then he tried the Fiat's doors: they were locked.

'Could you lend me a hat pin, Miss Nicolson?'

Furiously, she took a pin from her hat and handed it to him.

'Thank you,' he said. 'Keep an eye out, would you, please?'

It was hot; she crossed the road to stand in the shade. She took off her jacket, but found herself holding it to her chest as if for protection. Her mouth was dry and her nerves were strung out, taut as a wire. Out of the corner of her eye she glimpsed a police car, heading along the street. Jack Ransome noticed it too, and his hand stilled on the door handle of the Fiat. But the police car drove on and he crouched down once more beside the lock.

She could run now, abandon her suitcase, make a dash for it. She still had her handbag, with her purse, her passport and her now useless train ticket. But apart from her clothes and toiletries there was, inside her suitcase, hidden beneath the lining, an envelope containing English money, put aside for emergencies. And besides, would she make it to the railway station? Or would he try to stop her?

She rather thought he might. There was something determined about the set of his jaw; she found she didn't particularly want to provoke him. And if he was the sort of person who was caught up with the sort of people who used guns, mightn't he have a gun too?

Tall, lightly built but athletic-looking, he was bent over the door of the car, his mouth set, concentrating on his task. His dark blond hair swung damply over his forehead. His clothes were good; Freddie knew about clothes, Tessa had taught her, and the ones he was wearing were, though dusty and torn, expensively tailored. Her mind drifted back to that kiss, but she wrenched it away. Was he telling her the truth? *What* was he? And what did he mean to do with her?

She heard him call out softly, 'Miss Nicolson.'

He was holding open the driver's door of the Fiat. She crossed the road; he handed her back her hat pin and she stabbed it into her hat. 'I'll drive you to Bologna,' she said steadily. 'And then you may catch whichever train you want and I shall go home.'

'No trains. Roads are safer.'

She shook her head. 'I'm not going anywhere unless you tell me where we're heading.'

'I haven't decided yet. North, for a start.' He peered at her. 'You're not afraid, are you?'

'Of course not,' she said coldly.

'Good. You don't look like a quivering sort of girl. That's why I chose you.'

'Chose me?'

'I knew you were English, I read the label on your case. And you looked cool-headed. Not the hysterical type. You can drive, I assume?'

She gave him a filthy look and climbed into the car. He put her suitcase on the back seat while she fumbled with the controls. The car lurched, making him grab the dashboard. She jabbed at the accelerator and then they were off, weaving up the road. Freddie stared rigidly ahead, concentrating on negotiating her passage around parked cars and a barrow heaped with milk churns. It was more than a year since she had driven a car, and the heavy Fiat handled very differently to Tessa's small MG.

At the junction, Jack Ransome told her to turn left. They had been travelling for five minutes or so when he remarked, 'Don't you like changing gear?'

The engine was screaming. 'Not much,' she admitted.

'I'll do the gearstick, you do the pedals.'

He flicked the gearstick, barked out orders, and Freddie double-declutched. 'Best not burn out the gearbox,' he said.

She noticed how carefully he was holding himself. She glanced down; blood was seeping through her scarf on to the footwell. It would be awkward, she thought, if he died on her.

'When I find somewhere quiet,' she said, 'I'll stop and see if I can bandage your foot properly.'

More directions. They were heading north, out of the city. Catching sight of a signpost to Fiesole, Freddie recalled with a pang her visit to the town with Tessa only a couple of days before.

Soon they had left the houses behind and were in open countryside. Freddie felt some of her fear ebb away – though why she should feel less frightened, she did not know: out here, he could easily murder her and bury her body in the woods. At length, she saw ahead a track cutting off into a forest. Turning into it, she drove a short distance until she was sure the car could not be seen from the road. Then she parked. The narrow grassy track was surrounded by densely packed fir trees.

Jack got out of the car and, sitting down on the verge, began to unlace his shoe. He was very pale, Freddie noticed. If he passed out, she might be able to reverse the car back down the track to the road. And then she could drive to the nearest railway station and catch a train home.

But as he took off his shoe, he drew breath sharply, and she found herself feeling sorry for him, in spite of her annoyance. She took her suitcase out of the car and opened it on the grass beside him.

'I've some aspirins,' she said. 'There, in my handbag. Let me help you with your sock – sorry, I'll try not to hurt. Talk to me. It'll satisfy my curiosity and it might take your mind off it. And anyway, if I'm going to sacrifice a piece of my clothing to bandage your foot, the least you can do is to tell me what's going on.'

'Fair enough.' He frowned. 'Not sure where to start.'

'The usual places . . . age, parentage, birthplace, family, occupation.' She peeled off his sock. 'Oh, and how you came to be running through Florence with a gunshot wound in your leg.'

His forehead was filmed with sweat and there was a deep ragged gash in his shin, just above the ankle. Had she anything to clean the wound? She rummaged in her suitcase and found a hand towel and a small tin of Germolene.

'Okay,' he said. 'Twenty-two years old. Born in Norfolk. Parents still alive, last thing I heard. Two sisters and a brother — I'm fond of Marcia and Rose but brother George is as dull as ditchwater. Occupation — nothing much, really. I've travelled around a bit. I rather like Italy.'

Freddie dabbed at the wound with a towel. 'Your Italian's very good.'

'Thanks. Lived here for quite a while.'

'If we had some water, I could clean it up properly. I'll just try to mop it up a bit.'

'Girl Guide, were you, Miss Nicolson?'

'Yes, actually,' she said repressively. 'So. Go on.'

'Well. I know one or two people in the Foreign Office. And a couple of years ago they told me they'd like to have an idea of what Italy's going to do when war breaks out.'

'"When",' she repeated, looking up at him. 'Not "if"?'

'Yes, I'm afraid so.'

Oh Tessa, she thought.

He went on, 'They asked me to keep my ear to the

ground while I was in Italy. See which way the wind was blowing. So I did. It rather grew from there. Ask a few questions, talk to some people, try to get an idea of whether Mussolini's ready for war and which way he's likely to go. Pick up any information about how they're doing in the way of armaments, that sort of thing.'

Her heart gave an unpleasant thud. 'You're a spy,' she said flatly.

'Yes, I suppose I am.' He flinched. 'Ouch.'

She glared at him. 'Don't fuss.'

'Britain's been courting Italy for years. It's the most appalling miscalculation.' He sounded annoyed.

'Why?'

'Because what we should have been trying our utmost to do, these past few years, is to make a deal with the Soviet Union. The reason we haven't, of course, is because we're afraid of communism. The government hasn't seemed to realize that fascism's the greater threat. They appear to be coming round to it at last, but I've a horrible feeling we've left it too late.'

Max had said much the same thing. Freddie had cleaned up the wound as best she could. She surveyed it doubtfully. 'You ought to see a doctor. There might still be a bullet in it.'

'I don't think so, I'm sure it glanced off.' He grinned. 'Besides, I trust you completely, Miss Nicolson.'

'They didn't teach us how to stitch bullet wounds in Guides.'

He gave a bark of laughter. 'No. Damned shame.'

'So. You haven't explained . . .'

'The first few times were all right. I passed on my odds and ends back home and they patted me on the head and sent me back to Italy. But this time I must have loused up, because when I went back to my flat last night, there were a couple of goons waiting for me. I managed to get away, caught the first train out of Rome . . .'

'Rome?'

'Yes, that's where I live. The train only took me as far as Arrezzo, but I hitched a ride first thing this morning to the outskirts of Florence. I thought I'd lost them, damn it, but they were waiting for me outside the station. They chased me, and one of them managed to wing me on the ankle.'

She made him hold a wad of towelling over the wound while she tore a cotton skirt into strips. She had *liked* that skirt – two garments lost now, the skirt and the scarf she had given him in Florence. She, who tried to keep her life within sensible bounds, felt exasperated at finding herself caught up in someone else's misadventures.

As she wound strips of cotton round the towelling wad, he said, 'What about you?'

'Me?'

'Birthplace?'

'Italy.'

He raised his eyebrows. 'So where were you taking the train to?'

'England, ultimately. I've lived there since I was twelve.'

'Parents?'

She shook her head. 'They're both dead. I have a sister who lives in Florence.'

'Occupation?'

She pinned the makeshift bandage into place. 'I work for a lady called Miss Parrish. Typing letters, filing, that sort of thing.'

There, her life tidied up into a few neat sentences. It seemed rather thin. Jack looked dreadfully pale. If he fainted, would she really be able to abandon him here, where he might quite possibly die from loss of blood – or, perhaps equally as bad, be picked up by the Italian police? She thought not; it seemed inhuman, and, after all, he claimed to be doing something useful for his country – their country. Which meant that, like it or not, she was tied to him until they were able to leave Italy. But how would they leave Italy?

As she put her belongings back into her suitcase, she said slowly, 'You told me the trains weren't safe. But surely, when we cross the border, the police will look in the car. They might recognize you.'

He grinned at her. 'We're not going to drive across the border.'

'What are we going to do, then?'

'We're going to sail across it,' he said.

Jack Ransome had a friend who lived on the Ligurian coast, a few miles south of Rapallo. He was sure his friend would be able to find someone to ferry them across the sea to France. It went on all the time, fishermen smuggling this and that from one country to another, so why not drop off a stray Englishman and woman on a deserted beach on the Côte d'Azur?

They need drive little more than a hundred miles. He

knew the way, more or less; he was familiar with the north-west coast of Italy. They'd head west through Pistoia and Montecatini Terme and then take the coastal road to Rapallo – though it might be wise, he added as an afterthought, to keep well away from La Spezia and its important naval base. It should take a day or two, he estimated breezily. With luck, they'd find somewhere to stay the night.

The road took them through the foothills of the Apennines. In the distance, Freddie saw peaks that were, even in late May, topped with snow. Once or twice, passing a boy driving a flock of geese or a woman garbed in black, carrying a bundle of firewood, they drew up and asked directions. Freddie's driving began to take on a rhythm as the road peeled away beneath the wheels of the car. She changed gear smoothly now, learning, as the car swallowed up the miles, how to place the wheels exactly where she wanted to. It was going to be all right, she told herself. She would drive to Rapallo, and if Jack chose to sail to France then that would be his business, but she would not go with him. She did not intend to risk life and limb on a small boat on the Ligurian Sea; she would catch the train home.

In Prato, they stopped to buy bread and cheese and flasks of water and wine. They ate sitting on a grassy verge outside the town – or rather, Freddie ate and Jack swallowed several mouthfuls of wine. Then they drove on, skirting round Pistoia on smaller roads. The sun was high in the sky and eventually Jack dozed, his head propped against the side of the car. There was a greyish tinge to his skin. Freddie remembered the ragged wound and how he had been unable to eat, and how quickly he had swallowed the wine.

At mid-afternoon, seeing road signs to Montecatini Terme, Freddie drove into the outskirts of the town. Jack slept on as she pulled into a garage and bought petrol. She asked for directions to a pharmacy. Leaving Jack sleeping in the car, she crossed a piazza to the shop. She had checked the Italian for 'lint' and 'bandage' in her pocket dictionary, but her pronunciation must have been poor because the chemist, a thickset man with a sour expression, made an uncomprehending downward bending of the sides of his mouth. After she had repeated the words a couple of times and mimed making a bandage, he got slowly to his feet and thumped a couple of packets on to the counter. Then she remembered aspirin, which fortunately was much the same in Italian, and disinfectant – spying a bottle she thought might contain it, she went through the pantomime again and a small measure was poured out. Then the pharmacist said something – Freddie caught only the word *dottore*. She laughed, shaking her head. Oh no, she didn't need a doctor, not at all.

The chemist totted up her bill. Freddie could feel his unfriendly gaze on her as she scrabbled in her purse for coins. '*Inglesi?*' he said suddenly, and she put the money down on the counter, scooped up her purchases and walked out of the shop. As she crossed the piazza to the car, she looked back. He was standing in the open doorway, watching her. Then he spat on the paving stones. She looked ahead again and walked on, trying not to speed her pace.

Back at the car, Jack woke, blinking. Freddie climbed into the driver's seat and shut the door. As she sat down, she was trembling.

'I think I might have made a mistake,' she said.

He was instantly alert. 'Tell me.'

'I went to a pharmacy to buy bandages for your foot. I think the chemist was suspicious. I don't know, I'm not sure. He looked at me in a funny way and he guessed I was English. I'm sorry.'

'Not your fault.' He hauled himself upright. 'It probably doesn't matter, but we'd better drive on.' He gave her an encouraging smile. 'Get us out of town and then I'll sort my ankle out and take over the driving. I feel much better after that sleep.'

When they were a few miles out of Montecatini, they pulled into another farm track. Jack got out of the car to clean and bandage his ankle, but Freddie remained in the driver's seat. She felt exhausted; the disturbing episode in the pharmacy seemed to have sapped her reserves. Every sound – the distant revving of an engine, the bark of a dog – made her jump.

Jack came back to the car. 'That's better. Thanks for getting the stuff from the chemist. Move over and I'll drive.'

They changed seats, and as Jack started up the Fiat and they headed off once more, Freddie closed her eyes.

Later, she woke up, blinking. 'What time is it?' she asked.

'Seven-ish.'

'Where are we?'

'We can't be far from the coast.'

The thought cheered her. She imagined that they would find a little hotel and stay there for the night. She pictured a proper supper, a bath, a bed. Normality.

He glanced at her. 'I should apologize, dragging you off like this.'

'I was looking forward to a nice quiet train journey home. I like train journeys. You can get on with things.'

'Were you visiting your sister?'

'Yes.' She glanced out of the side window. The light had begun to fade and the intense blue sky of the afternoon had been replaced by a dusk of apricot and lavender. It seemed a long time since she had seen Tessa; she had to remind herself that it had been only that morning. She sighed. 'I came to Italy to try to persuade Tessa to come home with me.'

'But she wouldn't?'

Freddie shook her head. 'I had to try, though. What do your Foreign Office friends think will happen here if there's a war?'

He changed gear smoothly. 'They think – they hope – that Mussolini will at least stay neutral.'

'I hope they're right.'

'If they are, then your sister should be fine.'

She was grateful to him for that, even if she suspected he was not being entirely truthful and that he had said it to comfort her.

'I don't suppose,' he said thoughtfully, 'that I'll be able to come back to Italy for a while.'

'What will you do? Will you go back to Norfolk?'

'Good God, no. Living death. No, I think I'll join the army. That'll surprise my brother – Jack, doing something useful at last.'

'Are you the eldest?'

'Third out of the four. George first, then Marcia, then me, and last of all Rose.'

'Are the others married?'

'George and Marcia are. Marcia has two sons, my nephews. I daresay George and Alexandra – she's George's wife – will eventually stop quarrelling long enough to squeeze out an heir. Rose is only seven, so not at the marrying stage yet.'

'How nice, to have a little sister.'

'Oh, Rose is a poppet. Mad about dogs and horses.'

'How's your ankle?'

'Fine.'

But watching him as he drove, she saw how his jaw clenched each time he pressed down on the accelerator, and she said, 'I'm rather hungry. Could we stop and eat?'

'I'll find somewhere.'

He drove on for a few miles, and then, seeing a grassy slope dotted with silver birches, swung the car off the road and a short way up the slope. The trees cast long, thin shadows and the moon had come out, low and yellow and full. Sitting on the grass, which was lit by the beams of the car headlamps, Freddie tore their remaining bread in two and Jack divided the cheese with his penknife.

'I'll have another look at the bandage,' he said. Freddie stood up, yawning and stretching, and began to clear away the remains of the food. It was nearly dark, and she thought she heard the call of an owl, but whenever she tried to concentrate on it, it seemed to melt away, lost beneath the whisper of the birches.

And then she heard a different sound, the low rumble

of a vehicle, some way along the road they had just driven. Some instinct not to call attention to themselves made her turn off the engine, extinguishing the Fiat's headlamps. The sound of the approaching vehicle became louder. They did not move as it passed them on the road a short distance below. Inside the large black car were four men. She thought – she was not sure – that two of them were in uniform.

When the car had gone, she said, 'Do you think they might have been looking for us?'

'I don't know. It's probably nothing to do with us.' Jack dropped the spare bandages into his jacket pocket. 'But let's give it five minutes.'

They went back to the car. He was a spy, Freddie thought, and she had helped him to evade the police. She was on the run in a foreign country, driving a stolen car. Whatever she had intended, she was deeply involved, and if they were caught, she would not escape punishment. They shot spies, didn't they? There was a sick feeling in her stomach.

They waited, unspeaking. Then Jack said, 'I think we should keep away from the coastal road. I'll find us an inland route.' Freddie started up the engine and they drove on.

That night, they slept in the car. After driving for a couple of hours through the narrow roads that wove between the hills and along the valleys, they parked beside a stream that threaded through a stand of fir trees. They would have a few hours' rest, Jack said, and then he folded his arms and lay back in the seat, closing his eyes.

Though Freddie was very tired, her mind raced. Such a long, peculiar and upsetting day. Scenes from it were imprinted on her mind, like patterns on cloth. Tessa in her green dress, walking away from the station. The kiss: *I'm doing this for King and Country*. The chemist in Montecatini and the large black car on the coastal road.

She woke at dawn after dozing fitfully. Jack still slept; watching him, she found herself mentally sketching his profile: good jawline, nose almost straight with just a small bump at the bridge, nicely sculptured mouth, and that straw-blond hair falling over his forehead. A handsome face. She had kissed him, and now she was, in a sense, sleeping with him. It jolted her to realize that, in spite of her resentment at the high-handed way in which he had foisted himself on her, she found him attractive. She was sure it must be a very temporary aberration, brought on by the peculiar circumstances of their journey. He was stirring; hurriedly Freddie took her suitcase and climbed out of the car. Kneeling by the stream, she dipped her flannel in the icy water to wash her face.

They set off once more. In a small, dusty village they found a shop, where they bought food and drink. Jack spoke to the shopkeeper, who then offered them small chipped cups of rough, strong, scalding coffee that seemed to send a jolt through the veins. Though she badly needed the coffee, Freddie felt uncomfortable. The remoteness of these small villages in the foothills of the Apennines meant that few strangers passed this way. They did not fit into the tightly knit community of peasant farmers, and she suspected that their dishevelled appearance and their lack of the props of the tourist or hiker – cameras, rucksacks, walking boots – only made them stand out more.

They got back into the car. Freddie drove, Jack gave directions. Though he had no map, he seemed to know almost instinctively which way they should go. Freddie's shoulders were stiff from holding the wheel and her eyes felt gritty. Their pace was slower now, the roads more winding, narrower than those of the previous day, some of them unsurfaced. She forced herself to concentrate, but from time to time was almost overcome by a sense of unreality. She should have been in Paris. She should have been travelling on the Métro to the Gare du Nord, for the boat train and home. Instead, this stretch of road looked much like all the other roads they had driven earlier that morning, and this hill was as high, this valley as green and fertile as the last.

In the early afternoon, they were forced to head back towards the coast to find a garage. At length they came across a blacksmith's workshop among the small houses scattered along a roadside. A petrol pump stood across a stretch of dusty ground heaped with old tyres and rusting farm implements. Logs were stacked against a stone building, in the dark depths of which could be seen orange sparks and the gleam of a fire.

Freddie climbed out of the car while Jack went to ask for petrol. His limp had worsened, she noticed, and his walk was stiff and awkward. The door of the hut opened and a man in overalls came out. Jack spoke to him and the blacksmith said something, then frowned at the car. Freddie crossed the road to stretch her legs. A small girl came out of one of the houses to stare at her, thumb in mouth, then ran back indoors. She couldn't blame her, Freddie thought – she must look a fright.

Not far to go, she comforted herself. Jack had estimated that they must be a few miles inland from La Spezia. With a bit of luck they would reach Rapallo by the evening. Only a few more hours and this nightmare would be over. She saw that Jack and the blacksmith were still talking. Now Jack was frowning and the garage owner was waving his hands about. Freddie crossed back over the road to listen, but they were speaking too quickly for her to understand, and the blacksmith's Italian was heavily accented.

The blacksmith hooked the hose on to the petrol pump, then went back to the forge.

Jack crossed the courtyard to her. 'Apparently the police were here this morning.'

'The police?' Freddie felt a stab of fear. 'What did they want?'

'Us, from the sound of it. They were asking questions – had he seen a black Fiat, had any foreigners called at the garage.' Jack lowered his voice. 'This chap's a communist, so no lover of the Italian government or the police. Don't worry, it was several hours ago; they've moved on, we'll be fine.'

'Mr *Ransome*!' she cried, infuriated. 'They know about the car! They're looking for us!'

He gave her what she suspected was meant to be a reassuring smile. 'There must be hundreds of black Fiats in Italy. We'll be careful, we'll keep a lookout. There's not far to go, honestly. We'll be okay, I promise.'

'*Okay?*' Freddie's voice rose in a screech. She looked down at herself. Her sandals were scuffed and dirty, her dress unironed, and she felt dazed with lack of sleep. 'You call this *okay*?'

'Miss Nicolson, I'm sorry for getting you mixed up in this.' At least now he looked genuinely repentant. 'If you want to head off, I completely understand and I won't try to stop you.'

'I can't imagine,' she said sarcastically, 'that there's an hourly bus.'

'You're probably right. A lift on a farmer's cart, if you're lucky. Look, you mustn't worry. This chap's offered to show us a route around La Spezia that should keep us out of trouble.'

'How do we know we can trust him?'

'We don't. But I don't think we've a great deal of choice.'

She stared at him for a moment, and then, turning on her heel, walked quickly back to the car, slammed the door shut, and started up the engine. The blacksmith started his truck and Freddie swung the Fiat on to the road behind it. They headed inland, following the truck, deeper into the hills. All she wanted was to reach Rapallo, she thought, and then she could get away from him. She longed to get away from him.

Unable to stop herself, she groaned out loud. Jack said, 'What is it? Are you all right?'

'Did the blacksmith say the police knew about me?'

'Yes, I'm afraid so. A young Englishwoman . . . fair-skinned, dark hair and eyes. Seemed in a hurry. A rather good description, I thought.'

She sensed that he was smiling again, but refused to look at him. Instead, she fixed her eyes on the road as it unpeeled in front of her, climbing higher into the hills. If the police were looking for her as well as for Jack Ransome, it meant

279

that it would not be safe for her to cross the border by train. She would have no alternative but to sail to France on the wretched fishing boat. She wanted to groan again, but managed not to.

The road was pitted with deep potholes and the Fiat bounced and lurched. 'Keep the revs up,' said Jack. He was holding on to the dashboard; she saw him scowl as the car jolted.

They had followed the blacksmith's truck for several miles, heading into the deeply wooded foothills of the Apennines. Then the blacksmith had pulled in, giving them directions before he turned back along the way they had come. After his vehicle drove out of sight, the loneliness of the landscape seemed to increase. For several hours, they spoke little. Jack gave directions and now and then asked Freddie whether she needed to stop. Each time she shook her head. She drove as fast as the terrain permitted, her sense of urgency intensified by the knowledge that they were being hunted. Frequently she glanced into the rear-view mirror, but on these quiet roads there were few other vehicles. Once, their route took them along a rutted green lane through a forest. They passed painted caravans and horses standing beneath the dark boughs. A woman with a baby in her arms crouched beside a cooking pot slung over a bonfire, her gaze following them as the Fiat rattled over the rough ground.

They emerged from the covering of trees into open countryside. A bird of prey circled overhead, gliding on an air current, and the meadows were speckled with flowers of every hue. For a moment, Freddie forgot her fear, distracted by the beauty of the landscape. 'Some weather on its way, I'm afraid,' said Jack, and she saw, following his gaze, that to the east, above the hard grey peaks of the mountains, clouds were boiling up on the horizon.

It seemed to Freddie, as they drove on, that the Fiat had added to its customary chorus of squeaks and rattles a grating, intermittent whine. The clouds caught up with them and raindrops the size of pennies struck the windscreen. The windscreen wiper had worn away, so that Freddie seemed to peer out through a grey-brown blur of water and grime. She leaned forward, struggling to see the road clearly, easing off the accelerator. She was growing very tired, so much so that she had forgotten to be afraid.

The whine intensified. As they headed down a steep hill, Freddie felt the Fiat lurch sideways.

'Pull in,' Jack said sharply. 'There, under those trees.'

She struggled to steer the car to the side of the road. There she braked. Jack climbed out and crouched beside the front offside wheel.

'Blasted rust-bucket.'

'What is it?'

'The wheel nuts have worked loose. The rough ground must have shaken them free. I'll have to tighten them or we could lose the wheel.'

He opened the boot to search for tools. Freddie climbed out of the car.

'Can I do anything?'

'Not really. I should have a break, stretch your legs.'

She took her mackintosh out of her case and put it on and walked away from the car. It was raining hard, so she pulled up her hood. She had taken an apple from their dwindling store of food and she ate it as she wandered down the hillside. The road curved down towards a misty grey valley, and she wondered whether, had it been clearer, she would have been able to see as far as the coast. All her muscles ached, with tiredness and with tension. She seemed to have been travelling for ever; she could feel the movement of the car beneath the soles of her feet. When she looked back, Jack was still crouched by the Fiat. He would repair the car, she told herself, then they would drive the last few miles, and very soon she would be safe.

Rounding a bend in the road, she saw lights. She stopped, staring through the curtain of rain, trying to understand what she was looking at.

The lights were headlamps, and the cars — two or three, she was unsure — were stationary, strung across the road. They were — her heart seemed to pause — waiting for someone.

She ran back up the road to the Fiat. As she neared the car, Jack stood up. 'What is it?'

'Cars — police cars — on the road just down there!'

'Hell.' He scowled.

'We'll have to drive back the way we came.'

He shook his head. 'That's not possible, I'm afraid.'

She stared at him. 'Why not?'

'We've lost one of the wheel nuts and one of the others is so distorted I can't get it back into place. And there's no spare wheel. Besides,' he threw a spanner into the boot, 'if there's one roadblock, there could be others. There's nothing for it, we'll have to walk.'

'Walk?' Her voice rose.

'It must be ten miles or so to the coast. Can you do it?'
Mutely, she nodded.

They packed their remaining food into Freddie's suitcase
and then pushed the poor, faithful Fiat into the trees, where
it slid into a shallow gully. Then they began to walk down
the grassy hillside, away from the road. Jack carried her
suitcase; Freddie walked behind him.

The terrain was difficult, sometimes tussocky grass, at
other times steeply sloping with patches of scree. Every new
sound made her jump. *I've no time to play silly games*, she had
said the previous day, and yet, if she was honest, this adventure had not been without its exciting moments. The smooth
sweep of the road beneath the wheels of the car, the moonlight on the hills at night: these things had pleased her.

But there was no pleasure in this. Rain soaked through
her thin summer mackintosh, and her stockings were torn
and her sandals sodden. She was tired, wet, cold and frightened. Those cars blocking the road had scared her. This was
not a game any more, and her realization of their plight
wore away at her resistance to fear. They could so easily
have driven into the roadblock. If the wheel hadn't worked
loose they would not have seen the police cars in time.
They had left their trail behind them, witnessed by the
pharmacist at Montecatini Terme, the shopkeeper in the hill
village, and the blacksmith and the gypsies in the forest.
Easy enough for their pursuers to work out that they were
heading for the coast. The police would be watching all
the coastal roads. Perhaps they were searching these hills.

They might have dogs – she thought she heard something: a howl, a cry – but when she looked back, there was only the rain and the hills.

Heavy rain streamed from a charcoal sky. As the hours went on, Freddie continued to do what she seemed to have been doing for ever, putting one foot in front of the other, her eyes always fixed on Jack's tall figure as she plodded along in his wake. She should offer to take her suitcase, she thought dully, because of his wounded leg, yet she could not see how she could possibly scrape up the energy to carry the case as well as walk. Or she should tell him to discard the case – her things were probably ruined anyway – but she was too tired to speak. Every now and then he looked back at her and gave her an encouraging smile and asked her if she was all right, and she nodded. She looked at her watch, stumbling on the rough ground as she did so, and saw that it was almost eight o'clock. They had been walking for hours and the light was fading. The act of keeping going in the encroaching darkness took all her concentration, and her nerves were stretched to breaking point.

They reached a stream. Jack waded through the water. 'It's not deep,' he called back to her. 'Can you manage?'

Freddie stepped into the stream. Shallow water rushed over a bed of smooth stones and fine gravel. Looking back once more, she saw a flash of light halfway up the hillside – a car's headlamps, perhaps, or torchlight. Her heart pounded; she hurried to cross the stream.

Losing her footing on a slippery stone, she fell on her knees in the icy water and cried out.

'Miss Nicolson.' Jack held out his hand to her.

'Go away!' she screamed. 'Leave me alone!'

She was kneeling in the freezing water, her hands spread out for balance on the stream bed. She felt him hook his hands beneath her arms and she screamed again, 'Don't touch me!' but he took no notice, hauling her bodily out of the water and on to the bank.

There, she collapsed, bent double, her head in her hands, weeping. Through her tears she felt his hand on her shoulder, and heard him say calmly, 'I know this place. I've been here before. There's a shepherd's hut across the field. If we can make it there, we can warm up a bit. It's not far. Can you walk?'

She didn't think she would ever be able to walk again, wouldn't have minded giving up and dying there and then, but she snuffled, sucking back the tears, and nodded. He gave her his hand to help her to her feet, keeping hold of it as they crossed a water meadow and then a field. As they stumbled on, he talked, something about a summer he had spent here, working for a farmer and exploring the hills; she didn't pay much attention, but the sound of his voice cut through the rain and distracted her a little from her exhaustion.

'There it is,' he said, and Freddie looked up and saw the small stone hut in the far corner of the next field.

Reaching the hut, he pushed the door open and they went inside. The place smelled of sheep. Puffs of grimy wool adhered to rusty nails set into the walls, and the dirt floor was scattered with straw. Logs were stacked against a wall.

Freddie slid to a corner of the floor, wrapping her arms round her hunched knees. She was shuddering so violently her chin kept hitting her knees. She watched Jack make a fire – first some logs, arranged in a pyramid, then a bundle of twigs, and then some of the sheep's wool, stuffed into the cracks like thistledown.

His cigarette lighter clicked and there was a flare of flame.

'You are so ridiculously Richard Hannay,' she said. Her voice shook.

'Am I?' He smiled at her. 'Come closer – this'll soon get going.'

She shook her head. She couldn't move. She was too exhausted.

He fed more kindling on to the fire, and looked back over his shoulder to her. 'We're nearly there, I promise you.'

'Nearly where?' Her voice cracked. 'Nearly somewhere I never meant to go in the first place? I didn't want this – I want to go home. It's all your fault . . . they might have dogs!'

'Dogs?'

'The police . . .' She was crying again now. 'I hate those big dogs!'

'I don't think dogs are any use in the rain,' he said seriously. 'I don't think they can scent a trail.'

The fire was roaring. He sat down next to her and put his arm round her.

'Go away,' she said. Her teeth were chattering in a cartoonish fashion.

'No. You're freezing cold and you need to warm up. I'm

not trying anything on, I promise. Polar explorers curl up next to each other in the Antarctic. It's the best way of keeping warm.'

She sat for a moment, shivering, then she whispered, 'Is it true, what you said about the dogs?'

'That they can't scent a trail in the rain? Perfectly true.'

She managed to shuffle nearer to the fire. The heat seemed to reach her at last and she held out her hands to the warmth. She felt mortified for having cried. 'Sorry for making a fuss,' she muttered.

'I think,' he said, 'you're probably one of the least fussy girls I've ever met.'

She closed her eyes tightly. 'I hate − I hate *mess*.'

'Oh dear.' There was laughter in his voice. 'Then we won't get on. I seem to attract it.'

There flashed into her mind memories of voyages she had taken as a child, epic crossings of Europe driven by her father's restlessness, in Third Class railway carriages or on steamers puffing black smoke.

'When I was little,' she said, 'my father used to take us on these journeys. We'd wake up and he'd tell us we were going away. And there'd be a train or a boat or an ox cart − I remember an ox cart − and my mother was always so tired and my father would get angry because it never worked out how he wanted it to.' She took an inward breath. 'I don't *like* adventures. I don't *want* them.'

'I know.' He sounded penitent. 'I'm sorry. But some of it's been fun, hasn't it?'

'Fun?' she repeated, turning to stare at him. 'If this is your idea of fun, Jack, then it's completely different to mine!'

'No more after today, I promise you.'

'This boat . . .'

'It'll be fine.'

'It won't.' She shook her head. 'I just know it won't. I want to go home.'

'Miss Nicolson . . .'

'Freddie. My name's Freddie. Frederica.'

'Freddie? I had you down as an Anna or a Caroline, but Freddie's better. Listen, Freddie. This rain may be miserable, but it's good for us. With a bit of luck, the police won't have found the car. We'll be all right.'

'You keep saying that!'

'Don't you trust me?'

'No, Jack, not at all.'

'Are you hungry?'

She couldn't remember when she had last eaten. 'A bit.'

He opened her case and took out the remains of a loaf, a couple of apples and a flask of wine. 'Here, eat this,' he said, and tore the bread in half and gave her a piece. 'It'll make you feel warmer.' He uncorked the wine.

'I think you enjoy all this,' she said.

'Some of it,' he admitted. 'I'd be no use stuck in an office. I'd be crawling up the wall after a day.'

'How's your leg?'

'Hurts a bit.' He pulled back the turn-up of his trouser and peered cautiously at the bandage. 'I was in Greece, once, doing a bit of climbing, and I fell and broke my ankle. I more or less had to hop back to civilization. So it could be worse.'

'Your mother must despair.'

288

'Oh, I think my mother gave up despairing some time ago. Here. Have some of this.' He handed her the flask of wine.

Freddie drank deeply. The rough red wine warmed her; her clothes were starting to dry and she had stopped shaking at last. She had eaten the bread; she took several more mouthfuls of wine and then lay down on the floor, watching the flames dart and flicker. 'I'm not going to sleep,' she said. 'I'm just having a rest.' She closed her eyes and fell instantly asleep.

She woke once in the night to find Jack curled up beside her, his arm resting on her shoulder, her body fitting neatly against his. She lay still, aware of the rise and fall of his chest and the warmth of his enclosing arm. She remembered the kiss at the railway station, and those strange few moments the previous morning, when she had found herself wanting him. Dangerous thoughts . . . She reached out to put another log on the fire, careful not to disturb him, and then she closed her eyes, willing herself back to sleep.

They rose early the next day. After breakfasting on the remains of their food, they set off once more. The terrain was easier now, a series of gently undulating meadows, and then a farmhouse, with a gaggle of geese and children playing with a ball.

By midday the houses were closer together. They were walking on paved streets, rather than grass. They reached a café, where they stopped briefly for coffee. In the tiny

289

lavatory, Freddie peered at her bedraggled reflection in a scrap of mirror and tried to tidy her hair.

More houses, shops and streets. Ahead, there was a gap between the buildings, and the sky was silvery. Just there, said Jack, pointing, was the sea. Freddie could smell the salt in the air and hear the cries of the gulls.

Inside a bar, Jack ordered two brandies and asked to use the phone. A lengthy, coaxing conversation in Italian ensued as Freddie sat down at a window table and drank her brandy.

Jack came back to the table. 'She'll come and fetch us in the car.'

She, Freddie thought. Jack Ransome's friend was a she.

Half an hour later, he looked out of the window. 'There's Gabriella. Let's go.'

They went outside. A sports car had drawn up by the kerb. A young woman leaned out. Her hair was covered by a spotted silk scarf and her beautiful face was perfectly made up.

'Jack, you look terrible.'

'Thank you so much for this, Gaby. I appreciate it.'

She gave him a frosty look but offered her cheek to be kissed.

He said, 'Gabriella d'Aurizia, this is Freddie Nicolson. Freddie, meet Gabriella.'

'I do this for your friend, Jack, not for you,' said Gabriella haughtily. 'Quick, get in the car.'

Freddie climbed into the narrow back seat of the Lancia. Jack got into the passenger seat and Gabriella started the car. Freddie dozed, her eyelids jolted apart now and then by the fury of the quarrel taking place in the front seat,

290

and by the impetus of Gabriella driving at great speed round a particularly tight corner.

They reached a white stone villa surrounded by a garden, set back from the coastal road. Inside, they were led up stone steps, through a grand doorway and into a marble hall. A maid took Freddie's mackintosh, a manservant her suitcase. Another maid showed her up a wide sweep of stairs to an elegant white and gold bedroom and ran a bath in the adjacent room. The bath was hot and deep, the bubbles scented, and Freddie lay soaking, her eyes closed and her fingers gently sweeping the bubbles from side to side. Climbing out of the bath, she towelled herself dry and put on the bathrobe the maid had left out for her. She wiped away the steam from the mirror. Her dark hair lay flat and wet and straight and her skin was flushed by the heat. Beauty seemed a hard thing to define; why did some faces – Tessa's, for instance – make you want to look at them over and over again? And did her own possess any of that magnetism, that power?

She went back into the bedroom. A pair of black slacks and a peppermint-green silk blouse – Gabriella's, Freddie guessed – had been laid on the bed. She put them on and went downstairs.

The quarrel was still going on. Freddie followed the source of the raised voices.

'Ah, my dear Miss Nicolson,' said Gabriella, breaking off from a stream of invective and smiling at her. 'Are you hungry? I thought so. Then we shall eat.'

They lunched on the terrace, which looked out on to a beautiful garden. As they ate, every now and then Jack would say something, and Gabriella would make a sarcastic remark in response. Then a servant came to tell Gabriella that the doctor had arrived. Gabriella apologized to Freddie, and she and Jack went into the house.

When she returned, she said dismissively to Freddie, 'Jack is a very foolish man. I told him so. He could have been killed.' She poured Freddie another glass of wine. 'The doctor will mend his ankle, but what can you do with someone like that?' Freddie murmured agreeing noises.

Freddie spent the afternoon in the garden of the villa. It seemed an extraordinary contrast, almost too much to take in: the peace and tranquillity of the beautiful garden and the fear and exhaustion of the previous days. Over dinner, Gabriella told them that she had arranged for someone to take them to France the following morning. Freddie slept that night in the white and gold bedroom, where her head rested on plump pillows and a silk eiderdown kept her warm, and the only sound was the hush and whisper of the sea, drifting through an open window.

The maid woke her very early the next morning, drawing the curtains to let in the grey dawn light. Freddie glanced at her watch. It was five o'clock.

She drank the coffee and ate the roll and fruit the maid had brought to her on a tray. Then she washed and dressed. Her clothes, cleaned and ironed, had reappeared as if by magic.

She went downstairs. Gabriella and Jack were standing in the hallway. Jack had on outdoor clothing and was carrying a rucksack. Gabriella was wearing a flowered silk frock, silk stockings and high heels.

She smiled at Freddie. 'Miss Nicolson, I hope you slept well.'

'Very well, thank you.'

'We have to go, Freddie,' said Jack. 'There's a boat waiting for us and we need to catch the tide.'

Gabriella drove them along the coastal road. Eventually the car drew up in a small fishing village. Houses tumbled down the hillside, crouching round a horseshoe-shaped harbour. Boats bobbed on an inky sea, pearled by the dawn.

Heels clicking on the flagstones, Gabriella led them along the harbour arm. Two men were loading a boat called the *Rondine* with creels. Farewells were made and Gabriella took Freddie's hands in hers, kissed her cheeks and said that she hoped they would meet again in more pleasant circumstances. To Jack she gave a much longer kiss, and then she waved them both on to the boat.

They were told to stay in the cabin until they were out to sea. Freddie could hear the put-put of the petrol engine and the cries of gulls. The *Rondine*, Jack explained, would take them to a quiet spot on the Côte d'Azur. Someone would meet Freddie on the beach and would drive her to the railway station at Nice, from where she would be able to catch a train to Paris.

Then he said, 'There's been a change of plan. I won't be travelling back to England with you. I made a few phone calls last night and I have to take a detour. You'll be all right, won't you?'

'Perfectly. Glad to see the back of you.'

'I thought so.' He looked at her curiously. 'What will you do?'

'I shall go back to my home and my job and my friends. I shall lead a calm and measured existence. I can't wait.'

'It may not stay calm and measured much longer.'

She looked him in the eye. 'I like to feel useful, Jack. If there's a war, I'll find something to do.'

'I'm sure you will.' He glanced out of the porthole. 'Shall we go on deck?' He turned back and smiled at her. 'Of course we could, if we chose, avoid the whole thing.'

'What do you mean?'

'We could always run away together. Sit out the war in South America.'

'Don't be silly, Jack.'

He shrugged. 'Just a thought. Don't say I didn't offer.'

Freddie put on her hat and a cardigan and left the cabin to sit in the stern of the boat. Jack went to help the fishermen.

The sun rose in the sky and the Ligurian coast diminished to a narrow grey line, and the gulls that had followed the boat out of harbour flew back to land. Freddie thought of her rooms in South Kensington, waiting for her. Closing her eyes, she raised her face to the sun.

The hours passed and there was only the sea and the sky and once, in the distance, like black ticks on a blue page, a flotilla of fishing smacks. At midday they ate the food that Gabriella had given to Jack. The red wine must have made Freddie doze off. She was sleeping deeply when Jack shook her awake.

'Freddie, we're here.'

Opening her eyes, she looked out. Waves crashed on rocks to both sides of a small sandy bay. The fishermen had lowered the sails and the *Rondine* was gliding into the bay on her outboard motor.

'Have we reached France?' she asked.

'Yes. The car's waiting.'

On the clifftop, sunlight flashed on a car windscreen. 'They'll take her as close to shore as they can,' said Jack. 'Then you'll have to paddle, I'm afraid. Or I'll give you a piggyback, if you prefer.'

She threw him a withering look, then took off her sandals. A few minutes later, Jack slipped over the side of the boat. 'Here,' he said, and held out his arms to her.

She was lifted off the boat. The seawater felt cool and fresh as she waded to the shore, her sandals clutched in one hand. Jack was carrying her suitcase. Reaching the beach, he waved and called out, 'Hey, Auguste, *ça va?*' Looking up, Freddie saw a man running down the narrow cliff path.

Jack turned to her. 'Here.' He pressed into her hand a bundle of francs.

'Jack, I couldn't possibly . . .'

'It's for your train fare and hotels. I don't see why you should be out of pocket because of me. Take it.' He glanced at the boat. 'Auguste will look after you, Freddie. And – thank you. It's been . . .'

'An experience,' she finished for him drily. 'And one I hope never to repeat.'

'Is that so?' He grinned. 'I've rather enjoyed it. Goodbye, Freddie. *Bon voyage.*'

She held out her hand, but he ignored it and hugged

her instead. Auguste, who was young and slight and dark, joined them. A brief exchange of rapid French, Freddie and Auguste were introduced, and then Jack waded back to the boat.

Auguste took Freddie's suitcase and together they walked up the beach. The sand was warm and silky beneath her bare feet. Gulls wheeled in a cloudless sky. At the foot of the cliff Freddie looked back. Jack had reached the *Rondine*. He raised an arm in salute, and then the engine fired and the boat headed away from the land.

Chapter Nine

On August 23rd a pact was signed in Moscow by Germany and Russia. Both signatories guaranteed to remain neutral if the other country went to war. The pact, the residents of Mayfield Farm agreed over a long discussion at supper, gave the green light to Germany to invade Poland.

The Mickleboroughs went away for the weekend to stay with friends in London. David Mickleborough intended to join up, if one of the Services would have him. John and Romaine Pollen had already left the farm for America. They were pacifists, they said, and had no wish to become involved in someone else's war.

Rebecca cooked a supper of lamb chops and vegetables. She put some on a covered plate for Connor Byrne, which she took to the barn. After she had eaten her own supper and cleared up, she sat at the kitchen table, sketching the crockery on the draining board.

Connor came into the kitchen. His battered corduroys and check shirt were whitened by stone dust. He was too tall for the low-ceilinged room and had to bend his head as he washed up his dishes.

'You're a wonderful cook, Rebecca. Thank you.'

He looked over her shoulder at her sketch. 'I like it,' he said. 'It has a strength. But is it always pots and pans and scrubbing brushes with you?'

'I'm afraid so. I could measure out my life in them. I leave the gods and goddesses to you.'

He laughed. 'Where are the others?'

She told him, adding, 'And Noel and Olwen have gone to the pub, to get drunk.'

'Ah. I might have a drink myself. Would you have one with me?'

'Yes, why not?'

Connor went outside, returning a few minutes later with a bottle containing a few inches of whisky. He poured them each a glass, then stood in the doorway, looking out to the valley and the evening sun.

'You can't imagine it, can you?' he said.

Rebecca remembered photographs of the shattered town of Guernica. She said, 'What will you do, Connor?'

He came back inside the kitchen and sat down at the table. 'I shall go back to Ireland. I've booked my passage for a couple of days' time.'

'So soon?'

'Ireland will keep out of the war. We're too new a nation, and too poor. And I should be near my son.'

'Your son?'

'He's called Brendan. He's ten years old. He lives with his mother in Galway.'

Extraordinary events had broken through the barricades they had erected around themselves — the coming war, the absence of the others who lived at the farm.

'I didn't realize,' she said.

'It's nothing to boast about, is it, having left your wife and child.'

'I'm sorry, Connor. It must be hard.'

'And you, Rebecca? Have you children?'

She shook her head.

'Do you mind?'

'My husband didn't want them.' Which was an evasion, she knew. She tried again. 'I thought I didn't want children. But sometimes I regret it now. Tell me about your son, Connor. Tell me about Brendan.'

He smiled his lovely slow smile. 'I have a photograph.' He opened a worn leather wallet, took out something and passed it to her.

It was a snapshot of a little boy with wild, curling hair. The child was holding the hand of the woman standing beside him.

'He looks like you,' she said.

'Do you think so? Though Aoife is dark too.'

'Is that your wife's name? She's pretty.' She handed the photograph back to Connor.

'So she is.' He put the wallet back in his pocket and took a sip of whisky. 'I shouldn't have married. No woman wants a man who spends all his days hammering at bits of stone. And when he isn't, he's thinking about it. And he doesn't care where he lives or what he earns or what he owns so long as he has his bits of stone. But that wouldn't do for Aoife. She wanted me to have a real job. Sculpting wasn't a real job. I tried to do as she wished for a while, but I found myself turning into someone I didn't care for. So I left. They're better off without me, but I'm not divorced and I never will be. Aoife is a religious woman, you see. A marriage should last for life.'

'You must miss your little boy.'

'I do, very much. And if there's to be a war, I should be near them. I won't live with my wife again but I should at least be to hand. And you, Rebecca — what about you? Will you stay here?'

'I hope so.' He had spoken to her with a greater measure of candour than ever before and she felt obliged to lower her guard. 'My husband and I are getting divorced. For myself, I would have left it at a separation, but Milo wanted the divorce. Perhaps he's found someone else. I don't know. That was why I left him, because of all the someone elses.'

'He was a fool, then.'

The way he looked at her startled her and she felt herself flush. 'He was,' she said, 'in some ways. And in others, he was enchanting. I'd never met anyone like him. Milo has such a great capacity for enjoying life. But I wasn't enough for him. He was wealthy and successful and admired, and I think he felt that entitled him to have whatever he wanted.'

Connor took a packet of Senior Service out of his shirt pocket and offered it to her. They smoked and drank for a while, and then she said:

'I didn't leave him because of the mistresses. I left him because I didn't love him any more.'

300

Connor turned to her. His eyes were dark blue, flecked with gold. She had never noticed the gold flecks before.

'I should imagine the mistresses had something to do with it,' he said.

The whisky was making her feel pleasantly mellow. She gave a bark of laughter. 'It's true, they didn't endear him to me. But the odd thing is, it was something I did that stopped me loving him.'

'How long had you been married?'

'Sixteen years.'

He whistled. 'A good long time.'

'In the beginning it was good. I loved Milo so much. I thought he was my saviour.'

'We have to save ourselves, don't you think?'

'I expect so. I'm still trying.'

His smile crinkled up the corner of his eyes. 'Is that why you're here, Rebecca — for *penance*?'

'I like it here. Look at it — so glorious. The cottage where I stayed last autumn — now *that* was penance.'

'Bad, was it?'

In her mind's eye she saw the small stone cottage, proud and solitary. 'It was absolutely in the middle of nowhere,' she said, 'on a Derbyshire moorland. I'd gone there with a man called Harrison Grey. A complete washout he turned out to be. When I look back I think he only wanted me because of my car.' She shrugged. 'We used each other, and that's the truth of it. I was lonely and he couldn't drive. That's what our friendship was, a mutual exploitation. He walked out on me, and I haven't seen or heard from him since. Anyway, then I fell ill with bronchitis. I managed to

301

get myself back to London, and when I recovered, my friend, Simone, told me about the farm. I'm very fond of Simone. I do enjoy having a woman friend. I didn't have a close woman friend when I was married to Milo. I don't think I trusted him enough.'

Connor topped up her glass. 'That was never one of my sins, a roving eye. Plenty of others, but not that. What about your home? Couldn't you have stayed there?'

'I didn't think, I just left. I'm afraid I sometimes enjoy being dramatic.'

'I've always wondered whether beneath these polite phrases the English come out with, there's a great boiling of rage.'

'There was in me,' she said quietly. She glanced at his glass. 'You're hardly drinking anything at all. You're leaving it all to me.'

'That's because I've been a bad man in the past. I keep a bottle of the stuff in my room all the time. Sometimes I don't touch it for weeks, but I have it there to remind me.'

'Of what?'

'Of what it does to me, if I let it. I can shout and fight and curse with the best of them. I was unhappy, but that's no excuse.' He tapped his cigarette on the ashtray. 'I meant it when I said that Aoife was better off without me. I never laid a finger on her or the child, I swear, but I could feel such a rage in me that sometimes it frightened me. I stopped the hard drinking the day I left Ireland. So you'll help me out by finishing this off.'

'It's good whisky.'

He smiled. 'Only the best.'

The sun was setting; through the open door Rebecca could see the long blue-grey shadows of the trees.

'I loved our house,' she said. 'It was five miles from Oxford, a good place to live. It had once been a mill house – there was a river at the bottom of the garden. Wonderful countryside, so English, the best sort of English, I think. The house was, I suppose, my work of art. But after all that happened, it seemed so bound up with our marriage that I couldn't bear to stay there. It's sold now – the sale went through last month. I miss it sometimes, but not so much as I thought I would.'

'When you first came here, I didn't think you were Mayfield Farm's usual sort of tenant.'

'Why do you say that?'

'Most of us haven't two pennies to rub together.'

She sighed. 'It's true, I'm not badly off. Milo split the proceeds of the house sale with me so I could buy myself somewhere to live. But where would I go? I tried London and I hated it. We entertained a lot, Milo and I. He's a writer, and the pattern of my life was dictated by the progress of his books. Long walks when he was working out his plot, peace and quiet when he was deep in the story, elation and celebration when he finished. All that went when I left him. I felt cast adrift. I tried living in the countryside – my disastrous experiment with Harrison. I had' – she frowned – 'a breakdown. There, I've never told anyone that. Bronchitis seems so much more respectable than a nervous breakdown. It's made me afraid of being too much on my own.'

'When you came here,' he said, 'you had a bruised look about the eyes.'

303

'Did I? I was hanging on by my fingernails.' She swallowed a mouthful of whisky. She was, she realized without minding at all, a little drunk. She said quietly, 'I'm making it sound as though it was all Milo's fault, but it wasn't. The worst thing that happened was because of me.'

'You don't have to tell me if you don't want to, Rebecca. If it's the whisky talking and you might regret it tomorrow.'

'I won't regret it.'

A conclusion that surprised her, but he was a quiet, reserved man, and she sensed she could trust him. Then she asked him the same question she had asked the silver-haired hiker at the cottage.

'Do you think that if something you did made something terrible happen, it's your fault, even if you didn't mean it at all?'

'I don't know.' Connor shook his head slowly. 'It's a hard question. Do you?'

'I've thought about it a great deal since I came here, and I've come to the conclusion that some of the responsibility must be mine.' She took a deep breath. 'A year and a half ago I found out that Milo was having an affair. He'd had affairs before, and they'd hurt me a great deal, but this one was worse because there was a child, a baby boy – Milo's child. He told me he hadn't wanted the baby. He said he didn't want to leave me. I thought I might be able to forgive him – no, I didn't think that; I thought I'd won. But I was so angry. My rage – I can't describe it.'

'Like a creature,' he said. 'Like a wild beast that takes you by the throat.'

'Yes. Like that. So, one day I telephoned her – the girl,

Milo's mistress. I told her that Milo didn't care about her. And I told her that he was seeing someone else.'

'Was that true?'

'No. I could hear she was upset – I liked that.' Rebecca stopped, then took another mouthful of whisky. 'A few days later I found out that there'd been an accident. The girl, Tessa, and the baby – Milo's baby – had been in a car crash. She survived, but the baby died. He wasn't even three months old.'

'Dear God.' Connor let out a breath of air.

'The crash was on the Oxford road. Tessa had been driving to Oxford, I'm sure of it. I worked out the timings, and she must have set off very soon after I'd phoned her. She was going to see Milo, to find out whether what I'd told her was true. She was driving to Oxford because of what I'd said to her.'

'You're sure of this?'

'I'm as sure as anyone can be. I'll never be completely sure. At first, that was one of the hardest things. At first, I said all these things to myself. I hadn't been driving the car, so it wasn't my fault. I had every justification for doing what I did. Milo was my husband – she had given birth to my husband's child, which was a wicked thing to do. But the truth is, Connor, I did it because I hated her. God forgive me, I even hated the child.'

He reached across the table and took her hand. His fingers were warm and calloused, his touch reassuring. She thought how different he was from Milo, who would have wrestled aloud with the moral dilemma, tearing it this way and that. Connor's silences said more, perhaps. She knew, quite suddenly, how deeply she was attracted to him, and knew in the same instant that she was not yet ready for any serious relationship.

She gave his hand a squeeze and reclaimed her own. 'I've never told Milo about my phone call,' she said. 'I couldn't bear to. I was ashamed. I thought, after the accident, that I would stay with him. He needed me, you see. He'd lost his child. He's always retreated to me for comfort when things have gone wrong for him. He was on his best behaviour, those few months, but . . .'

'You'd stopped loving him.'

'Yes. He didn't go to the funeral. I went, but he didn't. He said he was too upset. He did grieve, for the child and for Tessa, I know he did. But so cowardly of him, Connor, to hide away like that. But then . . . he seemed to put it behind him. Milo's never had much of a capacity for guilt – there are times when I've envied him that. It was almost as if all that – the affair, the child – had never happened. It made me despise him. And I despised myself too, of course, for what I'd done and for not seeing him clearly before. And in the end, my secret was like a wall between us and I couldn't see over it.' She smiled bitterly. 'So as well as killing the baby, I killed my love for Milo.'

'You didn't kill the child,' he said. 'The car crash did, or God did, whichever way you choose to look at it. And there's only so much you can survive.'

'Yes. I've discovered that.' She was properly drunk now, and glad of it. She pushed her glass across the table to Connor and he poured in the last half-inch of whisky.

'I've never told anyone else,' she said.

306

'I'll not speak of it to anyone.'

'You don't hate me, then?'

'I couldn't hate you, Rebecca.' He smiled gently. 'You're a good person, I can see that.'

She shook her head. 'No.'

'Good people can do bad things. You must try to forgive yourself.'

'I can't.' She put down her glass. 'But thank you for listening to me.'

He smiled. 'I've always thought that was one of the best things about my religion, that you've someone to make your confession to.'

'Are you still religious?'

'I don't go to church any more.'

'That's not the same, Connor.'

He steepled his hands – they were large hands, inches longer and wider than her own, and ingrained with stone dust. 'As you know, I have my own gods.'

'Manannan mac Lir, the god of the sea . . .' She tottered over to the stove to put the kettle on. 'When I was at the cottage,' she said, 'I thought I saw an angel.'

'An angel? Well now, Rebecca.' He folded his arms and settled back in his chair. 'Tell me.'

She spooned coffee into the pot, then rested her back against the stove as the kettle boiled. 'He didn't look like an angel. No wings or halo. He looked like a hiker. No doubt the truth is he *was* a hiker. We often saw hikers on the moors. And I was very ill and had been on my own for days, and you lose track of time and imagine things, don't you? But he had such a sweet smile, I'll always remember that. After he'd gone, I felt better. I could see what to do, for the next day or two at least.'

'Did you speak to him?'

'Yes, for quite a while. He gave me some advice. He told me to go to the doctor, which was very sensible, and then he said I should try stepping outside. I couldn't think what on earth he meant, but I suppose that's what I've done. I've stepped outside my old life.' Rebecca poured boiling water on to the ground coffee. 'I've no idea where I'm going and it might all end in disaster, but at least I'm trying.' She stirred the coffee pot, and said softly, 'Such an odd thing – after he'd gone, I couldn't find his footprints. It had rained a lot, and there should have been footprints in the mud. And it came into my mind that he had been an angel.'

'It's a fine thought,' Connor said, 'an angel, taking to his wings over the moorland.'

'Isn't it? I often think about him. If I'm finding something hard, I try to imagine what he would tell me to do. I know it's silly, but that's what I do.' She took down two mugs and poured out the coffee. Then she said, 'I've come to the conclusion that my fate is to go on living with what I did. And when I'm feeling down, I think of him. I think of my angel.'

Two days later, Connor left the farm. His unfinished work was wrapped up in sacking, to be shipped to Ireland, if that should prove feasible.

Before he left, he tapped on the door of Rebecca's room. They wished each other good luck and goodbye, and then he said, 'I should have liked to have got to know you better. Would you write to me, Rebecca?'

'Yes, Connor, I'd love to,' she said.

Then he kissed her cheek and was gone.

She missed him. It took her by surprise, how much she missed him. In his absence there was an emptiness at the farm. He was a quiet man, she thought, but he seemed to leave a silence behind him.

On the first day of September, German troops marched into Poland. On the same day, the Luftwaffe destroyed many Polish aircraft while they stood on the ground. Bombers struck at roads, railways and towns. Britain and France, by treaty bound to come to Poland's aid in the event of attack, declared war two days later.

Sitting in Mayfield Farm's kitchen, Rebecca heard Neville Chamberlain tell the nation that Britain was now at war with Germany. When the prime minister had finished, David Mickleborough turned off the wireless. Olwen Wainwright cried, and her husband, who had fought in the Great War, muttered, 'Damned shame,' and got up and left the room. Outside in the sunshine, the Mickleborough boys ran round the yard, arms outstretched, pretending to be aeroplanes.

Rebecca went to her bedroom and wrote a letter to Meriel. Then she borrowed a bicycle and cycled into Tunbridge Wells. There was a queue for the phone box; while she waited, she rehearsed in her mind the conversation she was about to have. Of which was she more afraid — this, she wondered, or the war?

It was her turn. She went inside the phone box and, dialling the operator, did what she had put off doing for eighteen months: she phoned her mother.

Part Three

Golden Lads and Girls

1940–1944

Chapter Ten

These days, she was careful. She was Tessa Bruno now, nice and anonymous, a widow from an obscure hamlet in some little-known valley. Her papers were forged (this had horrified Freddie), but they served.

Freddie had tried to persuade her to return home. *Home* – a week, a day, an hour after crossing the border into Italy at the end of October 1938, Tessa had known that she was home again. Some of the load had seemed to fall from her back; the air she breathed was familiar and comforting.

She had stayed first with a fashion designer friend who lived by Lake Como. She had worked with Fabio in the past; he and his lover, Jean-Claude, were welcoming. The house was elegant, the garden, which went down to the lake, was beautiful. She walked a little, read a little, slept a great deal. But she realized after a while that Fabio *knew* – of course he did: he was a gossip, and the world of haute couture had always thrived on rumour. So she moved on, first to Venice, where she took, fleetingly, a distinguished widower for a lover. Something happened to her in Venice, though; some rawness rose to the surface, prompted by the dark, melancholy water of the canals and by islands that seemed to float on the winter fogs. Directionless and low in spirits, she left the city.

The months that followed were chaotic, a kaleidoscope of meetings and partings, lovers and journeys. She had thought at the time that she was trying to take her mind off things. Afterwards, she wondered whether she had been punishing herself.

One of her lovers, louche, wild and unpredictable, and living on the very edges of respectability, had procured for her the forged papers. Somewhere between Bologna and Florence she became Signora Bruno, a quiet, respectable widow. She found rooms in the Oltrarno and a job in a dress shop in the Via de' Tornabuoni. She learned how to eke out her small wages. She even cooked for herself, though she wasn't very good at it.

Coming back to Florence, she remembered Guido Zanetti. Guido had been her first lover; rediscovering the city in which they had grown up, she found herself also recalling the pleasure and pain of first love, the particular barbed sweetness. Through discreet enquiries, she learned that Domenico Zanetti had died and that Guido was now running the silk workshops in place of his father. He was living with his wife and child in the Zanetti palazzo in the Via Ricasoli. Guido would now be almost thirty. Perhaps his princely good looks would have faded. He would have thickened round the waist and his curling dark hair would have receded. A married man, he would have become comfortable and perhaps a little complacent. These days, they would have nothing in common.

In September 1939, after the German invasion of Poland, Italy, to Tessa's relief, remained neutral. Perhaps she would be able to keep the modest life she had chosen for herself. Perhaps the war would make little difference. The months passed. She avoided close friendships, using her assumed widowhood to fend off social invitations from the other girls in the shop. There was a man who worked in the second-hand bookshop below her rooms, in his thirties, cheerful, plump, bespectacled, who always said good morning to her. She had a coffee with him sometimes, in the narrow, gloomy shop with its smell of old paper and cobwebs. 'I'd ask you out to dinner,' he said to her one evening when he was closing up shop, 'if I thought there was the slightest chance you'd say yes, but there isn't, is there?'

She had learned not to take the first step. If you didn't go out to dinner with a man, you wouldn't kiss him. If you didn't ask him to your birthday party, you wouldn't end up going to bed with him. If you were careful, then you wouldn't fall in love with the wrong man and you wouldn't get hurt. Looking back, it seemed to Tessa that a lot of her lovers had been wrong men.

She was, during that hard winter of '39–'40, often very lonely. Sundays were the worst days, with their enforced idleness and the happy families in their finery, promenading through the streets. Hard to know what to do with herself on a Sunday – sewing, reading, washing clothes, a walk – and harder still to keep away the regret that pressed in on her, like the walls of her room.

There was a Sunday, bitterly cold, the sky a low, solid slab of grey, when she walked to the railway station to check the times of the trains. She would go back to England; she missed Freddie. Or she would go to Paris – she loved Paris. And yet the following morning, the clouds had cleared away and the blue of the sky shimmered in reflection on the waters of the Arno. She had always lived by her intuition and it felt right to be here now, in this city, in spite of her loneliness and in spite of the dangers. Was she running away? She supposed she was. Was she refusing to face up to reality, as Freddie had implied? No, she did not think so. You could almost touch the history here, the old loves and griefs and jealousies and regrets, imprinted in the stones on the streets, shimmering darkly in the shadows of an alleyway. Terrible things had happened here; this city did not judge her.

She knew she was waiting, waiting to find a purpose for her life.

Spring came, and there was a warmth in the air that lifted the heart. Deep down, Tessa had always guessed that Hitler would not content himself with Poland. In April, his armies invaded first Denmark, then Norway.

Tessa saved up and bought an old wireless from the flea market, and the man in the second-hand bookshop, who was a radio ham, tinkered with it until a tinny voice issued through the loudspeaker. You could almost feel the tension in the city: it seemed to vibrate through the air like the overwound string of a violin. At the dress shop, the other girls giggled and shrieked at the slightest thing, or wept as they wrote letters to their fiancés in the army.

The restlessness infected Tessa, too. She walked a lot, smoked a lot and wrote letters to Freddie in London, imploring her to go and live in the countryside – Land's End, John o'Groats, as far away as possible from the capital, where the bombs would fall. A few days after Norway's surrender, she went for a walk in the Boboli Gardens. She was heading down the long central path when she saw him. Guido was with his wife and little daughter. He was neither fat nor balding and she knew him instantly. She wondered whether to turn and run, to hide beneath the cypress trees at the side of the path. Something made her keep on, a need to test herself, perhaps. Perhaps he wouldn't recognize her. She was older, plainer – her cropped hair, her scarred forehead. Perhaps he had forgotten her.

They drew closer; his wife, slim and fair-haired, in a white skirt and jacket and a strawberry-coloured blouse and hat, was laughing. The child in the pram had flaxen curls and was wearing a frilly white dress. They passed – he hadn't known her; all that was over with. Of course it was over. It had been such a long time ago.

'Tessa.'

The sound of his voice; she remembered how once it had electrified her. She turned.

'Tessa, it *is* you!' He crossed the path to her.

'Hello, Guido,' she said. 'How are you?'

'I'm very well. And you?' There was confusion, as well as shock, in his eyes. And pleasure, too, she thought. 'How extraordinary to see you again!' he said. 'Where are you staying?'

Guido's wife said gently, 'My darling . . .'

'I beg your pardon. Maddalena, this is Tessa . . .'

'Tessa Bruno.' She took Maddalena Zanetti's white-lace-gloved hand. 'I'm so pleased to meet you, *signora*.'

'And I you, Signora Bruno.'

Tessa smiled at the child in the pram. 'What a beautiful little girl.'

'She's called Lucia,' said Maddalena, 'but we always call her Luciella.'

'How old is she?'

'She's nearly three.'

'You must be so proud of her.' Tessa explained to Maddalena Zanetti, 'Guido and I knew each other when we were children. We used to play together.'

'Are you visiting the city?' Guido asked. 'How long are you staying?'

'I live here,' she said. 'And now' – a quick glance at her watch – 'I'm so sorry, but I'm afraid I must hurry. So lovely to meet you both.' More handshakes. 'Goodbye, Guido. Goodbye, *signora*.'

She walked away down the path. Long ago, in the summer of 1933, she had been able to sense when he was looking at her. Glance across the dinner table and there he'd be, darkly handsome, restless, brooding. Walk home from school and something would seem to tug at her, and she would look up and see him across the piazza, as if an invisible cord tied them together. She could feel it now, the direction of his gaze like two pinpoints of heat between her shoulder blades. She pressed her nails into the palms of her hands as she hurried her steps.

*　　*　　*

Two days after their encounter in the Boboli Gardens, he was waiting in the street outside her rooms when she came home from work.

'Guido,' she said. 'How did you find me?'

'I asked around. It was easy enough. You work at Ornella's, don't you?' This was the name of the dress shop. 'I know everyone in the Via de' Tornabuoni,' he added. 'I'm surprised we haven't run into each other before.'

He glanced along the alleyway. Above them, lines of washing hung limply in the still air. A man in torn corduroy trousers and an oil-stained singlet tinkered with a motor-bike. A group of children were playing with an orange box, pretending it was a car, dragging it up and down the cobbles and squabbling over whose turn it was to ride inside. Guido's lip curled a little.

'I don't understand, Tessa,' he said. 'Why didn't you call me? Why didn't you tell me you'd come back?'

She sighed. 'Come inside, Guido. It's been a long day and I'm tired and I'd like to sit down.'

'Your husband . . .'

'I'm not married.'

She opened the door and he followed her into the building. Letting him into her rooms, she offered him a glass of wine.

'No thank you. Maddalena's parents are coming to dinner tonight. And I like to see Luciella before her nurse puts her to bed.' He did not sit, but walked to the window, glancing outside. 'You're not married, then. So you're widowed?'

'No.'

He frowned. 'Divorced?'

'No, neither. I've never married.' Tessa explained about Signora Bruno and the obscure hamlet in the little-known valley. 'I thought it best,' she added. 'It would be difficult for me in Florence just now, with an English surname. It's all right, Guido, I have papers in the name of Bruno.'

His eyes had narrowed. 'Forged papers?'

'Yes.'

'Tessa, what are you doing?'

'I needed an Italian name to find work. And to find somewhere to live — to do anything, in fact. It would have been hard for me, without papers.'

'You intend to remain here?'

'Yes, certainly. I'm very careful. I don't draw attention to myself. I try to make myself as anonymous as possible.'

'Anonymous? You?' He sounded angry. 'Don't be ridiculous, Tessa.'

'I've changed, Guido.' Her voice became cold. 'I'm not the same as I was before. Perhaps I shouldn't have told you. Perhaps I should have lied to you, the same as I've lied to everyone else.'

'Don't you understand that you're putting yourself in great danger? Forged papers, at a time like this? Good God, Tessa, this is madness!'

'This is what I choose to do. And really, it's no business of yours.' She looked at him coldly. 'Our friendship ended a long time ago, after all.'

He, too, looked furious. He picked up his hat. 'So it did. I apologize for troubling you.'

She went to the door and opened it. 'Goodbye, Guido,'

she said. She heard the echo of his footsteps as he ran down the stairs.

As soon as he had gone, her anger died. She pressed her lips together, feeling the sudden sinking of her mood. In the bedroom she opened a drawer and ran a hand over the things inside it. She had photographs, a pair of bootees, and a knitted rabbit. These were her mementoes of her son. There were other things that had belonged to Angelo, but Ray was keeping them safe for her until she could bear to look at them again.

She minded that she could not remember her last days with him. She hated that she could not remember the final time she had held him. Such a big part of such a small life, and yet those memories were gone, lost beneath a dense blackness. The doctors at the hospital had told her that amnesia was common in patients with head injuries. Her memory of the days preceding the crash might return and might not. The days and weeks that had followed the accident, when she had been at first unconscious and then drugged by strong painkillers, were lost too. One of the doctors had illustrated his explanation of her amnesia with the metaphor of a beach – the fine, clear, dry sand where the memories of the more distant past were vivid, then the ripples that shaped the sand closer to the water's edge, and then the accident and the days immediately before and after, consumed by the waves.

She had filled in some of the blanks by talking to friends. Because Angelo had had a cold, she had not worked that week. There had been a party, but she had not gone because the baby had been unwell and she had been tired. Max had called by the night before the accident. He had thought her a little down – too much time on her own, perhaps. She had always liked company.

The accident had taken place on the Oxford road. Tessa supposed she had been driving to Oxford to see Milo. She didn't think she could have been going to Freddie's school, because she never visited Freddie on a Monday afternoon, and besides, Freddie had told her that she had not expected her. She had even checked with her housemistress, Miss Fainlight, who had confirmed that Tessa had not phoned in the days leading up to the accident. Though it was possible, of course, that she had gone to Westdown on impulse.

So, then, Milo. She could have asked him whether they had had an arrangement to meet, but she had not. Many weeks had gone by before she had been well enough to think of phoning or writing to Milo, and during that time he had not visited her or written to her once. She had not contacted him because his silence had told her more clearly than any words that he no longer loved her. Her despair at his betrayal, along with the other, much greater loss, had dragged her down into a dark chasm. Eventually, despair had been replaced by anger. And then, quite soon afterwards, resignation and regret as she had realized that she must, as far as possible, put the past behind her and try to make something out the torn remnants of her life.

Three years had passed and yet she still seemed to hear the echo of her voice saying to Milo Rycroft, *Love lasts as long as it lasts, that's what I believe.* So naive, so destructive. These days, she rarely thought about him. All that remained was a wariness, and her perception of the enormity of her mistakes.

I've changed, Guido. I'm not the same as I was before. She had told him the truth: she was no longer the person she had once thought she was. Tessa Bruno would do as well as any other name. Tessa Nicolson had gone.

The next day, when she came home from work, he was waiting for her again. Dark suit, superbly tailored, silk tie, polished hand-made shoes. He was out of place, she thought, in the alleyway, with its washing lines and its graffiti.

He seemed to snap to attention as she approached him. 'I apologize for what I said to you yesterday,' he said stiffly. 'I was concerned, that's all.'

Guido had always been a proud man. Tessa knew that the apology must have cost him. 'Perhaps I was hasty too,' she conceded.

His expression was troubled. He spoke to her in a low voice. 'Things have changed, you see, Tessa. Florence has changed. If your papers were found to be forged, the police would think you were a spy.'

'I'll be careful, Guido, I promise.'

He looked up to where the sky was a slice of blue between the high walls of the buildings. 'It's a fine evening,' he said. 'Shall we walk?'

They headed along the Via Romana. Guido said, 'I meant what I said, Tessa. It isn't safe for you here. In a few weeks we may be at war.'

She threw him a quick glance. 'Do you think so?'

323

'I hope not – I pray not,' he muttered. 'Certain elements long for it, push for it. They scent easy glory.'

'And you, Guido? What do you think?'

He let out a breath. 'So far, we've stood aside from the war and profited from it. I had hoped that our government's cynicism and venality would allow us to continue that course. To declare on the side of the Axis would be utter folly. It would be insanity. It would destroy us.'

Half a dozen small boys raced past them, chasing after a lad on a go-cart. A dog snuffled among the dead leaves in the gutter.

Guido said, 'You told me yesterday that our friendship had ended. But if that's so, Tessa, then it was your choice.'

'No, that's not true.' She remembered her first miserable weeks in England – the school, the rain, the separation from almost everything she had held dear. 'I wrote to you,' she said, 'but you never wrote back.'

'I never received a single letter from you.'

She stopped in the street, frowning. 'I don't understand.'

'Not one. Nothing. And I wrote – oh, a dozen times.'

Was he lying? No, she did not think so. 'And I to you, Guido,' she said. 'I promise.' She remembered Westdown, with its spinster teachers and incomprehensible rules. She had not been allowed to walk to a postbox; she had had to hand her letters to a prefect to be posted.

'It was the school, I expect. Perhaps we weren't supposed to write to boys. Perhaps the teachers read our letters. Perhaps they tore them up.'

'In the end,' he said, 'I gave up. I thought you'd forgotten me.'

'No, Guido, never.'

'Then what a waste,' he said softly. 'Why did you come back to Florence, Tessa?'

'Because this is where I belong.'

'Not in England?'

'No. For a while I thought I did, but I was mistaken.'

'Weren't you happy there?'

'I was at first.' She smiled. 'I loved London. I liked earning my own living.'

'What did you do?'

'I was a model. I paraded around in front of rich ladies in department stores.' She struck a pose and he laughed.

'You were successful?'

'I was, yes. I was able to keep myself and pay Freddie's school fees. I was proud of that.'

'And now you work in a dress shop . . . Why, Tessa?'

Her mood plummeted again. 'Because something happened,' she said.

'That scar on your forehead – was that why you gave up modelling?'

Automatically she put up a hand, tugging down her fringe. 'I was in a car crash,' she said.

'Were you badly hurt?' She nodded. 'Poor Tessa,' he said.

She paused to run the tips of her fingers over the petals of the roses spilling over a wall. She said quietly, 'There were things that I did that I'm ashamed of.'

She appreciated that he held back from asking more questions. It allowed her to draw breath, to change the subject and say, 'But the years have been good to you, Guido. You've married. You have a beautiful daughter.'

'I've been fortunate, yes, it's true.'

'How did you meet Maddalena?'

Maddalena was the only daughter of a wealthy Florentine family, Guido told her. They had known each other since they were infants. The marriage had the blessing of both their families. Maddalena was beautiful, elegant and kind, a skilled housekeeper, a charming hostess, and a good mother to Luciella.

There was something flat, Tessa thought, about his description. It lacked passion. She imagined them, Guido and Maddalena, walking to church on a Sunday morning, she serene, composing her mind for the religious service, he a little bored, restless, as was his habit, his dark eyes flicking over the worshippers heading up the steps to the church, his thoughts unfocused, shifting.

They had reached the old city gate. 'I was so sorry to hear about your father, Guido,' Tessa said. 'I was fond of him. Was he ill for a long time?'

'Two years. It was dreadful to see him like that. My mother nursed him.'

'How is she?'

'Mamma's well. She and Faustina are living in the villa in Chianti now. Mamma's always preferred the countryside.'

'Faustina . . . how old is she?'

'Twenty-one.'

'Is she married – engaged?'

'Neither.' Guido turned down the corners of his mouth. 'Faustina doesn't seem to mind being buried in the middle of nowhere. It would drive me to drink.'

Tessa remembered Faustina Zanetti. *Hideously* bossy,

Freddie had used to complain when, as a young girl, she had had to play with her for an afternoon.

'And Sandro?' she asked.

'He's working in Bologna.' Guido smiled, a flash of white teeth. 'He builds roads and bridges. How's Freddie, Tessa?'

'She's very well. She works in an office in London. I miss her.'

His dark eyes, the colour of bitter chocolate, settled on her. 'Then go back to England,' he said softly.

'I can't,' she said. 'Guido, I can't.'

They walked for a while in silence. She said suddenly, 'When I look back, I can see what a strange situation it was. My mother and your mother. My mother used to go to your mother's house. They used to dine together, your father's wife and his mistress. I wonder whether your mother minded. She must have minded.'

'Perhaps she didn't know.'

'How can she not have known? We knew. You told me, don't you remember, Guido? You came back from university and one day you told me that my mother and your father were lovers. Stupid of me not to have noticed.'

'Perhaps I should have kept my thoughts to myself. You weren't much more than a child.'

I was old enough, she thought. When she looked back at her childhood, there were things that jarred. She had had such freedom, such an easy proximity to art and beauty, and yet at the same time too close an intimacy with the passion and malice of adult relationships. She had seen love without really understanding it, had watched her father

327

and mother hurt each other and thought it commonplace. Those things had shaped her, she saw that now.

On May 10th, Hitler's armies poured into the Low Countries and northern France. In Florence, fascist groups pasted posters to the walls, demanding that the Duce declare war on France and Britain. The talk in the dress shop where Tessa worked was of a war all but won, of the imminent capitulation of France and the inevitable defeat of Britain.

Some of the fountains and statues in the city had been swathed in padding; others had been entombed in a concrete shelter in the Boboli Gardens. Paintings had been taken from churches and galleries and transported to the safety of villas in the surrounding countryside, Botticelli goddesses jostling shoulders with Caravaggio bravos, wrapped in sacking, making their jolting journeys through country roads to cellars and dungeons, a diaspora of art.

The few remaining English residents packed their bags and scrambled to catch the last trains to the border. Tessa wrote a letter to Freddie and took it to the station. There, she asked one of the fleeing expatriates to post it when she arrived in England. A whistle blew, there was a billow of smoke, and Tessa watched the train pull away from the platform and disappear out of sight.

On June 10th, as French resistance to the Nazi invasion crumbled and the British began to evacuate their forces from the Channel ports, Mussolini declared war on the side of the Axis. There seemed, Tessa thought as she walked home from work, little sign of enthusiasm for war. Instead, the streets and piazzas were quieter than usual, the cafés half empty, heat and dread hanging over the city like a pall.

Back in her room, she sat by the window, looking out to where blue-black shadows, cast from the high walls of the buildings, pooled in the alleyway. Such a shabby end to a shabby decade, she thought. Mussolini's opportunism and Hitler's greed and violence had been underpinned by the irresolution and timidity of the other Western powers. So where did her loyalties lie – she, with her assumed name and forged papers? With the people she loved. With all that she felt in her heart to be right. But she was now an enemy alien living in a country at war with Great Britain. Mussolini's declaration had placed her in great danger.

She caught sight of Guido walking down the alley. She watched him for a while, noting the long lope of his stride and the firm set of his mouth, and then she went downstairs to let him into the building.

He waited until they were in her room before speaking. 'I leave Florence tomorrow,' he said. 'I'm to go to officer school in Modena.'

Tessa's hand stilled, pouring wine. 'How long have you known?'

'Not long.'

'How long will you be away?'

'I don't know.' He frowned. 'It depends where I'm posted. Mussolini waited until France is certain to fall before making his move. He believes Britain can't hold out on her own. He believes she'll seek terms with Germany in a few weeks' time – a month or two at most.'

Tessa thought of the men she had known in England – Ray,

329

Julian, Max, Paddy. Would they seek terms? She could not imagine it.

She handed him a glass and sat down. 'And you, Guido? What do you believe?'

'The Americans may come into the war. They stand aloof at the moment, but that might not last.' He sat down beside her, his fingertips drumming on the arm of the sofa. 'I had an argument with my father-in-law last night. He has always been a loyal supporter of Mussolini. He reminded me that there are a great many Italians in America. Why would they choose to fight their own countrymen? That was what he said to me. I told him that America will not wish to do business with a fascist Europe.'

'Who won the argument?'

'Neither of us. I could see that Maddalena was upset. She dislikes me arguing with her father, so I changed the subject.' His gaze rested on her. 'You have to leave Florence, Tessa. Sooner or later someone will ask questions. I've written to my mother.'

She looked at him, puzzled. 'I don't understand.'

'I told you that my mother and sister are living in our villa in Chianti. My mother has spent the years since my father's death bringing our tenant farms up to date. She encourages the *contadini* to use modern farming methods and she's set up a school and a clinic for their families. She is liked and respected there and no one will notice if an extra person comes to stay. Faustina has—'

She interrupted him. 'Guido, are you suggesting that I should go and stay with your mother?'

'Yes. You'll be safer there.' He took an envelope from the

330

inside pocket of his jacket. 'Faustina has written back to me. This is her reply – it arrived this morning. Read it, please.'

She did not take the letter. 'Guido, I know you mean to be kind, but I can't possibly go and live with your mother.'

'Why not?'

'It's impossible, you must see that.'

'Then you put me, as well as yourself, in danger.'

'No,' she said sharply. 'That's not true. What I do is my decision, my choice. It's no concern of yours.'

'You don't exist in isolation, Tessa. Do you think I've told Maddalena about you? Do you think I've told her that the first girl I ever loved has come back to Florence? No, of course not. If you stay in Florence, then I shall feel obliged to continue to visit you. I shall feel obliged to make sure you're safe and well. And if you should get into any difficulty, I doubt I would be able to stand aside.'

'This isn't fair!' she cried.

'We loved each other once. I can't forget that.'

She said angrily, 'I can look after myself! I always have.'

'Have you, Tessa?'

Instinctively, her hand went to her forehead. She stood up quickly and walked away from him. Her arms folded together, she stared out of the window. Outside in the street, a donkey pulled a cart heaped with empty bottles. In a doorway, two lovers kissed, their long, dark shadows pasted on the paving stones.

She heard the door close behind Guido as he left the room. Caught in a cobweb in a corner of the window frame, a butterfly struggled for freedom, its wings quivering.

331

Carefully she disentangled it and opened the window to let it out. Its flight was lurching and uneven, and she wondered whether, in releasing it, she had damaged its wings.

A year ago, she had told Freddie that she believed that England would be no safer than Florence in a time of war. She had also told her that she had needed to escape England's painful associations. Both these things had been true. But now, for the first time, she wondered whether she had done the right thing, or whether she should have left Italy along with the other English residents.

After the car crash, and after she had emerged from the blackest part of her grief and depression, all that had remained had been emptiness. She had neither laughed nor cried. Nothing had touched her. Whatever she had done – shrunk from the world or searched frantically for speed and sensation – there had endured a greyness inside her. It had seemed possible to her that she would never feel deeply again. She had known, as one knows a fact, that she loved Freddie. Rationally, she had also known that she loved Max and Ray and her other closest friends. But she had not felt love. And yet here, in Italy, some part of her had begun to come alive again.

She sat down on the sofa and lit a cigarette. In Guido's absence, something remained, some essence. She ran the palm of her hand across the sofa arm, where his hand had lain. *I doubt I would be able to stand aside*, he had said to her. There was a warning there. Time to leave. She would not wreck his life, or Maddalena's or Luciella's. Some lessons she had learned.

But where would she go and what would she do? She shrank from the thought of starting again, alone once more, carrying out the wearying business of finding somewhere to live and work to do.

She picked up Faustina Zanetti's letter and opened it. Faustina was practical but not unfriendly. She wrote that there was always room at the villa for an extra pair of hands and that Tessa would be welcome so long as she was prepared to work. War would lead to food shortages, so there would be plenty to do on the land. Or Tessa could, if she preferred, help at the school or the clinic. In return, she would receive food and lodging.

Italy's declaration of war had changed everything. Guido was right: she was no longer safe in Florence. She must melt into the countryside, she must hide herself away, because if she did not, she risked endangering others as well as herself. And if she were to leave Florence for the Zanetti villa, then she must let Freddie know where she had gone. Yet letters could be opened and read, and as Guido had pointed out, if her nationality were to be revealed, she might be accused of spying. She must be very, very careful.

Twelve days later, the Italian army advanced along the French Riviera, occupying Menton. That night, Tessa wrote to Faustina, accepting her offer of sanctuary.

The next time Freddie saw Jack Ransome was at the Dorchester, in the December of 1940, at the height of the London Blitz.

There were five of them at the table: herself and Angus

Corstophine, Julian Lawrence, Ray, and his girlfriend, Susan, who worked for the Home Service. Freddie was wearing her mother's garnets; they gleamed pleasingly against her black evening dress. There was a large party across the restaurant, sitting at a corner table. They were making a lot of noise, shrieks of laughter and now and then a burst of applause.

Susan was telling them about meeting Myra Hess on the stairs at Broadcasting House when from the corner table came a shout of 'Jack!'

Ray muttered, 'Good God, I can hardly hear myself think. Wish they'd put a sock in it.'

Freddie looked round at the man who was crossing the restaurant floor. It was Jack Ransome. He looked different – he was in army uniform, and he appeared cleaner, tidier, healthier than when she had last seen him eighteen months before. Jack, she thought – Jack, who had dragged her off on that appalling journey over the mountains. Jack, in London.

Angus had followed her gaze. 'Do you know him?'

'Jack Ransome? We've met. Do you?'

'I was at school with his elder brother.'

Freddie turned back to Susan. 'Was she wearing a marvellous dress?'

'A blouse and skirt, I'm afraid.'

'Wireless, Freddie,' said Julian. 'You don't need to dress up for the wireless.'

Freddie smiled. 'I always imagine Myra Hess wearing an evening gown whatever she's doing. Even the washing-up.'

The waiter served coffees and petits fours. Julian said, 'Has anyone heard from Max?'

'He said he might come later,' said Freddie.

After the invasion of the Low Countries and France during the summer of 1940, all enemy aliens living in Britain and deemed to be a threat to the state had been rounded up and imprisoned, Max among them. Once the threat of invasion had receded, the panic had died down and internees had begun to be released. Since he had left the internment camp on the Isle of Man, Max had worked for the Ministry of Information.

There was another roar of laughter from the corner table. Rising, Freddie kissed Angus's cheek. 'I'll be back in a moment, darling. I'll just go and say hello to Jack.'

She crossed the room to the corner table. 'Jack,' she said.

He looked round. 'Good Lord. Freddie Nicolson.' He stood up, smiling broadly. 'Well, fancy that. How marvellous to see you again.'

'How's your ankle?'

'Completely recovered, thanks to you. And you? You look wonderful.'

'I do feel rather better turned out than the last time we saw each other.'

Jack said to his friends, 'This is Miss Nicolson.' He reeled off a list of names to her. 'Are you dining here, Freddie?'

'We've almost finished. I think we're going on to dance. I must go – perhaps I'll see you later, Jack.'

She went back to her own table. Angus had saved her the nicest petit four, the one like a miniature chocolate eclair.

Freddie was now working as a clerk at the War Office. In October, she had been told to take a bundle of files to a room on the second floor. She had tapped on the door and a voice had told her to come in. The man sitting at the desk had glanced up briefly, and said, 'Thank you,' as she gave him the files. Then he had asked her her name. 'Nicolson,' she had told him. 'I'm Miss Nicolson.' 'My name's Angus Corstophine,' he had said. 'Would you come for a drink with me this evening, Miss Nicolson? Do take pity on me, I'm a very long way from home. I promise that I'm well behaved. It's just that you have such beautiful eyes.'

She had met him after work at Claridge's, where he was staying. After two martinis (Angus had drunk whisky), he had extracted from her a promise of dinner the following week and had then put her in a cab home. His full name was Angus James Macready Corstophine. Major Angus James Macready Corstophine. His home was a castle between Perth and Braemar, in which generations of Corstophines had lived. Angus was twelve years older than Freddie, tall, red-haired, blue-eyed. A regular soldier, he had been in France with the BEF and had escaped from Dunkirk on one of the last ships to evacuate the port. He visited the War Office now and then, but spent most of the rest of his time at a training camp in Scotland. He was interesting, considerate and a good conversationalist. He disliked dancing, but put up with it for her sake, would have preferred a long walk or an afternoon's fishing, and always sent her flowers the morning after they had dined together. The roses and orchids must come from someone's hothouse, she had concluded. Where else in the frozen, battered London of the winter of 1940 might he have found such beautiful things?

After they had dined, Ray and Susan left because Susan was working a late shift at the BBC. Now and then Freddie looked for Jack's crowd. She wondered whether one of those beautiful girls sitting at his table would have said, *Not here, Jack, let's go somewhere else*, and then he would disappear, as people did in wartime, and she would file away this brief meeting alongside that other one: surprising and chancy and not part of ordinary life.

But then, as the band struck up 'Let There Be Love', she saw him walking towards their table. Jack and Angus talked to each other, while Freddie danced with Julian. Then Jack asked whether they would like to share his table. They would, they decided.

Freddie found herself sitting between Angus and a woman called Marcelle Scott. Miss Scott was wearing an eau de Nil evening dress with a scattering of diamanté round the bust and her dark brown hair was pinned back into a knot at the nape of her neck. She had very lovely long, narrow, darting green eyes and her nails were painted an exact red, the same shade as her lips. She smoked a lot and played with the rings on her fingers.

Miss Scott said, 'We stayed with Jack once when we were in Italy. He made us walk for hours to see some stones – Greek or Roman or something. Denzil didn't mind, but I dislike the heat.'

Freddie said, 'Is Denzil your husband?'

'Good Lord, no.' Miss Scott glanced at her scarlet-tipped hand, with its several rings. 'These were my mother's. I'm not engaged or married. I can't see the point now, can you? The men would be away all the time.' She inhaled her cigarette. 'Some of us were touring Europe. Denny did most of the driving.'

337

'Where did you go?'

'The south of France, Switzerland, Italy . . . Jack and Denny wanted to go on to Greece but I had to get back to my father.'

'Is he unwell?'

'He's rather old and creaky, poor dear. How well do you know Jack, Miss Nicolson?'

'We were travelling companions once, that's all.' Briefly, Freddie summarized her encounter with Jack – visiting her sister in Florence, coming across Jack on the journey home, their parting in France – making it sound, she thought, as if they had shared egg and cress sandwiches in a railway carriage. She left out a great deal because she found that she did not want to be the object of Miss Scott's curiosity, and finished by saying, 'That was more than a year ago, and I haven't seen him since.'

'Jack can be terribly unreliable,' said Miss Scott. 'Do you know the Ransomes, Miss Nicolson?'

'Not at all.' Freddie remembered a conversation she had had with Jack when she was driving the stolen Fiat. 'I had the impression he didn't get on with his elder brother.'

'George? No. George is quite a bit older than Jack, of course. The joke is that Ransome mère et père only sleep together once every five years when they want to produce another child. George's wife, Alexandra, is completely ghastly. We came out in the same year. The hem of her frock once unravelled at a dance and she threw a tantrum. She winds George round her little finger. But some men like that, don't they?'

'I suppose so. Though it's funny, isn't it, how people only

say that about women. They don't often say *he* winds *her* round his little finger, do they?'

'Perhaps they don't.' Miss Scott looked at Freddie closely. 'Jack often brings us his waifs and strays, but they don't usually last long. I think you'll do, though. *Years* since I've seen Angus. Are you two dating?'

Waifs and strays, thought Freddie, but she said, 'Yes.'

'Are you in love with him, Miss Nicolson?'

'I don't think,' said Freddie, 'that's any of your business.'

'I expect you're right. You must forgive me, I'm afraid my curiosity sometimes gets the better of me.' Miss Scott did not look remotely abashed. 'I have a theory, you see, that couples never love each other equally. He loves her, or the other way round, but he isn't quite what she's looking for. If he persists, she's flattered, or perhaps she hasn't found anyone any better, and so she starts to think oh, I might as well, and so they become engaged and then they get married. Or they don't, and eventually he gives up and notices the girl who's been in love with him for ages. And because his ego's bruised, he becomes engaged to *her*, and marries *her*.' Miss Scott took another cigarette out of her case and, holding it between her first two fingers, gave a little smile. 'What do you think of my theory, Miss Nicolson?'

'You may be right some of the time. But sometimes love's mutual. Or it grows to be mutual.'

Miss Scott leaned towards the man on her far side, who lit her cigarette. Turning back to Freddie, she said, 'Would you like me to tell you who everyone is?'

'Please.'

'Ollie Piper and Jane Hedley are sitting at the end of the

table. They're to be married next week. Hasn't Jane lovely hair? I sometimes wish I was a blonde, but I don't think I'm nice enough.'

'Are blondes always nice?'

'I find they are. Jane and I went to school together. The wedding will be a bore but the party should be fun. The Hedleys always throw such marvellous parties. The tall man on Jane's other side is called Monty Douglas. Sweet, but not very bright. Inbreeding, my father says. And that's Denzil Beckford, sitting next to Monty. His family have the most divine house in Cornwall. We used to stay there in the summer – the garden goes all the way down to the sea. Betty Mulholland is on Denzil's other side. She's a sweet girl, Monty was in love with her for years. I think he still is, though he says he's not. Betty and Frances – she's the redhead – are sisters. They're both joining the WAAF. They've wanted to for ages but their parents wouldn't let them, but now they're afraid Betty and Frances might end up working in a factory so they're letting them go. They don't look at all alike, do they? Of course, their mother had an affair with Boy Trevelyan for simply years, so you never know.'

'And the pretty girl, in the pink dress?'

'She's called Clare Stuart. Do you think she's pretty? I don't. I can't bear girls who wrinkle up their noses like that. I always think they practise in front of the mirror, to make themselves look appealing.'

Freddie laughed. 'Isn't that rather harsh?'

'Perhaps, but I'm perfectly sure I'm right. Now, who else is there? Lewis . . .'

'Are you talking about me, Marcelle?'

A tall man in naval uniform had come to join them. His hand rested on Marcelle's shoulder. He had dark curly hair, a straight, narrow nose, and both his mouth and his hazel eyes curved up at the corners, which gave him, Freddie thought, an elfin appearance.

'I'm dishing the dirt,' said Miss Scott. 'I'm telling Miss Nicolson all about you.'

'Don't believe a word of it, Miss Nicolson.' He held out his hand to Freddie. 'My name's Lewis Coryton. I'm pleased to meet you.'

Miss Scott's eyes sparkled. 'I know all your secrets, Lewis.'

'I haven't any secrets,' he said calmly. 'There's nothing to tell.'

Marcelle made a disapproving face. 'If you're going to be dull, I shan't dance with you.'

'Darling Marcelle, I promise not to be dull at all.'

Miss Scott stood up, ruffled Lieutenant Coryton's curls and planted a kiss on his cheek. Before they went on to the dance floor, she spoke again to Freddie.

'Where do you work, Miss Nicolson?'

'The War Office.'

'I'm at the Ministry of Works. We should have lunch together. I'll write to you.'

The band struck up 'Oh Johnny'. Miss Scott and Lewis Coryton stepped on to the dance floor. The group round the table had thinned out. Angus was at the far end, deep in conversation with a man in army uniform. Freddie tried to catch his attention but he did not look up.

A voice said, 'Will you dance with me, Freddie?' and, turning, she saw Jack.

She smiled at him. 'Yes, Jack, I'd be delighted to.'

They threaded through the tables. Jack found a spot on the crowded dance floor.

'What did you think of my cousin?' he said.

'Your cousin?' She stared at him. 'Miss Scott is your cousin?'

'We used to climb trees together, Marcelle and I.'

Freddie could not imagine the immaculate Miss Scott going anywhere near a tree. She said, 'She told me that you sometimes bring along your waifs and strays. The implication was that I was one, and that most of them didn't last very long.'

He grinned. 'You shouldn't take any notice of Marcelle.'

'I felt as if I was sitting an exam.'

'I'm sure you passed. Marcelle can seem a little hard sometimes. She worries about her father.'

'She told me he was unwell.'

'He hasn't been right since the last war. Her mother's dead and Marcelle hasn't any brothers and sisters, so it all falls on her shoulders.'

'Then I shall forgive her. I would have forgiven her anyhow, because she made me laugh.'

As they danced, Freddie ran her gaze around the room. Max was standing near the dance floor; she waved to him.

With a flourish of saxophone and drum, the number came to an end. The soloist bowed, acknowledging the applause. When the music started up again, a slow, sentimental song, Jack took her in his arms.

'You changed your mind then,' she said 'about sitting out the war in South America.'

342

He looked down at her. 'It wouldn't have been any fun without you.'

'I can't help suspecting your idea of fun would probably include being cold and tired and rather frightened.'

'Be honest, Freddie,' he teased. 'You enjoyed it.'

'Maybe little bits of it.' She curled her finger and thumb an inch apart. '*Very* little bits.'

'What are you doing now?'

'I'm a secretary at the War Office. What about you?'

'I'm spending most of the time shut up in an army camp in Yorkshire.'

'That can't suit you at all, Jack. Can't you ask them to post you somewhere horrible and dangerous? Then you'd be perfectly happy.'

He pretended to look wounded. 'I'm afraid you have a poor impression of me.'

'I'm rather fond of smart restaurants and comfortable hotels. I don't care for sleeping in cars and existing on bread and cheese.'

'I don't believe you. I think that under that prim exterior you're a rebel at heart.'

'*Prim?*' As he steered her round a corner, she gave him a furious look.

'Genteel . . . proper . . .'

'You're making me sound like a maiden aunt!'

'A great deal prettier than my maiden aunts.'

'*Jack.*' He laughed.

The dance floor was crowded. Frequently another dancer called out, 'Hello, Jack, good to see you,' or clapped him on the shoulder in passing, and Jack waved or called out a greeting. Freddie had the same sensation she had experienced years ago, at the Ritz with Tessa, of being part of the most interesting and enviable clique in the room. She saw that Lieutenant Coryton was now dancing with Miss Stuart, and that Marcelle Scott had left the floor and was talking to Julian and Max. Angus was no longer in conversation with the army man, but was standing on his own to one side of the room. He had a habit of tapping his foot when he was bored. The foot was tapping now.

Jack said, 'Is Angus Corstophine your boyfriend?'

'Yes. You know each other?'

'A little. We were talking about Spain,' said Jack.

'Was that where you went?'

'Yes.'

'What were you doing there?'

'This and that.'

Spying, she thought. The British naval port of Gibraltar nestled by the entrance to the Mediterranean, on the southernmost tip of Spain. Wounded by years of civil war, Spain had thus far in the war declared herself neutral. It was very much in Britain's interests that she remain so.

She said, 'What was it like?'

'Grim.' For a moment his eyes clouded. 'The soul's been knocked out of it.'

'How long were you there?'

'Six months. It was a relief to come back to England, to be honest. And now my luck's taken another turn for the better, finding you again.'

'I bet you didn't think of me once after we parted in France.'

'Not true, actually.'

Something in his glance took her by surprise; she said lightly, 'Miss Scott warned me off you. She told me you were unreliable.'

'The nerve of it,' said Jack, though he didn't look put out.

'She as much as told me you were a feckless aristocrat.'

'Did she now?' Couples jostled tightly; he held her closer.

'I suppose aristocrats are often feckless.'

'It goes with the territory, you mean?' There was amusement in his voice. 'Whereas the middle classes have a tendency to be prim.'

'You are the most infuriating man. Anyway, I'm not middle class, I'm interestingly bohemian.'

'Of course you are, Freddie. How could I forget?'

'Though I'm not sure that I'm awfully good at being bohemian.'

'Oh, I'd say you were pretty adaptable. You rise to a challenge.'

'When I was at school, I used to long to be like my sister. She was so glamorous.' Freddie thought of Tessa's flat, with the framed photos and the black and white tiled fireplace. She smiled. 'I was Tessa's messenger.'

'Her messenger?'

'I used to deliver her letters to her boyfriends.' She laughed. 'Some of them were nice, but others were awful. I don't think Tessa realized how awful they were. One of them tried to kiss me and another offered to take me out to dinner when Tessa couldn't come.'

'Did you go?'

'Of course.' She glared at him. 'See. Not so prim.'

'And did you have a good time?'

'At first I felt very important. But then he got talking to his friends and he forgot about me so I went home on the tube on my own.'

'How old were you?'

'Fifteen. I didn't mind. I like travelling on my own.'

'You do, don't you? And your sister? How is she? Where is she?'

Freddie sighed. 'Tessa stayed in Italy, I'm afraid. I had a letter – she sent it to me via someone she knows in Sweden. She was rather cagey – she must have been afraid it might be read – but she told me she's gone to stay with friends in the countryside. I wrote back, but I've no idea whether my letter reached her.'

The dance ended with a drum roll, and they clapped. She said, 'It's good to see you again. Keep in touch, Jack.'

He promised that he would and she stood on her toes to kiss his cheek. 'You have a scar just there,' she said, and touched his eyebrow.

'I jumped out of a plane and landed in a tree.'

'Careless of you, Jack.'

'Wasn't it?' His grin had broadened. He thanked her for the dance and walked away.

She called out after him, 'You will take care, won't you?'

He looked back. 'Of course I will.'

There was the sting of frosty air and, in the distance, the crump, crump of bombs as they left the hotel. Icicles hung from broken gutters, and where the soft gleam of masked car headlamps caught the ice and the fractured shards of

346

glass in the windowpanes, they glittered like Christmas lights, giving the ruined buildings a deceptively festive air.

To either side of the front door of the Knightsbridge flat stood two box trees in pots, sculpted into balls and topped with a thick dollop of snow, like cream on a Christmas pudding.

The all-clear sounded as Angus unlocked the door of the building. Inside the flat there were oil paintings of fleshy men in curling wigs and women wearing low-cut necklines and arch expressions.

Angus said, 'I'll just put the lamps on, and then with a bit of luck we won't notice them looking at us. Feels like the inside of a fridge, doesn't it? I'll light the fire.'

Freddie sat down on a plum-coloured velvet sofa near the fireplace. In places the pile had worn away, giving the fabric a silvery sheen. Angus knelt and struck a match and put it to the kindling.

'I remember a winter at home when the water in the washbasins froze. London's never as cold as home.' Angus sat down beside her. 'Poor girl, you're freezing.' She liked the way he said 'girl', with its rolling of r's.

He poured them both a Scotch and they sat wrapped in each other's arms as the shadows of the flames flickered on the rug. He said, 'At Hogmanay, we light all the lamps and candles in the castle and we put torches outside in the garden. People tell me you can see the blaze for miles. There's food and music and dancing.'

'I thought you hated dancing.'

'Proper dancing. *Highland* dancing. At midnight they ring the bell in the tower and everyone has a dram. Then we go first-footing. That's down to the neighbours to bring in the New Year, you understand.'

'How far away are your neighbours, Angus?'

'Oh, the nearest is about two miles, that's all.'

'In the snow?'

'I've walked through snowdrifts up to my waist. It's how we keep ourselves warm in Scotland, whisky and walking. Though there are other ways.'

While they talked, his hand stroked her hair, and between phrases he kissed her. He said, 'I should like you to be there with me to see in the New Year one day. Do you think you might like that?'

She knelt up on the sofa and kissed him. 'I don't know, Angus. It sounds as though I might feel rather cold.'

'No you wouldn't. I would make sure of that.'

He took her whisky glass out of her hand and put it on a side table. Then he kissed her shoulder. 'Like bird's wings,' he said. 'This hollow, here.' He scooped her up in his arms and sat her on his knee. Then he eased down the zip at the back of her dress and looped the narrow straps of her gown over her shoulders and kissed her again.

'There, my beautiful Freddie,' he said. 'You would tell me if you wanted me to stop, wouldn't you?'

Into her mind came a memory of Marcelle Scott saying, *Are you in love with Angus, Miss Nicolson?* And her theory that love was always, inevitably, unequal.

But she said, 'I don't want you to stop, Angus. Not at all.' And she closed her eyes and gave a soft outward breath as the palm of his hand slid beneath the hem of her skirt.

* * *

In the night, she woke, and went to the kitchen for a glass of water. Sliding aside the blackout, careful not to let any light escape, she looked out. It was snowing, puffy white blobs floating down, covering the ruins and the rubble.

Her mind raced. Such an evening – Angus and Jack and the dancing. And this . . . She did not regret the loss of her virginity, but welcomed the sense it gave her of moving on, of having become properly adult. Angus had taken precautions – remembering Tessa, she had made sure of that. She looked out of the window at the snow, recalling the drift of his palm across her stomach and the feel of him inside her, and the words he had murmured in her ear, and the rise and fall of his breath as she had fallen asleep, enclosed in his arms.

Marcelle Scott wrote to her, asking whether they could meet for lunch. Freddie was surprised; she had taken Miss Scott's suggestion to be one of those well-meant gestures designed to show goodwill but never followed up.

They met in a small café in a road near Charing Cross station. To the side of the café a bomb had struck, shearing off one end of the building, like a sentence broken off part way through. Within the stubs of walls that had once made up a room, a blanket of snow had settled lightly on a tangled pyre of broken furniture, pram wheels and a piano keyboard.

Inside the café, trails of condensation ran down the windows. Marcelle Scott was sitting at a window table. She was wearing a black coat with a fur collar and a small black hat. There was a cup of tea in front of her.

'How good to see you again, Miss Nicolson,' she said. 'May I call you Freddie? I dislike formality, don't you? Is this place all right for you? I often come here for lunch. Most of the other girls bring sandwiches and Thermos flasks, but I hate to be stuck indoors all day.'

At the counter, they ordered bread and soup. Back at the table, Marcelle said, 'I hope you didn't mind me writing to you. I'd meant to write sooner, but my father was ill and I had to go home.'

'I'm sorry to hear that. Is he better?'

'Yes, much better, thank you.' Marcelle looked down, stirring her tea. 'I should go and live with Daddy. He'd be happier if I did so. Do you think it's selfish of me not to?'

'I don't know,' said Freddie. 'I couldn't judge.'

'Your parents are dead, aren't they?'

'They both died when I was a child.'

'Perhaps you're fortunate.' Marcelle bit her lip. 'No, I shouldn't say that, I'm sorry, you must forgive me.' She sighed. 'When I'm in Wiltshire, I imagine myself shrink-ing' – she drew thumb and forefinger closer together until only a small space remained – 'like this. I feel . . . reduced. If I lived there all the time, I'm afraid there'd be nothing left of me. I don't mind the war too much, you know. If it wasn't for the guilt, I'd be quite happy. Such a pointless emotion, guilt, I'm always trying to get rid of it.' She lit a cigarette. 'What did you think of my friends?'

'I liked them.'

'Lewis is madly in love with Clare Stuart, of course.'

'The girl in the pink dress? Oh, I see.'

As the soup was served, Marcelle confided, 'I used to be in love with him, actually.'

'With Lieutenant Coryton? He's rather attractive, isn't he? Are you still in love with him?'

'Not at all. He's a good friend and we write to each other. I fall in love rather a lot, it's a bad habit of mine. I expect you're far more sensible.'

'*Sensible*,' said Freddie. 'How damning. Jack called me prim.'

'You mustn't take any notice of Jack, he can be very impolite.'

They talked about their work and the war, and then it was time to return to the office. As they put on their coats, Marcelle said, 'I give a supper at my house most Fridays. Everyone brings something to eat. Would you like to come? You could bring Angus, of course. And your friend Mr Fischer.' She was pulling on her gloves. 'Yes. I should like you to ask Max Fischer whether he'd come.'

'Not Julian?'

'Julian's perfectly sweet, but no, I'm actually rather keen on your Max. He hasn't anyone, has he?'

'Not at the moment.'

'Someone told me he was in love with your sister.'

The curiosity in Marcelle's eyes told Freddie that the someone had told Marcelle rather more about Tessa, but she said only, 'He was, but that finished a long time ago. Years and years ago.'

Chapter Eleven

The Villa di Belcanto crowned a hill in the countryside south of Florence. In the fifteenth century the original buildings, which included a square tower, had been incorporated into an oblong villa with an inner courtyard and loggia. Further refinements had been added in the nineteeth century by Olivia Zanetti's forebears: an English park, an alley of chestnut trees and various outbuildings. Centuries of exposure to the wind and the sun had faded the exterior of the building to the soft pinkish-brown of hazelnut ice cream. Above the huge arched doorway the once brightly painted escutcheon – an octagon enclosing a morose-looking gryphon – had peeled and faded to muted greys and buffs.

To one side of the villa were farmlands, vineyards, olive groves and fields of maize. Across the valley the hills were thickly wooded, the oaks, chestnuts and scrub scored by ravines. The *fattoria*, the largest and most important of the estate's farms, was a short distance from the villa. The dozen other, smaller tenant farms were spread over a much wider area. Near the *fattoria* were barns, a dairy, workshops and a laundry, as well as several houses.

Horses, pigs, dairy cattle, chickens, geese and rabbits were reared on the estate. Fruit and vegetables were grown in the kitchen garden, cheese was made in the dairy, and honey was collected from the beehives. In the autumn, pigs were slaughtered, hams were dried and salted and sausages made. More than fifty people worked on the Belcanto estate: the cook, housekeeper, seamstress and other servants at the villa; the factor, Stefano, who lived with his wife and children at the *fattoria*; and the farmers and their families in the outlying farms.

In the spring, the rains swelled the streams and the young corn greened the wheat fields. Then the days lengthened and puffy clouds floated high in skies of azure blue. By midsummer, the ears of the corn had turned gold and the grapes were small and hard and green on the vines. The farmers watched the sky anxiously, fearful of hailstorms or sudden downpours that might destroy the crops. Then came the harvest, when sheaves of wheat were carried in ox carts to be stored safely in the barns. The petals of the poppies on the verges became limp and bruised, and in fields left shorn and dry, a mouse darted beneath a hedgerow to escape from the burning sun. In high summer, the heat swallowed up the landscape until everything green had been consumed, so that by August each blade of grass was bleached to the colour of sacking and the hills shimmered behind a blue-grey haze.

Then came the September rains, washing the dust from

the leaves of vine and olive and freshening the air. Tomatoes, figs and peaches were set out for drying in the courtyard of the *fattoria*, and pumpkins and melons ripened in the sun. Cobs of maize were strung up between the trees like huge amber-coloured necklaces. The grapes were gathered in, the fat bunches gleaming purple and green. Children ran between the rows of vines, collecting the scarlet leaves that would be fed to the cattle. In the evening, they celebrated with dancing and a feast.

The olives were the last crop to be harvested, in November. Except for babies and the infirm, everyone who lived on the estate went out to the fields, dropping the fruit into baskets slung round their waists. A cold wind made the grey-green leaves of the olives tremble. The first picking made the finest oil, the virgin pressing. The windfalls went into the second pressing. Soap was made from the third pressing, and the skins and kernels were formed into a cake that was used for fuel and fertilizer. The olive oil was stored in great terracotta jars in the cool of the cellars, kept apart from the wine in case one flavoured the other.

Then the winter came. The tramontana blew down from the northern mountains, a sharp, cold wind that seemed to find a way through the thick stone walls of the villa. Snowstorms covered the gnarled stubs of the vines and settled on the roof of the villa. On days like this, Tessa learned, it was impossible to remember warmth, impossible to believe that there had been a time when she had searched for a cool, dark corner, like a lizard fitting itself into a crevice in a stone wall.

* * *

Olivia Zanetti was now in her early sixties. Tall, thin, grey-haired and big-nosed, in appearance she reminded Tessa of Ottoline Morrell, to whom she had once been introduced at Ascot races – Ottoline Morrell without the dash and style and beautiful clothes.

From her office on the ground floor of the villa, Olivia ran the estate. The leather-bound ledgers stacked on the shelves detailed yields, sowing and harvesting times, weather conditions, expenditure and income, down to the last lira. She visited all the tenant farms weekly, travelling the stony unmade roads and farm tracks in a pony and trap. When the time came to slaughter the pigs, she selected the animals with the swineherd. When the olives were to be harvested, she tied a basket round her waist and picked from the trees. When one of the estate workers was ill, she sent for a doctor.

Deeply religious, Olivia attended Mass each morning. Her Christianity was of the practical kind, founded on a sense of responsibility and duty. Thoughtful and generous, she was, in her relations with other people, austere, rarely using endearments and limiting demonstrations of physical affection to the occasional peck on the cheek or touch of a hand. Tessa suspected that it was her natural reticence as well as her belief in the importance of Christian charity that made Olivia accept her own terse explanation of her assumed name and her forged papers with a nod and a murmured, 'I see. Very well.'

Not long after Italy's declaration of war, Olivia ordered the bricklayer and carpenter to wall off certain parts of the cellars and attics, so that food and valuables could be hidden.

Several times she travelled to Florence, to try to use her influence to alter a directive about the requisitioning of crops or the conscription of a peasant woman's husband or son into the army. She wrote daily to Sandro, who was stationed on the Dalmatian coast, and to Guido, in north Africa.

In a house near the *fattoria*, she had established a school for the children of the estate. A health clinic, with four beds, had been set up in the adjacent house. On Tessa's arrival at the villa, Olivia had spoken to her. Was she well, and what of Frederica? Then, businesslike, what work would Tessa prefer to do? She might help at the clinic, for instance, or at the school. Tessa plumped for the school. The clinic was very much Faustina's domain and she did not wish to tread on any toes.

Tessa's bedroom, on the second floor of the house, was high-ceilinged and whitewashed. There was a bed, a chair, a washstand and a cupboard, carved with armorial shields. Shutters kept out the sun in high summer, and thickly lined silk damask curtains contained the warmth in winter. At night, when she could not sleep, Tessa crept silently down to the courtyard in the centre of the villa. The high inner walls of the house surrounded the courtyard, forming the sides of a hollow rectangle. Along the four walls, an arched loggia offered shelter from both sun and rain. On a summer's night, the courtyard garden was magical. The scent of hoya and oleander sweetened the air, and the lemons growing on the trees in the terracotta pots hung swollen and heavy, golden in the moonlight. Far above, the rectangle of night sky sparkled with a thousand stars.

Tessa breakfasted, lunched and dined with the Zanettis. The discussion at mealtimes tended to revolve around the practical – the weather, the harvest, the difficulty in obtaining this or that – before turning to the deeper businesses of politics, religion and philosophy. The conversation of the Zanetti women was coolly intelligent, a surgical filleting of a subject until all facets were rigorously exposed, without acrimony. Doors were never slammed, tables were never stormed off from. Tessa's opinion would be courteously asked for, politely listened to, and then taken apart, piece by piece. Then Olivia would fold her napkin, press her hands together and say grace before leaving the table to go back to work.

At the school, Tessa was Signora Granelli's assistant. Signora Granelli taught the younger children. Tessa gave out paper and crayons, helped the pupils form their letters, and washed hands and faces.

Faustina Zanetti was thin-faced and sallow, and her limp, fine brown hair fell over intelligent grey eyes. Because the school and the clinic were side by side, Tessa and Faustina sometimes walked back to the villa together at the end of the day.

They were heading up the stony track one afternoon when Faustina said, 'When the war is over, I shall become a doctor. I shall study in Bologna or Parma – or Paris or Edinburgh, if need be.' She sniffed. 'I always wanted to go to university, but my father wouldn't let me. He didn't think a girl needed to study. Girls marry, that's what he thought.' She shrugged. 'Girls like you might marry, but not girls like me.'

'I've never married,' said Tessa. 'I've never wanted to.'

Faustina glared at her. Then she gave a snort of laughter. 'Apart from the unfortunate Signor Bruno.'

'Apart from him,' Tessa conceded with a smile. 'And I can't say he's much mourned.'

'I should like to be a surgeon.' Faustina walked on with long, fast strides. 'Dottore Berardi let me assist him last year when he performed an appendectomy. He thought I might faint, but I didn't.'

Tessa would have said, before she came to the Villa di Belcanto, that she preferred the town to the countryside. She would have said that she found domesticity dull and that she needed change and variety. A part of her had resented Guido's high-handedness in writing to his mother about her; a much larger part had recognized that the dangers of remaining in Florence had increased at the declaration of war.

At the villa, there was little contact with officialdom. In some ways the war existed distantly from the contained, self-sufficient world of the estate. In other ways it affected all of them. Husbands, sons and sweethearts had been conscripted into the army; there was a shortage of food in the cities and a shortage of petrol everywhere. The great events of the war – the German invasion of Russia in June 1941, Russia's consequent entrance into the conflict on the side of the Allies, and the continuing deadly dance of Allied and Axis troops back and forth across the North African desert – were listened to on the wireless, mostly in silence, as they tried to disentangle fact from propaganda. Everyone worried about someone.

On a mantelpiece in the Villa di Belcanto there was a photograph of Guido, Sandro and Faustina taken in the garden of the Zanettis' Florentine palazzo. Faustina scowled in a white dress and straw hat, Sandro looked serious. Only Guido gazed straight at the camera, his hands in his pockets and his shirt collar open, smiling and carefree.

Tessa had never been religious, wasn't sure whether she had been baptized, and if so, into which church, but even so, she prayed for the Zanetti brothers' safety. It couldn't do any harm, and besides, you never knew.

There was a child named Perlita who joined the nursery class in the January of 1942. Her mother, Emilia, worked in the Villa di Belcanto's laundry. On her first morning at school, Perlita stood in the cloakroom in which they kept their outdoor things, her great dark eyes peering out through a curtain of black hair, as the other children took off their coats or shawls and hung them on the pegs. She was wearing a knitted bonnet and mittens as well as her coat. She made no move to undress, but stood, as stiff as a wooden doll, terror in her eyes.

Tessa gently peeled off Perlita's layers of outdoor clothing, then took her by the hand and led her into the classroom. She sat beside Perlita's table for the rest of the day while Signora Granelli taught the class. Perlita did not say a word. When the nursery children were led into the bigger pupils' classroom for singing practice, Tessa held Perlita's hand while Perlita stood mute beside her. In the afternoon, the youngest pupils were given pieces of paper on which animal shapes were drawn, to colour in and cut out. Tessa helped Perlita cut out her lion because the child's small hands were not strong enough to work the scissors. When Tessa left her to help one of the other children, Perlita's gaze followed her, stricken. She had a habit of holding on to Tessa's skirts if Tessa hadn't a free hand. Signora Granelli nicknamed Perlita 'Tessa's shadow'.

After a week passed, Perlita spoke for the first time. Tessa clapped her hands and hugged her. It seemed as much of a triumph as getting your picture on the front cover of *Vogue*. Perlita spoke to Tessa first, and then, as her confidence grew, to Signora Granelli and the other children. One morning, when the children were running round the square of grass that was used as a playground, she went off to play with the other children, glancing back now and then for reassurance. By the time spring came, Perlita joined in the singing and dancing games. She would never be a chatterer, though; she measured her words carefully.

In April, Signora Granelli left the school to return to Pistoia, to nurse her brother, who had been wounded in action in North Africa. Tessa took over the teaching of the nursery class. After each school day had finished, Perlita helped her collect up the wax crayons, putting them in the old biscuit tin they used as a container. 'Are we all done, now?' Tessa would ask, and Perlita would give a solemn nod and slip her hand into Tessa's as they left the classroom.

Dust motes rose in the bands of sunlight that shone through the fanlight as Rebecca unlocked the front door to her mother's house in Abingdon. Inside, the air seemed stale and drained. There was a scattering of post on the tiles;

she put her mother's case by the umbrella stand, scooped up the letters and left them on the hall table.

She went back to the car. 'Here we are, Mummy, home again.' She heard herself adopting the tone of false brightness that, since her mother's illness, seemed to have become customary to her. She suspected that it irritated her mother, too, because Mrs Fainlight sighed heavily as Rebecca helped her out of the passenger seat.

Her mother's health had declined throughout the spring, eventually necessitating an operation – a hysterectomy – at the end of May. Meriel was unable to take time off during term time, so it had fallen to Rebecca to take care of her mother in the weeks after she left the nursing home.

They walked slowly up the front path together, Mrs Fainlight leaning on Rebecca's arm. In the hall, she sniffed and said, 'Oh dear! I would have thought you would have aired the house, Rebecca.'

'There wasn't time, Mummy. I came straight to the nursing home.'

'It seems so unreasonable of that place to keep you there until the last minute.'

Mrs Fainlight always referred to Mayfield Farm as 'that place'. Rebecca thought of pointing out that she had remained at the farm until early that morning because she was needed there to help grow the food that fed the country in wartime. But she did not.

Instead she said briskly, 'I'll give the house a quick once-over when you're settled, Mummy. It'll soon look spick and span.'

Her mother was pulling off her gloves. 'It needs more

than a quick once-over, I'm afraid. Mrs Roberts is a poor substitute for Gibson. I don't think you realize how difficult it's been.'

Mrs Fainlight's maid, Gibson, who had worked for the family since Rebecca and Meriel were children, had died at the end of 1941. Rebecca's search for a live-in help for her mother had been unsuccessful, partly because the wages offered could not match the money a woman might earn in a factory, and partly, Rebecca suspected, because the few candidates she had found had been put off by her mother's unpleasantness during the interview. Eventually Mrs Roberts had been engaged to clean and wash laundry for three hours each morning. But the house looked shabby, Rebecca thought, as she helped her mother up the stairs. All those letters on the hall tiles – it looked as if Mrs Roberts hadn't been round for some time. She would have to have a word.

In the bedroom, she opened a window to let in the fresh air. While she unpacked her mother's suitcase, Mrs Fainlight sat in the pink velvet armchair. She looked thin and tired, and Rebecca felt a wash of pity for her. Then there was the difficult business of helping her mother change into a nightgown. Mrs Fainlight's ideas of propriety were Edwardian, so everyday clothing had to be removed and night attire put on without Rebecca catching sight of any bare flesh. But at last it was done and her mother was tucked up in bed, too exhausted to argue or complain.

'I brought us some eggs from the farm,' Rebecca said. 'Shall I boil you one for lunch, Mummy?' Mrs Fainlight nodded.

Rebecca went downstairs to the kitchen. She boiled an

egg and put it with a piece of bread and butter on the tray, adding some rosebuds in a jug for decoration, and took it upstairs. Returning a quarter of an hour later with a cup of tea, she found the food eaten and her mother fast asleep.

In the kitchen, Rebecca drank her tea and then set about the cleaning. As she swept and polished and mopped, the familiar feeling of guilt, so integral to her relationship with her mother, settled over her. It had seemed sensible for Meriel to visit their mother while she was in the nursing home and for Rebecca to take over afterwards, but perhaps being *sensible* was a poor response to one's mother having a major operation. And yet David and Carlotta couldn't do everything, especially as Carlotta was pregnant and they had only the one land girl at the moment because the other one had German measles. Rebecca's work on the farm was not an indulgence, but a necessity.

But she knew in her heart how little she had looked forward to coming here. The problem was not only her difficult relationship with her mother but the boredom that always accompanied her sojourns in Abingdon. During her marriage to Milo, she had rarely spent more than a few hours at a time in her mother's house. Time seemed to stand still at Hatherden – Hatherden was the name of her mother's house, stolidly, unimaginatively Victorian. In the past, a couple of hours there had been dreadful to her.

But that was then and this was now. If the last few years had taught her nothing else, they had taught her to endure. She was stronger now. She was used to working outside in cold and rain, and she was also used to solitariness – indeed, it had become a part of her. The prospect of spending six weeks with her mother was merely unenticing. She would miss Mayfield.

The war had brought with it many changes. Of Mayfield Farm's original inhabitants, only the Mickleboroughs and Rebecca remained. David Mickleborough, who had been rejected by the armed services for health reasons, now put all his energies into making a success of the farm. They must run it efficiently, or it would be taken away from them. Officials from the local War Agricultural Committee visited regularly, to check that they were using every scrap of cultivable land.

Rebecca still made time to draw. It had become a habit, something she needed to do each day. She didn't feel right if she didn't draw. She remembered Connor gently teasing her for her choice of subject matter – *Is it always pots and pans with you, Rebecca?* Yes, it was, if she was too tired to think of anything else.

Almost two years ago, in the late summer of 1940, Mayfield Farm had found itself in the eye of a storm. The Battle of Britain had been fought in the skies over Kent and Sussex. One image had been burned into Rebecca's mind for ever, that of a plane, screaming and on fire, corkscrewing into the stand of beeches on the brow of the hill that could be seen from the farm's kitchen. She and David had run across the valley to the burning plane, she with her pitchfork in hand, thinking it might be of use. So futile: as they had approached the copse, they had stumbled over twisted pieces of metal from the downed Spitfire. The pilot, who had been twenty years old, had burned to death in the cockpit.

It had been a scene that she had since drawn and painted almost obsessively, and in many different ways. Sometimes the image focused on herself and David, running down the valley, the plane reduced to a grey smudged detail in a corner. In another version a black latticework of trees threaded through a boiling crimson sky. She had used oils for this painting; though she was unconfident of her technique with oils, their use had been necessary to obtain the solidity and density of colour she required. She had written to Connor that she thought she was trying to find the right way of portraying the scene, and he had responded that perhaps it was not quite that, that perhaps she was pointing out that something needed to be said, over and over again, about the death of a twenty-year-old airman in a copse on the High Weald.

She wrote to Connor, in Ireland, regularly. There had been a time when she had felt uncertain, when she had wondered whether her letters might bore him, but as the months and years had passed, her worries had vanished. He seemed to look forward to her letters as much as she looked forward to his. With Connor, to whom she had confided the worst part of herself, she found herself being honest in a way that she could not be with anyone else, even her sister. Her letters were a communication with someone whom she had, oddly, come to know better in his absence, as well as a gradual peeling-away of reserve. She and Connor had both hurt and been hurt; they had that in common.

She had finished cleaning the kitchen and was about to start on the sitting room when the doorbell rang. It was her mother's neighbour, Mrs Ridley. Rebecca showed her into the sitting room and went upstairs. Her mother was sitting up in bed when she came into the room.

'Was that the doorbell?'

'It's Mrs Ridley from next door,' explained Rebecca. 'She called in to see how you were. She's waiting downstairs.'

Mrs Fainlight looked flustered. 'I need to go to the bathroom.'

'I can ask her to come back later if you prefer, Mummy.'

'No, no.' Mrs Fainlight stared at Rebecca. 'I hope you didn't answer the door dressed like that, Rebecca. You look like a labourer!'

'I am a labourer. I work on a farm.' But her mother seemed genuinely upset, so Rebecca, who was wearing needlecord breeches and a cotton shirt, added, 'I've been cleaning, Mummy, that's all. I'm sure Mrs Ridley doesn't mind.'

'And you used to dress so nicely! You were such a pretty girl! Strangers used to stop me in the street and say how pretty you were. You've let yourself go since you've been at that place. It'll be hard enough at your age anyway, but if you look like that you'll never find another man.'

'I don't want to find another man.' Rebecca struggled to keep calm. 'One was enough.'

Mrs Fainlight muttered balefully, 'I always knew he wasn't good enough for you.'

Rebecca felt a rush of annoyance. 'Milo?' she said. 'Then you were right. Shall I help you to the bathroom?'

While Mrs Ridley was sitting with her mother, Rebecca took the opportunity to go to the shops. It was a fine, bright early summer's day, her favourite time of year. Clematis straggled over fences and her irritation faded as she walked into the centre of town. At the nursing home, the doctor had told her that a small tumour had been found in her mother's womb. The surgeon hoped that the hysterectomy would arrest the disease, but . . . The sentence had been left unfinished. Her mother appeared to believe that she would recover fully. It had occurred to Rebecca that she was trying not to worry her, but then her mother had always had a talent for ignoring difficult situations, so it could equally well be that. Whatever lay behind her refusal to discuss her illness, Rebecca felt she must respect it. Another item, she thought, to add to the list of things they never spoke about.

Back at the house, she showed Mrs Ridley out and unpacked her purchases. Her mother always kept her ration book inside her handbag. Opening the navy-blue bag, Rebecca breathed in face powder and eau de cologne, scents she had associated with her mother since childhood. As a girl, Rebecca had considered it a treat to be allowed to play with her mother's handbag, to take out the lipstick, compact, purse, notepad and little gold-tasselled pencil. It had seemed to her a repository of feminine mystique.

Feminine mystique seemed in short supply these days. There was her mother, womb-less and in pain, and there was she, with her breeches and calloused hands. She zipped the ration book into its compartment and clipped the handbag shut.

Mrs Fainlight recovered slowly from her operation. After the first few days, she insisted on dressing after breakfast and coming downstairs. In the afternoon, if it was fine, she dozed in a deckchair in the garden or they tackled the short walk to the postbox at the end of the street.

As her mother recovered, so did her critical spirit. Faults were found in Rebecca's housekeeping and cooking. Rebecca's clumsiness meant that there was too much noise, and her heavy footsteps woke Mrs Fainlight from her nap. These were old complaints, Rebecca having shot up in her teens so that she had become several inches taller than both her mother and Meriel, and her shoes three sizes larger. At fifteen and sixteen her mental image of herself had been of a lumbering, elephantine creature, when she would have liked to have been dainty. Only the discovery that boys admired her height and didn't give a damn about her shoe size had made her feel better.

Mrs Fainlight liked to stay up for dinner rather than take it in bed, though by that time of day she was tired and cantankerous. Rebecca made an effort, doing her hair and dressing for dinner, laying a tablecloth and napkins in the dining room. It depressed her that entire courses would pass by without any conversation between them other than requests to pass the salt or enquiries as to whether the food was all right, invariably answered by her mother with a grudging assent. The clink of cutlery, the scrape of a chair became unnaturally loud in the silence. Her mother seemed to find the meals difficult as well, because after the first few evenings she allowed the wireless to be put on while they ate. Even the succession of dismal news items – the fall of Tobruk to Axis forces in the third week of June had been particularly dispiriting – was an improvement, Rebecca felt, on the chink of glasses and the ticking of the grand-father clock.

The doctor called daily for the first week and every other day after that. Her mother's church had set up a rota of visitors, who called most afternoons. In their company, Mrs Fainlight softened and became less disapproving.

It was one of the congregation's visits that sparked off their quarrel – no, not a quarrel, Rebecca thought after-wards, but an explosion of long-suppressed acrimony. The visitor, a Mrs Macdonald, a toothy, earnest woman in her mid-twenties, had brought with her her baby son, Peter. Peter was a delightful little thing of fourteen months, who had just learned to walk and toddled round the garden pointing and exclaiming in nonsense language at the flowers and the neighbour's cat.

After their visitors had gone, Mrs Fainlight fell asleep in an armchair in the sun room. Waking after an hour, she scolded Rebecca for allowing her to sleep too long.

'I thought you could do with the rest, Mummy.'

'You know I find it difficult to sleep at night if I have too long a nap in the afternoon. And you've left the milk out, I can see it in the garden. Really, Rebecca, I'm not made of money, and we shall run out of coupons.'

Rebecca went out into the garden to fetch the tray. Coming back to the house, she put the kettle on and made tea. She took a cup to her mother, who looked at it suspiciously.

'I hope you haven't used the milk you left out in the garden.'

'Of course not, Mummy. I used cold, straight from the larder.'

Rebecca drank her own tea in the kitchen. Other mothers and daughters would have sat together, she thought, chatting about this and that. She felt a surge of envy for those families, and a wash of bitterness at her own situation. There was something about her that irritated her mother, she concluded, some fundamental ill-matching of character. The three hours before dinner stretched endlessly ahead of her.

She took a deep breath and went back into the sun room. 'Shall we play cards, Mummy?'

'I don't approve of card games, Rebecca.'

'Just for fun, I meant. I'm not suggesting we gamble our life savings away.'

She had meant it as a joke, but it sounded sarcastic. Her mother puckered her lips. 'You know perfectly well that when you were married to Milo you used to play for money.'

'Sixpences.'

'I suppose it's some compensation. At least you've stopped gambling.'

Rebecca became still. 'Some compensation for the divorce, do you mean?'

'Yes.' Mrs Fainlight shifted uneasily in her chair. 'I haven't told the church. I thought I'd best not.'

'Are you ashamed of me, Mummy?'

'There is no need for anyone to know, that's all.'

'It's all right, I promise I won't go into the sordid details with the old biddies from St Andrew's.'

'There's no need to be unpleasant, Rebecca.'

'I'm not. I'm merely stating a fact.'

There was a taut silence. Mrs Fainlight sat in her chair, rigidly furious. Then the words burst out of her.

'If only there had at least been a child! That dear little boy! That would have made up for some of it.'

Rebecca's fury bubbled up and boiled over. 'A child?' she repeated. 'Do you want to know why there wasn't a child? I'll tell you! It was because I couldn't have one!' Her voice rose. 'All those years we were married and not bothering to take any precautions –'

'*Rebecca!*'

'– and nothing happened! Milo has a child now, did you know that, Mummy?'

Mrs Fainlight looked frightened. 'No,' she whispered.

'Well he has! He married again, eighteen months ago. I didn't tell you because I knew you would crow. He married an American girl and he's teaching at an American university and they have a baby daughter called Helen. So if there wasn't a child, it was my fault, not Milo's. Just mine!'

Rebecca left the room. She took her jacket from a peg and walked out of the kitchen, concentrating all her will on not slamming the door.

Beyond Hatherden's back gardens lay fields. As she skirted a cornfield, the sea of wheat was blurred by the tears in her eyes. Her hand shook as she blew her nose.

She had learned of Milo's remarriage from Milo himself. He had written to tell her that he was marrying a girl named Mona Greer, whom he had met in Boston, where he was now a visiting professor. Rebecca supposed Mona Greer had been one of his students.

It had been Roger Thoday, Milo's editor, who had told

her about the child. She had run into Roger in Hatchards, one day when she was in London, visiting Simone Campbell. Milo and Mona, Roger had said, had a baby daughter called Helen. 'Didn't think you'd want to find out from the back flap of a book,' he had added. 'Not that it isn't damned difficult to publish anything these days, and Milo's last two haven't done so well, I'm afraid.'

A child. A daughter. *Helen Rycroft*. Rebecca had told herself she didn't mind. Milo was nothing to do with her now. And so typical of him, she thought, to cut and run to America when the war made things difficult at home.

Now, as she stumbled along the edge of the field, she wondered whether she did mind, after all. Milo had a prestigious appointment at an American university, a new wife and a baby daughter. The child to replace the child who had been lost. While she was still floundering, Milo had a new life. She had nothing.

She crossed a small patch of woodland and then found herself on a track between tall hedgerows festooned with honeysuckle and dog roses. It had not rained for a week and the mud on the rutted track had hardened. Rebecca walked on, her hurt and self-pity ebbing away with the tread of her feet on the ground. She did have something. She had plenty. She had an occupation and an art that increasingly absorbed her. She loved her sister and she loved her friends. She had her correspondence with Connor, which she treasured. She did not know what the future would bring, but then why should she? Few of them did, these days.

As for her mother . . . It was possible, wasn't it, that her mother had always seen failings in Milo to which she herself had for a long time been blind. It was also possible that some of her mother's tart remarks were born of protectiveness – that beneath the cantankerousness and criticism love might exist. Rebecca looked at her watch. It was a quarter past six. What would her angel tell her to do now? She tried to picture his face, his kind, gentle smile. He would tell her to go back to the house and cook dinner, she thought. And that she must keep trying, even though she and her mother grated on each other's nerves.

Slowly, taking her time, she walked back along the track, through the wood and along the edge of the field, then let herself in through the garden gate.

Mrs Fainlight was in the kitchen, at the sink, an apron round her waist, peeling potatoes. She looked up as Rebecca came in.

'I thought I'd get this out of the way.'

Rebecca recognized this as a peace offering. 'It's good of you, Mummy,' she said, 'but you mustn't tire yourself out.'

She took off her jacket and hung it on the peg. Then she floured the mackerel and chopped up a spring cabbage. They stood side by side as they worked. After a while, her mother said suddenly, 'These potatoes are quite rubbery. I've been very disappointed with Mr Wright's vegetables recently,' and Rebecca said, 'I thought I could dig you a little vegetable plot, Mummy. There's plenty of room in the border by the coal shed, and Meriel could nip over to do the weeding after I go back to Mayfield.'

Later, when Mrs Fainlight had gone to bed, Rebecca sat

at the kitchen table, drawing the wild flowers she had picked on her way back to the house. She had drunk a sherry and taken an aspirin and felt better. There was the sweep of her pencil on the paper, and, in the darkening midsummer evening, a distant music from someone's radio, seeping over the quiet gardens and through the open kitchen door.

Max's flat was above a grocery shop in Frith Street. Upstairs, on the landing, a small boy was playing with a toy train, kneeling on the floor as with great concentration he pushed the train along and made chuffing sounds.

Freddie rapped on Max's door. 'It's me! I know you're in there.' No response, so she gave an extra-loud knock. 'Max! Open the door!'

She heard the unsliding of a bolt. The child picked up his train and ran downstairs.

The door opened. Max looked angry. 'Come to check up on me?'

'I came to see how you were.'

'I am, as you see, tip-top.'

He made to shut the door. Freddie stuck her foot in it. Through the aperture she saw his room, the books, papers and clothing scattered over the floor, the empty bottles on the table.

'Oh yes,' she said crossly. 'Tip-bloody-top. You look awful, Max.'

'Go away, Freddie. Find someone else to fuss over.'

'Max.'

'Go away.'

'I won't.'

375

His eyes narrowed. 'I assume this is some sort of mercy visit.'

'Ray told me that you and Marcelle had split up.'

'I'm sure you know perfectly well that we haven't *split up*. Marcelle *dropped* me.' Max's lip curled. His gaze, bloodshot and contemptuous, rested on her. 'There are times when you remind me of Tessa. That same inability to face up to reality.'

She said nothing at first, but then she nodded. 'Okay. If that's how you feel.'

She had reached the top of the stairs when she heard him sigh. She looked back.

'Forgive me, Freddie. I'm a pig. I don't know why you bother with me. Come in, please. I'll make you coffee.'

Max's room smelled of stale cigarette ash and alcohol. As he filled the kettle and searched for clean mugs, Freddie looked through the mist of condensation on the windowpane to the street outside. Stair rods of rain fell from a charcoal-grey sky. It was late evening and shadows seeped into the boarded-up shop windows, spreading out towards the sandbagged buildings. There had been an excitement to the Blitz, a vividness that had persisted in spite of fear and discomfort. Since the Luftwaffe had turned its attention to the vast expanses of Russia, the raids on London had been far less frequent and severe, but fatigue and rationing and dreariness continued.

Freddie said, 'What happened?'

Max shrugged. 'Nothing much. We quarrelled. I can't remember the details. It would have gone something like this – I would have said or done something that annoyed

376

her, and she would have made a scene about something, anything, and I would have told her she was a spoiled brat. And then she would have told me to get lost.' He gave a crooked smile. 'I make myself ridiculous, reduced to foolishness by a girl half my age.'

'I don't see that age matters.'

'Experience should, surely? The rational part of me has always known that Marcelle and I have no chance of lasting. I know that for her I've always been some sort of second best. I am too old, too ugly, too foreign.' He waved a hand, cutting off her response. 'I'm afraid it's true, Freddie.'

She saw his hand shake as he spooned coffee into mugs. 'Oh, Max,' she said. 'How much have you had to drink?'

'Too much. Not enough. It's my vice. We all have our vices, Freddie, even you. Milk?'

'Please.'

He opened a bottle, sniffed it and made a face.

'It doesn't matter,' she said. 'Black is fine.'

He gave her a mug of coffee, then looked under cushions and ran a hand through the pockets of his jacket. 'Where are my cigarettes? You don't have any, do you, Freddie? No? Perhaps you don't have any vices after all.' He found a battered packet and extracted a cigarette from it. 'I don't know what Marcelle wants,' he said quietly. 'I'm not sure she does herself. She is a beautiful, interesting and troubled girl, who likes to pick quarrels. After all, it's not the first time we've split up.' He began another search, this time for matches, throwing papers and jackets aside, adding to the dishevelment of the room. 'She quarrels to take her mind off her anxiety about her father, yes, of course. And perhaps because she enjoys the sense of power it gives her. Not long ago, I took some photographs of her. She was wearing her coat with the fur collar. She looked like the Snow Queen. I expect I have a splinter of ice in my heart.'

'Poor Max.'

'No, not at all.' He struck a match. 'I don't deserve your sympathy, Freddie. Knowing all this, I still want her. She breaks my heart. As I said, I am ridiculous.'

'Shall I help you clear up a bit?'

'Certainly not. Sit down. Talk to me. There are so many other things that I should mind about far more than a silly, selfish girl.'

Freddie cleared a square of sofa and sat down. 'I'm not sure it works like that.'

'I have many friends and relations in Germany. I have no idea what's happened to them. I don't know whether they are alive or dead. Sometimes I feel like weeping for them. But the truth is, *she* occupies more of my thoughts.' He gave Freddie a keen look. 'I'm sorry for what I said about Tessa. I'm just a bitter old man. You know that I loved Tessa very much. I don't suppose you've heard anything?'

Freddie sighed. 'I had that first letter in 1940, and then another little note, very dog-eared, six months later. They were both sent via Tessa's friend in Sweden, and neither of them said very much, just that she was well and safe. She didn't mention any names – I suppose she's afraid of getting people into trouble. And since then, nothing, I'm afraid.' She felt as she always did when she thought of Tessa, a terrible sense of loss as well as fear. 'But I know what you mean, Max. I mind if I can't find a seat on the bus and I mind when I've run out of shampoo and there's none in the shops. Even though the only thing I really want is to know that Tessa's all right.' She took a mouthful of coffee. It tasted bitter, of chicory. Then she said, 'Actually, I've come to say goodbye.'

'You're going away?'

'I'm being posted to Birmingham. I'm going to train to be a mechanic — they're going to teach me how to make aeroplanes.'

'Good God.' His brows rose. 'No more shuffling paper in the War Office, then?'

'I've been sick of it for ages. And I'm an unskilled mobile woman, I'm afraid, so I can be sent anywhere. It's rather a depressing description, don't you think?'

'And deeply inaccurate.' His eyes, a kind and tender brown, studied her. 'Will you like making aeroplanes, do you think, Freddie?'

'I hope so. I'll mind leaving my friends, though.' She smiled at him. 'Even the bad-tempered ones. I'm trying to say goodbye to everyone before I go.'

He took out another cigarette and tapped it against the packet. 'Do you plan to see Marcelle?'

'Yes, I should think so.'

'Would you take her a message from me?'

'Max . . .'

'She won't answer my phone calls. Please, Freddie.'

She ached for him. His black hair had greyed at the sides and needed cutting. There were bluish shadows round his eyes. His face was thin and angular; he had the look, Freddie thought, of a tired and rather ragged crow.

She said, 'I will if you want, of course, but mightn't it be a better idea to wait for her to contact you?'

'Play hard to get, you mean?'

'Let her stew. She might appreciate you more. Why don't you wait for her to apologize to you?'

'Because she won't. Not ever. I know this.' Max looked desperately sad as well as a little ashamed. 'I know that I love her more than she loves me. So I will go on running after her like a faithful little dog, even though it makes her despise me.'

She couldn't stop herself saying, 'But is that sort of love worth having?'

'If it's all that's on offer, then yes.'

Freddie left a quarter of an hour later with Max's note in her pocket. She caught the tube to South Kensington and headed on foot from there to Cheyne Walk in Chelsea. She caught the rotting, oily scent of the river as she neared Marcelle Scott's house. There were two planks nailed across the front door so Freddie ran down the basement steps and rapped on the kitchen window.

Marcelle let her in. She was wearing a black cocktail dress; around her neck she wore a jade necklace that echoed the green of her eyes. 'Freddie,' she said, and offered a cheek to be kissed.

The kitchen was large and cold. Betty Mulholland, in a pale blue slip, was standing by the sink, pinning her hair into curls and dabbing them with sugar solution to set.

'Lewis is asleep upstairs,' said Marcelle.

Freddie remembered Lewis Coryton from that night at the Dorchester, his dark hair and elfin features.

'We're trying to be terribly quiet,' whispered Betty. 'Poor Lewis hasn't had any sleep for weeks. He's on the Atlantic crossings, you see. He's had an awful time.'

Freddie explained about being sent to the Midlands. Betty exclaimed and said wasn't it awful, she was being posted to Plymouth, miles and miles away from Frances, who was at an airbase in East Anglia. Then she went upstairs to dress.

Marcelle was putting away clean crockery. Freddie took Max's letter out of her pocket. 'Max gave me this for you.'

'You've seen him?'

'Yes, just now.' She waited for Marcelle to ask her how Max was; when she didn't, Freddie said anyway, 'He's not good.'

Marcelle put a soup tureen on a shelf and shut the cupboard door. Then she slit open the envelope. Briefly she scanned the note, then dropped it on the kitchen table and went back to putting away dishes.

Freddie said, 'Will you speak to him?'

'I don't know. I may do.'

'He misses you.'

'I'd rather not talk about it, actually.'

'I want to talk about it.'

Marcelle said softly, 'It's no business of yours, Freddie.'

'But it is. Max is my friend.'

'Of course, I'd forgotten. Max Fischer, the great friend of the Nicolson sisters.' There was mockery in Marcelle's voice.

Max had been in love with Tessa for years, but Freddie couldn't remember ever seeing him as unhappy then as he was now. The difference had been, Freddie thought, that

Tessa hadn't been unkind to him. Never intentionally, anyway.

Marcelle was polishing knives with a tea towel. Her hair fell in smooth coils to her shoulders and her fingernails were painted with the bright red polish she always wore. Freddie wondered where she found such nail polish in wartime – or had she hoarded it, dozens of bright red bottles to last her through till peace was declared?

'If you don't care for him,' she said, 'then wouldn't it be kinder to tell him so, once and for all?'

Marcelle turned to look at her. 'I'm very fond of Max.' Her cheeks had turned pink.

'I don't think being fond is enough. He *loves* you. Don't you see, when it's like that, it's no good. That's when people get hurt, really, dreadfully hurt.'

The kitchen door opened. Lewis Coryton, wrapped in a red silk dressing gown that presumably belonged to Marcelle, stood in the hallway, blinking.

'*Desperate* for a cup of tea,' he said.

'I'll make you some, darling Lewis.' Marcelle filled the kettle.

Lewis frowned at Freddie. 'I remember. Freddie something – Freddie *Nicolson*.'

'Hello, Lewis.' She offered him her hand.

'You were at the Dorchester,' he said. 'You were wearing a long black frock and you had a purple necklace, like damsons.'

'Such an elephantine memory, Lewis,' said Marcelle acidly.

Freddie felt pleased that Lewis remembered her. She recalled that she had thought him a good-looking man,

382

back then. He was still good-looking, even with his hair tousled and wearing the ridiculous red dressing gown.

Betty hurried back into the room. 'My earrings. Have you seen my earrings?'

'On the windowsill,' said Marcelle.

Betty threaded diamonds into her ear lobes. 'Are you coming with us, Freddie? Denny's going to be there. And Clare, isn't she, Lewis? And what about those RAF boys we met on the train?'

'They said they'd come.' Marcelle poured boiling water into the teapot.

'Jack?' asked Betty.

'I don't think so.'

'Stockings,' muttered Betty. 'I must find a decent pair of stockings.' She dashed upstairs again.

Marcelle poured out a cup of tea and gave it to Lewis. Lewis said, 'I'd better go and have a bath. Good to see you again, Freddie. You'll be around tonight, won't you?'

She gave a non-committal reply. When Lewis had gone, Freddie said to Marcelle, 'You've seen Jack?'

'My cousin Jack? Yes, of course.' As she poured out the tea, Marcelle frowned. 'You know him a little, don't you? I'd forgotten.'

'He's been in London?'

'Yes, for weeks. We've had such a mad time. I'm quite worn out with parties and things.' Marcelle's voice was hard and glassy. 'I'm hoping he'll fall in love with Frances. With Jack's fair hair and Francie's red, they'd have such beautiful children, don't you think?' She took a lipstick and compact out of her bag. 'Do you want to come tonight,

383

Freddie? I expect I could dig out something that might fit you.'

'No thanks. I'm quite tired, actually. I think I'll have an early night.'

Freddie left shortly afterwards. It was still raining, so she put up the hood of her mackintosh and dug her hands into her pockets as she walked.

For the first time, she found herself longing to leave London. She had existed on the periphery of Jack and Marcelle's crowd since that night at the Dorchester. Now, walking through the rain, she felt a powerful antipathy towards Marcelle. Though rationally she knew that Max's misery was in part self-inflicted, she despised Marcelle's carelessness towards him. There was a detachment that characterized Marcelle, that made it easy, perhaps, for her to wound. And didn't Jack, who was Marcelle's cousin, betray a similar quality? She had been useful to Jack, back in 1939, but he had dropped her as soon as he no longer needed her. Perhaps she shouldn't feel hurt that he had been in London and had not contacted her, as he had promised, but she did. The memory of their flight from Florence to France remained vivid for her, but he, she suspected, had forgotten it as soon as they had parted. On the boat sailing for France, he had said to her, *We could always run away together.* What would have happened if she had said yes? Might they be living in Buenos Aires or Valparaiso, he earning a living doing something raffish and disreputable, she with a gardenia tucked behind an ear, drinking cocktails on a beach? Or would he have moved on after a month or two, freeing himself from anything that had even a tang of permanence?

But was she all that different? The thought discomforted her. Her relationship with Angus had ended three months after they had first become lovers, after she had turned down his proposal of marriage. She had loved him, but she had not loved him enough. Since then, though she had had boyfriends – a soldier she had met in a dance hall, a Canadian airman she had got talking to one day on the bus – the friendships had never lasted long. The soldier had been posted to Devon and the airman had been shot down, flying his bomber over Germany. Her longest relationship had been with an American journalist who had been staying in London to report on the impact of the war on Britain. It had been he who had broken it off. 'You're a nice girl, Freddie,' he had said to her at the end of an evening, 'and a beautiful one, too, but I feel as if I'm talking to you through a glass wall. You English. Nothing touches you, does it? It's almost as if you're waiting for something, but I've no idea what. Not me, for sure. You've put up your defences and you're damned if you're going to let anyone breach them.'

Tessa had believed that marriage was to be avoided at all costs; had she, observing her sister's example, come to the conclusion that it was love that must be avoided, rather than marriage? Or was it simply that she was waiting, as her American journalist had said, for something – to see Tessa again? – and that all that waiting and hoping took up most of her emotional energy.

She minded that Max had said 'loved' and not 'love', as if Tessa existed now only in the past. She minded that Ray, who had once been in love with Tessa, now rarely mentioned her. She minded most of all that, after three years of separation, the remembered Tessa seemed to have faded, so that now, when she tried to picture her, she saw more and more often the images that existed in photographs and magazines. As if Tessa was solidifying, freezing, caught in that particular time of her life, cut off from her future.

She couldn't wait to leave London, she thought. She wanted to start again, to be with new people, doing new things. She flung back the hood of her raincoat and ran down the steps to the tube.

Chapter Twelve

Maddalena Zanetti was sitting on a sofa in the *salotto*, the drawing room of the villa. Olivia was beside her, while Faustina sprawled in an armchair. Guido was walking up and down the room, his little daughter on his shoulders. Every time he walked beneath a chandelier, Luciella reached up and tried to touch it, and then Guido roared out a warning and Luciella shrieked with excitement.

'You'll overtire her, my dear,' said Maddalena. 'She won't eat her supper.'

Guido swung his daughter, helpless with laughter, down to the floor. Tessa sat on the rug beside her. While Luciella showed Tessa her dolls' tea service – the tiny cups, saucers and plates made from bone china and painted with flowers – behind them a conversation went on. There was a tension, Tessa thought, between Guido and his wife, a lack of unity, a tendency to confute her remarks on his side, and to silence on hers. The same tension had existed earlier that day, when the family had lunched together shortly after Guido,

387

Maddalena, the child and her nurse had arrived at the villa. Yes, Maddalena had told them, her parents were well. Yes, things were difficult in the cities just now, with food shortages and suchlike, but she hoped they would soon improve. From Guido there had been a contemptuous snort, and Olivia, to smooth things over, had reminded them that she would, of course, give them food to take back to Florence.

Guido had been shipped back to Italy in the middle of the year, having been wounded in North Africa. Olivia and Faustina had visited him, first at the military hospital, and then in Florence. Now, he had two weeks' leave, after which he would return to the army.

'So wonderful,' said Olivia, 'for you to be here, Guido.'

Faustina, who liked to stir, said, 'I think Guido's raring to go. I think he prefers to be heroic.'

'Hardly *heroic*,' said Guido sharply, glaring at Faustina. 'Merely not cowering in some backwater, like a mouse in a hole.'

Faustina twisted a lock of lank hair around a finger. 'You always were hopeless at being bored, Guido.'

'I'd choose danger over boredom any day.'

'The rest of us have to put up with it, you know.' Faustina shuffled upright to grab a biscuit from a plate. 'Women especially. Most of what women have to do is very boring.'

'Besides, it's not a question of boredom. It's a question of *honour*.'

Maddalena said quietly, 'Guido, not now.'

Guido picked up a tiny silver spoon, then put it down again. 'I would prefer to return to North Africa.' His voice was taut. 'Maddalena doesn't want me to.'

'Is that so unreasonable?' Suddenly Maddalena's eyes blazed. 'Why should I want you to be sent to the front? Why should I want you to be killed, Guido? Of what possible benefit would that be to either Luciella or me?'

'I dislike being manipulated. I dislike—'

'Guido,' said Tessa softly.

Maddalena stood up. 'What is more important to you? Your wife and child – or your honour?'

'That's unfair,' said Guido coldly. 'You know it is.'

'If you will excuse me, Olivia.' Maddalena's voice shook. 'Luciella must have her supper. And I have a headache.' She swept the child up into her arms and walked out of the door.

Olivia murmured, 'The heat . . .'

There was a long silence. Then: 'I'm sorry, Mother,' said Guido. Rising, he too left the room.

It was the end of the first week of September and it had not rained for a month. Dusty white roads snaked up hillsides of bleached dry grass, while above, high in a metallic blue sky, the sun was a flat pale disc. Inside the villa, curtains hung limply in the humid air and sunlight squeezed through the slats in the shutters to fall in blazing stripes on the floor.

There was, Tessa thought that evening, the scent of disaster in the air. Maddalena, her face white and angry, had bundled the child, her nurse and their cases into the car, and had driven off to her parents' country home near Impruneta. Guido had not come out to the courtyard to see them off.

Later, after dinner, the family listened to the wireless. Reports told of an Axis defeat in North Africa, at Alam

389

Halfa. A temporary setback, the newsreader claimed, but after Olivia had switched off the wireless, they sat in the airless heat, finding little to talk about.

Tessa could not sleep that night. In the early hours of the morning, she put on a pair of slacks and a sleeveless top and went downstairs. In the kitchen, she poured herself a glass of water, then cupped her hands beneath the tap, splashing the cold water on her face and running her wet hands through her hair. Leaving the kitchen, she walked through rooms and passageways. The marble floors were cool beneath her bare feet, and from the centre of the house, a light drew her towards the courtyard garden.

Guido was sitting on a stone bench between the terra-cotta pots, in the paved square that was open to the night sky. An oil lamp stood beneath the arches of the loggia; moths fluttered around it, dusty and copper-coloured. Softly Tessa said his name.

Guido turned. 'Tessa,' he said. 'Couldn't you sleep either?'

'It's too hot.' She put down the glass of water and sat on the bench beside him. 'This sort of weather always feels as if it's building up to something.'

'There's going to be a thunderstorm. Look.'

Gazing up at the rectangle of sky above them, she saw that the stars were now masked by clouds.

'I went out for a walk,' said Guido. 'Had to clear my head.'

'How's your leg?'

'Fine. It still aches a bit, but the doctors said walking was the best thing.' He rolled up his right trouser leg. His calf was a patchwork of scars, livid and red, the tissue lumpy and uneven where the cuts and gashes had knitted together.

Tessa remembered Guido swimming in the pool at the Villa Millefiore, how she had liked to watch the smooth movement of his perfectly muscled limbs, and how, when he had climbed out of the pool, the water had beaded and slid from his tanned skin.

'Poor Guido,' she said.

'I was lucky. I didn't lose the leg.'

'It must have hurt.'

'A hell of a lot, then they gave me morphine.' Suddenly, he laughed. 'What a pair we are – walking wounded.'

Reaching out a hand, he brushed back her fringe and ran his thumb across the scar on her forehead. She had to bite her lip to stop herself flinching.

'You are as beautiful as you always were,' he said gently. 'Never believe anything else.'

She shook her head, looking down.

'And you, Tessa – apart from your head, where were you hurt?'

'My leg, my arm . . . my collarbone.'

'Here, too, I think.' Guido fisted his hand and put it to his ribs, where his heart was.

She said, 'You shouldn't have let Maddalena leave on her own. You should have gone with her.'

'Perhaps.'

'Not perhaps, certainly. She was worried about you. Can you blame her?'

'Tessa, keep out of what you don't understand.' He sounded angry.

'I understand that Maddalena loves you and cares for you.'

Rising, Guido went to stand a couple of yards away, looking up at the sky. 'The clouds are thickening.' She sensed him trying to control his annoyance. 'Don't you just long for rain?'

A breeze rippled the leaves of the oleanders and lemon trees. Tessa shook back her hair, loving the feel of the cool air on her bare arms and face. 'I'm never tired of the sun,' she said. 'I lived too long in England.'

Guido took his cigarette case out of his jacket pocket and offered it to her. Tessa heard the click of his lighter and saw the light flare in the darkness. The leaves whispered as the breeze got up strength, spiralling into the courtyard.

He sat back down beside her. 'It isn't the first time Maddalena and I have argued. In fact' – he gave an unamused laugh – 'it's getting to be a habit.'

'That's because you've been apart for so long. And because you've been so unwell. It must have been frightening for her. Fear can make people angry.'

Guido stared out at the courtyard, his eyes brooding. 'We always quarrel about the same thing. Maddalena's father is very wealthy. He's never had to work for his living. He's the sort of man who always knows the right people, and who always says the right thing to them. I despise him.'

'You must have known what he was like when you married Maddalena.'

'I suppose so.' He made an irritated gesture. 'I didn't think it mattered then. I didn't think it mattered to us.'

'But it does now?'

'A word in his ear and I could be posted off to the back of beyond in the foothills of the Alps, where the most dangerous thing I'd have to do would be to chase after the odd peasant who was trying to evade excise duties.'

'And Maddalena would like you to do that?'

'Yes. But I can't, Tessa. I couldn't live with myself. Honour . . .' Guido gave a sour laugh. 'What a pompous ass I must have sounded this afternoon. The men who started this war, who pursue it, haven't a shred of honour. God knows what will happen if we suffer another defeat in the desert. There's a limit to how many more troops Germany can send there. They're overextended already, they're fighting on too many fronts at once, and right now they need every man they have in Russia.' He fell silent, then said, 'A cold wind always comes before a change in the weather. I can feel the weather turning. The British know the Americans are waiting in the wings. All those men, all those planes and tanks and guns. If the Allies take North Africa, what will happen then?'

Tessa thought of the map of the Mediterranean, the bead necklace of islands strung out between the North African coast and the toe of Italy.

'You think they'll come here?'

'Yes, I do.'

'What does Maddalena think?'

'She's never had much interest in politics. I felt the same when I was younger. But now I can't help feeling it's an affectation to claim to have no interest.' He gave a wry smile. 'I've fallen out with my wife over a war I've never believed in. No wonder she finds me infuriating. But, you see, my men are still out there, in the desert. They're putting up with hardships my father-in-law and his kind can't even imagine. And I owe it to them to go back.' He flicked ash on the paving stones. 'When Maddalena was packing to leave, we quarrelled again. She said to me . . .' He broke off, shaking his head.

'What, Guido?'

He picked up a leaf that had blown on to the paving stones and crushed it in his fist. 'She said that if I wouldn't stay in Italy for her, wouldn't I at least consider doing so for Luciella.'

'Oh, Guido.'

'I told her that what I was doing *was* for her and Luciella. What sort of a father – what sort of a husband – would I be if I turned my back on everything I believe in? In loyalty, in trust – if I betrayed *that*?' He waited for Tessa to speak; when she did not, he said bitterly, 'You're a woman. I expect you sympathize with Maddalena.'

'I do. But I sympathize with you, too, Guido.' She frowned. 'I used to think I was living according to my principles. I was rather proud of them. My principles weren't the same as other people's, but that didn't matter to me.'

'And now?'

'My principles almost destroyed me. I don't know that I care about that sort of thing any more.'

'You don't seem to me to have changed all that much, Tessa. You're quieter – sadder, too. But underneath, much the same.'

She stubbed out her cigarette in a plant pot. 'Perhaps I should have gone back to England.'

'Perhaps you belong here.'

'Perhaps.' She shrugged. 'I understand loyalty better now. It's taken me a long time, but I do. I used to think that if a love affair turned sour, then you should walk away from it, move on. That you shouldn't get tied down. That was what my childhood taught me, so that's what I did, every time. I thought I was being loyal to myself, that I was being loyal to my principles.'

'And then?' When she did not respond, he said, 'There is an "and then", isn't there, Tessa?'

'Eventually I met someone I couldn't walk away from.' She hunched up her knees, wrapping her arms round them. 'He was clever, handsome and charming. And he was married. I knew a lot of men who were clever, handsome and charming, and several of them were married. I told myself it wasn't a problem because I didn't want to take them away from their wives.' She looked up at the sky. 'How we fool ourselves when we fall in love. Perhaps it was because of the moon and the frost. Sometimes there seemed to be a kind of enchantment in those quiet English places.'

'What happened?'

'Nothing good,' she said sadly.

A crackle of lightning lit the courtyard with a lavender glow. 'I hope it pours,' Guido said, looking up. 'We could do with a good downpour.'

'Stefano will be worrying about hail, because of the grapes.'

'So you're becoming a countrywoman, Tessa. Well, well, I'd never have imagined it.' His voice was gently mocking. Then he sighed and said, 'Who knows why we fall in love? The moon and the frost are as good a reason as any.

I know what you must think – Maddalena and I, child-hood friends, wealthy family. You must think we married for dynastic reasons, that we married to suit our families.'

'No, Guido.' Her tone was fond. 'I know you. You would have married for love.'

There was a distant rumble of thunder, like someone moving furniture in an empty room. And between them, a sense of shared loss, of awareness of what could have been.

'If Mussolini were to be deposed,' said Guido, 'that would hurt Maddalena's family. They have been loyal patriots. You say you understand loyalty, Tessa, so tell me what I should do. Should I stay here with my family, so I can protect them if things go wrong for them, or should I return to the desert and my men?'

She studied his profile, made more severe by the dark shadows cast by the night. 'I can't tell you, Guido. You have to decide, I'm afraid.'

Another thunderclap, louder this time, closely followed by a crackle of lightning.

'When Freddie visited me,' said Tessa, 'we went to the Villa Millefiore. The garden's all overgrown now. It was still beautiful, though.'

He glanced at her, amused. 'I remember the afternoon you made me jump into the pool with my clothes on.'

'You were always so vain, Guido. I couldn't resist it.'

'It was the first time we kissed.'

Their clothes wet from swimming, the scent of the laurel, and the sunlight fracturing into diamonds above them. And the heat, just like today, and his body, moulding close to hers. She felt an intense pang of longing for the past, for untroubled times.

Guido said softly, 'I regret not following you to London. I should have done so. I should have found a way.'

'It wouldn't have worked.' She said it without pain, stating a fact.

'We could have made it work.'

If she had reached out and touched him then, what would have happened? But she did not do so, and instead, rising, said crisply, 'Guido, I was your father's lover's daughter. How could we possibly have made it work? No. You and I, we existed in different worlds.' Lightning split the sky and the first drop of rain made a dark circle on a paving stone. 'And anyway,' she said, 'we weren't suited.'

'How can you say that?'

'Because it's true. We both like our own way too much. If you quarrel with Maddalena, then how much more would you have quarrelled with me?'

'You were never cynical before, Tessa.'

'I don't mean to be cynical. But I know myself, and I'm not made for marriage. I never have been.'

'How can you know if you've never tried?'

'I'm too fond of my freedom. I find it hard to compromise — I don't know how to, I never have. And if you're married, you have to make compromises, both of you do, or it doesn't work.'

Droplets of rain fell with an audible patter on to the flagstones. Tessa looked up, taking a deep breath of the fresher air, which was scented with lemon. The dust and the heat were being washed away.

'You see, it wouldn't have worked for me,' she said quietly. 'I don't know much, but I do know that.'

'So what will you do with your life, Tessa? The war won't go on for ever. When it's over, what then?'

'That hardly seems worth thinking of.'

'My mother tells me you teach at the school.'

'I do. I love it.'

'So you'll spend your days looking after other women's children, without ever having one of your own?'

The plants in their pots moved violently in the rush of wind. 'Tessa?' he said.

The rain was falling heavier now; it beat against her face. 'I told you I'd never married, Guido,' she said. 'I didn't say I'd never had a child.'

In the clamour of the coming storm, she did not hear his footsteps as he crossed the courtyard to her.

'Tessa? I don't understand.'

'It's perfectly possible to have a child without being married.' Her voice was cool and disengaged, almost taunting, and she saw the shock in his eyes. 'You don't know anything about me, Guido. I told you, I've changed. Whatever assumptions you've made about me, they're wrong. Whatever memories you have mean nothing now, nothing at all.'

She walked away. From the shelter of the loggia she looked back at him. 'I do know this, though,' she said fiercely. 'This is what you must do. Look after your child. Keep her safe, Guido. Don't ever let anything bad happen to her. Nothing else matters, nothing at all.'

*　　*　　*

When the Pollens had left Mayfield Farm on the outbreak of war, they had also left behind the kiln that John Pollen had built, along with some of the coloured glass that Romaine had used for making stained-glass windows. The glass was in shards and fragments, sorted by colour into old Oxo tins. There was something appealing about the translucency of the glass and Rebecca sometimes found herself going into the room with the kiln, taking a piece out of one of the tins and holding it up to the window, so that the light poured through it.

One day, she tried to fit together some of the fragments to make a picture. She worked on the bench where John Pollen had made his pots, shuffling round the jigsaw pieces, taking care not to cut her fingers. Later, she searched through the workshop, looking for the lead that Romaine Pollen had used to join the pieces of glass together. She found only a few stubs – either Romaine had run down her stocks before leaving Mayfield, or she had taken the lead, which must have been expensive, with her. It occurred to Rebecca that she might be able to make her glass picture without using lead, in John Pollen's kiln. One night, she fired up the kiln. The next day, when the glass had cooled, she took it out. It had fused and joined, the colours melting together.

It was a hard autumn. Mayfield Farm stood on an exposed site, buffeted by wind and rain. Gales blew up the Weald from the Channel, turning the clay soil to sticky mud. Yet the fields still needed ploughing and the crops must be sown. In the worst weather, Rebecca wrapped herself up in coats and jumpers, scarf, gloves and a hat, and put on two pairs of socks and a pair of old hiking boots before going out to the fields. Using David Mickleborough's shotgun, she learned to shoot the crows that tried to steal the seeds, as well as rabbits for the pot. She celebrated the Allied victory of El Alamein in North Africa at the beginning of November with the Mickleboroughs and the land girls, toasting the occasion with home-made cider.

Throughout the winter, Rebecca experimented with fusing glass. Sometimes the pieces failed to join together, while at other times the glass fused but then cracked while cooling. Opening the door of the kiln after a firing, she always felt excitement as she lifted out the piece she had made. Glass, she discovered, could be a forgiving medium. Her mistakes could be melted and used again. Even the most dismal failure might spark off a new idea, another direction to take.

She and Meriel spent alternate weekends with their mother in Abingdon. Hatherden always seemed to Rebecca draughty and uncomfortable. She felt the cold there, which she rarely did at the farm. The chills had settled out of Mayfield over the centuries; in comparison, her mother's house seemed raw, cobbled together, its contents utilitarian and worn, bought to be long-lasting and economical. This, she remembered, had been one of the things that had first attracted her to Milo: that he had taken it for granted that one cared about one's appearance and surroundings. It had been a revelation to her, an entrance into a new world where pleasure was not always burdened with guilt.

And yet, in this bleak fourth winter of the war, the habits she had learned in childhood, the penny-pinching and the making-do, were vital once more. She found it easy to slip back into the old ways, to use up every crumb of a loaf of bread, to scoop the last drop of egg white from the shell with her fingertip so that nothing was wasted. Sometimes, when she thought of the sixteen years of her marriage to Milo, they shrank. They had been a part of her life, a colourful and exciting part, full of passion and anguish, but only a part. It did not necessarily follow, as she had once feared, that her future must be dull and pallid.

'I so enjoyed reading your account of your trip to the Burren,' she wrote to Connor Byrne. 'And how lovely that Brendan went with you. What a wild and wonderful place it sounds! I should like to go there one day, when the war is over. I imagine it peopled by the old gods, elemental creatures of stone and wind and sea. I picture the two of you walking along the shore, looking for shells and sea glass.'

In his letter, Connor had enclosed a photograph of himself and Brendan at the Burren. Brendan was an attractive boy, but it was to his father's image that Rebecca's gaze was always drawn. In the picture, Connor was smiling. Wrapped up in an overcoat and scarf, his wild dark hair was blown about by the wind, as the sea struck the rocks behind him.

Winter sunlight shone through the glass that Rebecca had taken from the kiln that morning. Coloured shapes, greens and bronzes and gold, roughly triangular in form, reduced the valley, woodland and hills of the Weald to pure form. The glass captured the light, freezing it. She thought with a rush of excitement, I could make it sand-beaten, like sea glass. I could make it look as liquid as water. I could make it into shapes and forms, as alive as Connor's stone gods.

'It's made with beetroot, I'm afraid,' said Meriel. She put the cake tin on her mother's kitchen table. 'It seems rather strange, doesn't it, a pudding made of beetroot, but the recipe said it tasted very nice.'

It was the Easter holidays and most of Westdown's pupils had gone home for four weeks. Though it was Rebecca's weekend for staying at Hatherden, Meriel had phoned that morning to ask whether she might come to lunch.

They ate in the back room, which looked out over the garden. Because the room was south-facing and had large windows, it was Hatherden's warmest. As Rebecca served meat loaf and carrots, Meriel told them about her recent visit to her friend Monica in Cleethorpes.

'Monica was frightfully upset because one of the other WVS girls had been rather unkind.' A long, involved story followed: the rota for the WVS van; an implication that Monica hadn't been pulling her weight; Monica's cat being unwell, which had necessitated a long wait at the vet's; the unkindness of talking about someone behind their back.

During the pudding course, conversation limped rather. Mrs Fainlight looked tired and Meriel had fallen silent – whether because of the peculiarity of the beetroot pudding or because something was distracting her Rebecca was unsure. She suspected the latter.

After lunch, Mrs Fainlight went up to her bedroom for a nap and Meriel helped Rebecca clear the table. In the kitchen, Rebecca filled the sink with water and began to wash up.

Meriel rummaged through her bag for cigarettes and matches. 'I had to talk to you,' she said suddenly. 'The most frightful thing.'

'What?'

'It's Deborah.' Meriel seemed unable to go on. She shoved a cigarette between her lips and struck a match.

Rebecca scrubbed at a solidified patch of gravy on a plate. 'Dr Hughes's wife?'

Meriel nodded. 'She's dead.'

'*Dead?*' Rebecca stared at her sister.

'Yes. I heard yesterday afternoon. Milly Fawkes told me.' Millicent Fawkes was another housemistress. 'Apparently Deborah was staying with her cousin in Worthing and there was a bombing raid and the house was hit.'

'Oh, Meriel, how dreadful.'

'Deborah and her cousin were killed instantly. She never would go to the air-raid shelter, I remember Dr Hughes telling me, and I suppose her cousin must have stayed to keep her company.'

Rebecca put the kettle on for tea. 'Poor Dr Hughes.'

'I feel so sorry for him. They had been married for twenty years.' Meriel dried some glasses and put them away in the cupboard. 'I know one shouldn't speak ill of the dead, but Deborah could be very hard work.'

'She was rather an invalid, wasn't she?'

Meriel nodded. 'That was why she went to Worthing, for the sea air.'

'Have you spoken to Dr Hughes?'

403

'I telephoned last night but he was expecting a call from Deborah's mother, so I only had time to give him my condolences.'

'How did he seem?'

'Terribly shocked, poor man. Do you think . . .' Meriel smoked with great concentration, 'do you think I should offer to help him sort out her things? It's such an awful job for a man to do on his own, and Deborah didn't have any sisters and her mother is quite old and infirm. I don't want to intrude, of course, and someone else may offer, but . . .'

'I think it would be a very kind thing to do,' said Rebecca firmly.

'I only met Deborah a couple of times and I have to admit I didn't take to her, but you can't help thinking, what a rotten way to go, miles from home and when she was having a little holiday. I didn't want to say anything in front of Mummy in case I felt upset. The truth is, I'm upset because he's upset. Deborah was so difficult and demanding, it's hard to mind for her, but I do mind for him.' Meriel looked at Rebecca. 'Do you think that's awful of me?'

'Not at all.' Rebecca gave Meriel's shoulder a comforting pat. 'I think it's perfectly understandable.'

The train ground to a halt between Rugby and Coventry. Freddie was sharing a compartment with a sleeping soldier and a man in a houndstooth jacket and trilby hat. When she had boarded the train at Euston, there had been two middle-aged women as well, which was why she had chosen that compartment. At Westdown School, Miss Fainlight had instructed her pupils always to choose a train compartment in which other women were sitting, and Freddie had maintained the habit. But the two women had left the train at Rugby and now the man in the houndstooth jacket was holding out a crumpled paper bag to her and saying, 'Do have a sweetie, miss.'

'No thank you,' she said.

'You young ladies, always worrying about your figures.' She knew what was coming next, and it did. 'You don't need to worry, if I may make so bold, miss.'

She was probably, she thought, supposed to simper and say thank you. Instead, she glanced through the window to where a brown river, swollen with rain, meandered between fields and reeds. Mentally she urged the train to move again.

'Where are you heading for, miss?'

'Birmingham,' she said.

'Well fancy that, so am I. You don't sound like a Brummie, if I may say so. Ciggie?' A cigarette packet was proffered, a hand almost accidentally brushed her knee.

Her book was in her bag in the luggage rack. She wondered whether to get it down and hide behind it, but didn't fancy reaching up: she suspected he would try to look up her skirt.

'No thanks,' she said.

'Do you like to go to the pictures?'

'Sometimes. With my boyfriend.'

'I bet a girl like you has lots of boyfriends.'

'Plenty,' she said coldly.

The train shuddered, then started up, dragging itself a

short distance along the track before coming to a halt again. 'Excuse me,' Freddie said, and left the compartment.

She walked along the corridor from one carriage to another. If she took her time, perhaps the man in the houndstooth jacket, like the soldier, would fall asleep before she returned. She was tired and wouldn't have minded a nap herself. She stifled a yawn as she passed through the shifting rubber and metal tunnel that joined two carriages.

Something made her look through a compartment window, and she saw, dozing in a corner seat, a man in naval uniform: Lewis Coryton.

She opened the door. The compartment was empty but for Lewis. She thought he might not recognize her, but he focused and gave a slow, sleepy smile.

'Good Lord. Freddie Nicolson.'

'Hello, Lewis.' She went into the carriage.

He rose and gave her his hand.

'I'm awfully glad to see you,' she said.

'And I'm delighted to see you. Bloody boring journey. I'm beginning to wonder if this thing's ever going to move again. Have you just got on the train?'

'No, since Euston. I've had to escape because a man in my compartment keeps offering me cigarettes and sweets – ciggies and sweeties, he calls them.'

'You should come and sit here with me.'

'I'd love to. I'll go and get my bag.'

Lewis offered to come with her. They walked back down the corridor to Freddie's carriage. The man in the houndstooth jacket gave her a wounded look as Lewis took down her bag while she stood in the open doorway. As they headed back to Lewis's compartment, they glanced at each other and began to laugh.

'He was a knee-patter,' said Freddie, as Lewis shut the door of the compartment behind him. 'I expect he was a bottom-pincher as well.'

Lewis took a silver flask out of his pocket and offered it to her.

'What is it?'

'Rum. What else would a naval man have? Go on, it'll warm you up.'

Freddie took a mouthful, enjoying the rum's fiery sweep down her throat. 'How are you, Lewis? Are you on leave?'

'I'm on my way back to my ship. I've just had two weeks – terrific.'

'How's Clare?'

He scowled. 'We finished a couple of months ago.'

'I'm sorry.'

He took a swallow from the flask. 'I was pretty cut up at first but I'm okay now. Her parents never approved of me anyway. Clare has some heart thing, did you know, and she was always rather under their thumb.'

'Heart thing?'

'A murmur. She used to faint. She's their only child and they worry about her health. And of course, they want the best for her. And that wasn't me.' He took another swig of rum, then screwed the top back on the flask and put it in his pocket. 'She's seeing someone else now, some bloke her parents have always wanted her to marry.'

'Oh, Lewis.'

'Being away at sea for months at a time didn't help.' He shrugged. 'Plenty more fish, so they say.'

'Are you sure you're all right?'

'Honestly, I'm fine. What about you, Freddie? Where are you these days?'

'I'm living in Birmingham.'

'Do you like it?'

'Yes, I do. I've made some good friends there and there's plenty to do, and to be honest, I'd had enough of London. I'm working in a factory now.'

'Are you?' His hazel eyes glittered. 'How's it going?'

'All right, I think. I'm a Qualified Semi-Skilled Mechanic.'

'Good for you. You don't find it . . . well, I would have thought it was rather hard going for a girl.'

'It is hard,' she admitted. 'I found it very tiring at first, but I'm used to it now. It's terribly noisy – they have the radio on all the time, Music While You Work, but you can hardly hear it because of all the machines. And my overalls sparkle, because of the metal dust. Look.' She showed him her hands, the dark line beneath each fingernail. 'The dust gets under my nails. I can't shift it – I scrubbed them for ages, because of Ray's wedding.'

'Ray Leavington's married again?'

'Yesterday. A quiet ceremony, as they say in the papers. That's why I was in London. Max says it's the triumph of optimism over realism.'

'Was it fun?'

'Actually, yes. Almost like old times.'

'That evening at the Dorchester, I wondered if there was anything going on between you and Jack.'

'Me and Jack?' Freddie laughed. 'Goodness, no. Jack and I always end up arguing. Anyway, I haven't seen him for years.'

'I think he's abroad. Someone told me he's doing something very hush-hush.'

Hush-hush and dangerous, no doubt. She saw, looking out, that the window had misted up with condensation, reducing the countryside beyond to a blur of greens and browns.

'I wish this train would get a move on,' she said.

'Have you to be somewhere?'

'Not really; just, you know, washing and ironing to do, letters to write.'

Lewis pulled down the window and stuck his head out. 'Nothing doing out there, as far as I can see. Some chaps hanging around, talking. I wonder if the engine's broken down?'

'That's the thing,' she said fretfully. 'Everything seems so unreliable.'

'Too much making do and mending, I'm afraid.'

'I like to plan. I like to be organized.'

'You don't like surprises, then, Freddie?'

'Not the sort of surprises that mean you end up sitting for hours in the middle of nowhere. How about you? How's your ship? Are you still sailing across the Atlantic?'

He was, he told her. She sensed that he didn't want to talk about it and was searching for a change of subject when he said suddenly, 'I'm on a destroyer now. It's better, I suppose, you don't feel as exposed as you do on a corvette. It can still feel pretty hellish, though not always in the way most people assume. I mean, I don't necessarily find it worst at the obvious times, like when we're under fire, though that can be terrifying. But at least you're doing something and you don't have much time to think. It's when I'm on watch at night that it gets to me. You feel as if you're the only person left in the world. Everything looks grey and all you can see around you for miles and miles and miles is empty sea. It makes me feel – I don't know, hopeless. As if there's nothing else and there's never going to be anything else.'

'Oh, Lewis,' she said gently.

'Sorry.' He smiled at her. 'I'm talking rot, aren't I? When I was seeing Clare, if I got the blues I'd try to think about her. What I was going to write to her, that sort of thing.'

'You can write to me, if you like. I know it's not the same, but if it takes your mind off things . . . And I enjoy writing to people.'

'You'd write to me? I should like that enormously. Decent of you, Freddie.' He had brightened, but then his face fell again and he grimaced. 'I'm afraid my nerve's going. You see these chaps in the pub, drinking themselves to a stupor before they go back to their ship. I don't want to end up like them.'

She thought of the flask of rum and the way he had closed his eyes before tilting his head back to swallow. She took her pencil and notebook out of her handbag and scribbled down her address.

'Here,' she said, and tore off the page and gave it to him. 'Write to me if you feel like it. You can write anything you want, I don't mind. It's always nice to get a letter.'

Lewis put the piece of paper in a pocket. 'Do you write to a lot of people?'

'Max and Julian, of course, and some of the girls I knew when I was working in London.' She paused before saying, 'And sometimes I write letters to my sister, Tessa, as well, though I've no idea whether they get to her.'

'Where does she live?'

'In Italy. Last thing I heard, she was staying with some friends in a villa south of Florence.' She frowned. 'I can feel myself starting to hope now, and that's almost worse. I can feel myself starting to think that one day the war might be over. I've hardly thought about it before because it always seemed as if it would go on for ever.'

'If the Eighth Army takes Tunisia – and it's looking on the cards – then Rommel will be forced to surrender. Then we'll have the whole of North Africa and we can start thinking about Europe. You're thinking Italy next?'

Freddie ran her hand across the window, sweeping away an arc of condensation. 'It's starting to look that way, isn't it?' She looked back at him and smiled. 'Would you like some cake, Lewis? Ray's wife, Susan, gave me some slices of wedding cake.'

They ate them while the train remained motionless and the sky outside darkened to Prussian blue. Lewis pulled down the blinds and they talked about leaving the train and walking off over the fields – there was something about the idea that appealed to both of them. 'But as soon as we make a run for it,' Lewis pointed out, 'the wretched thing will heave itself into life again, you can count on it.' Then they pondered the possibility that they might have to stay on the train all night – Lewis had heard of a train that had been marooned in a Cumbrian blizzard for a week. And it occurred to her, talking to him, watching his quick, amused smile and the way his eyes lit up when she said something that entertained him, that the journey wasn't tedious any more, and that she wouldn't have minded if the train had remained where it was, on the darkening river plain, for hours more.

But at last, quite suddenly, the engine gave an almighty heave, as if it had drawn breath, and they began to move again. The long day and the rhythm of the train made Freddie's eyelids droop. When eventually the engine drew into New Street station and she opened her eyes, Lewis was sitting beside her and her head was resting on his shoulder.

'You looked like you needed a pillow,' he said.

'Thanks.' Blearily, she stood up. He took her bag down from the rack as she buttoned her jacket, and opened the carriage door for her. 'I'll write to you,' she said.

They shook hands. Freddie stepped down on to the platform and walked away. But as she approached the ticket barrier, she heard running footsteps behind her. Looking round, she saw Lewis weaving through the crowds towards her.

She felt a rush of elation. 'Your train,' she said.

'Damn the train. I've realized that I want to spend the rest of the evening with you. Do you mind, Freddie?'

She shook her head. 'Not at all.'

'Good. I hoped you'd say that.'

They stood face to face on the platform. His hand brushed

against hers. Then the pistons on the train turned, a plume of steam issued from the funnel and it pulled out of the station.

Lewis watched as the train became a dark smudge, draped in smoke. He laughed. 'There's bound to be another one.'

Freddie insisted on checking the times before they left the station. 'I don't want you peeling potatoes for a month, Lewis, or whatever it is they do to sailors who've gone AWOL.' There was a train to Liverpool in an hour.

They linked arms as they walked out of the station. They went into a hotel a short way down the road. The bar room was high-ceilinged and cavernous, the walls painted a dirty cream. The mahogany bartop was scratched and marked, and there were water rings on the lid of the upright piano that stood against the wall. Soldiers and sailors with their sweethearts and businessmen with attaché cases were standing up and chatting; others were dozing, propped against their suitcases, or were slumped in their seats, drinking and smoking.

Lewis brought the drinks to the table.

Freddie said, 'Do you usually do things like that?'

'What, missing trains? I probably do. I'm afraid I forgot that you don't like surprises.'

'*Sometimes* I don't like surprises.'

'Best surprise I've had for quite a while, seeing you on that train.' He looked round. 'Bit of a dive, I'm afraid. Next time I'll take you somewhere more glamorous.'

'Next time?' she repeated.

'There will be a next time, won't there, Freddie?'

413

She found herself saying, 'Yes, I hope so.'

'Good.' He took out cigarettes, offered them to her. 'Sometimes I can't quite make you out,' he said.

'What do you mean?'

'I thought you were like the others, but I'm not so sure now.'

'Which others? Marcelle and her friends?'

He nodded, lighting their cigarettes.

'I've rather fallen out with Marcelle,' she said.

'What about?'

She shrugged. 'This and that. We were friends for a while but we're not any more. I used to think . . .'

'What?'

'That I could make myself fit in anywhere. When I first came to England, when I first went to boarding school, I hardly said a word for a fortnight. I just watched and listened, and eventually I worked out the right things to say. But I appear to have lost the knack – or perhaps it's that I don't care any more. I'm tired, and I can't be bothered to say the things people seem to want me to say.'

He was looking at her curiously. 'You weren't born in England, then?'

'No, in Italy. I was twelve when I came here.' She gave a half-smile. 'It was rather a shock. So cold, and all the other girls seemed so – well, normal, I suppose, but because of that they seemed extraordinary to me. They had families with a mother and a father and they'd lived in the same house all their lives instead of moving around from place to place.'

'Good grief.'

'What is it?'

He shook his head slowly. 'So for the past few hours I've been on my best behaviour, hiding the skeletons in my closet, and you've probably been thinking, that Lewis, he's a dull old stick.'

She laughed. 'No, not at all. Have you skeletons?'

'A few. An uncle who ran guns to Ireland – oh, and one of my forebears is supposed to have jumped ship in Shanghai. I should go there, sometime, find out if there are any Corytons running around. I'm not exactly out of the top drawer, Freddie.'

'Neither am I.' There was pleasure in feeling an affinity with him.

'I sometimes think,' he said, 'that the others have a sort of checklist.'

'What do you mean?'

'People like Marcelle and her friends. Titled parents – tick. Mouldering pile in Wiltshire – tick. Ancestral portraits – tick. My mother died when I was two, my father had scarpered a year before. I was brought up by my three aunts. There was Auntie Florrie, who ran a pub in Bermondsey, and Auntie Lol, who was a dancer, and Aunt Kate, who was a schoolteacher – oh, and she was a communist and a pacifist. I used to shuttle between them – off to Auntie Florrie when Auntie Lol was on tour, back to Kate when Uncle Morton was hitting the bottle.'

'Who did you like best?'

'Kate. I knew where I was with her. She got me reading, took me to museums and art galleries. She made sure I got

415

a scholarship to a decent school. I'd have been nothing if it wasn't for her.'

Freddie shook her head. 'I don't believe that. You seem a terribly energetic person, Lewis.'

'I don't like to let the grass grow under my feet, it's true. Anyway, Kate died when I was sixteen, from pneumonia. I was at school when they told me. Bloody awful. And poor old Auntie Florrie pegged it a couple of years ago. The pub was flattened by a bomb – she was in the shelter, but she lost heart afterwards, gave up rather. And Lol went to America before the war. I get a letter now and then.' He stubbed out his cigarette. 'I always think there are so many threads tying people like Jack and Marcelle together. They always seem to have . . . safety nets.'

'Do you mind?'

'Not really.' He sat back in the chair, looking at her. 'Let's see how much we've in common. Tell me your three favourite films, Freddie.'

She screwed up her eyes, then said, 'Casablanca . . . Gaslight . . . so deliciously creepy . . . oh, and Now Voyager. I ran out of hankies.'

'Not Gone With the Wind? Women always say Gone With the Wind.'

'Scarlett's too flouncy. If I were friends with her, I'd get awfully tired of her.'

'Songs, then.'

'That's not fair, it's your turn, Lewis. Oh well, here goes. "Jealousy" – I do like a tango. And "Apple Blossom Time". Corny, I know, but I love it. And "As Time Goes By".'

'Because of Casablanca.'

'Exactly.' She glanced at the piano. 'It's a shame no one's playing.'

'Do you?'

'I'm afraid not. What about you?'

He shook his head. 'My Auntie Lol taught me to sing, though.' And he began to hum, at first in a low murmur, and then louder, the melody of 'As Time Goes By'. To begin with, people gave him a glance and then went back to their conversations, but then one of the soldiers' sweethearts joined in, her voice a light soprano to Lewis's rich baritone, and then, it seemed to Freddie, as she watched and listened, torn between embarrassment and laughter, most of the occupants of the bar were singing. And so was she, because it was irresistible, and *he* was irresistible, and she knew, as he stood up and took her hand, addressing her in song, his gestures theatrical, but funny and oddly sincere as well, that she was falling for him, and that sense and caution were slipping aside in a way that had never happened to her before.

At the end of the song, the whole bar burst into applause and Lewis bowed. Freddie had to look away. Her heart was pounding. She felt giddy, short of oxygen.

She stood up, shaky on her feet. 'We should go.'

They walked to the station. Outside, Lewis said, 'Here, take this for the taxi,' and offered her a ten-shilling note, which she tried to refuse, telling him she could catch the bus.

'Take it, Freddie. It's my fault you're up late. If you don't take it, then I'll insist on walking you home and then I will end up peeling potatoes.'

Then he said, 'It's been the most terrific evening. Thank you.' And as they stood, like a rock in a river, while the late-night travellers poured into the station on either side of them, he kissed her. His lips were cool against hers, the pressure of his hands on her back was light, and there was that delicious sinking, drowning feeling all over again.

Chapter Thirteen

The first of the children had arrived in the spring, half a dozen of them, in age between four and eleven, refugees from the bombed city of Genoa. Their clothing was torn and filthy, their skin marked by rashes and boils, and there were lice in their hair. Tessa and Faustina bathed them, dressed their scratches and sores and found them clean clothes. They shaved off the hair of those with the worst infestations and went through the matted locks of the others with a fine-toothed comb. Then the children were fed bread and milk. Afterwards they were put to bed in a large room in the villa that had been transformed into a dormitory. That first night, most of them cried themselves to sleep.

Three weeks later, another ten children arrived, as well as two babes in arms and their mothers. One of the children was a boy of around six years old called Tommaso. Tommaso's hair writhed with lice: you could almost see it move. He ate like a wild animal, stuffing food into his mouth with both hands, glancing furtively around as if afraid someone might steal his supper. He had sores on his face that never healed because he picked at the scabs. And he did not speak. Tessa remembered Perlita, and her week of silence, but Tommaso was not like Perlita. He did not cry, like the other children, and nor did he smile, but bared his teeth in a grimace. The only sound he made was a strange keening. At school, he did not join in the lessons with the others, but rocked back and forth on a bench, picking at a sore on his eyebrow, now and then erupting into his mournful howl. When anyone came too close to him, he would try to bite them, a sudden quick lunge like a lizard shooting its tongue out at a fly.

Lina, the teaching assistant who had escorted the children from Naples to the Villa di Belcanto, said that Tommaso shouldn't be allowed to stay in the class until he had settled down because he upset the other children. Reluctantly, Tessa was forced to agree. From then on, he spent most of his day at the laundry, under the watchful eye of the mothers and grandmothers who worked there. He liked to be taken into the garden in the wheeled wicker basket they used for carrying the wet linen to the washing line. Sometimes, when the basket was pulled fast, he gave an odd, nasal sort of laugh, which was if anything more disturbing than the howl. The trouble was, Tessa said to Faustina one evening, that they didn't know what Tommaso had been like before the air raid. He might have been brought up by loving parents or he might have been beaten. His family had presumably died in the bombing raid, because he had been found wandering alone round the ruined streets of Naples.

Even his name was not his own: the sisters of the charitable order who had taken him in and fed him had chosen it for him, before sending him to the comparative safety of the countryside with Lina and the other children.

On fine evenings, Tessa often took the little boy out for a ride in the wicker laundry basket. She pushed him over the grass and Tommaso laughed his unsettling laugh while she talked to him about the things they saw. When something frightened him – the bark of a dog or a rustling in the undergrowth – he would scramble out of the basket and run away and hide in a box hedge. He had made a sort of nest inside the hedge, of dried leaves and twigs, and he hid things there – a rusty tin full of rainwater, a tattered old piece of blanket, a crust of bread. One evening, alarmed by the rattle of an army truck over the nearby road, he refused to come out of his den. Tessa sat on the grass beside the box hedge until the sky darkened and Tommaso fell asleep, and then she scooped him up in her arms and took him indoors.

Dr Berardi told Tessa that Tommaso was an imbecile and should be put in an institution. Tessa told Dr Berardi that he was the imbecile, not Tommaso. If everything that was familiar had been taken away from you, if you had scavenged for food in the rubble and slept out alone night after night, perhaps you might want to hide in some little hole where you felt safe. And perhaps you'd shovel down your supper as quickly as you could, because you'd be afraid that others might take it from you. Tessa knew that Tommaso wasn't lost, that he was in there somewhere. She just had to find a way of coaxing him out.

That summer the Allied army, victorious in North Africa, headed towards Italy, using the islands of Pantelleria and Sicily as airbases and stepping stones across the Mediterranean. Fierce fighting was still taking place on Sicily when the radio announced the fall of Mussolini, deposed following a meeting of the fascist grand council. Marshal Badoglio, a hero of the First World War, set up a government, the fascist militia was disbanded and martial law imposed.

At the villa, they hid jars of olives and sides of ham behind the false walls that had earlier been built in the cellars and attics. Stores of food were buried in pits dug in the ground. Secret caches of food, clothing and shoes were concealed on the outlying farms. It was hard to buy clothing and thread – a few items, perhaps, picked up from the second-hand markets on Olivia or Faustina's visits to Florence – and it was almost impossible to find shoes. They made nappies for the babies out of old sheets and towels, and shirts and dresses for the children out of curtains. Because they couldn't buy knitting wool any more, the women of the Belcanto estate spun their own wool. Some of the older women owned small, portable spinning wheels, which they tucked under their arms, spinning as they walked from farm to farm, their fingers constantly working. One of the women, a great-grandmother a foot and a half shorter than Tessa, with a face as wrinkled as a walnut shell, taught her to spin. There was something hypnotic, Tessa discovered, about the whirl of the bobbin and the puffy, lumpy sheep's wool narrowing into a length of yarn.

Now and then Allied planes flew over the villa. Some of the children looked up, captivated, but Tommaso howled and hid in his box hedge. In the distance, there was the dull thunk-thunk of bombs, but no bombs fell on Belcanto land.

Returning to the villa one hot summer's evening after a trip to Florence, Faustina swept back limp rat's tails of hair from her face as she threw herself into an armchair. The hem of her dress was white with dust.

'It's all too exhausting,' she said. 'How can we be sure, living here, what's truth and what's lies? How can we know what's really going on?'

Tessa poured out two glasses of cold white wine and handed one to Faustina. 'How was Florence?'

'Jumpy. You feel that anything could happen. There were riots a few days ago. Maddelena leaves the house as little as possible.'

'How is she?'

'She's well and so is Luciella. She worries, though. Her father has gone into hiding. She was glad of the food I brought.' Faustina scrabbled in her pocket and drew out a crumpled piece of paper, which she handed to Tessa. 'The Allied planes were dropping these over the city.'

Tessa read the leaflet's headline aloud. '*Out with the Germans – or fire and steel.*'

'If only it were that simple – wave goodbye to one army and welcome the next one in.' Faustina gave a contemptuous snort. 'Ah, my hair!' Irritably she pushed it out of her eyes again. 'I'm going to cut it all off,' she said crossly. She delved in her bag and drew out a pair of nail scissors.

'Faustina, you can't.'

'Can't I? Watch me. I only wear it like this because Mother believes unmarried girls should have long hair. So ridiculously old-fashioned. I should have got rid of it years ago.' She began to hack at her hair with the scissors.

'If you really want to cut it short, then let me do it,' said Tessa, holding out her hand for the scissors. 'And not with those.'

'What does it matter? I should shave it off, like we do with the children when they have lice.'

Tessa went to fetch a comb and her own long-bladed scissors. Walking along the cool, dark corridors of the villa to her room, she thought of the leaflet Faustina had shown her. *Out with the Germans – or fire and steel.* The bombings of Turin, Genoa and many other Italian cities had demonstrated all too clearly what fire and steel could do.

Tessa had Faustina sit on a stool while she combed out her hair. 'You can cut it as short as you like,' said Faustina.

'I'll cut it so that it suits you. Tell me what you heard in Florence.'

'Lots of rumours. There's been a *coup d'état*, or the communists are murdering the fascists in this city or that, or Hitler's committed suicide. Now *that* would be nice.'

Faustina bobbed her head and Tessa said, 'Keep still, or you'll end up with one side longer than the other.'

'I don't care.'

'Of course you do,' said Tessa calmly. 'You'll look wonderful when I've finished with you. All that hair dragged back from your face never suited you – your forehead's too high.'

'That's because I'm so clever,' said Faustina smugly. 'You're such an optimist, Tessa. I don't think a different hairstyle is going to change things much.'

Tessa combed and snipped. 'Was there any other news?'

'I went to the hospital to get lint and bandages, and some of the people there were saying that the Allies will land on the coast of Tuscany. Absolute rubbish, of course – why would they sail to Tuscany when all they have to do is to cross the Straits of Messina? And Guido . . .'

'Guido?' The scissors paused.

After recovering from his leg wound, Guido had not returned to North Africa, but had been stationed in Bologna, at a military training school.

'Maddalena had a letter from him. She let me read it.'

'How did he sound? Is he well?'

'He said so. Fed up, but then, you know Guido, he never could sit still.'

Faustina ran her fingers through her hair and then rose and peered in a mirror. 'Oh. Thank you, Tessa.'

The short, feathery hair framed her face, softening her sharp features. 'You look fashionably gamine,' said Tessa.

Faustina turned to face her. Her smile faded. 'They're saying in Florence that Badoglio has waited too long and that he should have come to terms with the Allies weeks ago. They're asking what the government will do when the Allies land on the mainland, and whether there'll be an armistice, and if so, what the Germans will do then. When I was at the hospital I talked to one of the surgeons. He told me that German troops are pouring over the northern borders into Italy. You know what that means, don't you? That they're preparing to fight for every inch of Italian soil.'

There was no newspaper, no post. Some of the telephone lines had been cut. Train travel had become near impossible and barricades had been put up across roads.

After the fall of Sicily at the end of August, Allied troops landed on Reggio, on the Calabrian coast. Five days later, on the afternoon of September 8th, the news of the Italian armistice was announced. That night, on the houses and farms of the estate, there was rejoicing. Bonfires were lit, and there was drinking and dancing.

They buried their store of petrol in a pit in the orchard and took the tyres off the huge old Alfa that Olivia's father had driven when he was alive. No use – only days after the announcement of the surrender, German troops came to the villa to requisition the car. The captain was polite but unbending – no matter that the Alfa lacked tyres; they would find some. The next day two soldiers arrived at the villa with tyres and petrol and drove the car away.

Hope, too, began to trickle away. They heard the narrowing of their options on the radio news, BBC and Swiss. In the fine early autumn weather, columns of German tanks and armoured cars headed south through country roads, towards the Allied beachheads south of Naples. You wouldn't send your troops south if you didn't mean to fight.

On September 10th, the German army entered the city of Rome. The occupation was uncontested. Other northern and central Italian cities were seized, and on September 12th, in a daring raid, Mussolini was released from captivity by German paratroopers. Three days later, he proclaimed his return to power and established a fascist government at Salo, on Lake Garda.

Strangers headed down the quiet tracks of the Belcanto estate. They called at the villa and the farmhouses, asking for food and clothing and for somewhere to stay the night. They were Italian soldiers, who, hearing of the armistice and then learning that they were required to report to German headquarters, had torn off their uniforms and set off to make their way home however they could. They were Allied prisoners of war, who, fearing deportation to Germany, had broken out of their prison camps and were travelling south to the Allied lines. The woodland on the Belcanto estate bristled with fugitives. Now and then a husband or a son, absent for years in France or Yugoslavia, reappeared on one of the estate's farms. An English prisoner, wearing a peasant's tattered clothing, hoed a field or cleared away stones on a smallholding in repayment for food and lodging. More rumours: of British prisoners of war who had been shot trying to escape, and of Italian soldiers who, failing to leave their barracks quickly enough, had been herded into wagons or trucks and driven north to an unknown destination.

At the villa, they had heard nothing of the fate of Guido and Sandro.

One morning, an Australian prisoner of war knocked at the door of the clinic. His name was Sam Robbins, and he had a high fever and an open wound on the side of his body, inflicted while scrambling through the barbed wire that surrounded his camp. Faustina washed out the wound and bandaged it and they made up a bed for him on the top floor of the villa.

Any Italian sheltering a prisoner of war was required to tell the nearest German command of their whereabouts within twenty-four hours. Failure to do so would result in trial by a court martial. Once, when Sam was very ill and feverish, Tessa helped Olivia make up his bed. 'Why are you doing this for me?' she heard Sam ask Olivia. 'Why? You could get yourself killed.'

Olivia smoothed out the deep embroidered border of a pillow. 'I'm doing this for someone else's son,' she said. 'I'm doing it because I pray that some other mother is doing the same for mine.'

He was walking along one of the tracks that intersected the road leading to the villa. He was tall and rangy, and he had straw-coloured hair and red sunburned skin and the bridge of his nose was peeling. He was wearing a patched, ragged coat, boots and a tattered pair of trousers. He might be a deserter or he might be an escaped prisoner. Or he might be a fascist spy.

Suddenly he stopped and said, 'Hello, Tessa.'

Tessa froze. The fair-haired man was walking towards her, grinning, his hand outstretched.

'Desmond Fitzgerald,' he said. 'Paddy's friend. Do you remember?'

Desmond Fitzgerald . . . Paddy's friend. Tessa cried, 'The Mirabelle!'

Then she clapped her hand over her mouth. 'It was years ago – Julian nearly hit Max.'

'I'd lost a fortune on some nag.' Desmond sounded wistful. 'I went on to my sister's chap's birthday party later on and there was a pyramid of champagne glasses and some clown knocked the lot over and I cut my foot on a piece of glass. I was hobbling about for weeks. Terrific evening.'

She hugged him. 'How wonderful to see you. What on earth are you doing here, Desmond?'

'I'm on the run.' He looked pleased with himself. 'What about you?'

'I live here,' she said.

She asked him whether he would like some breakfast, and he said, rather, he was ravenous, hadn't eaten for twenty-four hours, and so they headed to the villa. As they walked, he told her his story. A lieutenant in a cavalry regiment, he had been captured at Tobruk more than a year ago. He had been transported to Italy and had ended up in a prison camp between Bologna and Florence. 'Not a bad place,' he said philosophically. 'Some of the guards were decent chaps, but the food was rotten. No worse than school, though.'

On the day after the armistice, the guards had warned them that German troops were coming to take over the camp. 'So we made a hole in the barbed wire and hoofed it,' said Desmond. 'None of us fancied spending the rest of the war in the Fatherland.'

Some of their number had been recaptured the next day, but Desmond and a friend had headed south, with the intention of reaching the Allied lines. His friend had sprained his ankle, sliding down a mountainous gully, and though he had tried, using a stick as a crutch, to continue, in the end they had parted and the friend had remained in hiding at a farm.

Desmond had carried on alone. He had had a piece of luck, and had spent a morning sleeping in a hay wagon as it trundled along country lanes, but mostly he had walked, using footpaths rather than the roads and sleeping in hay barns or at farmhouses, where he had been given food and wine and shelter for the night. He had worked for a few days on some of the farms, and before he had left, his various hosts had always recommended a safe route and somewhere to stay the next night. Old so-and-so was a mean devil and might give you his most vinegary wine, but his wife was a wonderful cook. Keep away from this or that place, the owners had friends in the *fascisti*. He had had some lucky escapes: the previous day he had dived into a river just in time to hide from a column of German troops.

'Countryside's crawling with them,' he said. 'They're everywhere.'

While they walked, Tessa looked at him now and then, unable to believe that he was here. Desmond Fitzgerald was a little piece of her old life, her London life, which during her years in Italy had become increasingly distant and unreal.

He seemed to feel the same way. Grinning, he shook his head slowly. 'I still can't believe it. Tessa Nicolson, in bloody Italy. How long have you been here?'

She told him. They had reached the villa. She saw that he was frowning. She said, 'What is it?'

'Then you won't have heard about poor old Paddy.'

A sinking of the heart. Tessa shook her head.

'He was shot down in the Battle of Britain, I'm afraid. September 1940. His plane was hit and he ended up in the sea.' Desmond rubbed the flaking skin on the bridge of his nose. 'Sorry. I hate to be the bearer of such lousy news. It would have been quick, that's the thing.'

She thought, oh *Paddy*. She remembered the time he had flown her to Paris, and how she had screamed with pleasure as they had bounced along the runway, landing at Le Bourget airfield. She remembered Paddy's ambition and his love of life and his short temper – the dinner party he had ruined by getting drunk and making fun of the other guests, the fight he had started in a pub. And his whoop of joy whenever he had driven fast along an empty road, and the unexpected tenderness of his lovemaking.

This was the trouble with running away. You became out of touch. What of all her other English friends? Though logic had told her that their lives, like hers, must have changed, a part of her had preferred to imagine them just the same, untouched. Here she was, immured in her castle, and she hadn't a clue. Anything could have happened.

At the villa, in the kitchen, Tessa put out food for Desmond. While she was making coffee, she asked him about the others, about Ray and Max and Julian and, of course, Freddie.

But he didn't know them. They moved in different circles, the arcs of their separate lives hardly intersecting. They had

431

a few friends in common, she discovered. Someone had been left behind at Dunkirk and someone else, a model, had died with her small daughter in the Blitz. And London wasn't quite itself any more, though there was still plenty of fun to be had.

Then they talked about the war. He said, 'I'm afraid it's going to be a long, hard slog. Winter's coming, so that'll make the job tougher.' He would head off tomorrow morning, he told her. He would have the best chance of reaching the Allied lines if he got a move on. The longer it took, the more enemy troops would have concentrated in the south and the more difficult it would be to get through them.

'I can't bear the idea of going back to the prison camp,' he said. 'It's been a bloody hard slog since I left it, but I can't tell you how marvellous it's been to be out in the open again. These last few weeks, people have been so kind to me. My Italian's pretty damned poor and their English was non-existent, and it was obvious from the way most of them lived that they hardly had two pennies to rub together. They didn't know me from Adam, and yet they took me in, fed me, hid me. Incredible.' Desmond shook his head slowly. 'Just incredible.'

He left at dawn the next day. The autumn air was cooler and the trees on the hillsides glittered copper and gold. Tessa kissed him and wished him luck. As he reached the edge of the woodland, he looked back over his shoulder and waved to her. Then the forest swallowed him up.

A week later, a letter arrived at the villa, delivered by

hand. The address of the Belcanto estate and a few sentences were scrawled on a single sheet of paper. It had been thrown from the window of a train carriage and then passed from hand to hand, travelling a slow, difficult route from northern Italy to Tuscany.

The letter was from Sandro. He had been taken prisoner after he had refused to join the fascist army. He had written the letter on a train bound for some unknown destination. He was well, he told them, and he sent his love to them.

Another letter arrived, this time from Maddalena. An army comrade of Guido's had visited her in Florence. He had told her that after the armistice, Guido had left his barracks in Bologna. No one knew where he had gone, and no one had seen or heard from him since. As for herself, Maddalena was taking her daughter north, to stay with an aunt near Rimini. It frightened her to be in Florence now without either her father or Guido. She needed company, she wrote. She was tired of being alone.

Lewis's train was more than two hours late. The two small boys sitting next to Freddie in the waiting room were taking sly kicks at each other. At each kick they howled histrionically. Their mother said to Freddie, 'If that bloody train takes much longer, I'll end up throttling them. Gilbert! Brian! Cut that out!' She smacked both boys' legs. 'Do you want me to tell your dad you've been naughty? Do you?'

A blurred mumbling from the tannoy; Freddie went outside to listen. Catching sight of Lewis among the crowds coming through the ticket barrier, she ran towards him. She sensed his impatience in the flick of his eyes to his watch and the sharp wave of his travel pass beneath the inspector's nose.

'Sorry!' he called out, seeing her. 'Sorry for making you wait so long, Freddie. Blasted trains!'

'It doesn't matter.'

They kissed, then a soldier's carelessly slung kitbag struck her on the back, jolting her.

Lewis growled at the soldier, who muttered an apology.

'Are you all right, Freddie?'

'I'm fine.'

'Stupid idiot.'

'Honestly, I'm fine. Oh, it's lovely to see you again!'

'You look so beautiful.'

'You're very generous, Lewis,' she said with a smile. 'I've run out of lipstick and I couldn't find a pair of stockings without ladders.'

'I hate seeing a girl's face plastered with lipstick and powder.'

His comment irritated her. When men said that, what they really meant was that they hated being able to tell if a girl was wearing lipstick and powder. They didn't care if it just made you look pretty.

'Not much left of the morning,' he said, looking at his watch.

They emerged from the station into driving rain that bounced off the streets. Lewis looked disconsolate. 'What lousy weather.'

'You can't organize the weather, Lewis.'

'Pouring with rain and no point in escaping into a gallery or a museum because there's nothing there.'

There began to be a hollow feeling inside her. This was not how she had pictured their reunion. Had she imagined her feelings for Lewis? Had she conjured them up out of loneliness and boredom?

She steeled herself to face up to it straight away. 'Are you disappointed with me?' she asked.

He turned to her, rain dripping from the peak of his cap. 'Disappointed? How could I be?'

'People don't always match up to their memories.'

'Freddie, you're *better* than my memory. Why? Is that how you feel about me?'

'No, of course not. You don't seem very happy, that's all.'

'Sorry.' Lewis groaned. 'Sorry I've been moaning. The journey took forever and there were no damned seats and all I wanted was to be here with you.' He took her in his arms, hugging her. 'How could I possibly be disappointed with you? You're perfect. I wanted the day to be perfect too. Freddie, I've been ticking off the hours. I wanted the train to be on time, and blue skies and frost – it didn't seem too much to ask.'

She kissed his cold cheek. 'I won't blame you for the weather.'

They found a café on Euston Road. After ordering coffee, Lewis asked Freddie about her job. She had been transferred to a factory in Slough the previous month. The factory made propellers.

'It's fine,' she said. But then added, 'I miss my Birmingham friends. It's nice being in a lodging house, though. Some of the others in the house complain about the rooms, but I'm so glad not to be in the hostel any more. It's a relief to have a room of my own.'

'What are the people like?

She shrugged. 'They're okay.'

'No they're not.' The corners of Lewis's mouth tilted in a smile. 'Something's up, isn't it?'

'It's very boring . . .'

'You won't bore me.'

'I will. Men always hate hearing about girls falling out with each other. They don't understand and they find it tedious.'

'I don't care what you talk about. It's wonderful just to hear your voice.'

'Okay. But if you're bored, say so. There's a girl called Shirley who everyone else hates. Half a dozen of us work at the same bench. If we go out to the pictures, they never ask Shirley.'

'What's wrong with her?'

'She's just odd. That's the thing: if she was bossy or unkind, I'd probably ignore her as well. But she isn't. She never quite says the right thing and her clothes are awful and her hair's all wrong. So the other girls shut her out, and I hate that.'

'Ganging up on someone, you mean? I admire you for sticking to your principles, Freddie.'

'Do you?' she said glumly. 'I'm thinking of throwing them aside. All it means is that I end up sitting with Shirley at break time, and goodness, Lewis, she can be tiresome.'

He gave a crack of laughter. 'There was a chap like that

on my first ship. Couldn't get a thing right, and the first lieutenant was a bully and made life hell for him. I felt sorry for the fellow, but my God, he seemed to walk into it.' He looked out of the window. 'Seems to be easing off a bit. Shall we make a dash for it?'

They caught a bus to Oxford Street. In Selfridges, Freddie looked in the haberdashery department for buttons for her raincoat, but there weren't any the right size. Then Lewis said he wanted to buy her something, and she said there was no need, and they had something approaching an argument. In the end she said, oh well, something small, which she knew was ungracious, but though they wandered round the various floors, there wasn't anything nice, which made Lewis irritable again. To cheer him up, she suggested they have lunch.

In the restaurant, they met a couple that Lewis knew, a fellow naval officer from Dartmouth, and the officer's wife, a pretty woman with curling brown hair, who was expecting a baby. Because the restaurant was crowded, the four of them shared a table. During the conversation, which was mostly about the navy, Freddie felt herself taking a step back. In their chance meeting on the train three months earlier, Lewis had seemed to admit a vulnerability, and she had liked him better for that. But now, watching him with his friends, he seemed much like every other cocky young man she had been out with in the last few years – handsome, yes, but too eager to impress, to amuse, to put on a show. She sensed that he, too, wasn't concentrating on the conversation: every now and then his gaze darted round the restaurant and then, seeing her looking at him, he gave her his friendly, confident smile. They were better when it was just the two of them, perhaps – or maybe it was simply that they were both very tired. It frightened her to realize how little she really knew him, and it frightened her too to acknowledge to herself how much expectation and hope she had invested in this day.

After the meal was over, they parted from the couple. Lewis said, 'Sorry about that.'

'It doesn't matter.'

'Good of you to say so.' He shook his head. 'Christ, that was difficult.'

'Why?'

'Trevor was engaged to someone else when I knew him at Dartmouth. And then, a couple of years ago, Clare told me he'd got engaged to another girl.'

'Two fiancées?'

'And a wife now. I've no idea whether Sally knows about the others. I kept thinking I was going to put my foot in it.'

Because it was still raining, they went to see a film, *The Man in Grey*, at a cinema in Leicester Square. During the film, Lewis took her hand, threading his fingers through hers. Sitting with him in the darkness, she remembered what it was that had attracted her to him: a sort of solidity, an intuition that beneath his easy-going exterior he was substantial and serious. She recalled waking in the railway carriage to find her head on his shoulder. It had been both deeply pleasurable and restful at the same time. In the flickering light of the cinema, she looked at him, trying to work out what it was about his appearance that she found

438

so compelling. He was not Clark Gable handsome, but there was a puckish cast to his features: they were changeable, and his smile was quick and there was often a light in his eyes. Yes, perhaps it was that.

Without words, she found it easier to be close to him. She knew that she was tired and jittery, had felt like that for a long time, worn out by the long hours at work and by the constant demands and discomfort the war imposed upon civilians. She became unpleasant when she was tired, she thought, overly critical and quick to judge. Even worse than prim: prim and judgemental – dear God.

It was dark by the time they emerged from the cinema. They walked arm in arm along Charing Cross Road, ducking into a second-hand bookshop when it began to rain again.

Lewis searched through a row of paperback thrillers while Freddie browsed the shelves. Her eye was caught by a name on a spine and she took the book down. On the dust cover was a painting instantly recognizable as an Italian land-scape, the blackish-green of the cypress trees against a cobalt-blue sky. The book was called *The Dark and Distant Hills*, and it was by Milo Rycroft.

It took her a moment to place the name. Then she remem-bered. Milo Rycroft had been a friend of Tessa's. His phone number had been listed in Tessa's diary. He hadn't come to Angelo's funeral, but his wife had. *I thought I would come to represent him*, she had said. What had her name been? Rebecca, that was it. Rebecca Rycroft.

'Found something?' said Lewis.

Freddie showed him the book. 'My sister knew him.' She

turned it over in her hands. 'Milo Rycroft,' she said, half to herself. 'I hadn't really thought about him.'

'What do you mean?'

She looked him in the eye, her chin jutting. 'I suppose Marcelle's told you about Tessa.'

'She said something. She told me your sister had had a baby who had died. Why? Did you think I'd disapprove?'

'Do you?'

'No, of course not.' He looked hurt. 'Disapproving or approving doesn't come into it. It just doesn't.'

'Sorry.' She felt ashamed of herself for leaping to conclusions. 'Sorry, Lewis.'

'A rotten thing to happen to anyone, that's what I thought.'

Unexpectedly, tears sprang to her eyes and she had to blink to send them back. She felt him stroke her hair; his lips brushed against hers.

Then he took the book from her, turning it over in his hands and skimming through the brief description of the novel on the inner flap of the dust cover. 'It's set in Tuscany,' he said. 'That's where your sister lives, isn't it?'

'Yes.' Again, she almost wanted to cry. 'I worry about her all the time,' she said. 'She's always there, in my mind, though I try to think about other things.'

'If she's sensible . . . if she keeps her head down . . .'

'Tessa's *never* been sensible. And I don't think she's ever in her entire life even *considered* keeping her head down.'

'You sound angry with her.'

'She just went off!' The words burst out of her. 'She just left me!'

He was looking at her closely. 'Poor old Freddie,' he said, and kissed her again. Then: 'Let me get this for you. I've thought of somewhere where we'll be able to talk properly.'

They walked to a bus stop. 'I don't know what you'll think of this place,' he said. 'I don't even know if it still exists. When I was at Winchester, my Aunt Kate used to meet me at the station at the end of term and take me to this funny little café for lunch.'

The bus took them to Bloomsbury, near the British Museum. The café was in the basement of a tall house, which, like the rest of London, looked dilapidated. Wooden supports held up the roof of the front porch, and the stone steps running down to the basement had fractured.

Inside, there were half a dozen tables. Freddie sat down at a free one as Lewis went to the counter. Books were crammed on the shelves that covered the walls. There was a black enamel stove with a snaking metal chimney, and a Russian samovar on the counter. The contents of the café appeared to be in an advanced state of decay – the leather cushions on the chairs had split, the spines of many of the books were attached by a cat's-cradle of threads, and rain leaked through the gaps around the window.

An older woman, wearing several holey cardigans and with her grey hair pinned up in a straggling bun, was serving at the counter.

Lewis ordered tea and took it to their table. 'Sonia's a communist,' he said, cocking his head towards the woman with the cardigans. 'Delighted that Uncle Joe's on the same side as us now. She and Aunt Kate were great friends.' He glanced round. 'When I was a kid, I used to think this place smelled funny.'

'Woodsmoke and cigarette ash.'

'And condensation and wet wool. What do you think? Do you like it?'

She reached across the table and took his hand. 'I love it. I could sit here for hours, it's so lovely and warm.'

'I'm glad. How old were you when your sister's baby died?'

'Eighteen.'

'Just a kid, then. It must have been bloody hard for you, losing your nephew like that.'

It struck her that no one else had ever said that to her. Lewis had recognized that she had suffered a loss as well.

'It was awful,' she said. 'The worst thing was having to arrange the funeral. I didn't know whether I was doing the right thing – whether Tessa would have preferred something else. I hope I'll never have to do anything so awful again in my entire life.'

She hadn't thought about Tessa's men friends for a long time, but now she did. She could not remember Milo Rycroft among the crowd who had come to Tessa's flat or among those who had dined with her at the Ritz or the Mirabelle. Which was interesting in itself. *You sound angry with her*, Lewis had said, and he had been right. She had been angry with Tessa for leaving her and she had been angry with her for refusing to tell her the name of the baby's father. It had made her feel as if she was being treated like a child; she had felt distrusted. Tessa had told her that she had loved Angelo's father, but it seemed to Freddie that Tessa's love

442

had left so much destruction in its wake. It had even opened up a distance between the two of them.

Lewis said suddenly, 'I'm sorry if I've been a bit off today. I haven't been sleeping well.' He laughed. 'No one sleeps well on board ship – too noisy, and the nights are too interrupted. But I used to be able to get my three or four hours. I can't now. I lie awake, thinking about things. I try to think of you, Freddie, but sometimes even that is pretty hopeless. I seem to catch these brief glimpses of you. That night at the Dorchester, and then, do you remember, Marcelle's house, just for a minute or two. Then that evening on the train. You don't seem to belong anywhere in particular, you don't seem to need anyone in particular. I'm afraid you'll slip out of my grasp. And I couldn't bear that to happen.'

His hands gripped hers tightly. She gave a shake of her head. 'I'm not going to slip out of your grasp, Lewis.'

'No?' He gave a half-smile. 'Then that's just as well. Because you see, Freddie, I've fallen in love with you.'

Now and then, Tessa almost remembered. It was an odd feeling, almost remembering, like thistledown that floated away, propelled on the air currents made by the movements of your hands as you tried to grasp it.

The almost memories came to her first thing in the mornings. She would open her eyes and fix her gaze on the pale square of curtain where the light showed through. In her mind's eye she saw a long, straight road ahead of her, grey with rain. At the side of the road, something moved – a flag or a sign, blue and orange in colour. Then it would dissolve and she would close her eyes and try to sink back into the relaxed, dreamy state that had given birth to the almost memories. Angelo had had a cold, she would say to herself. She hadn't been able to work and the weather had been bad. It had felt oppressive to be in the flat with the rain and the baby crying because he couldn't feed properly. Max had come to see her – but she couldn't remember Max coming to see her, only that he had afterwards told her he had.

It was like glimpsing something out of the corner of her eye. A flash, a glimmer, and a thought forming, gathering shape. It seemed to her that she must look at it obliquely, because if she tried too hard it might disappear and never come back.

In the winter, when the snow had lain thick on the ground, she had walked down the valley each night after darkness had fallen. She had worn her mother's fur coat and a pair of rubber boots and she had carried two large baskets. The shorn, knotted trunks of the vines had made rows of black marks through the smooth surface of the snow, like dots waiting to be joined up.

Reaching the edge of the wood, she had walked a short way beneath the trees and waited. Soon a muted light had shown and she had heard the crunch of footsteps. Then one of the men – Desmond, Roy or Chris, perhaps – had come out of the shadows. They all looked like brigands, were often unshaven, their hair wild and their clothing a ragged piling-on of anything that might give warmth. She gave them the food from her baskets, they talked for a while, and then they melted back into the forest and she returned to the villa.

As wars went, Tessa supposed this one was more complicated than most. A world war and a civil war were being played out simultaneously in one narrow, mountainous country. There were the Allied troops, struggling to hold on to the beachhead at Anzio and at the same time engaged in bitter fighting to break through the heavily defended Gustav Line, south of Rome. There were the partisan bands forming up in the woods and mountains, a ragtag mixture of Italian deserters and patriots and Allied prisoners of war, who liked now and again to take a potshot at the fascist militias or blow up a bridge or ambush a German convoy. The reprisals against the partisans and their families were swift and cruel.

There were more than a hundred men hiding in the wooded hills on the Belcanto estate. Tessa knew many of them by name. They were of numerous nationalities – British, Canadian, Australian, New Zealander, Indian, French. Some, including Desmond Fitzgerald, had tried more than once to reach the Allied lines, but had been forced to turn back. Desmond had returned to Tuscany halfway through December, having been recaptured before escaping a second time.

As the fighting raged south of Rome, more and more refugees fled north. Their homes, towns and villages had been pulverized to rubble in the battle. Men, women and children, hollow-faced and hungry, some injured in the bombings and many unwell, all worn out by exhaustion and deprivation, came to the farms and villa in search of food and shelter. Olivia never turned anyone away. But their stores were beginning to run low, and she dreaded, Olivia confided to Faustina and Tessa, being forced to choose between continuing to feed those who lived on the estate and helping the refugees.

POWs, deserters and partisans called at the clinic. There might be a quiet knock on the door early in the morning, or Faustina might look out to the small garden behind the clinic and see a wounded man hiding in the shade of the chestnut tree. They patched up the sick and injured and tried to find them a place of safety in which to recuperate. At the end of May, warning leaflets were dropped from aeroplanes. Anyone giving food or shelter to a partisan would be shot. Any house sheltering a rebel would be destroyed.

There was an afternoon when Tessa was returning to the villa after visiting one of the farms. Her route took her along the border of a field. As she neared the villa she heard the slamming of car doors and the crunch of boots on gravel. In the lee of a tall hedgerow, she paused. Cautiously she stepped forward until she could see between the branches. Two German armoured cars were standing outside the entrance to the villa; half a dozen soldiers were crossing the front courtyard. One soldier had remained with the cars. As Tessa watched, he took off his forage cap, scratched his head boredly, then swung round, his gun raised, until he was facing the hedgerow.

Tessa took a step back. A path ran beside the field, down to the valley. As she hurried away from the villa, she seemed to feel the heat of the soldier's gaze on her back. Her spine tingled.

But no voice called out and no gunshot ripped through the air. When she looked behind her, the path was empty. Quickly she took cover in a chestnut copse. She guessed that the German soldiers were searching the villa. Perhaps some rumour had reached the ears of those in authority that the Zanettis were sympathetic to the partisans, or that an escaped prisoner of war could hope for shelter at the Villa di Belcanto. It only took a whisper, coaxed by bribery or coerced by threat. Thank God no fugitives were hiding in the villa at present. But some of the clothes hanging in Tessa's wardrobe had English labels, and her address book, with its list of English names and a letter she had received from Freddie in early 1941, was hidden behind a loose brick in the fireplace. Scratch away and anyone might discover who she really was. They all knew of people who had been taken from their homes, accused of treachery or spying, imprisoned or put to death.

Above her, between the green leaves of the chestnuts, gleamed scraps of sapphire-blue sky. In places, sunlight pierced the tree cover and fell in pools of radiance on the forest floor. Not so long ago, she had cared little whether she lived or died. But now she discovered in herself a fierce desire to live, to be free, to survive the war.

Dusk had fallen before she felt it safe to return to the villa. Faustina met her in the courtyard. The German troops had been looking for three escaped prisoners, she told Tessa. They were searching all the houses and farms in the area.

In her room, Tessa checked that her address book was still in its hiding place. It was. She let out a breath and sat down on the edge of the bed. The muscles in her legs trembled; she pressed her fingers against her mouth.

She thought of Guido. Had he been taken prisoner – but if so, wouldn't they have heard something through the Red Cross? Or was he hiding out in the mountains, along with so many other Italian soldiers? She remembered the conversation they had had that late summer's evening in the courtyard, Guido's passion, his belief in loyalty and principle. Loyalty and principle were dangerous qualities now. A great many people were dying for them.

Let him be alive, she thought, let him be safe. Please, let him still be alive.

The battlefield was coming closer. You kept yourself busy. It wasn't as if there was a shortage of things to do. Days and nights were interrupted by the bombing formations that flew low over the countryside. The hills and valleys seemed to shake with the force of the explosions. Fighter planes aimed their machine guns at roads and bridges and passing cars. Plumes of smoke rose into the sky from a ruined house or the wreckage of a plane. Sometimes the silver bubble of a parachute floated to earth.

When the planes swooped close to the villa, they hurried the children down to the cellar. There were now twenty children at Belcanto, including a six-week-old baby girl, Cara, whose mother had died in childbirth. Cara had a way of drifting off to sleep while she fed; Tessa had to jiggle her and tickle her feet to keep her awake.

When the bombs fell close to the villa, some of the children cried and screamed, but others, by now accustomed to the noise, went on playing, scarcely glancing up at the sky. Tessa made sure to take Tommaso's hand as soon as she heard the low rumble of the bombers. She didn't want him running off to hide in his den in the box hedge.

Inside the cellar, she tried to distract the children by telling them stories or playing singing games with them. The cool stone room was lit by candles, the one small high window protected by a grid. Shadows blackened the corners. One day, Tessa was reading to the children when she felt someone bury their head in her lap. Looking down, she saw that it was Tommaso. Which was a kind of miracle, she thought, as she stroked his curly head.

June 5th, the day after Rome fell to the Allies.

It was Faustina who found him, though she didn't recognize him at first. It was dusk, and bats were flickering over the roofs of the buildings. Faustina was getting ready to leave the clinic for the villa when there was a knock at the door. Opening it, she heard running footsteps and saw two men disappearing around the corner of the road. Then she saw a third man curled up on the dusty verge across from the clinic. She heard the panicky rasp of his breathing as she crossed the road to him.

'It's all right,' she said gently. 'You're safe now. Try to breathe slowly, that's right, in, then out, slowly, yes, that's good.'

As she smoothed back his ragged black hair from his face, she drew in her own breath sharply. 'Guido,' she said. 'Oh, *Guido*.'

* * *

449

They carried him into the clinic, where they cut off his clothing. He had been shot in the shoulder and Faustina suspected that he was suffering from pneumonia.

Stefano, the factor, was dispatched to fetch Dr Berardi. While they were waiting for the doctor, Faustina unwound the makeshift bandage from Guido's shoulder. As she worked, she talked to her brother. 'So typical, Guido, going off like that without telling anyone where you were. Mother was worried but I knew you'd turn up like a bad penny. Trust you to make a dramatic entrance — and just when I was about to have my dinner.' A flicker of a smile crossed Guido's strained face.

Dr Berardi removed the bullet from Guido's shoulder and stitched up the wound. Faustina's diagnosis of pneumonia was confirmed. The *dottore* took Faustina and Olivia aside. If he were to survive, Guido would need careful nursing for many weeks. He would need rest and quiet and the chance to recover his strength.

That first night, they nursed him at the clinic. Early the following morning, Stefano and one of the other men carried him, wrapped up in blankets, and laid him carefully on the back of the cart. Olivia said her farewells, and then Stefano drove Faustina, Tessa and Guido away from the villa and along the road.

The plan, concocted by the three women the previous night, was that they would transport Guido to the most remote farmhouse on the estate. They would take turns looking after him, two or three days at a time. The small stone farmhouse — two rooms and a store for logs and tools — had been deserted for many years, but the bulk of the building was intact. Woodland lay to one side of it, and to the other was a broad valley. Few people passed that way. If necessary, the forest would provide shelter and a hiding place.

The cart turned off the road and headed along a grassy track. Another half-mile or so and then the track faded to a footpath. Guido lay motionless in the back of the cart. Now and then Faustina told Stefano to halt so that she could check on her brother. Then their journey began again, up and up. The meadows were jewelled with flowers and the air was fresher. Spreading down the far side of the hill, a dense, dark green, was the forest.

Soon, even the footpath disappeared and there was nothing to mark their way.

In the early hours of the morning, when she rose to check on Guido, Tessa heard the birds singing in the woods. As she bathed his feverish body and wiped the beads of sweat from his skin, her head was filled with birdsong, and the hush-hush of the trees in the forest, and Guido's breathing, the laboured inward breath and the short, gasping outward one. When the gasps became quicker she held his hand and counted for him, in one two three, out one two three, until his breathing eased.

When his fever began to abate, he asked where he was. Then he blinked and said, 'Tessa? Is it you?' but closed his eyes before she could reply. She remembered how she had felt in the hospital, after the accident, all clarity gone, nothing understood. Guido's cheekbones jutted through his skin and there wasn't an ounce of spare flesh on him. He was sunburned nut-brown and there were old scars on his body. When she gave him a back rub, as Faustina had instructed her to, she felt the rise and hollow of his ribs. When he coughed, she held a cup to his mouth so that he could take a sip of water. It was a different sort of intimacy, this, she thought, a different sort of knowledge, and it seemed like a gift to her.

She slept on the floor beside his camp bed – well, *slept*: flickering in and out of consciousness, she woke whenever he stirred or moaned and placed a cool cloth on his forehead, talking to him until he grew calmer. When he seemed to take a turn for the worse one night, his skin clammy and his breath short, she bathed him with tepid water as the fever rose. There was a ferocity in her nursing of him, a refusal to be beaten. She wasn't going to let him die, she wouldn't let him slip away. By morning, his temperature had fallen and he was sleeping soundly.

It felt odd, leaving Guido with Faustina or Olivia and returning to the villa. Her life there seemed less real than these strange days at the farmhouse.

Once, from the farmhouse, she saw a shepherd, his flock of sheep puffs of smoke against the green grass across the valley. Another day, she caught sight of two figures walking over the hill, their black shapes like cut-out paper dolls. She estimated the distance from the house to the woodland and wondered whether she would be strong enough to support Guido across the grass so that they could hide beneath the trees. But the two figures walked on, disappearing over the brow of the hill, and eventually, when she was sure they would not return, she left the window and went to sit by his bed again.

The great events of the war – the fall of Rome and the Allied landings in Normandy just two days later – seemed a long way away. Sitting beside Guido at night, Tessa thought instead about love, and the way it died, and the way that sometimes, in spite of distance and misunderstanding, it persisted. How it might drape a glamour over everything, as the moon and the frost had done the first night she had met Milo, and how once the magic had fallen away, you might not even remember why you had loved that person in the first place. In recent years, when she had thought of Milo, she had seen only vanity, egotism and greed.

Yet though love might last, it could also change. She had been seventeen years old when she had fallen in love with Guido Zanetti. She had loved him then because he swam the fastest, because he had jumped into the pool with his clothes on, and because the way he had looked at her had made her melt inside.

Though much had altered, worn away by time and experience, she acknowledged, as she sat by his bedside, that she still loved him. She loved him for his resolution and his courage, but also for his vulnerability. Funny that, she thought, that you could fall in love with a man all over again because of the questions in his eyes.

He said, 'Tessa?'

She was standing at the window. She turned to him and smiled. 'Hello, Guido. How are you feeling?'

'Better.'

He looked puzzled, so she explained. 'You've been ill. Olivia and Faustina and I have been looking after you.'

He tried to shuffle upright. She went to help him, propping pillows behind his back. She sat down on the side of the camp bed and put her hand on his forehead. It felt cooler.

He said, 'How long have I been here?'

'Ten days.'

He looked dismayed. 'I can't remember . . .'

'Two of your friends brought you to the clinic.'

He frowned. 'I'd been shot.'

'Yes, in your shoulder. The wound's healing well.' She didn't want to tire him, talking to him. 'Do you think you could eat something?'

'I'll try.'

Tessa heated up some soup on the oil stove. She fed him spoonfuls, a sip at a time.

After half a dozen mouthfuls, Guido shook his head. 'Christ . . . spoon-fed like a baby!'

'You'll be able to do it yourself in a day or two, I promise you.' She put aside the bowl and spoon. 'You just have to be patient.'

The corners of his eyes crinkled when he smiled. 'You know patience was never my strong point.' Suddenly he clutched her hand. 'Luciella, Maddalena – have you heard from them?'

'They're both well. Olivia had a letter from Maddalena only a week ago.'

'Thank God.' He exhaled, closing his eyes.

'They're living in Rimini now.'

'Rimini.' His lids flew open.

'Maddalena took Luciella there to stay with her aunt. She thought it would be safer. You mustn't worry. As soon as you're well enough, you can write to them.'

'Was she very angry with me?'

'I don't know. She misses you, I'm sure, Guido.'

His voice lowered. 'When I left the barracks, I knew that I was deserting her, too.'

Tessa picked up the soup bowl. 'Try to eat a little more. The more you eat, the quicker you'll regain your strength.'

She told him about the letter Sandro had thrown from the train. 'So we know he's alive,' she added.

'*Was* alive, then.' Guido looked angry. 'Sandro was never cut out to be a soldier.'

'Were you?'

He tried to shrug, but winced at the pain in his shoulder. 'I didn't mind too much at first. But then I grew sick of it. I prefer things to be clear-cut, you see, and most of the time, war's a bloody mess.'

'Hush,' she said. 'Try not to think about it.'

His gaze turned to the window. 'When we were boys,' he said softly, 'Sandro and I used to play in these woods. Once, we got lost. My grandmother had to send the men to look for us. It was midnight before they found us. When we were older, we learned every tree and path. We could find our way in the dark.'

He lay down again, closing his eyes. Tessa knew that she could have drawn from memory the angle of his cheek-bone and the curve of his chin. She covered his hand with her own and watched the rise and fall of his breath.

*   *   *

'At first,' Guido told her, 'after I left the barracks, I told myself that I was doing the sensible thing. I'd hide out in the hills, wait till things settled down. But in my heart, I knew that the longer I waited, the more difficult it would be to travel south. So in the end, I just stayed where I was.

'I began to come across others like myself, deserters and men who were avoiding the draft. Eventually there were a couple of dozen of us. In the winter, it was so cold. We built shelters, but we had to be careful when we lit fires in case someone saw the smoke. And it was hard to find dry fuel.'

He smiled at Tessa. 'When the snow fell, I used to dream about being here, at Belcanto, in the summer. I'd try to imagine lying here, like I am now, on the grass, in the sun. And then, thank God, spring came at last. We had a piece of luck – we raided an ammunition dump and were able to take away explosives and weapons. We used the dynamite to blow up railway tracks and derail a troop train. We learned, after a while, that we were more effective when we operated in small groups. We ambushed a staff car, brought down telephone lines. We learned to bury the men we'd killed, because if no bodies were found then reprisals were less likely. But then I fell ill. I had a cough that wouldn't shift. We were all exhausted and half starved. I didn't want to be a burden on the others. Stupid of me – I was a danger to myself and everyone else.'

'And then?' she said. 'What happened to you, Guido?'

'Someone came up with a plan to blow up a bridge. I argued against it – it would be too well guarded and we didn't have enough weapons – but in the end we went ahead. It was a disaster. We were heavily outnumbered and we hadn't a chance. I was shot in the shoulder and some of the men were killed and others were taken prisoner. Which is pretty much a death sentence. Afterwards, the hills weren't safe for us any more, so we split up. A couple of friends helped me travel south. I'd never have made it here without them.'

He was silent for such a long time that Tessa thought he had fallen asleep. But then he said, 'I told you I used to dream about being here. But I had other dreams, as well. I'd remember that night in the courtyard, when we were together, in the thunderstorm. I tried to see you in my mind's eye. I tried to remember exactly how you looked and what you said. Only I always gave it a different ending. In my daydreams you didn't walk away from me, Tessa. You stayed with me, beneath the loggia, and we held each other as we watched the rain.'

She lay down beside him on the camp bed, fitting her head into the crook of his good shoulder. As she felt the beating of his heart, her own slowed. She closed her eyes, and the world was reduced to the rise and fall of his breath.

Faustina said that Guido's lungs were clear now and the shoulder wound was knitting up nicely. Guido measured out his returning strength by the distance he could walk. To begin with, two circuits of the farmhouse. Then he had to come in and lie down on the bed, his heart pounding, sweat on his brow. The next day he walked into the woods, along the winding path beneath the trees.

Sometimes planes circled and swooped in the sky and

they heard the crump-crump of bombs and saw columns of smoke rising in the blue-green distance. Tessa and Guido liked to lie in a glade in the woods, with the dappled shade of the branches above them. They could stay there for hours, just touching and kissing. She had forgotten all the different ways you could kiss, like a rainbow of colours. Soft kisses and hungry kisses and kisses that made her burn inside. Kisses as transient and light as a powder puff, sweeping over the skin.

They kissed like teenagers, she thought. Teenagers who were half afraid of taking the next step. Teenagers who thought they had all the time in the world.

Walk a few yards into the woods and the canopy of leaves and branches formed a green roof, lit by flickering fragments of sky. On the forest floor, thickets of briar and scrub formed barricades.

Guido knew the paths that wove through the forest, the green tunnels of leaf and branch and undergrowth. He knew how, after a short distance, the land rose up in a steep escarpment. Saplings grew out of the cliff face and ivy struggled to grip the bare soil. He took her hand, leading the way. On the top of the escarpment, in a grove of birches, they kissed.

They were heading back to the farmhouse when they heard voices. Guido's hand tightened on her wrist. They stood as motionless as the trees.

Three men in field-grey uniform were walking down the brow of the hill towards the farmhouse. Guido put a finger to his lips. *Don't move*, he mouthed. Tessa wished she hadn't worn pink. Shocking pink, Schiaparelli pink. It wasn't the sort of colour you saw in woodland. What if one of the soldiers looked into the forest and caught a glimpse of it?

The German soldiers went into the farmhouse. Tessa heard a whoop of delight. One of the men came out to stand on the front step, a bottle of wine in one hand and a loaf of bread in the other. He sat down on the step to eat. He was young and fair-haired and his uniform was ragged and dirty. The others followed him, arms full of booty, and the three of them sat on the grass between the house and the woodland. Tessa could smell the tobacco they smoked. Her muscles ached from standing still so long.

At last they gathered up their kitbags and headed off down the hill. She heard Guido exhale. After several minutes had passed, they walked back to the house.

Inside, baskets and storage jars had been emptied and clothing and bedlinen flung about. They stood face to face, their fingers threading together. His lips floated over her mouth and brow. Then he unbuttoned her blouse and the palms of his hands ran over her skin.

She had known him so long. More than ten years had passed since they had first made love in the garden of the Villa Millefiore. And yet as he made love to her now, she thought she had hardly known him at all. She was learning him anew, learning the shadows and secrets of his body, the taste of his skin and the touch of his hand. She was learning what it was to be perfectly in tune with a man, to close her eyes and know that she was a part of him and he was a part of her, and together they were one.

* * *

459

Afterwards, she said:

'I want to tell you about my son. His name was Angelo, Angelo Frederick Nicolson. I always thought it was such a long name for such a tiny baby. He died in the car crash. It was my fault. I was driving. Something like that, you lose a part of yourself. I can't remember the day of the accident at all. Afterwards, people told me that the weather was bad and the car skidded. And I've always been afraid that I went out that day on a whim, because I was bored of the rain and being stuck in the flat. I can't bear to think that Angelo died for a trivial reason. He died and I lived, and after it happened I so often wished I'd died with him.'

He kissed the top of her head. 'And do you now, Tessa?'

She said, 'Not now. Not any more.'

'I regret not following you to England,' he said. 'I regret letting you leave. I regret that I was too proud to go after you. You think we would have quarrelled – I'm not so sure. I think it would have been an adventure. I think we would never have tired of each other.'

Her head rested on his shoulder and his breathing slowed until she knew that he slept. She felt against her back the ridges and canvas of the camp bed and saw, on the floor, their clothing, where they had torn it off, a splash of pink blouse, a sandal kicked into the doorway. Her eyelids dipped open and shut as she listened to the birdsong and the sough of the breeze in the trees.

The next morning, Guido left the farmhouse. He would head south, he said, towards the Allied lines. If he came across any partisan bands en route, he would join them.

460

Tessa walked with him through the woods until they reached the foot of the escarpment. They said their good-byes and then Guido went on alone. Love lasts as long as it lasts, she thought, as she watched him climb to the top of the escarpment. He looked back and waved to her.

When she could no longer see him, she closed her eyes tightly. *Be safe, Guido,* she whispered, *and be careful. And when all this is over, go back to your wife and child and be happy.*

Chapter Fourteen

Charing Cross station was busy, queues snaking out of the ticket hall and along the street. Rebecca walked to the Embankment to save changing trains. The tube station was crowded too, the waiting passengers so deeply packed on the District Line platform that two trains came and went before she was able to get on. She checked her watch: it was a quarter to two. Visiting times at the nursing home in which her mother had been incarcerated for the past fortnight were distinctly mean – between three and four in the afternoons at weekends, and half an hour in the evenings. She wouldn't stay for the evening; it would be difficult with the trains so unreliable, and she was needed at the farm, and Meriel had said, when they had last spoken on the telephone, that they had filled Mummy up so with painkillers she hardly knew you were there.

Great events had recently taken place, but all had for Rebecca been muted, overshadowed by her mother's illness. Though she had expressed both relief and joy at the Allied landings in Normandy, she had felt distanced from the news. Two weeks ago, Mrs Fainlight had collapsed at home and had been taken to hospital. X-rays had shown tumours in her ribs and left hip. The bone in her hip joint was crumbling, and in time would no longer be able to support her weight. After a fortnight, she had been moved from the local hospital to a nursing home in Kensington, where she would remain until, the consultant had told Rebecca and Meriel, her condition had stabilized. And then what? Rebecca had asked him. He had seemed put out by her bluntness and had steepled his fingers. They must understand that their mother's condition was terminal. They would hope to relieve her pain but could not arrest the course of her cancer. If Mrs Fainlight wished to return home, then she would no longer be able to care for herself. Arrangements must be made. Leaving the nursing home, both sisters had cried. It had struck Rebecca later that they had taken it in turns, Meriel as they had walked to the bus stop, and Rebecca on the bus itself. As if in recognition that they were now all that was left to each other, and that one of them must be capable of flagging down the right bus and asking for tickets.

She was early. She stopped for a cup of tea in a small café near Holland Park. There was a fug of cigarette smoke and the tea tasted of dishwater, but Rebecca drank it all the same. A tired-looking woman sat at the adjacent table. She was doing her make-up, making forceful circular strokes on her cheeks and forehead with a greyish powder puff, which now and then was scrubbed vigorously into the edges of an almost empty compact. The compact went back

464

inside the woman's handbag and a pot of rouge was taken out. Again, it looked empty. Then mascara and a stub of lipstick. Rebecca's hand itched for a pencil to sketch the transformation, the scrub of the powder, the tight pressing together and release of the lips, and the frowning peer into the hand mirror. When she was done, the woman stood up and smoothed her dress down over her hips. Then, swaying on high heels, she left the café.

There was still half an hour to kill, and the territory was familiar to Rebecca from her stay in London after her separation from Milo, so she decided to go for a walk. She passed the café in which she had sometimes breakfasted when she had been unable to face the hotel dining room, and a small haberdasher's where she had bought buttons and stockings. When she looked back at her former self, she felt a mixture of pity and impatience. She had been so purposeless, and so easily wounded.

She walked on. London looked dreary and derelict. Few buildings had not suffered some war damage and many were mere shells. Bombs had opened up great gaps between the houses, flattened expanses, sometimes cratered, in which lay heaps of rubble, broken bricks, splintered wood and fractured stones. Tall green weeds grew among the debris. Children played on the bomb sites, their dirty clothing too small or overlarge, the girls' cardigans holed, the seats of the boys' shorts worn away or patched. They shrieked, pushing and jeering at each other as they ran through the ruined buildings. A boy of eight or nine was urinating into a puddle, the expression on his thin, ratty face a mixture of concentration and glee.

Rebecca realized that she had become disorientated. Streets that should have been there had disappeared and buildings that had once been landmarks were now unrecognizable. The children seemed to notice her confusion. A boy paused, standing on top of a heap of rubble, and a girl pushing a set of pram wheels stared at her. Something splashed in a puddle as Rebecca walked past; one of the children had thrown a stone at her. The boy stooped and picked up a piece of broken brick. Rebecca saw a flicker of excitement in the girl's eyes. The girl picked up her skirts and walked beside Rebecca, waggling her bottom in an exaggerated way and pursing her lips. The onlooking children roared with laughter. Then the brick struck the back of Rebecca's raincoat and she yelled at the boy to bugger off, and they all howled and screamed and whirled round in a great arc, like feral starlings.

At last she recognized her surroundings: she was only a few minutes away from the nursing home. She brushed the mud off the back of her coat and hurried on. In the nursing home, her mother, shrunken and diminished by illness, was propped up on pillows, hair brushed, best nightie on. Rebecca's purpose, this visit, was to try to find out whether her mother wanted to go home or whether she preferred to stay where she was. The conversation did not go according to plan. Mrs Fainlight was unusually chatty, almost elated. Had Rebecca read the newspaper – the war was sure to be over soon. There was a particular paragraph – Rebecca was required to search through the paper, to find the article and then read it aloud. *Well*, said her mother expectantly, looking at her, and Rebecca said, yes, it sounds thrilling, doesn't it, Mummy? Then Mrs Fainlight told a long story about one of the nurses, who came from Shrewsbury, where she herself had lived when she was a girl. The story had failed to reach any conclusion when she closed her eyes and quite suddenly fell asleep. A few minutes later a nurse stuck her head round the door and said, 'Well, you have tired her out, haven't you?' and by then it was almost four o'clock, so Rebecca kissed her mother and left the room.

She pondered trying to speak to one of the doctors again, but abandoned the idea, knowing it would be pointless. It was up to her and Meriel now; she would start ringing round the nursing agencies on Monday. If going home was what her mother wanted, then that was what they would do. She would look after her in term time; perhaps Meriel would take over in the school holidays.

It was a relief to leave the nursing home, which smelled of floor polish and disinfectant. She did not want to go back yet inside the airless, crowded tube, so she walked instead. She felt the familiar guilt return, but now it was mixed with grief. In her relationship with her mother there had always been an intense desire to please, coupled with the knowledge that something about her inevitably disappointed.

She walked a short way along Kensington Road and then turned down Gloucester Road. Here, the street scene seemed ordinary, lacking the menace of her earlier walk across the bomb site. The sun was shining and the sky was blue, and in the gardens, roses were in flower. On Gloucester Road itself, people were going in and out of the shops and a queue was forming outside the butcher's. A platinum blonde was leaning out of a third-storey window, calling to someone on the pavement below. On a side street on the far side of the road, two young girls came out of a house. They were fourteen, fifteen or so. One was wearing a blue dress and swinging a shopping basket, the other was in green stripes.

Rebecca heard a strange noise. Thrum, thrum – the humming intensified into a whine. People looked up. Then silence, and then, just before the massive explosion, Rebecca saw a dark shape in the sky.

The force of the blast threw her against a wall. She saw a flash of light, the spray of debris, a body flying through the air. Deafened, she seemed to watch the scene in slow motion: a car sucked upwards as if by a giant vacuum cleaner, along with a bicycle, a pram and a road sign – and the graceful arc of the blonde woman's body as she was pulled out of the window and dropped on to the road.

Rebecca's hearing returned. People were screaming, sirens were sounding, and there was the rush and pitter-patter of fragments of brick, wood and glass falling to earth. When they stopped falling, Rebecca stood up. She checked that she wasn't hurt. She saw that the epicentre of the blast had been between the side road and Gloucester Road. She remembered the two girls, the one in the blue dress and the one in green stripes. She took a few steps. She wasn't sure whether the pinkish-red things on the pavement were from the butcher's shop, or whether they were parts of people. She retched. Then, carefully, she made her way over

468

to the other side of the road, where she saw a piece of green and white cloth.

The girl in the green dress was dead. Rebecca could not see any sign of the girl in blue. She began to dig with her hands into the pile of fallen bricks and masonry. White dust flew into the air and the broken bricks cut her hands. She was kneeling in the rubble and dust, dragging out pieces of wood and throwing them aside, leaning forward to put all her weight into moving blocks of half a dozen bricks. She dug with urgency, afraid the girl would suffocate before she reached her. Though she was aware of the arrival of police cars and heavy rescue vehicles, she did not look round, but concentrated all her strength and attention on her task.

At last a piece of fabric, white with dust, was revealed. She scrabbled harder now, scooping up dust and fragments, using a length of planking to scrape aside broken glass. There was the girl's leg, smooth and white.

A voice said, 'That's all right, love. We'll take over now,' but she kept on digging. She could feel herself tiring, her muscles no longer working properly, and she wanted to weep with frustration.

The man crouched down beside her and put his hand on her shoulder.

'You've done well, but you need to let us have a go. We'll get her out quicker, you see.' Then he helped her to her feet.

She insisted on staying and watching as the firemen worked to prise the girl out of the rubble. Someone put a blanket round her shoulders and someone else placed a cup of tea into her hands. Her teeth rattled against the rim of the cup.

When they had freed the girl from the rubble, Rebecca saw that she was almost naked, her dress torn into tatters by the force of the blast. Her body, marbled by dust, looked untouched.

One of the firemen put his fingers against her neck.

'Is she alive?' said Rebecca.

The fireman nodded. 'Just about. Do you know her?'

Rebecca shook her head. As two women lifted the girl on to a stretcher and carried her to an ambulance, Rebecca walked away from the scene, slipping on the debris and weaving round fallen walls and wrecked vehicles. Eventually finding herself in Cromwell Road, she headed for South Kensington tube station. Her handbag was still hooked around her shoulder, so she took it down and got out the money for her fare. She felt oddly calm now, and when the man in the ticket office asked her whether she was all right, she was surprised, and nodded, saying, 'Yes, thank you, perfectly all right.' But when she alighted at the Embankment, she could not for a moment remember which way to walk, and stood on the pavement looking this way and that, as her thoughts slid around like broken glass in rubble.

At Charing Cross station, by a miracle, a train to Tunbridge Wells was waiting. Rebecca found a compartment. There was a woman of around her own age sitting in the opposite seat. The woman was wearing a grey skirt and jacket and a grey hat with a bunch of artificial cherries. She looked at Rebecca and said, 'Are you all right, dear?' and Rebecca,

who by then felt very tired, said once more, rather irritably, 'Perfectly all right, thank you.'

'You're rather dusty,' said the woman.

Rebecca looked down at herself. She saw that she was
covered in white dust, like the girl in the rubble. 'I didn't
realize,' she said. 'There was a bomb. A flying bomb.'

'Here,' said the woman. She offered Rebecca a handkerchief and mirror.

Rebecca stared into the mirror. She looked extraordinary,
she thought. Her hair and skin were almost entirely white;
the only colour was the green of her eyes.

'Oh dear,' she said, embarrassed. 'I do look a fright.'

She tried to wipe off the dust with the handkerchief,
but couldn't do it because her hand was shaking too much.
The woman in the hat took the handkerchief and cleaned
Rebecca's face for her. Rebecca remembered how, when
they were children, her mother had used to clean her
own and Meriel's faces by spitting on her handkerchief and
then scrubbing them. The woman in the hat with the cherries didn't spit.

The train rumbled through the green Kent countryside.
Rebecca closed her eyes and went into a half-sleep. Thoughts
flashed through her head, vivid and luminous. The boy
peeing in the puddle . . . her mother, animated, talking
about the nurse from Shrewsbury . . . the woman in the
café putting on her make-up. And for some reason she
couldn't fathom, she found herself remembering a trip
she had once taken to London with Milo, where she had
bought two costumes, a brown tweed and a red.

She thought of the girl in the blue dress. She remembered

471

how important it had seemed to free her. Why? she asked herself. Did you think it would even things up? Did you think it would make it better, a life saved for the one lost? Had her frantic scrabbling in the rubble been an act of atonement, perhaps?

No, she thought. It was nothing like that: I only wanted her to live.

After the fall of Rome, the Wehrmacht had fled north through Tuscany, pursued by the Allied Fifth and Eighth Armies. Now the Villa di Belcanto had been absorbed into the battlefield. A unit of German infantrymen had requisitioned the house, setting up gun emplacements inside barns and behind walls. Their captain, a civilized man, tried to ensure that his men did not harass the women of the villa.

The building that had once housed the school was now being used to store ammunition and fuel. Tessa and Faustina had carried the children's beds, clothing and playthings to the stable block. In the evening, they packed small suitcases for themselves. Into her case Tessa put a few items of clothing and a spare pair of shoes, her address book, a bar of soap and a hand towel, a hairbrush and some hair grips. What else? She opened the drawer of her dressing table and stared at its contents, then lifted her gaze to the mirror. Her hair had grown long during her years in Italy and was bleached flaxen by the sun. She wore it pinned into a knot on the back of her head. Her face was tanned and freckled, and her dress, an old blue cotton one she had made herself, had faded and worn at the seams. There were scratches on her arms – she could not remember where she had got them – and crinkles at the corners of her eyes. Twenty-eight years old, she thought, and lines round her eyes. Mama had always said that the Italian sun was bad for an English complexion. No wonder the soldiers now occupying the villa by and large left her alone. Tessa's hand hovered over the drawer. Then she took out a small pair of scissors, some tweezers, and a red lipstick, the colour of poppies. She clipped her case shut and went downstairs.

Two days ago, a bomb had landed in the courtyard of the *fattoria*. The force of the blast had brought down the front wall of the farm building, exposing the rooms inside, and had shattered every window in the surrounding houses. Cracks had appeared in the front façade of the villa, which had taken the greatest force of the blast. The Villa di Belcanto as Tessa remembered it, a place of coolness and grace and elegance, a refuge from the outside world, no longer existed. Indoors, broken glass littered the floors. A rain storm had soaked the silk curtains – Zanetti silk – so that they drooped, their vivid colours dimmed, white watermarks on the damask. The soldiers had taken chairs, blankets and china to their encampments in the outhouses and gardens, and to the *salotto*, which they now used as a mess. Men dozed on sofas or roamed the house, searching for food or wine. A pack of playing cards was scattered across a rug; in a fireplace, papers smouldered, crisping black in the flames.

Outside, beneath the trees, military lorries were parked, camouflaged with branches. Soldiers lounged in the shade, sleeping or smoking, the top halves of their bodies naked or their battledress unbuttoned in the heat. Someone had taken the portable gramophone from the house, and a Mozart quartet drifted through the hot evening air. The music was punctuated by the distant rat-tat-tat of gunfire.

Now and then, the sound of the guns grew louder and the soldiers hurried off to their emplacements. Then the noise would start again, deafening, a tidal wave of sound and vibration. Not far away, in the valley, the bright, flaring blots of shells arced through the sky.

In the stable block, Tessa packed another case, this time for the children, with a change of underwear and socks for each child. She found jerseys and raincoats, folded clothing and nappies for the babies and packed them into the pram. After she had checked that the children were sleeping, she went to the kitchen.

Faustina was wrapping cheese and sausages in straw and packing them into baskets. Tessa helped her. They talked about this and that: the heat, a trip Tessa had taken years ago to Morocco, a girl they both remembered from Mrs Hamilton's luncheons at the villa, and the dreadful food at those luncheons. Not the war, though.

At eleven o'clock Tessa went to bed. Lying awake on the narrow camp bed, she wondered how they would find enough milk for the babies. And how Olivia, who was unwell, would manage if they had to walk a long way. And how the younger children would cope.

But where should they go, and when? These questions troubled her. She had spoken to the German captain earlier in the day. He had advised her to take the children away from the villa, because its exposed position on a hilltop made it a military objective.

Tessa could not make up her mind. Might they be risking the children's lives if they took them away from the comparative safety of the villa? But then how long would it be before the villa itself became part of the battleground? And if and when they left, where should they go and which route should they choose, when the hills were exposed and the roads mined and machine-gunned?

She would decide tomorrow, she told herself. Now, she must sleep. She wondered where Guido was and what he was doing. She felt a sudden intense longing to hear his voice and see his smile, to feel the warmth of his arms around her. Their love for each other had always been mistimed, she thought, and had never had much of a future. Though Guido had spoken of his regrets in not following her to England, she herself had no such regrets. Guido belonged to Florence. He would not have been happy anywhere else. He was not a vagabond, a wanderer, as she was.

Tessa closed her eyes and willed herself to sleep.

Early the following morning, there was a moment of silence. Tessa looked at her watch. It was a quarter past five.

She went outside. At the back of the house, a part of the garden had so far survived the war untouched. Lavender grew in narrow beds and roses tumbled over archways. From the gravel path she could see down to the valley. The shells were landing closer now: one had struck the olive grove on the slope of the hill, splintering the gnarled grey trunks of the trees. Beside the road, cypress trees flared like black flames. The dawn sunlight made the dew on the grass sparkle like jewels. Tessa thought how new the world looked, how clean.

Just before she had woken, she had been dreaming. She looked out at the valley, searching her memory. A voice echoed. *He's found someone else. Some little trollop in Oxford.* It had been as if the voice had spoken in the next room.

Who had it been? Milo's wife, of course. Tessa remembered why she had been driving to Oxford. She had been going to see Milo, because she had been afraid she had lost him. It had been raining hard and Angelo had been crying because of his cold, and she had been tired and upset. She remembered the rain on the windscreen, and the metal sign, flapping in the wind, and a cyclist in a yellow oilskin, the headlamp on his bike like a single gleaming Cyclops eye. And the lorry, crawling up the hill.

Then the guns in their emplacements began to fire again, shattering the silence, and she turned on her heel and went back to the stable block.

They left the villa at mid-morning. A shell had struck the terrace where Tessa had walked that morning and the unit's captain had ordered all fuel and ammunition to be moved into the cellar. So there was no place any more of even the slightest safety. Olivia had spoken to the captain, who had told her to take the children away. They must not stay here, he had said, running a hand over his unshaven chin. Everyone must watch out for themselves.

They set out for Greve, a straggling crocodile of women and children. The children wore sun hats and carried their jerseys, and the grown-ups – Tessa, Olivia, Faustina, Perlita's mother, Emilia, and Maria, who worked in the laundry – took the suitcases and baskets. Emilia, who was short and sturdy, pushed the pram across the uneven ground.

They walked along the edge of the field, parallel to the road. Dog roses formed a tangled hedge and poppies grew in the thick grass. They were making for the higher ground, where the rough scrub and thickets, scored with ditches and gullies, might offer shelter. Now the planes were firing incessantly at the roads. When she looked back, Tessa saw the grey smear of a body lying on a verge. Well then, she wouldn't look back. She wouldn't think about anything other than putting one foot in front of the other and making sure the children reached safety.

They left the fields and began to climb up the hillside. Every so often Tessa scanned the children, counting them, checking that no one had been left behind. In a copse of birch saplings, they stopped to rest. It was midday, and the sun glared overhead. Some of the children ran in and out of the trees; others lay in the shade, sucking their thumbs. Tessa made sure that everyone had a drink of water and a piece of bread and sausage. She gave Olivia, who looked white with fatigue, extra mouthfuls of water. The babies slept in the pram, and just then it didn't seem too bad. Faustina, who was good at that sort of thing, read the map and checked the compass. Six miles to go, she said in a low voice. It would be better if they reached Greve by nightfall. They should move on.

Tessa gathered the children, counted them again, and made sure they still had their jerseys. It might be too hot for them now, but the weather could change overnight.

Two of the children cried, so Tessa held their hands and sang to them. Soon they were all singing, even Faustina, who couldn't hit a note in tune. Then there was a roar as a plane plunged down through the sky, and they ran for a shallow ditch. Bullets ricocheted off the ground. Tessa's knees were pressed into the stones and there was dust in her mouth.

The plane soared up and disappeared. They climbed out of the ditch and walked on in silence now. Soon the track narrowed, threading through pine trees, and they stopped to confer. They would not be able to take the pram through the trees. Emilia said she would push it along one of the lower paths. Perlita must stay with Tessa, higher up, where it was safer. Olivia decided to walk with Emilia. The hill paths were too steep for her.

A low, muttered conversation passed between Olivia and Faustina. Then the two women embraced and Olivia headed back down the slope with Emilia. Olivia was holding the handle of the pram. There were tears in Faustina's eyes. She picked up the smallest child and began to walk up the narrow path. The girls walked hand in hand and the boys kicked at fir cones. Faustina strode ahead, leading the way.

It was cooler beneath the pines. The rough path was carpeted with needles. The children revived a little in the shade. They should rest again, perhaps, here, where it was cooler – but then, to one side of her, Tessa caught a glimpse of movement in the trees. Soldiers were darting between the pines. In the shadows, she could not tell the colour of their uniforms. She hurried the children along, counting them once more, tripping over the numbers because she was frightened now. She had a sudden, overpowering urge to go home, but she could not think where home was.

They emerged into the glare of the sun. The path headed upwards and lizards darted on the rocks. The planes seemed to have turned their attention elsewhere. As the trees thinned out, Tessa looked back. Shells were falling steadily now, lower in the valley. Smoke plumed into the air.

Faustina sat down on a fallen tree trunk, the map spread out in front of her. Her hair clung to her forehead with perspiration. Tessa gave everyone water and a piece of fruit. It was almost three o'clock in the afternoon and the heat thickened the air. Some of the children slept, using their jerseys as pillows. Tessa put a plaster on a blister, shook a stone out of a shoe. One of the girls drew in the dust with a stick; another cradled her doll. Tommaso lay on his back, his knees bent, his dark eyes looking up at the sky. 'You shouldn't look at the sun, you'll hurt your eyes,' Tessa said gently to him, and tipped his sun hat over his face. But a moment later he pushed it back and lay there staring at the sky again.

Tessa sat down next to Faustina. Faustina smiled and squeezed her hand but did not speak. Perlita crawled up to Tessa, crouching against her skirts. Tessa stroked the child's hair and closed her eyes. She remembered her dream and the still, quiet comfort of the garden early that morning. So that's what happened, she thought. She remembered how hard it had been, caring for Angelo on her own, how different the reality of motherhood had been to what she had imagined. How young she had been, how ignorant, and how unsupported. She had driven to Oxford because

479

of Mrs Rycroft's telephone call, because she had loved Milo Rycroft, and because she had been frightened that she was losing him. It hadn't been trivial at all. Love was never trivial, she knew that now. If she had learned nothing else, she had learned that.

Greve was about three miles away, said Faustina, standing, dusting herself down. They must hurry on. Tessa counted the children: eighteen, that was right. She took the hands of the smallest; Perlita whimpered and trailed a few yards behind. Faustina hoisted a little boy on to her back and they headed down the hillside. It was impossible to think of anything now other than the act of putting one foot in front of the other. Not Guido, not Angelo. There was just this moment and the heat and the path.

The planes came from behind them, a formation of half a dozen, their roar deafening, resounding off the hillside. They ran down to a shallow gully, coralling the children into it, calling to them to crouch down. One, two, three, four – once again, Tessa counted. Where was Perlita? Looking up, she saw that the child was standing a short way up the hillside, on the path, transfixed with terror. Tessa ran out of the gully and swept her up. The planes had gone – but there, looking up, a glaring light arced overhead.

Then they were back in the ditch. Perlita was safe. Tessa looked down at herself. There was a splash of red on the blue fabric of her dress, at her waist. Confused, she touched the splash. When she turned her palm up it was red.

She felt very tired and rather cold. She sat down on the ground. Faustina came across and knelt down beside her. Faustina touched the red patch and said something. Tessa couldn't hear what she was saying. She wanted to tell Faustina that she supposed she had been hurt, and that she needed to rest before she walked on, but she couldn't get the words out.

It wasn't painful. It was just that she felt so cold. She lay down in the gully. For a moment her gaze focused on the tops of the trees and the blue sky. Then the darkness spread, erasing them.

Chapter Fifteen

Faustina Zanetti's letter arrived at Freddie's lodgings at the beginning of September. She had written to break the news of Tessa's death. Her sister had been killed, Faustina wrote, escorting a party of children from the Zanetti villa to Greve. She had been struck by a fragment of shell, which had severed an artery. She had died almost instantly, and without pain. Faustina finished her letter by conveying her deep regret at Tessa's passing, and her own abiding affection for her. 'Tessa was a hero,' she wrote. 'She was strong and loyal and courageous and we shall always remember her and always miss her.'

Freddie sat on the bed in her room at the lodging house and read Faustina's letter through. Then she tried to read it again, but couldn't get to the end because she was crying.

She wrote to Ray and Max and Julian, and to some of Tessa's other friends, though there seemed to be fewer of them now. Julian, who was on sick leave after being injured in an RAF bombing raid over Germany, phoned to tell her that a dozen of them were getting together one evening to remember Tessa, in the Ritz, which Tessa had always loved. Freddie told him that she was too busy. Which was true: at the factory, she worked six days a week, from eight in the morning to six in the evening. When there was a rush on, she worked an extra hour's overtime. On her days off she mostly slept – or, before, she had mostly slept. Now, all her days and nights were broken.

She didn't tell anyone at work about Tessa. Her small group of friends had some time ago left the factory, one to have a baby, another to look after a brother who had been wounded in Normandy, a third to be posted else-where. She didn't try to make new friends. At the factory, she tried to think of nothing. She avoided talking to anyone during her tea breaks, and it was a relief to her now that the workshop was too noisy for conversation. She felt bitter when she thought of the months and years she had hoped for Tessa. When she remembered her elation in early August, when the Allies had liberated Florence, she felt angry. Tessa had already been dead by then. She had not known, she had gone on hoping, and it had all been futile.

She wrote to Lewis, telling him about Tessa. No letter came in return. His letters were often delayed: weeks would pass and there would be nothing, and then a flurry of half a dozen would arrive at once. But this time she wondered whether she had lost him, too. It seemed perfectly possible to her that his ship had been torpedoed and he had drowned. Or he might just have decided it wasn't worth his while, this stuttering, intermittent love affair.

One day, she was sitting at her workbench at the factory

when she began to cry. Once she had started crying she couldn't stop, and in the end they called a doctor, who sent her home and told her not to come back to work for a fortnight. At the lodging house, she still cried, blowing her nose until she ran out of handkerchiefs. Her landlady brought her cups of tea and she tried to drink them. The following morning, Ray's wife, Susan, came to the lodging house, packed her a case, and took her back to their flat in Piccadilly.

Freddie had always thought Susan rather shallow and superficial, but she was kind and tactful and Freddie felt ashamed of herself for not appreciating her more before. Ray was in France and Susan was at the BBC a lot of the time, and she had never known Tessa, which spared her, thought Freddie, a lot of those *do-you-remember-when* conversations she didn't want to have. So many people thought that they had known Tessa. So many people seemed to think they had owned her. They tried to share with her their own grief, as well as their memories. Susan asked her whether she wanted to talk about her sister, and Freddie said no, she didn't, thanks, and after that, when they conversed, it was about the BBC or Susan's family and hobbies.

In the daytime, while Susan was at work, Freddie went out. She didn't go anywhere in particular, just wandered around. She felt in tune with the exhaustion and the end-of-your-rope feeling that had settled over London. The coming of the V1 and V2 rocket bombs had returned the city to the horrors of the Blitz, and yet, four years on, few of them had any reserves left. She sometimes pondered what she would do if a bomb flew over her head, whether she'd go to a shelter or not, but none did, so she never found out.

'Phone,' said Susan. 'It's for you.'

Freddie took the receiver. A voice on the other end of the line said, 'Freddie?'

'Lewis? Is that you?'

'I've been looking for you everywhere. It's taken me ages to track you down.'

'I wrote several times – I'm sorry.'

'I'm not cross, I was just worried.'

'The line's good,' she said inconsequentially. 'Are you in Liverpool?'

'I'm in London. I came as soon as I could. I'm staying at Marcelle's house. Come and have dinner with me.'

'I'm not hungry.' She knew she sounded brusque, so she added, 'I'm sorry, Lewis, but I'm really not hungry.'

'Well I'm famished. I've a table booked at Quaglino's for eight. Put on a frock and hop in a taxi and I'll meet you there.'

At Quaglino's, the waiter showed Freddie to a corner table. Lewis rose and kissed her. 'Freddie,' he said. He hugged her tightly. 'I'm so sorry about your sister.'

'Kind of you,' she said automatically, and sat down.

The waiter came to take their order. When he had gone, Lewis said, 'Rotten for you, all this. Marcelle told me you hadn't been well.'

'Marcelle?' She looked at him, vaguely surprised.

'News gets round.'

'I'm not ill, I'm just tired. I don't know why it was a

shock when I'd been worrying about Tessa for years, but it was.'

'It was bound to be a shock,' he said kindly. 'You'd waited so long. You were so faithful.'

'When I was younger,' she traced a pattern on the table-cloth, 'after the baby died, I tried to find out who his father was. I blamed him, you see, for everything that happened to Tessa.'

'And did you find out?'

'No. I look back now and I wonder what I was doing. As if it could have made any difference. As if I could have made any difference. Tessa always did what she wanted to. She never listened to anyone.'

He took her hand. 'I want to make it better for you, Freddie.'

'You can't.'

The waiter brought their soup; when he had gone, Freddie said, her voice hard, 'How can you make it better? You can't bring Tessa back.'

'I know that. I didn't mean to suggest that.' He frowned, and she saw again that vulnerability in his eyes. She didn't want to see it, because it might hurt her, and she had been hurt enough.

'What I'm trying to say is that you don't have to feel you're alone. Let me look after you, Freddie.'

'I don't need anyone to look after me.'

'No, of course you don't.'

They were both silent. She regretted her sharpness; she didn't like that part of herself. 'I love you, Lewis,' she said quietly. 'But I can't seem to feel it now. I can't feel anything.'

'It'll pass, Freddie. Believe me, it will. It'll take a while but it'll pass.'

'Everyone says that.'

'Perhaps everyone's right.'

She looked down at her soup bowl. 'I'm afraid I've haven't got it left in me. I'm afraid I'd be no use to you.'

'I don't want you to be useful, I just want you to be *there*. Marry me, Freddie.'

Her heart skipped a beat. 'Lewis . . .'

He pressed her hand. 'It's funny, I've always doubted I'd get through the war in one piece, yet it still shocks me when I hear of something happening to someone else.'

'You're all right now, aren't you?'

'Oh yes, I'm fine.' But he looked troubled. 'I always feel as if I'm *waiting*.'

'For what?'

'For my number to be up, for one thing.' He gave an uneasy laugh. 'I feel sick with fear when we're at sea and sick with apprehension when I'm waiting to go to sea. I suppose I'm waiting for all this to be over.'

She was clinging to his hand as if only that would stop her drowning.

'The thing is,' he said, 'I've spent the last five years of my life waiting, and I hate it. I waited for Clare for years and years, but I won't wait for ever for you, Freddie. I've had enough of that. If you don't want to marry me, then tell me now. But just think about it first. Do you want to get through this war with nothing? I don't. I know what I want. I want something better. I want a home and a family and a future. Do you think you might want the same things?

I think you do, deep down. I think you're as sick of things happening to you as I am. I think you know that there are times when we have to take life by the scruff of the neck and give it a shake.' He waved away the waiter, who was hovering to take their soup bowls, and leaned forward across the table, his eyes burning. 'I think you want the same as me, Freddie. If you do, then for God's sake say so. We could make a new life together, I know we could. Because I love you. I love you and I want you and I want us to be together all the time. So, what's your answer? Will you marry me?'

She was tired of being alone. She was still holding his hand; she wanted never to let it go.

'Yes, Lewis,' she said.

Part Four

Stepping Outside

1945–1951

Chapter Sixteen

They were married in February 1945. The wedding was at a church in Slough. Lewis looked handsome in his naval uniform and Freddie wore a violet-blue coat over a cream-coloured knee-length dress. Her wedding dress was a cut-down evening frock and the coat had once belonged to Tessa, before the war. Freddie loved its rich colour, wished it hadn't been too early for violets but carried a bunch of snowdrops instead. There were thirty guests to the wedding breakfast, naval men who were friends of Lewis's, as well as Susan Leavington (Ray was still on active service in Europe), Julian, Max, the Douglases (Monty and Betty had married the previous autumn), and some of Freddie's Birmingham friends. And Marcelle Scott. Lewis had insisted – it had been Marcelle who had got together the crowd at the Dorchester back in the December of 1940. If it hadn't been for her, he pointed out, they might never have met.

At three o'clock in the afternoon they headed off through snow flurries for their honeymoon. A friend had given

493

Lewis the key to his house in Surrey. Freddie had imagined a bungalow, or perhaps a semi, but the house was vast and old and set in its own parkland. Inside, the rooms were cold and damp, but the beautiful fabric of the building showed through the neglect. Carved balusters curved upwards beside a sweeping staircase, and Freddie ran her fingertips across the ripples of linenfold panelling. Lewis lit a fire in the library and they lay on a rug in front of it, reading passages to each other from books picked at random from the shelves – dull Victorian sermons and essays on housekeeping – giggling like teenagers as the tension of the day was forgotten. That night, they made love in a four-poster bed. The walls of the bedroom were covered in silk the colour of aquamarines. Lewis's lovemaking was sweet and passionate, and afterwards, lying in his arms, Freddie drifted off to sleep.

Had they been happy that day, she and him? She thought they had, though later she recalled that Lewis had been disappointed that he had been given only forty-eight hours' leave, and he had been disappointed too with the meagre buffet the hotel had put on. And he hadn't wanted her to go back to work, and they had argued before he had returned to his ship, she explaining that for her, sitting alone in some lodging house in Portsmouth or Devonport would be worse than the factory; he proud, suspicious that her desire for independence indicated a lack of faith in him.

Mrs Fainlight died three weeks after VE Day. During the last year of their mother's life, Rebecca and Meriel had looked after her at home, with the help of a nurse during the nights. Afterwards, there was the dispiriting business of sorting through Hatherdene's contents. Neither sister had room for the large, heavy furniture their parents had bought on their marriage. In the end, Meriel had taken a tea set and some pictures and a chair with a tapestry cushion, sewn by her mother. Rebecca had walked through the house, trying to decide what she wanted to keep. The truth was that she wanted nothing. The contents of the house seemed so weighted with emotions she did not wish to revisit: a stupefying dullness, a constriction of ambition and an absence of joy and excitement. In the end, she chose some gardening tools and a set of literary classics she had enjoyed reading as a girl. The tools were of good quality, and she and her mother had shared their pleasure in the garden during the last years of Mrs Fainlight's life. They gave the furniture to the WVS and the house was sold.

The death of her mother and the ending of the war left Rebecca feeling restless. She decided not to return to Mayfield Farm; the place had always been a stopgap – a stopgap that had lasted for seven years – and she knew that she needed to take a new direction. She began to look for a place of her own, but the severe housing shortage that followed the end of the war meant that her search took more than a year.

In the autumn of 1946, an estate agent sent her the particulars of a cottage between Andover and Hungerford. After collecting the keys, Rebecca drove north-west through narrow, winding Hampshire lanes. The countryside was an attractive mixture of woodland and chalk hills.

The cottage, though, was not attractive. Small and square and squat, built of red brick in the early 1920s, it was almost defiantly charmless. But it was the presence of the workshop beside the cottage that had persuaded Rebecca to view the property. Made of the same red brick, but roofed in corrugated iron, it had before the war been used as a blacksmith's forge.

As she unlocked the door, a starling flew out. The interior of the workshop was dim and cluttered; she should have taken a torch. Her eyes grew accustomed to the light and she made out a galvanized pail, rusty tools and, like the skeleton of some prehistoric beast, a harrow. A grey smear of ashes on flagstones marked the place where the blacksmith's anvil had once stood. Beyond, there were heaps of sodden newspapers and rotting straw, and she could see daylight through the holes in the roof. Scooping away a cobweb, Rebecca rubbed a smeared pane with her glove. Light poured into the space. She knew then that it would make the perfect glass studio. The end wall would be all window. She would build her kiln on the flagstones and her workbench would run the length of the long side wall.

The cottage itself had been requisitioned during the war by the RAF and still bore the marks of its occupation – a gas mask hanging from a peg, a pair of binoculars in a leather case. There was a kitchen, sitting room, dining room and two bedrooms. There was also an inside lav, thank heavens, but no bathroom. Behind the house was a quarter of an acre of overgrown garden, mostly lawn that had gone to seed, as well as a tangle of brambles and nettles. Beyond the garden was a beech wood – she liked the way the one ran seamlessly into the other.

The cottage cost five hundred and twenty pounds. Rebecca's share of the profits from the sale of her mother's house had been around three hundred and fifty pounds. She still had a substantial sum of money in the bank from the sale of the Mill House – she had spent little during her years at Mayfield Farm and had worked in exchange for her board and lodging – so she could comfortably afford to buy the cottage. The following weekend she bid successfully at auction. Once the paperwork was complete, she had her belongings from the Mill House taken out of storage and moved into the cottage. Reacquainting herself with chairs, tables and sofas she had last seen when she was married to Milo, she reflected that she seemed doomed to be haunted by her previous lives. You could never entirely get away from the past. She was glad of her kitchen and dining things, though, her good saucepans, china and glasses, and at least she wasn't having to pay for storage any more.

On fine evenings, she watched from the kitchen window the rabbits lolloping in the grass. Sometimes a jay swooped down from a branch, blue feathers flashing. The postman and the villagers always referred to the cottage as The Forge, so that was what it remained. She made the house habitable first, then started on the studio. She cleared out the rubbish and burned it, and dragged the rusty harrow into the long grass, where it had a certain sculptural quality, she thought. There were birds' nests between the walls and roof, and there were rats. She borrowed a shotgun from a farmer and polished off the rats, and scoured the country-side for sheets of corrugated iron to repair the roof. There was a severe shortage of building materials – a shortage of everything, in fact, including food, so she dug a vegetable patch and scoured the hedgerows for berries. She found a carpenter to make a window frame to fit the end wall of the building, and a lad from the village helped her build the kiln. Then she moved into the studio and set to work.

After his discharge from the navy, Lewis, along with thousands of other ex-servicemen, began to look for work. A friend who owned a garage in Bristol offered him a job, but after three months, with petrol rationing still gripping tightly and no materials available to manufacture new cars, Lewis left. He didn't want make-work, he said to Freddie; he didn't want to be sitting there twiddling his thumbs just because his friend, who was a decent fellow, wanted to help him.

They moved back to London. They went out, cheered themselves up, attended the christening party the Leavingtons put on to celebrate the birth of their son, had a few raucous evenings with ex-navy men. Freddie suggested they give a supper party – they owed quite a few invitations – but Lewis looked round the tiny furnished flat in which they were living and said no, better wait till things looked up. Freddie was about to say that people didn't care about china that didn't match and having to squeeze round a table, but then she saw that Lewis had that look in his eye. It was a look she was coming to know well, a mixture of resentment and bitterness, coupled with shame.

He found a job as a salesman, travelling round the country, selling recipe books. He was good at it – attractive and well-spoken – and the housewives who answered his knock on the door were charmed by him. There was a need for a decent modern recipe book, he told Freddie – all those women who'd joined the Forces or worked in factories were at home now and had no idea how to cook for their families. But as the months passed, his enthusiasm faded. The long absences from home, the nights in grim boarding houses, the snatched meals and poor pay and lack of any decent social life all wore at him. Then a new sales manager was appointed. Lewis had applied for the job, but it went to a friend of the boss. The fellow was a fool, Lewis said angrily, had them running round all over the place, Exeter one day, Hull the next. Shortly afterwards he gave in his notice.

They moved to Southampton. In a pub one evening, Lewis met a man called Barney Gosling. Barney was ex-army, almost bald, his pink scalp scattered with fine tufts of grey hair – much, in fact, like the feathers of a gosling. He was the proprietor of a magazine called *Boating and Fishing World*. He took a shine to Lewis and offered him a job on the magazine. Lewis was to help run the office, write some articles, take a few photographs. Barney hadn't appointed anyone to help sell the magazine, so Lewis took that on as well. At last he had found a job he enjoyed. The magazine limped rather, its circulation a meagre couple of thousand, but Lewis was confident it would grow. He began to talk about using his severance pay to put down a deposit on a house in Southampton, and they became part of a new social circle, Barney's friends, who were from what Tessa had called the huntin' and fishin' set, landed outdoorsy people who kept packs of dogs and a horse or two. Freddie noticed that in their company, Lewis censored his background. He spoke of his friends from Winchester, not his trio of aunts. He always offered to buy the first round of drinks, always made sure to bring a present to their hostess. Freddie loved him for his generosity, but worried about money. If she tried to discuss her worries with him, Lewis brushed them away. Everything was fine, he said. They were getting on at last, meeting the right people.

Then, six months after they had moved to Southampton, Barney, who'd always liked a drink, got blind drunk one evening, tearful drunk, and told Lewis that the magazine wasn't making a bean, was haemorrhaging money, and there wasn't a job for him any more. The two men parted with a handshake. Two weeks later, Lewis started work in an insurance office. The wages were half of what Barney had paid, and when at weekends they headed off to the seaside, Freddie listened to the misery in Lewis's voice as they tramped up and down the shingle, talking. He felt trapped, he said. He couldn't get used to sitting still all day. The work was dull and repetitive; it occupied neither his mind nor his energy, and his thoughts drifted. And they weren't good thoughts, Freddie. Throw it in, she said, cupping his face with her hands, looking him in the eyes. Let's do something different.

There was an article in the newspaper about the large numbers of ex-officers who had gone into the teaching profession. Lewis couldn't imagine why he hadn't thought of it before. A prep school in Leicestershire was advertising for a teacher of maths and physics, so he applied for the job and was appointed.

Throughout this time, as they zigzagged across the country in search of something better, they had lived in cold, tired lodging houses and bed-sitting rooms with metered electricity, and in dark, dank cottages with no electricity at all. The Leicester school offered accommodation along with the post. Packing, Freddie felt a rush of optimism. Perhaps their luck was changing. She imagined a pretty little lodge and verdant countryside. Lewis would enjoy teaching, and the enthusiasm that he brought to any halfway worthwhile task would fire his pupils. And perhaps there would be work for her, a few hours in the bursar's office or helping the matron. Because she, too, was finding it hard to adapt, had struggled with the boredom of eking out household tasks to fill her rather solitary days, wasn't used, after years of working in offices and factories, to being on her own so much. And she hated the quarrels that started up whenever she talked to Lewis about looking for work, found his cold anger a little frightening, if she was honest with herself, because it showed a side of him she had not previously known existed. Their discussions these days tipped so easily over into quarrels. You wouldn't be bored, he told her, if you had a baby. She wasn't ready for a baby, she said. When? he asked. Soon, she said. It wasn't that she didn't want a baby, it was just that she knew, remembering Tessa and Angelo, that babies needed routine and consistency. And so far, she and Lewis had known only dislocation.

So, then, the school. A few miles out of Market

Harborough, the straggle of undistinguished buildings lay at the bottom of a misty valley. Their accommodation was not the pretty lodge Freddie had hoped for, but a cold, cramped flat in the attic of one of the houses. On their arrival, Lewis discovered that he was required to teach rugby and PE as well as maths and physics. Oh, and some religious education too.

He stuck it out for two terms. Something poisoned the atmosphere of the school, something hard to put a finger on, like the mist that hung over the fields. The headmaster and the deputy, both veterans of the First World War, disliked small boys. The French teacher liked them rather too much, and was given to inviting his favourites to tea in his study, where he ruffled his hand through pale blond curls or squeezed a thigh. The other masters were cynics or drunkards or their nerves were shot. The school survived because the fees were low and because the fathers of the pupils, who were servicemen or businessmen who worked abroad, were mostly old boys. Freddie detected in the fathers a spirit of well, it was rotten for me, so why shouldn't it be rotten for you too.

Lewis stood out like a sore thumb, because he tried. He got a rugby tournament going, and even read through the Bible in the evenings so he knew what he was talking about in RE lessons. But the grey, lacklustre disposition of the place infected him. He drank more, slept badly. He didn't confide in her any more. When she tried to talk to him, he snapped at her. Though he didn't dissolve into tears like poor old Barney, she witnessed the school slowly eroding his spirit.

A pattern had been set up on their wedding day, one of dashed expectations and let-downs. The difference between the two of them, Freddie thought, was that she managed her expectations, kept them small. All those years back and forth across the ice-cold Atlantic, all that fear and horror, should have entitled Lewis to more than a series of low-paid and dispiriting jobs. The knowledge that thousands of other ex-servicemen were going through the same upheaval did not comfort him. She couldn't blame him for hating it – anyone would have hated it – but she minded that she couldn't console him, and that his disappointment made him withdraw from her. She still loved him, still remembered the Lewis who had sung to her in the pub, the Lewis who had made love to her on their wedding night in a room the colour of aquamarines, but sometimes she found herself questioning whether this angry, resentful Lewis loved her back.

In the London museums, there were necklaces more than two thousand years old, the blue glass beads interspersed with glass fish and frogs and a plump blue naked woman with spotted wings. There was a bowl made of coloured glass strips like the striations of stone in a cliff, and an Italian plate dotted with squares and stripes, like liquorice allsorts. And there were Lalique bowls, as palely translucent as ice, the fine, geometric shape of a dandelion seed enclosed in their hearts.

In the spring of 1947, Rebecca travelled to the east coast of Scotland to stay with a group of glass artists. She studied the techniques of fusing and slumping, how to polish and sand-blast glass, and how to cast it in a kiln. John and Romaine Pollen had returned from the United States and were now living in Cornwall, in St Ives, near the Wainwrights, so in the summer Rebecca went to visit them. She and Romaine walked along cliff paths where the waves pounded themselves to a white froth on the rocks below. Before she left, John showed her how to make ceramic moulds and Romaine gave her the name of the London gallery in which she showed her work.

Is it always pots and pans with you? Connor Byrne had asked her once, and yes, in a way it still was. She liked to use the ordinary to make something beautiful. She owned small metal skillets in which she had once baked French pancakes in her dinner-party days at the Mill House; now she used them as moulds to make glass dishes. She bought sheets of window glass from a builder's merchant and set strands of copper wire between the layers so that the fronds gleamed through the greenish, undulant surface.

'I tried placing dried leaves between layers of transparent glass,' she wrote to Connor. 'The firing burned off the plant material, and left an imprint like the ghosts of leaves.'

Connor had remained in Ireland after the end of the war. Aoife had been unwell, and there had been some trouble with Brendan, which had resulted in a ticking-off from the police. 'Nothing bad,' Connor wrote, 'but I remember myself at that age, and how one thing can lead to another if you get in with the wrong crowd.' He had looked forward to seeing her again, he wrote. He regretted that they had been so long parted.

Rebecca was working in the studio one morning when

a letter arrived. She slit open the envelope. The letter was from Meriel, and it told her that she and Dr Hughes were engaged to be married.

Freddie and Lewis were living in Lymington in Hampshire, on the south coast, on the western side of the Solent estuary. A man called Jerry Colvin had set up a boatyard there in a peeling wharf near the seawater baths. Not far away, gulls dived and shrieked and the mudflats glistened like icing. Jerry had been in the boatbuilding business before the war and had captained Lewis's first corvette. Boatbuilding was the business to be in, Jerry said. As soon as the country got herself back on her feet again, men would want to own a boat, a nice little dinghy or a yacht to play around in at the weekends. Freddie liked Jerry: he was a quiet, gentle, courteous man, though there was a brittleness about him, and his fingertips were red and ragged beneath his bitten nails.

This was the opportunity he had been waiting for, Lewis told her. He loved to be practical, loved to get his hands dirty. He and Jerry would share the sales work between them – Jerry had contacts. Jerry would do the paperwork, and his shipwright, Walter, would teach Lewis his craft. The boatyard was made up of two long, single-storey, black-stained wooden sheds. The slipway to the estuary led out of the larger building; the office was in the smaller one.

They bought a house. Freddie worried about the financial commitment, but Lewis insisted. Anyone of any standing owned rather than rented, he said; it would give them permanence and a place in society. He reminded her that he had put his severance pay aside for a deposit.

The house was small, detached and red-roofed and stood on the southern fringes of Lymington. Through the upstairs windows, you could see the sea. Freddie liked the way the sea changed according to the sun and the wind, shimmering like azure silk or whipped up into sullen white-topped waves. They could settle here, she thought. This was a new beginning.

She liked that Lewis came home from the boatyard whistling cheerfully, and that sometimes, closing the front door behind him, he swept her up in his arms and carried her up the stairs to the bedroom. Often, she walked over to the boathouse at midday. On fine days, she and Lewis sat outside, looking out across the estuary, eating the sandwiches Freddie brought with her. If it was raining, they sheltered in the boathouse, which smelled of salt and tar. Sometimes, when Jerry was in town and it was Walter's day off, they made love in the boathouse, locked together in the half-darkness, while the water slap-slapped against the slipway. The angry stranger had vanished. She felt herself falling in love with him all over again.

Lewis insisted Freddie engage a daily help, and on Saturday nights they went out to dinner or to a party. Charming and sociable, Lewis made friends in the town among the community of bankers and solicitors and businessmen. His friends came with their wives to the small house with the red roof for supper parties and for cocktails. Freddie couldn't find much in common with the wives. She tried, complimenting them on their dresses and hair, asking after their families. Mostly the wives talked about their children and their gardens. Freddie had never before had a garden, didn't know what to do with one. The only garden she had ever known well had been the one at the Villa Millefiore in Fiesole, and she doubted whether she would be able recreate its grand, crumbling elegance in a square grassy plot in Hampshire.

But after six months or so, Lewis stopped whistling on the way home from work, and he didn't want her to come to the boathouse at lunchtime any more. He worked longer hours, weekends too. Freddie's housekeeping money was cut – Lewis was sorry: a sale Jerry had been depending on hadn't worked out, but he was sure things would soon look up. Freddie told the daily help she wasn't needed any more. They managed, they got by, but she began to feel as if they were living on the edge of something, and what had once been solid was shifting beneath them.

Dressing for her wedding, Meriel snagged her stocking with her thumbnail. 'Oh blast,' she said. 'My one good pair.'

'Have mine,' said Rebecca.

'No, no. I can wear my lisle.'

'Nonsense.' Rebecca peeled off a stocking and gave it to her sister. 'Take it.'

They were in Meriel's flat at Westdown School. Meriel was wearing a cornflower-blue skirt and jacket and a white blouse and hat. After she had changed the stocking, she stared in the mirror and tugged at the hem of her skirt.

'You do think . . .'

Rebecca flicked open her compact and powdered her nose. 'What?'

'That I'm doing the right thing? That it isn't rather ridiculous, to get married at fifty-one?'

'It isn't ridiculous at all. I think it's wonderful.' Rebecca hugged Meriel. 'You look so pretty.'

'Oh, nonsense.' Meriel's frown deepened. 'And you don't think I'm being disloyal to David?' David Rutherford had been Meriel's fiancé who had died at the Somme.

'I think David would have wanted you to be happy.'

Meriel chewed her lipstick. 'I wish Mummy could have been here, don't you?'

Rebecca snapped the compact shut. 'Yes. Though she was dreadful at my wedding. Do you remember?'

'She was so rude about the food. And to Milo. And you? You don't mind? All this fuss. It's been such hard work for you.'

Rebecca had planned the reception, which was to be held at Dr Hughes's house, and had organized the catering and made Meriel's wedding cake. But this was not, she sensed, what Meriel meant. What Meriel really meant was, do you mind that I'm getting married when your marriage to Milo ended in divorce? Do you mind this extraordinary reversal of fortune?

'Of course I don't mind,' she said firmly. 'It's all been great fun.'

A car horn sounded and Rebecca peered out of the window. 'It's the taxi.' She turned to Meriel. 'Are you ready?'

Sitting in the car beside her sister, Rebecca looked down at her hands. They were, as always, calloused and scored with small cuts. She should have made time to fit in a manicure, she thought. She was gasping for a cigarette, and it felt odd to be wearing a skirt and jacket instead of corduroy trousers and a cotton shirt. For the wedding, she had chosen the cherry-red costume she had bought in Selfridges before the war. She had lost weight and had had to take in the skirt at the waistband and put new darts in the bust of the jacket. The costume was made of wool, rather hot for a warm August day, and now she felt the familiar heat boil up inside her. Beads of perspiration sprang to her upper lip and she would have liked to have torn off the stiff, uncomfortable clothes.

She put Meriel's bouquet down on the seat between them. 'Do you mind if I open a window?'

Meriel, too, looked hot. 'Please do. I feel like a boiled pudding.'

Rebecca wound down the car window, stuck her head out, and the flush died away. She thought she understood Meriel's doubts about marrying in her fifties. They arose, she suspected, from an uncertainty about what a woman was supposed to be at this point in her life. For herself, at forty-nine, menopausal and divorced, the line between letting oneself go and clinging ridiculously to youth some-times seemed so narrow. Articles in fashion magazines and the clothes stocked by shops emphasized the beauty of youth and a woman's expected decline into frumpiness once she had reached her forties and fifties. One was no longer supposed to be desirable. One was no longer supposed to desire. The thought depressed her, even though she had some time ago accepted that in all probability she would live the rest of her life alone. Connor was still in Ireland; the feelings she had had for him now seemed rather ridiculous, a lonely woman's fantasy, making too much out of something that, when you looked at it objectively, had been nothing much at all.

They were out of vermouth and Lewis had said they must have vermouth. Freddie thought she had checked the bottle a couple of days ago and it had been half full, but she must have been mistaken.

She looked inside her purse. There was a shilling and a threepenny bit. A bottle of vermouth cost about seven shillings. She opened her handbag, ran her fingers around the lining, and drew out a penny and a halfpenny. Then she checked the pockets of her mackintosh and the small brass bowl on the hall table where Lewis sometimes put odd pennies. Both were empty.

She opened the kitchen drawer where she put aside money for the milkman and baker. Even if she used the four sixpences there, she would still be almost three shillings short. The canapés were lined up on the table and the glasses – washed, dried and polished – stood on the draining board. Freddie chewed a nail, thinking. Then she went back to the sitting room and ran a hand round the sofa in the hope that some loose change might have fallen between the cushions, but drew out only a sweet wrapping and a pencil. There wasn't such a thing as loose change any more; every penny counted.

She could go to the boatyard and see if Lewis had some cash, but was reluctant to do so. These days, he didn't like being interrupted at work. And Jerry or Walter might be there and it would humiliate Lewis if she asked him for money in front of them. Anyway, he might not have anything. She wondered whether they could do without vermouth, but it was supposed to be a cocktail party, and it would be hard to make decent cocktails without it.

She went upstairs to their bedroom and sat down on the bed, letting the coins fall on to the eiderdown. Her gaze fixed on the framed photograph on the dressing table, their wedding day, Lewis in his naval uniform, she in the violet-blue coat. After a while, she brushed her hair and carefully applied lipstick and powder, then scooped up the coins and went downstairs.

Outside, a blustery wind tugged the leaves from the trees. The mud and salt marsh that bordered the estuary always had a drenched look, whether the sun was shining or not. Sea and land merged into each other in inlets and estuaries and reed beds. When the tide was out, the river shrank to a narrow snaking channel between mudflats. She loved their house, but there was something in the landscape that was alien to her. The sea clawed at the solid ground, hemming it in, devouring it, and some days the wind cut like a knife.

Looking up, she saw that the tide was out. The light on the sea shifted and the clouds cast shade on the marshes, and the land looked transient, evanescent, liable at any moment to dissolve into nothing.

That evening she didn't even try with Lewis's friends. She handed round canapés while Lewis poured drinks, and thought all the time what a sham it was, this pretence of sophisticated and moneyed living, while she scrabbled about for coins under sofa cushions. The wives chattered about the servant problem and Freddie dumped the dirty plates in the kitchen sink and stared out of the window as inky clouds scudded across an opalescent sky.

By half past eight the guests were leaving. Goodbyes were called, vague suggestions of suppers and drinks murmured, and cars started up. Lewis shut the front door, Freddie took a tray into the sitting room. There was a time, she thought, when she would have said, it was fun, wasn't it, even if she hadn't meant it. Tonight she said nothing as she picked up glasses and put them on the tray.

Lewis poured himself a drink. He said, 'You could have made a bit more effort.'

She looked round sharply. 'I made a lot of effort. It took me all day to clean the house and cook the food.'

'I didn't mean that.' He gave the expansive sweep of his hand that told her he had drunk too much. 'I meant tonight. You hardly said a word.'

'I was tired.'

'Tired? For God's sake, Freddie, we're all tired. I'm working seven days a week.'

She tried to swallow back her annoyance. She sat down. 'I'm worried, Lewis.'

'Really? What about?'

'Money, mostly.'

'Money.' He laughed. 'No point in worrying about money.'

'I couldn't afford the bottle of vermouth. I had to tell Ronnie at the pub I'd give him the rest tomorrow.'

'More like the end of the month. Or the end of the year.'

There was a blankness in his eyes that disturbed her: she couldn't tell whether he was angry or whether he was laughing at her.

She opted for laughter. 'I don't think it's funny.'

'No, not funny at all.' He held up the whisky bottle. 'Drink?'

'No thanks.'

'You just need to keep an eye on the housekeeping,' he said.

Keep an eye on the housekeeping. All her life she had been careful with money. Her mother's daughter and Tessa's sister: of course she was careful with money.

'You don't give me enough money at the moment, Lewis. Not if you want to have parties.'

Suddenly he was in front of her, one hand on the arm of the chair, crouching down, his gaze a few inches from her own. 'There isn't any more money, Freddie. I've nothing to give. Don't you see?'

Shocked, she said quickly, 'I only meant five or ten shillings, that's all.'

'No, sorry, can't even do five bob.' He moved away from her. 'Boatyard's going bust.'

Now she needed the drink. She slid off the chair and sloshed some whisky into a glass, took a swallow, then turned to face him. 'You don't mean that,' she said. 'You're just going through a bad patch. Jerry will get in more work.'

'I haven't seen Jerry for three weeks.'

She stared at him. 'What do you mean?'

'Just that. It's three weeks since he came to the boatyard.'

'Where is he?'

'I've no idea.'

'But you must know.'

'I don't. Haven't seen him. No letter, no phone call.'

'His house . . .'

'He's not there. It's locked up, curtains drawn.' Lewis refilled his glass, then lay down on the sofa, his head on a cushion, the glass balanced on his chest. He closed his eyes. 'Jerry's done a runner,' he drawled. 'Either that or he's topped himself and is lying in his house as dead as a doornail.'

'Don't joke,' she said sharply.

'I'm not joking. I've been thinking of breaking into the place.' He opened his eyes and glanced at his watch. 'Might pop over tonight, actually.'

'*Lewis.*'

'Even if he hasn't croaked, I need to get my hands on the books from the yard. There's damn-all paperwork in the office. Jerry must have taken it home with him.'

She whispered, 'Three weeks . . . Why didn't you tell me?'

'I didn't want to worry you. I know you hate us having financial difficulties.'

She did: it was true. The same experiences that made her careful with money had also made her fear debt. She felt a wash of shame. Was she so rigid in her opinions, so fearful of penury and so unsympathetic to his difficulties that he had felt unable to confide in her? Or was it his pride that was at fault?

'You should have told me,' she said.

He shrugged. 'I was hoping something would turn up. That's what tonight was for. Tim Renwick's been talking about buying a yacht for months. Damned skinflint just told me he's changed his mind.'

She perched on the edge of the sofa, looking down at him. The corners of his mouth were turned down and his hazel eyes were clouded. 'Let me do something, Lewis,' she said. 'Let me help you.'

He took her hand and planted a kiss on her palm. 'Just keep smiling. That's the best, kiddo.'

'I meant, I could look for a job.'

He dropped her hand, saying angrily, 'Not that again!'

'We need to be practical. Part-time, if you like.'

'No, Freddie.'

'Lewis, I want to work. I *enjoy* working.'

'Tell me, what would you do?'

She raised her shoulders. 'Anything. I wouldn't mind – a shop, an office, cleaning . . .'

'*Cleaning!*' His eyes narrowed. 'My wife, *cleaning*. What do you think people would say?'

'I wouldn't care what they said. We can't be fussy, we need the money, you just said so yourself.'

He stood up suddenly, brushing against her. 'This is a small town,' he said coldly. 'We'd never be asked anywhere ever again if people thought I'd sent you out charring.'

'Then let me help you at the boatyard. If Jerry's not coming to work any more, you need someone to do the accounts. I've worked in offices before, I know what to do. It would free you up to get more orders in.'

'No.' Lewis swallowed the remainder of his whisky.

Then he said, his voice quiet and angry, 'You still don't understand, do you? I didn't ask you to marry me to have you skivvying for me or anyone else. This is my sanctuary.' His first struck his palm. 'This, our home, where I get away from all the rubbish in my life. This house, and you.'

Now, she felt afraid. She whispered, 'But you're not here, Lewis, you're out working. And when you are here, you hardly speak to me.'

'That's rot, and you know it.'

'I meant, we don't talk properly. Not telling me about Jerry — keeping something like that from me. It was wrong of you.'

'I told you, I didn't want to worry you.' He put his empty glass down on the table. 'I'll sort it out. But in my own way and my own time.'

He went into the hall and put on his coat. She followed him. 'Where are you going?'

'To Jerry's house. To see if the stupid sod's left any clue where he's gone.'

He went out of the front door. It was raining now, thick drops barrelling into the road. 'Lewis!' she called, but he had gone. She went back into the sitting room and poured herself another whisky and drank it quickly, even though she felt sick.

He wasn't there when she woke in the morning. He must have come home, because his side of the bed was rumpled and the suit he had worn at the party was on a hanger. Lewis was very neat: navy habits.

Freddie sat up. Her head was aching. The whisky must have sent her to sleep – she was still wearing her watch, bracelet and necklace and there was a sour taste in her mouth. She looked at the watch. It was early, ten to six. She went to the bathroom and sluiced cold water over her face. She remembered their quarrel, the things they had said, their anger. She would have said, before her marriage, that she disliked and avoided quarrels. She had not thought herself a quarrelling person.

She put on her dressing gown and went downstairs. It was cold, as if autumn had suddenly made up its mind to turn into winter. Lewis wasn't in the house, she knew that even before she checked the rooms. She could always tell when he was there, just as she had always been able to tell with Tessa, something to do with their larger-than-life, generous natures, unlike hers, which was small and shrivelled and mean.

She made herself a cup of tea in the kitchen and drank it standing, her back to the sink. Last night's dirty glasses and plates stood on the table. She thought of running the water to wash them, but didn't. *Boatyard's going bust. Jerry's done a runner.* Lewis had a way of falling into a gloom and seeing the worst. Surely it couldn't be as bad as he feared. He had been working such long hours, struggling on on his own, no wonder he felt so anxious. And betrayed – he had looked on Jerry as a friend.

She cut some bread to make sandwiches and wrapped them up in greaseproof paper, then went back to the bedroom to dress. As she left the house, she saw that the wind had dropped and that the sun gleamed on a smoothly shimmering sea.

The sky was huge and blue, and her spirits rose. They would sort it out, she thought. It would get better. They still loved each other – surely, surely that was what mattered. All they needed was a bit of luck. She pushed to the back of her mind the thought that sprang up: that she had believed it would get better throughout the three and a half years of their marriage, and it never had.

She cycled to the boatyard. The tide was in, and the water slopped lazily up and down the wooden walls of the jetty. Gulls bobbed on the grey water and fishing boats creaked along the narrow channel, motors phutting. A black cat sat on top of a wooden post, licking its paws.

Freddie propped her bicycle against a wall and went inside the office. Lewis was sitting at the desk, which was covered in papers. He looked up as she came into the room.

'I brought these,' she said. She put the sandwiches on his desk. 'I wasn't sure whether you'd had any breakfast.'

'Thanks.' He looked white and drawn. Standing up, he put his arms round her, holding her tightly. 'Oh, Freddie,' he murmured. He stroked her hair, and she breathed in the familiar scent of his skin, mixed with the salt and tar of the yard.

'I'm out of cigarettes,' he said. 'Do you have any?'

'No. I'll cycle to the station, if you like, get some from the machine.'

'It doesn't matter.' He stepped back, looking down at her. 'I'm sorry, Freddie. Sorry for being so vile last night. I shouldn't get angry with *you*. It's not your fault everything's such a mess, it's mine.'

Gently, she stroked his face. 'I'm sorry too. You try so hard, Lewis. You mustn't blame yourself. You've just been unlucky.'

He gave her a crooked smile. 'I'll make some coffee, shall I?'

'Please.'

He put the kettle on. She said, 'Did you go to Jerry's house?'

'Yes.' Again he smiled. 'A nice, clean break-in.'

'Did you find anything?'

'The books, but no sign of Jerry. No bodies in the bath, thank goodness, and nothing to tell me where he's gone.'

'You don't think he could have . . .'

'What?'

'That he's trying to drum up business. That he's travelling, meeting customers, and he's forgotten to let you know.'

'It's possible, I suppose.'

His back was to her as he spooned instant coffee into mugs. She could tell by the set of his shoulders that he didn't believe what he was saying.

She said desperately, 'Or perhaps he's fallen ill.'

Lewis went to the desk. 'I found these in his house.' He picked up a pile of envelopes. 'Jerry hasn't much family, just a sister in London. These are her letters to him. I read them, I'm afraid – I know it's not the thing, but I need to know what's going on.'

'Did you find out anything?'

He shook his head. 'Nothing much. There's a phone number, though – I thought I'd give her a call.'

'I'll do it, if you like.' She saw that he was about to

object, and added quickly, 'She might feel easier, speaking to a woman.'

He frowned. 'Perhaps you're right.'

The kettle had boiled; he made the coffee. She sat down on a canvas chair and made herself say, 'You said the business was going bust, Lewis. Is it really that bad?'

'No.' He laughed. 'We'll muddle on somehow. You mustn't worry. Last night – it was the drink talking.'

'Perhaps Tim will go ahead with his boat after all.'

'Yes, perhaps.'

He looked exhausted and rather ill. She said, 'Why don't you call it a day and have a break? You look so tired. It's a lovely morning; we could go out somewhere, forget about everything.'

'Can't. I need to make sense of these.' He waved at the ledger books and the piles of bills and receipts on the desk. 'I'd only worry about it, you see. Jerry's left them in a mess. As soon as it's sorted, we'll go away to London for a weekend, see our friends, I promise, Freddie.'

'At least eat the sandwiches.'

'Yes. Thanks.'

She watched him as he worked. It was cold in the wooden building; she was glad she had worn a coat and gloves. Her gaze ran over the shelves behind the desk, the line of files and ledger books. The sharp white light from the estuary glittered in the narrow gaps between the planking of the walls.

Suddenly Lewis looked up from the desk. 'Why has it got to be so hard, Freddie?' he said. He looked distraught. 'Why couldn't something have worked out just for once?

520

It's not as if I don't try. I sometimes think I've been chewed up and spat out and left to rot by this bloody country. Christ, if I could think of anywhere else to go, I'd be off like a shot.'

She went to him, running her fingers through his hair, kneading her thumbs into his tense shoulder muscles. He pressed his face into her side and let out a breath.

'I don't want to let you down.'

'You won't. Please, darling, please don't even think about that.'

'I feel such a failure. I don't know what I'll do if all this hits the buffers.'

'If the worst happens, then we'll just start again. We've done it before and we can do it again.'

He looked up at her, seemed about to say something, then stopped.

'How bad is it really?' she said gently. 'You can tell me. It'll seem better if we share it.'

His finger jabbed at the order book. 'The work's not coming in. If we get nothing new in the next few days, I'm going to have to tell Walter I've no work for him. I've been keeping him busy with small repair jobs.'

'Perhaps you could find more of those, to keep you going.'

'Yes, jolly good idea.' His cheerfulness seemed forced.

'Are there any debts?' She tensed as she waited for his answer.

He ran a hand over his chin. 'The bank, of course.'

'How much do you owe them?'

'Fifty quid or so, that's all.'

She kissed him. 'That's not so bad, fifty pounds.' Though she could not see how they could possibly repay it. 'We'll manage, I know we will.'

He seemed to cheer up. He drew her on to his knee. She felt him relax as they kissed.

'I expect I'm making a mountain out of a molehill,' he said. 'I'll tell you what we'll do. I'll build us a boat and we'll sail the world. We'll go to all the places we've always dreamed of seeing. What do you think, Freddie?'

Later, she left the boathouse and cycled to the phone kiosk on the harbour.

She dialled the operator. Jerry's sister was called Mrs Davidson, and she lived in Bayswater. Freddie asked the operator to put her through to the number on Mrs Davidson's letter.

The phone rang out a few times, then a man answered. Freddie asked to speak to Mrs Davidson.

'Who is it, please?'

'My name's Frederica Coryton. I'm calling from Lymington.'

A pause. Then, 'From the boatyard?'

'Yes. I really do need to speak to Mrs Davidson. It's urgent.'

'I'll go and get her. Hang on, please.'

A longer pause. Freddie heard the high-pitched voices of children and – she strained to make out words but could not – adults talking.

The phone was picked up again. 'Hello? Mrs Davidson speaking.'

'This is Mrs Coryton. From—'

'The boatyard, yes.' The words were well enunciated and crisp. 'How can I help you, Mrs Coryton?'

'I was hoping to speak to your brother, Jerry.'

'He's not here.'

'Do you know where he is?'

'I'm afraid I haven't heard from him for some time.'

'Have you any idea how I can get in touch with him?'

'I'm afraid not. I'm sorry. And now you must excuse me, I have people to lunch.'

Freddie thanked Mrs Davidson and put the phone down. Her optimism of the early morning had evaporated; she shivered as she left the kiosk and climbed on to her bicycle. Mrs Davidson had been too pat, she thought, too incurious. Mrs Davidson had been lying.

It was six o'clock in the evening, the tail end of a drizzly day that had reduced London to shades of grey. Rebecca was heading down Jermyn Street when she caught sight of a man coming out of the Cavendish Hotel. He was wearing a raincoat and he was bareheaded. She knew him by the way he walked, the bounce in his stride.

She called out, 'Milo!'

He turned. 'Good Lord, Rebecca, how extraordinary.' He gave her a piercing look; she suspected he was thinking how much she'd aged.

'What a surprise.' She kissed his cheek. 'What are you doing in London, Milo?'

'Some publicity stuff . . . a meeting with Roger. And you?'

'I'm here for a few days, visiting a friend.' She was staying with Simone.

'Marvellous. You're looking very well, I must say.'

'And you.' Though he had put on weight, she thought.

Milo glanced at his watch. 'You've time for a drink, haven't you, Rebecca?'

'Yes. Thank you.'

They went into the Cavendish. Rebecca excused herself and headed for the ladies' room. Looking into the mirror, she ran her hands through her hair, touched up her lipstick and dabbed on a little powder. Then she made her way to the bar.

Milo had ordered a gin and lemon for her and a whisky and soda for himself. They chinked their glasses in a toast.

Milo said, 'I used to think it terribly déclassé to mix anything other than water with whisky. The soda's an American habit, I'm afraid.'

'You don't sound American. I thought you'd have an accent, after so long.'

'People seem to like the English accent, so I've hung on to it.' He sat back in his chair, looking at her. 'I've been trying to work out how many years it's been since we saw each other.'

'That awful time at the lawyer's, before the war. I expect I was horrid to you.'

'I expect I deserved it.'

In the bright light of the bar, Rebecca noticed his thinning hair and the pouchy folds beneath his eyes. Her golden boy, Milo Rycroft, with whom she had fallen in love at the Chelsea Arts Ball, was going bald.

She said, 'How are Mona and Helen?'

'Fine. Blooming. And so's the new baby.'

She stared at him. 'Milo. When was this?'

'Laura's nine months old.'

'Laura . . . that's a pretty name.'

'She was christened Laurabeth. Mona chose it.' Milo took out his wallet, drew out a snapshot and handed it to Rebecca.

She looked at the photograph. The elder girl, Helen, stood beside her mother; the baby, Laurabeth, sat on Mona's knee. The girls, both of whom were pretty, had the same thick dark hair as their mother. Mona was pretty too, but Rebecca noted a certain steeliness in her expression, which might, she thought, mean that Mona was better able to manage Milo than she herself had been.

'They're very sweet,' she said. She gave the snapshot back to Milo.

'I can never see much of me in them. Though Helen's a great reader. Likes to hide away with a book. Mona isn't keen on it, says it's bad for her eyes.'

'You must be so proud of them.'

'Yes.' He put the photo back in his wallet. 'To tell the truth, I don't think I'm cut out to be a father. I'm too selfish.'

'Now there's an insight,' she said drily.

Milo shrugged. 'I know I'm selfish. It's hardly a revelation. I can't write if I'm not selfish. I need peace and quiet and someone to cook my meals and iron my shirts. Someone who isn't offended if I need to go for a long walk on my own. Otherwise I can't do it. There's a way of thinking that allows me to write, makes it not too much effort. Lets me get to it.'

'A sort of quietness,' she said. 'Not just a lack of noise, but a mental quietness.'

'Yes.' He looked at her, surprised. 'That's it. I can't write if the phones are ringing and the children are talking. Mona's very good, keeps them out of my way, but they're still there, I always know they're there.'

'Can't you work at the university?'

'I do try,' he said fretfully, 'but the students seem to interrupt me rather a lot.'

'Oh dear, Milo.' She couldn't help smiling. 'You still have your Maenads, then?'

He said ruefully, 'I think they look on me as a father figure. They expect me to listen to their problems – and such dreary little problems, Rebecca: boyfriends, and fallings-out with girls in the dorm. I could write a book about it but it would bore me stiff. It's been a relief to come here, to tell the truth. Three weeks without having to think of anyone but myself. And I wanted to see England again.'

'Have you missed us?'

'More than I thought I would. Though London – it's been a shock. I mean, it's more than three years since the war ended and the place still looks a bloody mess. I can hardly recognize some of it.' He sounded aggrieved.

'We haven't any money, Milo,' she said patiently. 'And we're worn out. It was a hard few years. It still is hard, actually.'

'Of course. I didn't mean . . .' He paused, then said, 'I

suppose I've got used to the American can-do spirit. And I can't help thinking that if this were America, they'd have made things better by now.'

Rebecca thought of the Spitfire corkscrewing nose-first into the copse near Mayfield Farm, and of the girl she had tried to dig out of the rubble, turned to a marble statue by the white dust.

She changed the subject. 'So your work's going well?'

'Splendidly.'

There was a silence. She found her gaze drifting to the clock above the bar. Twenty past six. She was to have supper at Simone's at seven.

She was about to take her leave when he said suddenly, 'Actually, I haven't had anything published in five years. Some essays, reviews, a few short stories, but nothing *proper*. Not a novel.'

He sounded defeated, she thought. And weary. 'Let me get you another drink,' she suggested.

'Just a soda, then.' As he raised a hand to signal to the waiter, he added quickly, 'Bit of liver trouble. Mona doesn't let me drink anything at home. She doesn't drink herself – she did before we married but she hasn't since the children. Says it's a bad example. We don't keep anything in the house.'

'I'm sorry to hear you've been unwell, Milo.'

'I was in hospital for a fortnight.' He frowned. 'I'd never been ill before. It shook me up. I'm supposed to lose weight. Mona keeps an eye on what I eat.' He took a pack of cigarettes out of his pocket. 'She doesn't like me smoking, either. I still do at college, though.'

527

He offered the packet to Rebecca. She took one. 'Thanks.'

He lit their cigarettes. 'I've often wondered whether that's why I can't seem to write now.'

'Giving up the booze and fags?'

He smiled. 'That too. But no, I meant this.' He glanced round the room. 'Maybe I'd be able to write if I came back to England.'

'Would Mona agree to that?'

'Never. All her family are in Boston. Her parents, her brothers and sisters.'

'Oh, Milo,' she said.

'I know.' He sighed. 'I can't write about America because I don't understand it well enough and I can't write about England because I don't know it any more.'

'Then write about something else. Write about families.'

'I don't think . . .'

'I know you've always tried to avoid family life, but it doesn't sound as if you've done too well at that recently,' she said tartly. 'Or write about love, Milo. You must have learned something about love.'

He was silent for a moment. He blew out a stream of smoke through his nostrils. 'I could write about regret,' he said.

So could I, Rebecca thought. She did not speak.

Milo looked down at his glass. 'Sometimes I think about Tessa,' he said. 'I can't really remember what she looked like. I say to myself, blond hair, tall and slim and that amazing smile. But I can't *see* her.'

'Was Tessa the love of your life, Milo?' She managed to say it without bitterness.

'I don't know. I don't think I'm very good at knowing that sort of thing.' He looked across the table at Rebecca. 'I regret that I hurt her. And I regret that I hurt you. I regret not being able to see what was important at the time. You get dissatisfied with something and you change it, and what you end up with isn't necessarily any better than what you started with. I regret very much what happened to Tessa and the child. Sometimes I find myself feeling responsible.'

She thought how easily she could say it now, how easily she could tell him what had happened. *I phoned Tessa Nicolson and told her you were seeing someone else. That was why she was on the Oxford road that afternoon, because of my phone call.* Would it free her?

She opened her mouth to speak. Then, from behind her, a voice called out, 'Milo Rycroft! By all that's marvellous, Milo Rycroft!'

Looking over her shoulder, Rebecca saw that a tall, toothy, grey-haired man was advancing towards them.

Milo's expression changed. The sadness, the air of defeat, dropped away and she saw her old Milo: bumptious, Tiggerish, revelling in the sheer delight of being clever, handsome, famous Milo Rycroft.

'Godfrey!' he cried, rising, holding out a hand. 'Rebecca, you remember Godfrey Warburton. How are you, Godfrey?'

'Very well, old chap, very well. And you? Are are you still stunning the Yanks with your literary brilliance?'

'Well . . .' said Milo modestly. He seemed to notice then that Rebecca was putting on her coat. 'You're not going, are you, Rebecca?' he said. 'I thought we should have dinner.'

'I can't, I'm afraid, I have an engagement. But it was lovely to talk to you, Milo. Give my regards to Mona.'

She gave her cheek to Milo to kiss and shook Godfrey Warburton's hand. Out in the street, walking away from the hotel, she reflected that Milo hadn't asked her what she was doing with her life. Once that would have upset her; now it amused her. She wished him well, but she had the sense of having made a narrow escape.

The opening lines of a poem unfurled in her head. *Fear no more the heat o' the sun, nor the furious winter's rages . . .* And the final couplet, devastating in its unblinking honesty: *Golden lads and girls all must, as chimney sweepers, come to dust.*

Chapter Seventeen

Freddie found a job, six hours a week, working for a woman named Mrs Mayer. Renate – Mrs Mayer preferred that Freddie called her Renate – lived in the countryside towards Beaulieu Heath. It was a longish cycle ride, but there were advantages to that. Lewis didn't know Mrs Mayer and neither did any of Lewis's friends. Freddie told him that Mrs Mayer was a friend, and that they drank coffee together and talked. Which was true. She didn't tell Lewis, however, that during her two mornings a week at Renate's house, she mopped floors, cleaned the bathrooms and the kitchen, and cooked lunch. Nor did she tell him that the ten shillings she earned each week bought him his dinner. He didn't query how she managed to buy food, because he didn't know how much food cost, had never cooked, had gone seamlessly from boarding school to university to the navy, and then marriage.

Renate Mayer was a widow in her late seventies. Her husband had been an academic, a professor of chemistry.

They had had no children, and before the war, and before Renate had become unwell, she and her husband had travelled widely. Mrs Mayer's house was modern in design, light and airy, with huge glass windows and a balcony off the big bedroom at the back of the house. There were no curtains, just cream and grey blinds, and no carpets. Scattered on the wood and ceramic-tiled floors were rugs of striking design, woven in dark reds, browns and greys. Beside the fireplaces and on the stairs stood huge bulbous pots, charcoal grey incised with geometric patterns, and plates the colour of earth, their glazes softly iridescent. The vases and plates were by Bernard Leach, Renate told her. Twice a week, Freddie dusted them.

On the walls of the house were photographs and paintings – an abstract in oils, the turquoises and greens set off by flashes of orange, and a nude in black and white, all curves and shadows, her face turned away from the camera. Freddie mentioned that she knew Max Fischer, and Renate said that she had met him once at a gallery, and that she admired his work. After that, they were friends.

Renate suffered from a rheumatic disease. Sometimes, when Freddie arrived at the house at nine o'clock, she was still, very slowly, getting up. On bad days it might take her an hour to dress. She didn't want help, preferred to manage by herself, though she liked Freddie to talk to her while with great difficulty she threaded a swollen hand through a sleeve or did up a button.

That winter, the rain hurled itself at the picture window at the back of Renate Mayer's house. Outside, the tall trees in the garden blurred and blackened and tossed their windswept heads. If it was one of Renate's bad days, she crouched in a chair, her curled hands on her lap, her gaze flicking now and then to the window, as if something was waiting to pounce on her. If she sensed that Renate was too tired to talk, Freddie worked in silence, dusting the vases, her cloth following the smooth, rounded shapes. She liked being in Renate's house. It was peaceful. The light and air and the simple, beautiful objects created a feeling of calm, unlike in her own home, where there was a brittleness, a fragility, and where she seemed to walk a narrow path, aware that some day soon something might just snap.

Lewis had not heard from Jerry Colvin. There had been no letter, no phone call, and Jerry's house remained closed up. Lewis told her that he was sorting things out. They just had to hang on, that was all, till something turned up. It disturbed Freddie to realize that she no longer trusted him; it shamed her to know that she kept secrets from him.

It was the second Saturday of the New Year. Lewis spent the day working while Freddie did the washing, shopped, changed her library books and wrote letters. He came back to the house at four o'clock. They had a cup of tea together and then, because they were to go out to dinner, Freddie ironed his shirt and mended her stockings while Lewis fixed an electric lamp that kept cutting out. Going outside to the shed to fetch a screwdriver, he saw her letters on the hall table and offered to post them. It was dark, she pointed out, it could wait till tomorrow. It was no trouble, he said, it was a fine night and he could do with a breath of fresh air.

They were dining with the Renwicks that evening. Tim Renwick was a solicitor and his wife, Diane, did a lot of charity work. They had a large Georgian house in the centre of Lymington. Two other couples had been invited to dinner, friends of Tim's from university days; the wife of one of the friends was pregnant. Diane served roast leg of pork, and when one of Tim's friends asked her where she had managed to get such a fine big joint, Diane tapped the side of her nose and laughed.

Freddie noticed that Lewis was drinking more than usual. Or rather, more than he had drunk before this level of drinking became usual. He talked a lot and his voice was rather loud and some of his anecdotes didn't seem to have much point to them. But then, all the men were drinking heavily and a couple of the wives too, though not Freddie or the pregnant wife. Perhaps she should have another drink, Freddie thought, and then she might feel like talking and Lewis wouldn't accuse her of not making an effort. She drank another glass of wine rather quickly, and felt herself relax, felt her conversation lift, so that she flirted a little with the men and made some of the wives laugh.

It was past midnight when they left the Renwicks' house. Walking home, Lewis put his arm round her waist and kissed her. 'Was I all right?' she said, and he said, 'You were terrific. Adorable. Thank you, darling.'

Because there was a full moon, they saw the car parked outside their house as they turned the corner of the road. It was a few moments before they realized it was a police car.

534

'Christ, what the hell's going on?' muttered Lewis. He hurried his footsteps, then began to run.

Freddie was wearing heels and couldn't keep up with him. As she neared the house, she saw that the driver had stepped out of the car and was talking to Lewis. Her imagination conjured up disasters – perhaps Jerry Colvin's body had been found in one of the hundreds of little reedy inlets that let into this coast.

As she reached him, Lewis turned to her, his eyes wild.

'It's the boatyard,' he said. 'There's been a fire. The whole bloody place has gone up.'

There was nothing left. It had been a dry fortnight and the wooden sheds had burned down in hours. Had they looked out from one of the windows at the Renwicks' house, they might have seen the orange glow over the estuary.

The next morning, she and Lewis walked down to the yard. White-faced, Lewis stared at the tangled, unrecognizable things that protruded from the heap of ashes and charcoal. There was an acrid stench in the air, and when they walked through the debris, dusty smoke puffed up. It made Freddie think of the Blitz. Blackened fragments of paper floated on the brown water of the estuary. A handful of small boys had gathered on the wharf and were throwing stones at them.

The police and the fire brigade interviewed Lewis. Phone calls were made, letters were written to the insurers and forms were filled in. The loss adjuster, a short, thin man called Mr Simpson, came to the house. He and Lewis were enclosed in the sitting room all morning. Preparing lunch in the kitchen, Freddie found herself straining to hear what they were saying. When the sitting room door opened, she jumped.

Mr Simpson wanted to speak to her, Lewis said. Did she mind?

No, of course not, she said, though for some reason her heart lurched. Mr Simpson cleared his throat and looked down at his notes. Mr Coryton had told him that he had returned home at about four o'clock on Saturday afternoon. The inflexion in his voice turned the statement to a question.

Yes, she said.

Perhaps Mrs Coryton would like to talk him through the events of the remainder of the day.

Freddie listed them, the mundane domestic details, the cup of tea, the ironing, the broken lamp. They had left home to walk to the Renwicks' house at twenty to eight, she said.

Another clearing of the throat. 'And your husband was with you all this time, Mrs Coryton?'

'How much longer is this going on?' Lewis interrupted angrily. 'Can't you see my wife's upset?'

'It's all right,' Freddie said quickly. 'Lewis went out to the shed to get a screwdriver to fix the lamp, but otherwise, yes, we were together all the time.'

Mr Simpson thanked her. Lewis showed him to the front door. In the kitchen, Freddie cut up potatoes, put them in a pan, and in that time remembered.

Lewis came back into the kitchen. 'The letters,' she said, glancing round at him. 'Did you remember to tell him about the letters?'

536

'Letters? What letters?' He lifted a lid, peered into a saucepan.

'My letters. You took them to the postbox, remember.'

'Don't worry, I told the obnoxious little creep everything.' He caught her round the waist, kissing the back of her neck. 'I came clean, guv'nor. It's a fair cop.'

'And you told him . . .' She broke off.

'What, Freddie?'

'Well, that the yard's in trouble financially.'

'Of course not.' His gaze cooled and he let her go. 'It would only have stirred up trouble. And all the books went up with the boatyard. I didn't see any point in complicating things.'

'But if they were to find out . . . it might look bad.'

'Then we'd better hope they don't find out, hadn't we?' He reached up and took a glass out of a cupboard. 'Tell you what, darling, why don't we go away for the weekend, take our mind off things? It's months since we went to London.'

She watched him take the whisky bottle out from beneath the sink and unscrew the top. She said, 'I think you should tell them.'

He spun round, fury in his eyes. 'Shut up, Freddie. You don't know what you're talking about.'

She took a step back, as if his words had been a physical blow. Had he any love left for her that he could speak to her like that?

There was a silence; Lewis seemed to fight to regain control. He said, 'Everything's going to be all right, do you understand?' He poured an inch of whisky into his glass. 'Everything's going to be all right.'

Then he laughed. 'They asked me a lot of questions about Jerry. I had to tell them he'd done a bunk. I think they think he set the place on fire. Bloody ridiculous – I mean, can you imagine dear old Jerry doing a thing like that? It'll have been someone careless, tossing a cigarette end near the place. Those wooden buildings, they go up like tinder.'

They took the train to London the next day. They stayed in a West End hotel – the insurance money would pay for it, said Lewis. Reaching their room, he tipped the porter, and then, when they were alone, he took off his tie and undid the top button of his shirt. Then he gave a deep sigh, flung himself on the bed and fell asleep.

Freddie washed her hands and face and put on fresh lipstick. She slipped out of the room, closing the door quietly behind her.

She went to Green Park. The weather wasn't particularly nice, cold and damp, but she hardly noticed. She needed to think. She couldn't think any more when she was with Lewis. She needed to reassure herself and to stop feeling frightened. She walked for a while and then sat down on a bench. Lewis had told the truth, she said to herself. He had told the loss adjuster that he had gone out to post the letters, he had said so. It had been sensible of him not to mention the boatyard's precarious financial state. As he had said, why complicate things?

But it was no good, she was unable to shake off her unease. It wasn't only the fire at the boatyard or even the tone of voice with which he had spoken to her – *Shut up,*

Freddie, you don't know what you're talking about – that troubled her. She was no longer able to see a future for herself. She and Lewis had made so many new starts, and the promise of all those new starts had soured, and a bitter taste had seeped into their marriage. Lewis did not share his problems with her and she had stopped confiding in him. They lived separate lives within the same house. Their ambitions were not the same, and neither, she had begun to fear, was their morality. Beneath her ribs something was tightly wound up, as if her heart had tied itself into a knot. And she was so tired – tired of trying to make the best of things, tired of the pretence that everything was all right.

She walked back to the hotel. Lewis wasn't in their room, so she went downstairs and wandered around for a while, looking for him. Eventually she saw him sitting at the bar.

He rose as she entered the room. He looked annoyed. 'Where were you?' he said.

'I went for a walk.'

'Hell of a long walk. You could have told me, Freddie.'

'You were asleep.'

'You could have left a note.'

'I didn't think there was any point. I needed some time to myself, that's all.'

He said coldly, 'Do you want a drink?'

'No thanks. I'm going to have a bath.'

'I phoned Marcelle.'

She looked back at him. 'Did you?'

'She told me she's having a few people round tonight. She's asked us to come.'

'I'd rather not.'

'I accepted the invitation.' As he looked at her, his voice hardened. 'It's only a few drinks. I would have thought you could make the effort.'

She noticed that the other people in the room were staring at them, and she felt tired again and said, 'Yes, all right then, if we must.'

Back in their room, she ran a bath, shook some salts into it. Her fingers were bluish; she had not realized how cold she was. She lay in the water and felt the fear ebb and flow, washing over her in waves. Had she ever felt quite so alone before? After the accident, she thought, when Tessa had been so ill, perhaps then. But this aloneness had a different quality – for all their absences and partings, and for all the secrets Tessa had kept, they had never been out of tune with one another. She and Lewis were out of tune: she no longer knew what he felt for her. And did she still love him? She must do, or he would not have the power to hurt her so. When she lay back in the warm, scented water, closing her eyes, she wanted to fall asleep, to block out all her worries, not to think any more. But the water cooled, and eventually she climbed out, dripping on to the bath mat, and wrapped herself in a towel and went into the bedroom.

A sort of defiance came over her as she opened the wardrobe and ran her gaze along the clothes on the rack. She had brought with her to London her favourite dress, a black and white striped silk with a nipped-in waist and calf-length full skirt. The dress had been bought in the spring, when they had had money – or they had *seemed* to have money: perhaps that too had been a chimera. She held up her mother's garnets against the dress, admiring their crimson gleam.

She was sitting at the dressing table, doing her make-up, when Lewis came up into the room. He took out a clean shirt, found cufflinks. He glanced across at her.

'You don't think that's a bit much for a cocktail party?'

'What?'

'That necklace.'

It probably was. Freddie studied her reflection in the mirror. The jewels were oversized, dark and sultry, almost tarty, a marriage of Victorian showiness and gloom. Marcelle would be wearing a neat row of pearls.

'No,' she said coolly, 'I don't.'

In the taxi to Marcelle Scott's Chelsea house, they hardly spoke. The house had changed since Freddie had last seen it, the ravages of wartime plastered over and tidied away. Marcelle was wearing a pale green dress, a pearl necklace and earrings. They were greeted with exclamations and kisses. Then a waitress in black offered them a drink. Freddie said, 'Look, Lewis, there's Betty Douglas,' but when she turned aside, he had gone. She watched him, heading from one cluster of guests to another, working the room, smiling now, his bad mood forgotten, talking, charming, laughing.

The noise of chatter and laughter echoed against the high ceiling. She had been to parties here before, in the days when she and Marcelle had been friends. She found herself absorbed into a circle of guests. There was a man called Alan Lockyear, who farmed in the north of England, a woman called Pamela, who owned a dress shop, and Pamela's fiancé, Gus Morris. There were also George and Alexandra — because of the noise, Freddie had not caught their surname – he tall, balding and red-faced, liable to speak at length if not headed off, she slender and lovely, her pale skin freckled and her chestnut hair twisted into a French pleat, her eyes bored, sulky, raking the room.

Alan, Pamela and Gus melted away, but George was still telling her what he planned to do to his house in Norfolk. It sounded as if it was a large house – he mentioned a ballroom and stables. His voice, which was monotonous in tone, was hypnotic, and Freddie found her attention drifting.

'The problem's the cornices and mouldings,' said George. 'Impossible to find decent craftsmen these days. The thing is, should we make a start or should we wait till after Rose's birthday? Marcia tells me we'll need the ballroom for her twenty-first, d'you see.'

'Georgie,' Alexandra said irritably. 'Rose doesn't want a birthday party. She told me.'

'I'm sure she does, darling. Anyway, that's beside the point.'

Rose, thought Freddie, and her attention snapped back. Rose, Marcia, George and Alexandra. And a house in Norfolk.

She said, 'Do you have a brother called Jack?'

George tucked in his chin and raised his eyebrows. 'I do, actually. He's here somewhere. Do you know him?'

Jack was here. Yes, she knew him, said Freddie. Suddenly, she longed to see him. She noticed that Lewis was talking to Denzil Beckford – her gaze moved on and she caught a glimpse of fair hair.

She murmured an excuse to George and Alexandra and threaded through the crowds. 'Jack,' she said.

He turned. 'Freddie!' His face broke into a smile. She remembered that smile: the amusement in it, and the hint of cockiness. And his blue eyes, and the touch of vanity in his well-cut suit and Italian silk tie. She was looking at him, drinking him in, noticing what had changed and what was just the same.

'Well, this is just perfect,' he said. 'How are you, Freddie? You look wonderful. Are you sure I can't persuade you to run away with me again?'

With no warning, and to her utter horror, tears stung her eyes. She stood there, blinking, speechless.

'Oh God,' said Jack. He ran a hand through his hair, staring at her. 'I'm so sorry, Freddie. Here, let me get you another drink.'

By the time he came back with the glasses, she had got herself under control. He said, 'I'm a tactless idiot, talking about Italy, all that. You were thinking of your sister, weren't you? Here, have a swig of this.'

She swallowed a mouthful of gin and let him think that she had been crying because of Tessa, though she hadn't – she had wept, she thought, because of her discovery that the past, and that extraordinary journey she had undertaken with Jack Ransome in Italy, now seemed so safe, so free of complexity, compared to the tangled maze of her marriage.

'Marcelle told me about Tessa,' he said. 'I was so sorry, Freddie.'

Marcelle Scott, she thought, the fountainhead of all gossip. But she was touched that he remembered Tessa's name. 'Thank you, Jack.' She changed the subject quickly. 'I've been talking to your brother George. He was telling me about ceiling mouldings.'

Jack gave a bark of laughter. 'That's enough to make anyone weep with boredom.' He looked at her closely. 'Are you sure you're all right?'

'Yes, honestly. I'm just a little tired.'

'Let's go and find somewhere quieter.'

He led her to a small sitting room at the back of the house. A plump, purple-nosed man, his waistcoat buttons undone, slept in an armchair. A young girl, twelve or so, was lying on a rug, reading a book.

'Hello, Peggy,' said Jack, and the girl smiled at him and then went back to her book.

They sat down by the window. Jack said, 'Is Lewis here?'

'Yes, somewhere. He was talking to Denny.'

'Where are you two living?'

'On the south coast, in Lymington.'

'Do you like it there?'

Another discovery: that she did not want to go back to Lymington. That she was afraid of going back.

'Very much,' she said. 'It's nice having our own house at last. And lovely to be near the sea.'

'What's Lewis doing these days?'

'He owned a boatyard.'

Jack frowned. 'Owned?'

'There was a fire, ten days ago.'

'Was there much damage?'

'Everything's gone. The office, the yard, everything.'

'Good Lord, that's terrible. Poor old Lewis, what a blow.'

'Yes.'

'The place was insured, presumably?'

'Oh yes.' Her mind flicked back to Mr Simpson's visit, and Lewis telling her the insurers' suspicions about Jerry Colvin. Was it possible? Could Jerry have burned down the boathouse?

She smiled at him. 'What about you, Jack? What are you doing? I don't suppose there's so much scope for your talents these days.'

'Oh, you'd be surprised. Governments always like to know what other governments are doing, even those who are supposed to be our friends. After the war, I worked for the Diplomatic Service for a couple of years. And then, I don't know, all of a sudden I'd had enough. It began to seem a little . . . well, tacky. All that deception. Necessary in wartime, but less forgivable now. It starts to affect the way you think. You find yourself looking at people and wondering what they're really like, what goes on beneath the surface. So I resigned, and I went back to Italy.'

'To Rome?'

'Yes. I was there during the war, you see, and for one thing, I wanted to make sure the people who'd helped me back then were doing all right. Oh, and I wrote a book.'

'A book?'

'Don't sound so surprised, I can string a few sentences together. I suppose it's a sort of travel memoir, though that sounds hideously pompous.'

'Goodness, Jack, how impressive. And — marriage? Children?'

'I'm afraid not.'

'You haven't been able to persuade Gabriella to marry you, then?'

'Gaby's got more sense. Anyway, I was waiting for you, Freddie. When I heard you'd hitched yourself to Lewis Coryton, I was distraught.'

They talked about Jack's family, about his place in Rome, and about mutual friends. Then the man with the waist-coat gave a sudden loud snore, sat up and said, 'What time is it? Supposed to be meeting the in-laws,' and left the room.

Freddie looked at the clock. It was half past eight. 'I'd better go and find Lewis,' she said. 'It's been so good to talk to you, Jack. So lovely to see you again.'

She kissed his cheek and returned to the drawing room. The crowds had thinned out; there were only a dozen people left, and a quick glance told her that Lewis was not among them. She began to search the various ground-floor rooms. Then she went downstairs to the basement, where in the kitchen an older woman, her sleeves rolled up, was washing glasses. She thought she should try the bathroom. She went upstairs, but it was empty.

There was an unpleasant falling sensation in her stomach as the truth sank in: that he had left without telling her. She kept thinking she must be mistaken, he couldn't possibly have done such a thing, that soon she'd look up and there he would be, checking his watch, in a hurry to move on to the next event. But he did not appear, and she stood in the drawing room, irresolute, her fingers crushing together the strands of garnets.

'Freddie?'

She looked up. Jack had come to stand by her side. 'Where's Lewis?' he said.

'I don't know.' She gave a little laugh. Had Lewis been angry with her for talking to Jack for so long? 'He seems to have gone.'

'Gone?'

'Yes.' She couldn't think of anything more to say. She had lost the energy for pretence.

'Where are you staying?'

She told him the name of the hotel.

'Might he have gone back there?'

'I don't think so. You know Lewis, he likes to have a proper night out.' Though recently she had begun to think that she did not know Lewis at all.

She said, 'He was talking to Denny. Perhaps they've gone on somewhere.'

'Denny was meeting some people at the Criterion. Shall we try there first?'

'You don't have to come, Jack. I could just get a taxi back to the hotel.'

He was looking at her in a way that discomforted her. As if he could see through her, see the way her life was slipping out of control.

'I'd like to catch up with Lewis,' he said easily. 'It's been years.'

Outside in the street, he hailed a taxi. On the journey to Piccadilly, Freddie sat, trying to absorb her shock and hurt. Jack talked about this and that, and every now and then she said yes or no or goodness me, and all the time she thought about Lewis walking off, as if she was unimportant to him.

Inside the Criterion restaurant, all gold and mosaics and draped velvet curtains, Jack spoke to the head waiter, asking for Mr Beckford's table. They were led to the centre of the room. And there was Lewis, sitting near Denzil Beckford, and Freddie was speechless, torn between anger and tears and a desire to run to him, to make it better between them, somehow, anyhow.

Lewis said, 'Hello, Freddie,' as though nothing out of the ordinary had happened, and then, 'Well, fancy that, Jack Ransome.'

Extra chairs were fetched and place settings laid. Freddie watched Lewis carefully. Sometimes he smiled, then he laughed. Some of her tension slipped away. Her happiness had come to depend on Lewis's mood. She had been wound up like a spring since the loss adjuster's visit – no, before that, since the boathouse had burned down, or since Lewis had told her the business was going bankrupt and Jerry had disappeared.

A few drinks, some conversation and her spirits lifted, and somehow, miraculously, it turned into the sort of evening you recall years later, saying, *Do you remember when . . . ?* It was going to be all right, she told herself. She should trust Lewis and stop imagining things. There was nothing to worry about. When the insurance money came through, they could sell the Lymington house and move back to London. Lewis was always happier in London.

Theirs was the last group to leave the restaurant. It was midnight, and as, in the cloakroom, Lewis helped her on with her coat, he said, 'I've asked Jack to come and stay with us. He said he would. It'll be fun, won't it, Freddie?'

And she kissed him, saying, 'Yes, it'll be great fun.'

They went back to Lymington. They put the house on the market and Lewis wrote letters to friends and acquaintances who worked in London, looking for openings.

A few days after their return, Jack came to visit. The three of them went for walks along the estuary and on Beaulieu Heath. Jack had a car; one day they drove to Bournemouth and strolled along the front, eating ice-cream cornets, while a storm brewed up and charcoal-coloured clouds seethed on the horizon. Higher in the sky, bands of lighter grey gleamed. The waves drew themselves up before crashing down on to the sand. In the evening, Freddie cooked supper, and after they had eaten, they played cards and then the two men walked to the pub. In Jack's company, the atmosphere in the house lifted, became easier.

A letter arrived from the insurance company. Lewis ripped open the envelope. 'Is it the cheque?' said Freddie.

'No, damn it.' He frowned, scanning the lines. 'They want me to drop over to their office in Southampton.'

'Why, Lewis?' Her fragile calm slipped away; she felt frightened again.

'Nothing important. Oh for God's sake, Freddie, don't give me that dying swan look. It'll only be some more bloody pain-in-the-neck form-filling.'

'When do you want to go, Lewis?'

Jack's voice. She looked up. He was standing in the kitchen doorway.

'Today, I suppose.' Lewis glanced at his watch. 'Get it over and done with.'

'Let me give you a lift to Southampton.'

'It's all right, I'll catch the train.' Lewis stuffed the letter into his pocket. 'You stay here and keep Freddie company. It shouldn't take me more a couple of hours.'

Lewis left half an hour later. Freddie finished clearing up the breakfast things while Jack drove him to the station. She watched the motion of her hands, swooshing soapy water over plates and bowls.

Jack came back to the house. They could go to Hurst Beach, he suggested. He loved shingle beaches in the winter – if, that was, she didn't mind the cold. Freddie put on her duffel coat and scarf. She needed to get out of the house.

They drove west. Jack parked at one end of the shingle spit, and they decided to walk to the castle at the far end. They tramped along, their shoes sinking into the pebbles. It was a bright morning – winter had decided to take a day off for once – and the sea was rippled like grey-green silk. Only a few other people populated the vast expanse of shingle – a man walking his dog, a couple collecting shells. Across the water they could see the Isle of Wight; some days, Freddie said to Jack, when she and Lewis had come here, the island had been lost in the sea mist.

Jack said, 'Rough on Lewis, this business with the boatyard.'

'Yes.'

'He told me you were selling the house.'

'He wants to go back to London and buy a place there.'

'And you, Freddie? Is that what you want?'

'Yes, I suppose so.'

She heard the hiss of the salt water as it rushed back, draining through the pebbles, carrying the smaller stones into the waves. She heard Jack say, 'What are you afraid of, Freddie?'

She looked at him and laughed. 'Afraid? I'm not afraid.'

He shrugged. 'On edge, then, if you prefer. Is it money?'

'Is it so obvious?'

'You wouldn't be the only one. George had to sell off some of the family silver.'

'Lewis and I haven't any family silver to sell off. Well —' that false laugh again — 'there are my garnets, but Victoriana is so deeply unfashionable now, I can't imagine they'd raise much.' Her mind drifted to Lewis, at the insurance office. What questions were they asking him? What had he told them?

They headed on, their shoes crunching on the pebbles. Walking on the shingle was slow and tiring, and after half an hour they seemed to be no nearer the old Napoleonic fortress at the end of the spit. There was a rotting wooden breakwater; they sat down on it.

Jack said, 'I don't think many of us found it easy to settle after the war.'

She glanced at him. 'You too, Jack?'

'You can put it so that it sounds all right, can't you? Work for the Diplomatic Service for a couple of years, write a few books, do a bit of journalism, and it skates over how sometimes you found yourself floundering.'

'I can't imagine you floundering. You always seem to have an answer for everything.'

'Do I? Then how irritating of me. No wonder you get annoyed with me.'

'Not *annoyed* . . .'

'Feckless, you called me.' He was smiling. 'And the first time we met, you stamped on my foot.'

The first time they had met, he had kissed her. Somehow, sitting next to him on the breakwater, their bodies now and then touching, it seemed dangerous to remind him of that.

He told her something of his experiences in Italy during the war. His task had been to liaise with the partisan bands who were hiding out in the forests and mountains. He had brought them clothing and equipment and had trained them to use their weapons. He had been wounded once, captured twice and escaped twice, and had narrowly avoided being shot as a spy. There were experiences he knew he would never forget – coming across a village where women and children had been put to death, their bodies left in the street, in reprisal for sheltering partisans – and other times that had restored his faith in human nature. He told her about the generosity of the Italian people, who had possessed so little themselves.

He asked her about Tessa. She explained that for most of the war, Tessa had been living at Olivia Zanetti's villa in Chianti. That she had taught first the local children and then refugee children too at the school on the Zanetti estate. That she had been admired and much loved, and that she had died escorting a party of children to safety. The villa where she had been living had been completely destroyed during the war, but Olivia Zanetti herself, her daughter and her two sons, Guido and Sandro, had survived. Though Sandro had spent much of the last years of the war in a POW camp, Guido had remained at liberty, hiding out in the hills until the Allied forces reached Tuscany.

He said, 'Have you been back there?'

'To Italy? No.'

'Why not?'

'Because we couldn't afford it, for one thing.' She decided to tell him the truth. 'And because I'm not sure I could bear it.'

'It might help.' His voice was gentle. 'Think about it. If you change your mind, I've a spare room at my flat in Rome.'

'Have you, Jack?'

'For Lewis as well, of course.'

'Of course.' She tried to imagine going to Rome with Lewis, seeing sights that had once been familiar to her, but she couldn't hold on to it, it seemed unlikely somehow.

Then he said, 'What's going on between you and Lewis?'

'Nothing.' She looked out to sea. 'Nothing's going on.'

'Freddie, I heard the way he spoke to you this morning. And at Marcelle's, he walked out on you.'

She made a brushing motion with her hand. 'Lewis is just worried, that's all, because of the boathouse.'

'Has he any particular reason to worry?'

'No, no, not at all. He hates the delay, the form-filling.'

'I came down here because I was concerned about you. I wanted to see that you were all right.'

She noticed the way the smallest pebbles gleamed like jewels as the wavelets receded. 'As you see, Jack, I'm fine.'

'No you're not, Freddie. There's something in you that I've always admired – your courage, your resolution in facing up to difficulties – and that's gone. Or you've hidden it away, at least.'

She made herself speak calmly. 'What nonsense you're talking. Lewis and I will work it out. And it's really none of your business.'

Jack stood up and, gathering a handful of pebbles, walked to the sea's edge. She watched the breeze tug at his fair hair and the easy grace of his movements as he skimmed stones across the water; something inside her seemed to crumple and fold, and she found herself rising and going to his side.

'It's just so bloody lonely here sometimes!' The words flew out of her, pent up for so long. 'Sometimes I hate it. Everyone says they love the seaside, and how lucky we are, but I can't see it, Jack.'

He dropped the pebbles and hugged her tightly. He stroked her hair; within the strong grasp of his arms, she felt safe at last.

'Dear Freddie,' he said. She thought she felt his lips touch the top of her head – surely not? – and she looked up at him questioningly, and suddenly they were kissing, their mouths searching and hungry, each crushed against the other, his hands gripping her waist hard as the waves sucked and rushed beside them.

It was she who pulled away first. 'Jack, we mustn't,' she said, and she turned aside, but he caught her hand, pulling her back to him. They kissed again, gently this time, until she laid her head against his shoulder, closing her eyes.

'Listen to me, Freddie,' he said softly. 'I almost told you this before, but I've always funked it. So I'm telling you now. I know my timing's rotten and that you're married and that I shouldn't be saying anything at all, but I have to, you see. I love you. I think I've loved you from the moment I saw you standing outside Santa Maria Novella station. All that stuff about choosing you because you were English and you looked sensible − what guff. There was something − I don't know − liking, attraction, *love*, I believe, right from the start.'

'Jack,' she whispered. 'Please. You mustn't − you really mustn't.'

He gripped her upper arms, looking down at her. 'I wouldn't have said a word if I'd thought you were happy. But I've been watching you for the last few days and you're not happy, are you, Freddie?'

'Jack, please.' She put up her hand, silencing him, shaking her head. 'I don't want to talk about it. Let's just enjoy today.' She felt exhausted, on the verge of tears, yet at the same time exhilarated and more alive than she had felt for a very long time.

They walked on, arm in arm, towards the castle, stopping for Freddie to gather up some shells, another time to take off their shoes and tip out the small stones that had accumulated inside, and then, stupidly, crazily, to run down to the sea and paddle in the freezing-cold water. Sitting on the shingle, watching him fool around, she questioned

555

herself. He had told her he loved her. Why did that knowledge so transform and elate? Did she, in fact, love him too? Was it possible? She remembered the attraction she had felt for him in that very first kiss, outside the station in Florence, and she remembered waking beside him in the car, on their journey, and wanting him. She remembered their parting in France and, more than a year later, dancing with him at the Dorchester. She could recall every word they had said to each other and every time they had touched: these things were incised in her memory as if engraved by a diamond on glass. *When I found out you'd hitched yourself to Lewis Coryton, I was distraught* . . . And at the Dorchester, she had said to him, *I bet you didn't think of me once after we parted in France*, and he had looked at her with a seriousness that had startled her. *Not true, actually*, he had said.

As they walked back to the car, and during the drive to Lymington, neither of them spoke much. Once, Jack reached across and squeezed her hand, but she thought he seemed preoccupied.

At the house, he parked the car. She saw that Lewis had come out of the front door.

'I'll leave tomorrow,' Jack said. 'It would be wrong of me to stay. I'll miss you, Freddie.'

Lewis had returned from his visit to Southampton in good spirits. The insurers had asked him to check through and sign the inventory of items lost in the fire. Then they had asked him a few more questions about Jerry. He expected the cheque to arrive within the week.

During the days that followed, she tried not to think of

Jack. She felt ashamed of herself for having kissed him. She was married to Lewis; she *loved* Lewis.

An unspoken truce existed between them. High drifts of cloud scudded through pale blue winter skies and Lewis talked of the future. They would leave Lymington as soon as they could, he said. This place had only bad memories for him. *I feel as if I'm always waiting for something to happen*, he had said to her the night she had accepted his proposal of marriage. Now they were waiting once more. For time to pass, for it all to blow over.

Another letter arrived from the insurers. Lewis slit open the envelope and drew out a cheque and let out a great sigh of relief. A new start, he said. He waved the cheque. That was what this was – a new start.

The next day, he caught a train to London, for a preliminary recce, he told Freddie. She stayed behind in Lymington. It was one of her mornings with Renate, and at the weekend a couple were coming to view the house, so she needed to clean.

She stayed to eat lunch with Renate and did some shopping in the town on her way back. It was dark by the time she reached home, and it had been raining. She towelled her wet hair and was coming downstairs from the bathroom when she heard the knock at the door.

She opened it. A man stood there: forty-ish, stocky, khaki raincoat, trilby, thin black moustache. Behind him, parked on the roadside, was a large black car.

She guessed he had stopped to ask for directions. 'Yes?' she said. 'Can I help you?'

'Mrs Coryton?'

Not directions, then. 'Yes.'

'Is your husband at home?'

'I'm afraid not. He should be back tomorrow evening, if you'd like to leave a message, Mr . . .'

'Kite, Frank Kite. May I come in?'

There was something about him she disliked. 'That isn't convenient,' she said.

Frank Kite glanced up and down the road. 'I don't think you'd want to have this conversation on your doorstep. The neighbours might overhear.' His eyes, a watery greyish-brown, rested on her. 'Hubby's been a very naughty boy, Mrs Coryton.'

She let him into the house. Her heart was hammering.

Mr Kite came into the hall, shutting the door behind him, brushing raindrops from the sheeny fabric of his coat. 'Good to get out of that rain,' he said. 'A cup of tea would be nice, Mrs Coryton.'

Automatically, she went into the kitchen and put the kettle on. As she opened the cupboard, her hand shook and the cup and saucer clinked together. *Hubby's been a very naughty boy.* She stared out of the window. She wanted to walk out of the back door and keep on walking until she felt safe again.

A sound behind her made her turn. Frank Kite was standing in the doorway. 'Nice little place you've got here,' he said.

She put the tea on the table beside him. He picked up the cup and drank two large mouthfuls, not seeming to notice that it was scalding hot.

'Put the house up for sale, haven't you? I saw the sign.'

She said nothing, just pressed her lips together, watching him warily as she might have watched a wild dog.

Another gulp of tea. 'You're to give Lewis a message,' he said. 'Tell him not to forget the money he owes Frank. I'm worried he's thinking of doing a bunk, you see. That would be very foolish of him, because if he did, then I'd make sure the insurers knew he'd started the fire at the boatyard.'

Her heart skipped a beat. 'That's not true. It was an accident.'

'Don't be naive, Mrs Coryton. Lewis owes rather a lot of money and the place was going down the pan.'

'I don't believe you.'

'Don't you? Are you sure?' Reaching out a hand, he stroked her cheek. 'You better had, honey, because it's the truth.'

'Jerry . . .' she whispered.

'Poor old Jerry's in a nuthouse in St Albans. Has been for the last three months. He had a nervous breakdown, you see.' Then he put down the cup, said, 'I like a girl who makes a nice cup of tea,' buttoned up his raincoat and walked out of the house.

Sitting in the cold front room, the fire unlit, Freddie recalled the night of the fire. The broken lamp, the letters. They had passed two postboxes on their walk to the Renwicks' house, so why had Lewis insisted on posting her letters only an hour earlier? How long had he been out of the house? Ten minutes, fifteen – more? She could not remember. She had been bathing, doing her hair. A fit man like Lewis could have run to the boatyard and back in twenty minutes. Or he could have taken her bicycle and reached it in five. Plenty of time to put a match to kindling. These were all things that, since the night of the fire, she had tried not to think about, but they had been there, whispering like moths at the back of her mind, making her jittery, anxious, frightened. Now the fear returned tenfold.

She found a torch, put on her mackintosh and left the house. She walked to the estuary, to where the boatyard had once stood. Wet, charred planks lay on the slipway and black puddles slicked the floor of what had once been the office. She knew then, with a dull certainty, that Lewis hadn't told the insurers that he had gone out that night. She knew that he had lied to her. If Frank Kite spoke to the insurers, as he had threatened, would she be able to lie for Lewis?

She shone the torch out along the estuary, towards the salt marshes. She felt trapped by this landscape, the uncertainty of it, the slipperiness of it, the way the tide changed it twice daily, swallowing it up. The wind blew and the reeds shifted, waving their feathery heads, and she felt a rush of fear and revulsion, and she turned round and headed back to the house.

At seven o'clock, she heard Lewis's key in the door.

He called out to her. 'Freddie, where are you? I'm back. Freddie?'

She went into the hall. 'There you are,' he said. 'Come here.' He kissed her. Then he sniffed. 'Is that dinner? I'm starving.'

She said, 'A man called Frank Kite came to see you.'

She saw it in his eyes, a closing-off. He hung his coat and hat on the peg. 'He came *here*?' he said.

'Yes.'

'When?'

'This afternoon.'

Turning round to her, he said angrily, 'He shouldn't have come here!'

'He gave me a message for you.'

Now his expression was wary. 'A message?'

She watched his face as she said, 'He said you owed him money, Lewis. And he told me you set fire to the boatyard.'

He pushed past her, into the sitting room and poured himself a drink. 'He's a crook, Freddie.'

'Did you? Did you set fire to the boatyard?'

He laughed. 'No, of course not.'

'But you do owe him money.'

She saw him lick his lips. 'Yes.'

'How much?'

He swallowed a mouthful of whisky. 'About five hundred.'

'Five hundred pounds!' She sat down on the sofa. She felt nauseous. 'You said he was a crook. Why would you borrow so much money from a crook?'

'Why do you think?' He sat next to her. 'Because the bank refused to help me. We'd have folded six months ago if I hadn't got hold of some cash. What else could I do? Do you think I'd have taken money from a man like Frank Kite if there had been any other way?'

'You could have *told* me.'

'What, and have you know it was all going wrong? See

on your face that oh-so-patient expression – poor old Lewis, he's made a mess of things again?'

She said angrily, 'Did you set fire to the boatyard, Lewis?'

'Stop it, Freddie. Give me a break.' He took a packet of Senior Service out of his pocket, tipped out a cigarette and put it between his lips.

'I need you to tell me the truth.' Her fists were clenched. 'You have to tell me. We have to be able to trust each other.'

'Trust?' He turned to look at her. 'Do you trust me, Freddie? Do you, honestly?'

She could not answer him.

'Thought so,' he said sourly.

'Did you tell the insurers you went out that night? Did you, Lewis?'

He flicked his lighter. Then, frowning, he gave a small shake of the head.

'Oh God.' She put her hands to her mouth.

'They wouldn't have paid up if I had.' Suddenly his anger disappeared and he sounded very tired. 'They were nosing around. The bank had told them I owed them fifty quid, and I couldn't invent fictional boats that we'd built; it would have been far too easy for them to check up on me.'

She whispered, 'You lied to me.'

'Yes. I'm sorry. I shouldn't have. I couldn't think what else to do. I was afraid we'd lose everything.' He drew on his cigarette. 'The business . . . the house . . . I could cope with losing them, Freddie, but I couldn't bear losing you.'

She thought of Jack Ransome and felt a frisson of fear. 'Lewis . . .'

'Oh, I've known that I've been losing you for a long time now.' He gave a small smile.

'No, Lewis.'

'You know that I'm right,' he said quietly. 'I can see it in your eyes, Freddie. I wish it hadn't been like this, such a bloody battle, trying to keep going, always having to put on a show.'

'You don't have to put on a show for me.'

'Don't I? I was sick of you being disappointed in me, sick of trying and failing. I was afraid that if you knew what was going on you'd walk out on me. Actually, Freddie, I'm still afraid of that. I'm afraid that after this conversation's over, you'll get up and walk out the door.'

'I won't.' The words squeezed out of her. 'I won't, Lewis, I promise.'

'We'll lose the house, Freddie.'

'The house?'

'Kite's interest rates are extortionate. The debt's doubled since I took it out. It'll swallow up the insurance money and whatever we make on the house.' He looked ashen, exhausted.

She said, 'I need you to tell me the truth, Lewis. I need to know what happened at the boatyard.'

'I can't, Freddie.' He ran a hand over his face.

'Listen to me.' She took his hands in hers, pressing them hard. 'We'll start again. And this time it'll come out right, I know it will. But I need you to tell me.'

After a silence, he said, 'I hadn't realized it was so bad till I got the books from Jerry's house. I knew that if I didn't find a way of raising some money, then we'd lose the house. First time I thought of burning the place down, I thought just what you're thinking now. Can't do that, it's criminal. But then, after a while, I began to think, why not? It wasn't as if it would hurt anyone, just the blasted insurers and they're a bunch of crooks anyway. That chap who came round, Simpson, I asked him what he'd done in the war. Sat at home filling in forms, that's what. Why should men like that prosper when men like me are knocked back over and over again? I'd tried so hard, Freddie. Kept to the rules, played the game, and it didn't get me anywhere. So I did it. Set it up during the day so that all I had to do was put a match to it when I nipped out before going to the Renwicks'. I needed to have an alibi, you see. I needed to be well out of the way when the place went up.' He smiled. 'I didn't know I had it in me to do something like that. But to tell the truth, it wasn't nearly as hard as some of the things I've had to do in the past. Fishing my friends out of the sea when they were covered in oil and burning alive – now that was hard.'

In the early hours of the morning, she lay awake, thinking. She was not like Tessa; she had known that when she had kissed Jack Ransome on the beach and she knew it now. She had worked out a long time ago that Tessa's lover, Angelo's father, must have been a married man. Sometimes love just happens, Tessa had said, that time they had spoken in the garden of the Villa Millefiore. And so, she had learned, it might. Love had happened to her a week ago on Hurst Beach, crushingly, joyously, and now she understood at last what Tessa had meant. But there lay the difference. Tessa

564

had followed her love, had given herself to it, heart and soul, and her affair had left such destruction in its wake. She, Freddie, could not do the same. She no longer knew which was better and which was worse – Tessa's belief in the supreme importance of love, or her own conviction that she must be faithful to a marriage that had hurt and deceived. But she did not have a choice. Secret trysts and assignations in hotel rooms: these were not for her. She knew herself too well, knew what she was, and because of that, she would walk away from what she longed for most.

The phone box was at the end of the street: she asked the operator to put her through to Jack Ransome's London number. Waiting, a part of her wanted him not to be in, wanted to put off the moment for as long as possible.

The operator said, 'You're through, caller,' and she heard his voice.

'Hello?'

'Hello, Jack.'

'Freddie. It's good to hear you. How are you?'

'I'm well. And you?'

'Terrific.'

But there was a question in his voice, and she steeled herself and said, 'I don't want you to come here any more, Jack. I don't want you to visit us again.'

A silence, then, 'If you're angry about what happened . . .'

'I'm not angry. But it mustn't happen again. Things have been difficult and I was lonely; it was nothing more than that. It wasn't *important*.'

'It was to me.'

She imagined him at the other end of the phone, puzzled, aware of the beginnings of hurt, and she hardened her voice. 'I'm sorry if I gave you the wrong impression. It was a mistake, that's all.'

'A mistake?'

'Yes.'

'You see,' she could almost hear his frown, 'I've been thinking about it a lot, these last couple of days. Some of the time I've been thinking what a heel I am, kissing a friend's wife, but other times I've been thinking you deserve something more than a marriage that isn't working out right.'

'Lewis and I are fine.'

'I don't believe you.'

'You must.' Suddenly, she was angry. 'What do you know about either of us? What do you know about *me*? You turn up in my life now and then, whenever you feel like it, and you tangle everything up, and then you go away again. I know hardly anything about you, Jack. I've never seen your home – if you have a home – and I haven't met the people you're closest to. I tried to work out the amount of time we've spent together and it came to about a week. Do you honestly think that I'd betray Lewis for someone I've known for a *week*?'

'I'll tell you what I think, Freddie.' His voice was low and steady. 'I think it doesn't work like that. I don't think you can work out whether you love someone with some sort of mathematical equation. You can know that you want someone after an hour. And you can know someone for

566

ten years and then discover one day that it's over, that there's nothing left, that it's all run dry.'

'That's romantic nonsense, and you know it,' she said sharply. 'Don't think for a minute that you can come into our lives and ruin what Lewis and I have.'

She heard his intake of breath on the other end of the phone. He said coldly, 'I had no intention of doing that. I'm sorry if it looks that way.'

'It does, rather.'

'Let me ask you one thing, Freddie. Do you love Lewis?'

She looked out of the window of the kiosk, to the marshes and mudflats. She whispered, 'Yes.' And then, more firmly, 'Yes, I do. Very much.'

'Then if that's what you really want, I won't trouble you any more. Goodbye, Freddie.' He put the phone down.

Chapter Eighteen

There were lights showing in the window of the Pimlico gallery. Rebecca paused for a moment, then took a deep breath and went inside. The room was full of people, and she could not at first see Connor Byrne. Her stomach gave an anxious squeeze. Perhaps, after such a long separation, she would not recognize him. Perhaps he would not recognize her – she had changed in the intervening nine years. She knew she had aged.

She worked her way through the crowds, her eye caught by a sculpture coiled like a snail or a seashell, and then a tall black stone, run though with a hole the shape of an egg.

In the centre of the room, stern and monumental, a huge grey granite form prompted a flash of recognition.

A voice at her shoulder said, 'Manannan mac Lir, the sea god of the Manx. I thought you might want to make his acquaintance again, Rebecca.'

She turned. Connor was wearing a dark suit and a shirt

and tie. His curly hair, which was run through with silver, had been tamed to a parting at the side.

'Oh Connor,' she said, and all her nervousness fell away. 'How wonderful to see you again. And looking so handsome.'

His eyes sparkled. 'I'm trussed up so like a turkey, I can hardly breathe.'

'You look very smart.'

'Ah, Rebecca, you always were a kind woman.' He took her hands in his, pressing them. 'I'm so glad you came.'

'I wouldn't have missed it for the world.'

A tall, fair-haired man joined them. Connor introduced him as his agent, Adrian Calder. The three of them talked for a while and then Adrian led Connor away to meet some of the other guests.

Rebecca found a quiet spot by a wall. She watched Connor as he shook people's hands and made conversation. She remembered that there had always been something in him that had spoken to her. She had told him about her angel, when she had told no one else. She found herself recalling her meeting with Milo, and her impulse to tell him about her phone call to Tessa Nicolson, which, like a crack in glass, had altered the direction of all their lives. She had been thankful afterwards that Godfrey Warburton, crashing bore though he was, had prevented her. Her confession would have slid off Milo as a drop of water slides from a feather. But she had kept with her the intuition that she must find a way of sending out a message to whoever might want to hear.

A voice said, 'May I introduce myself? My name's Michael Lyndhurst. Dr Michael Lyndhurst.'

'Rebecca Rycroft.' She held out her hand.

He was fifty-ish, tall, handsome, distinguished-looking. 'Are you interested in sculpture, um . . .' he glanced at her left hand, 'Mrs Rycroft?'

'Yes, very. I've known Connor for some years.'

'Is your husband here?' He made to look round.

It was always best, she had found, to get it over with straight away. 'Actually, I'm divorced,' she said.

Some men saw possibilities in her status. Dr Lyndhurst, it appeared, fell into that category. He smiled.

'Let me get you another drink,' he said.

When he came back, they talked for a while about the exhibition and then moved on to the books and plays they admired. He was well-spoken and informed, but she found it hard to concentrate, her gaze always returning to the room, picking out Connor, reacquainting herself with the way he moved and the shape of his smile.

By eight o'clock the crowds had thinned out. Rebecca made her excuses to Dr Lyndhurst and went to say goodbye to Connor. Then she collected her coat and went outside.

Dr Lyndhurst was waiting on the pavement. He said, 'I thought I would take you to dinner, Mrs Rycroft.'

'It's kind of you,' she said, 'but no thank you.'

'If you've an engagement, perhaps tomorrow night.'

'I'm sorry, that's not possible.'

He frowned, then said coldly, 'I wouldn't have wasted my time if I'd known you were going to be like this.'

The gallery door opened and Connor came out. Dr Lyndhurst walked away.

Connor's gaze followed him. 'Was that fellow bothering you?'

'Hardly at all.' Rebecca sighed. 'There's a type of man who seems to believe that if he takes the trouble to talk to a woman of my age then he's entitled to go to bed with her too.'

'I'll punch him on the chin, if you like.'

'Oh, he's not worth that.' She smiled at Connor. 'Shouldn't you still be talking to the great and the good?'

'I expect so, but I'd prefer to take you to dinner, if you'd let me.'

'I'd be delighted to.'

They went to an Italian restaurant in Soho. The circular tables were dotted round a darkened basement; a jazz trio played in the corner.

Rebecca asked after Connor's family. Aoife and Brendan were both well, he told her. Brendan was due to start at university in Dublin in the autumn.

'He's to study history,' said Connor. 'He's a clever lad. I'm proud of him.'

'You're a good father to him, Connor.'

'No, that's not true. A good father would have stayed with his mother.' He lit cigarettes for both of them. 'Aoife has taken a part-time job in a draper's shop. I told her she didn't have to go out to work. I told her I would always look after her and Brendan.'

'Perhaps she wants to go to work. She'll miss Brendan. Perhaps she wants to have something else to do.'

Connor shook his head. 'Aoife's always been very traditional. She's always believed that the man should support the family and the wife should look after the home and children.'

'But your arrangement isn't traditional,' she pointed out gently. 'Perhaps she's accepted that.'

He did not immediately answer. Then he said, 'She told me that she prays every day that I'll come back to her. She'll never accept it, Rebecca. And it makes her unwell.'

'Oh, Connor.'

'I wondered whether she took the job to make me feel guilty. And then I felt ashamed of myself for thinking of that.'

'Do you feel guilty?'

'Sometimes. And if it gives her peace, poor woman, then I'm glad of it.'

'Maybe that's the price of freedom. None of us has everything we want.'

He nodded. 'I'd have come back here before, but I was concerned about Aoife. Tell me how you are, Rebecca. Tell me about your sister and her husband. Tell me about your work.'

So she did. After they had eaten, Connor ordered brandies and they drank them as they listened to the music.

'I loved your exhibition, Connor,' she said. 'It would be so hard to choose which of the works I liked most, though I think I'll always have a soft spot for your sea god. I remember you and David Mickleborough hauling the slab of granite into the barn with ropes and pulleys. I remember looking through the window of the barn and seeing that face – so strong and stern. You told me to come in and meet him. That was the first time we talked properly.'

'I was daunted by you, Rebecca. There was always something wild about you.'

'Wild?' She laughed. 'Oh, Connor, no, I was terribly tame. With my tweeds and my twinsets and my daily help and my smart little dinner parties, I wasn't wild at all. I didn't know how to be wild. I've learned, though, I think.'

He shook his head. 'No, there was always a wildness in you. I used to see you at Mayfield, out there in the field with a gale blowing and the rain pouring down, and there you'd be, stabbing your spade into the earth.'

'I expect I was imagining it was Milo.'

He laughed. 'You looked like a goddess, all wild black hair and pale skin and those flashing green eyes.'

She reached across the table and took his hand. 'I've always liked to be outdoors. Perhaps it was being stuck in the Mill House all day that drove me a little mad.'

'Do you still think of him?'

'Milo? No, hardly at all. Did I tell you that I met him in London once, a while ago? He has two daughters now. They're called Helen and Laurabeth.' Rebecca wrinkled her nose. 'Mona chose Laurabeth. Milo was always very disapproving about made-up Christian names. So funny to think of him as a family man.'

'You're a wicked woman, Rebecca.' He turned her hand over in his, rubbing his thumb across her palm. She felt the dry warmth of his skin, the cuts and calluses that scarred his hand, like her own.

He said, 'Do you know, I must have tried to draw you a hundred times, when I was in Ireland, and I never got it quite right. There's that arch to your brow that I'd forgotten, and those hollows at the corners of your mouth. I'd have to look at you long and hard to know you well enough to draw you.'

Something miraculous was happening, she thought, a change, a transformation, that she had not dared to hope for.

She said, 'Would you, Connor?'

'I am awed by your beauty, you see.'

'Oh Connor.' There were tears in her eyes. 'I'm old and worn out. I was beautiful once, but I'm not any more.'

He shook his head. 'You were beautiful then and you are beautiful now. And you will still be beautiful in ten and in twenty years' time. I know that. If I'd written down everything I wanted to say to you over these years of parting, then my letters would have been a mile long. I love you, Rebecca, and I want you to be there when I open my eyes in the morning. And if I should wake in the night I want your face to be the one I search for. I'm tired of being alone, and I'm tired of being away from you. I want to be with you all the time. I don't know how we'll work it out, you and I, me with my wife and child, you with your husband, me with my stones and you with your glass, but that's what I want. Do you think you might want that too?'

'Yes,' she said, and her heart sang. 'Yes, Connor.'

Freddie and Lewis left Lymington in the summer of 1949. They had had an offer on the house and Lewis had found work at an aeronautical engineering firm in Croydon. Throughout those last months in Lymington, Freddie had been afraid of the knock on the door, the ring of the phone – the police, the insurers, Frank Kite – their past catching up with them.

They rented a small flat in St John's Wood. Freddie found a job at an art gallery in Cork Street. The gallery was owned by a man called Caspar de Courcy, who wore velvet smoking jackets and spotted bow ties. Mr de Courcy had a mean streak – his friend Tony, who shared the flat over the gallery, let slip to Freddie one day that she was being paid half as much as her predecessor. Mr de Courcy had been doubtful about giving Freddie the assistant's job (he found male employees more reliable, he said) until Freddie mentioned that she was Gerald Nicolson's daughter. His eyes had gleamed: 'You don't own any of his work, I don't suppose?' She told him that she didn't, unfortunately. Her mother had sold what paintings she had possessed to pay for her daughters' clothing and education, and though Tessa could presumably have afforded to buy some of her father's work during her modelling days, she had not. Tessa had remembered too clearly, perhaps, Gerald Nicolson's hot temper and sarcastic tongue to want reminders of him.

Mr de Courcy gave her the job anyway. Her father's paintings, Freddie discovered, had risen in value in the years since his death. There was a childishly boastful side to de Courcy's nature; once or twice she caught him murmuring to a prospective customer, 'Yes, Gerald Nicolson's daughter, frightfully clever girl.'

She knew that Lewis didn't like her working in the gallery, but she did so anyway because both things, the job and the move to London, had been essential to her. She had needed to get her life under control again, and that meant earning her own money. And oh, the relief of being back in London, the normality of it, the rightness of it – no more marshes and mudflats, just the familiar old streets and buildings, the shops and the offices and the people and the necessary distraction they provided. Because they needed distraction these days, she and Lewis; there was so much they did not talk about, so much thin ice to be skirted round.

To begin with, Lewis's mood was low. They rarely went out, spending the evenings reading books or walking in one of the parks. Sometimes at night Freddie woke to find his side of the bed empty and heard him walking round the flat and the low rumble of the wireless. He had paid off Frank Kite with the insurance money and the profit they had made from the sale of the house. But some grubbiness persisted; something had seeped into their lives, poisoning them, and a ring at the doorbell late at night could still startle her, reminding her what fear was, that ice-cold finger down the spine, that shifting of dry land beneath her feet.

The turn of the decade seemed to provide some relief. Lewis was promoted at work and was at last achieving the success he had always sought. They moved into a larger flat and he began to contact old friends. He seemed happier, more content, more like the old Lewis. Though Freddie went with him to parties and restaurants, she preferred the company of Julian, Max and the Leavingtons, those friends who had once been Tessa's and now were hers. Julian had married and was the father of a little boy; Ray and Susan's second child, a girl, was born in July 1950.

That summer, Max held a retrospective exhibition of his work in a Soho gallery. Many of the photographs displayed were of Tessa, his muse: Tessa standing by the Serpentine, laughing; Tessa modelling evening gowns for Dior; and there was Tessa with the zebra, in the photograph that had once been in her Highbury flat. There was also a picture Freddie had not seen before. Max had taken it shortly before Tessa had left for Italy. She was sitting on a bed, wearing a pair of slacks and a short-sleeved jersey. Her arms were wrapped around her bent knees. She was wearing no make-up and her hair was falling back from her face, showing the scar on her forehead. And yet her beauty and her fragility shone through. The label beneath said: 'Tessa Nicolson 1916–1944'.

One morning, Freddie was in the small office behind Mr de Courcy's gallery, writing out a receipt for a sale, when she heard the doorbell chime. She went out to the shop. The customer was tall and fair-haired, and for a moment her heart stood still, but then, as he turned to her, she saw that it was not Jack.

He introduced himself. His name was Desmond Fitzgerald and he had known Tessa when she lived in Italy. They arranged to meet after Freddie had finished work.

Desmond Fitzgerald took her for dinner at the Savoy. He'd been meaning to speak to her for ages, he said, but he'd had a high old time finding her. He told her about his acquaintance with Tessa, from the moment they had met at the Mirabelle before the war to the day that Faustina Zanetti had told him that Tessa had died. 'Rotten thing to happen,' he said. There were tears in his eyes. 'Utterly rotten.' Then he blew his nose and told Freddie how, along with many other British and Allied prisoners of war, he had hidden for almost a year in the woods on the Zanetti estate. And how Tessa had brought them food during the winter. 'We had to take turns going to wait for her each night,' he said. 'Or the entire bloody lot of us would have hared along just to get a glimpse of her. She was a wonderful woman, Freddie, one of the best, and you should be proud of her.'

After dinner, they parted. Desmond shook her hand and they promised to keep in touch. Travelling home in the taxi Desmond had insisted on hiring for her, Freddie found herself remembering how, after their mother had died, she and Tessa had talked about her to keep her alive. Talking about Tessa to Desmond Fitzgerald, learning about Tessa's life in Italy, she felt closer to her.

She and Lewis were at dinner once, with Marcelle Scott and her friends, when someone asked after Jack. 'Jack's gone back to Italy,' Marcelle said. 'He left, oh, *ages* ago.'

Freddie found herself asking, 'Does he ever come back here? Does he ever visit?'

'No, not at all.' Marcelle looked disapproving. 'I'm rather cross with him, actually. He doesn't usually stay away so long.'

October, 1950. She had come home from work and was cutting up onions and carrots to make a stew. She heard Lewis's key turn in the lock.

He came into the kitchen. 'Freddie, we need to talk.'

'In a moment.' She scooped up chopped onions and dropped them into the saucepan. 'Just give me five minutes to get this going.'

He turned off the gas. 'Now, please, Freddie.'

She wiped her hands on her apron and followed him into the sitting room. 'Sit down,' he said. He took out the gin bottle and two glasses.

'It's all right, I don't want a drink,' she said.

'Marcelle and I have fallen in love.'

She watched Lewis pour gin, slice up lemons. His words were shocking and incomprehensible. She could not take them in.

She shook her head. 'I don't understand.'

'Marcelle and I are in love,' he said evenly, 'and we want to get married.'

'But you can't. You're married to me.'

'I'd like a divorce, Freddie.'

He put the glass on the table beside her. She stared at it, then drew back her hand and swept it off so that it shattered on the floor. 'You're married to me!'

'This isn't a marriage.' He sat down on the sofa opposite her. 'It hasn't been a marriage for years. You don't trust me and you don't need me. I'm sorry if it hurts you, but you know that it's true. You've changed, Freddie. You're not the girl I married. The things we both wanted, you don't want any more. It's my fault, of course, I accept that. But the thing is, whenever I'm with you, I can see you blaming me. I can see you remembering what I did. You don't mean to be patronizing, Freddie, but you are. When I'm with Marcelle, it's different. She doesn't know. And even if she did, she wouldn't judge me.'

She rose then, her muscles as stiff as if she had climbed a steep hill, and went into the kitchen. She took the dustpan

580

and brush out of the broom cupboard and went back into the sitting room. Kneeling down on the floor, she began to pick up the broken pieces of glass.

She said, 'So what are you saying? Are you leaving me?'

'Yes. I'll go tonight. That would be better.'

She looked up at him, eyes narrowed. 'Better for whom, Lewis?'

'For both of us.'

'You and Marcelle . . .' she said the name with venom, 'how long has this been going on?'

He looked ashamed. 'Since the beginning of the year.'

Ten months, she thought. *Ten months*. She was holding a shard of glass; she squeezed it in her hand. Blood dripped from her clenched palm. Lewis went to help her, but she rose to her feet, pushing past him, and walked to the bedroom, shutting the door behind her, wrapping her hand in her apron and pressing the bunched cloth into the cut, needing it to hurt.

Rebecca had been turning over the idea in the back of her mind since her conversation with Meriel on her wedding day. She had begun to make a series of figures from cast glass. There were seven of them in total, and they were all representations of women, *real* women – old, young, fat, thin, pregnant, barren, plain, beautiful – rather than the idealized women of art.

She used different techniques to create each figure. The first was kiln-cast from a clay model; broad-cheekboned and full-lipped, she tilted her face to the sun, her eyes closed. Her long hair fell in tight curls past her shoulders, as on the heads of the painted figures in Egyptian tombs. Rebecca called the piece 'Isis'. The next woman was wide-hipped and there were creases around her eyes and mouth. The glass she used was richly coloured, turquoises and emeralds, bronzes and browns. This piece was called 'Elizabeth'. She thought of naming her pregnant model 'Mona', decided not to, and called her 'Gaia' instead.

She made the glass sculptures over the course of a year. Connor helped her shape the moulds. At night, she dreamed of her seven women, striding over the Oxfordshire downs near the Mill House, strong and proud, stars in their eyes and moonlight piercing their transparent faces.

The final piece was technically the most difficult. It was to be a head and shoulders rather than full-figure. First Rebecca sculpted the head in wax, and then she coated the wax in a mixture of plaster and silica. When the plaster had hardened, she melted out the wax, using steam from a kettle, so that a hollow mould remained. This she filled with pieces of glass.

Then, the trickiest part. She abandoned her first three attempts, which either shattered in the kiln or failed to produce the effect she wanted. The fourth time, she part filled the mould with glass, then put a layer of crumbled clay halfway across the head. Then she filled up the remainder of the mould with more glass.

Taking the cooled and hardened object from the kiln, she controlled her excitement as she removed the plaster mould. The glass head emerged from its covering, pellucid and full of light. Then, very carefully, using first her fingers and then a soft paintbrush, she dug out the crumbled clay and saw that, as she had intended, the head was riven through with a deliberate fissure.

Freddie moved out of the flat and found rooms in South Kensington. The grim legal business of divorce was gone through, the bargaining, the settlement. She wanted nothing from Lewis. She wanted, when the divorce came through, to feel free.

Except that she didn't. You couldn't erase six years of marriage with a piece of paper. You couldn't erase the contempt she felt for Lewis or the hatred she felt towards Marcelle Scott. For months it obsessed her. Working at the gallery, travelling home on the bus, scenes ran through her head, imagined confrontations with Marcelle. In her fantasies, her words flowed fluently, scornful and crushing, while Marcelle cowered, begging for forgiveness.

Then, one day, she woke in the morning and wasn't angry any more. Instead, she was exhausted. It was an effort to clean her teeth, to dress, to go to work. She cried a lot, and, in the evenings, when she came home from the gallery, couldn't be bothered to cook, so made herself a bowl of Weetabix or a piece of toast. Her tiredness lasted for months; her doctor, writing a prescription for iron tablets, told her that her fatigue was a reaction to the trauma of the divorce. But when she looked back, she thought it was more than that. Tessa's death, the struggles of the early years of her marriage to Lewis, the fire at the boatyard: these events had heaped themselves one upon the other.

In the summer of 1951, she went to France with Ray and Susan and their children. Afterwards, this holiday seemed to her a turning point. Ray had rented a villa in Provence; Freddie helped Susan with the children and went for walks and read books. But often she did nothing but lie in the shade, a straw hat pulled over her head, her body slathered with sun cream, thinking, dozing, resting.

Often she thought about Jack. In the immediate aftermath of Lewis's desertion, she had felt too raw even to consider contacting him. Her instinct had been to retreat, not to expose herself to hurt again. And when eventually she had begun to emerge from her depression, it seemed to her that she had left it too late. More than two years had passed since they had kissed on the beach, more than two years since she had told him she did not love him. She had left him no room for doubt. Jack would have forgotten her. He would have found someone else. He had probably not been serious in the first place – Jack was so rarely serious.

She received a letter from Faustina, who had kept in touch after the war. Faustina was now married and living in Paris, where she worked as a paediatrician. She wrote that Olivia Zanetti had died. 'She was never really well after the war. It took its toll on her.' But she had some happy news as well – her sister-in-law, Maddalena, had just given birth to a boy. Guido had chosen his name – he was to be called Domenico, after their father.

Slowly, Freddie felt herself recovering. Back in London, she spent her Saturdays wandering round art galleries and antique shops. She liked to hunt for treasures in the Petticoat Lane street market. Now and then, someone asked her out on a date. None of her boyfriends lasted. They seemed to her too young, too callow, too inexperienced. Her American journalist in the war had been right, she thought. Nothing touched her; she had put up her defences. So *English*. She did not find in these men that deep-rooted attraction that she had felt at first for Lewis, and had later known with Jack.

Jack, she thought. Oh God, how she missed him.

Browsing one Saturday, she looked into the window of an art gallery in Lisle Street at the glass head of a woman. Her features were African and her long hair was tightly braided. The face was arresting, haughty and sublime.

Freddie went inside the gallery. More glass figures were displayed along one wall. A young man in a pinstriped suit approached her. 'Are you familiar with the work of Rebecca Rycroft?' he said.

Rebecca Rycroft. She knew the name, of course. Rebecca Rycroft was married to Milo Rycroft, Tessa's friend, the writer. Rebecca Rycroft had attended Angelo's funeral.

'No, not at all,' she said.

'Terribly collectible. The Americans are frightfully interested.'

'How wonderful,' said Freddie politely.

She walked from one glass sculpture to the next. The seven figures of women varied in size and style. Some were coloured, while others were made of transparent glass, but they had in common a power and strength. Each piece was entitled with a girl's name: Isis, Elizabeth, Gaia, Rachel. All the names were emblematic, Freddie noticed.

Until the last one. She had reached the plinth holding the seventh sculpture, a head and shoulders. The glass was opaque, bluish, like ice. The face would have been serene and beautiful, were it not for the fissure that ran through the glass, almost tearing it apart.

Freddie read the title printed on the label. *Tessa*. Her heart stilled.

Easy enough to murmur something about a commission and get Rebecca Rycroft's telephone number from the man in the pinstriped suit. Walking to the phone box at the end of the road, she remembered the other time she had called Mrs Rycroft, after Tessa's accident.

There was a queue outside the kiosk. Waiting, Freddie ran it all through in her mind. Milo Rycroft, Rebecca Rycroft, the glass Tessa with the deliberate crack running through it.

It was her turn. She went inside the phone box and dialled the operator.

Rebecca Rycroft lived in Hampshire, some way from the nearest railway station, so Freddie borrowed Max's large old Alvis and drove down. After Weyhill, the roads narrowed until they were no wider than the wheelbase of the car. Tall hedgerows of hazels and spindles, heavy with fruit, barricaded both sides of the road. Now and then the sunlight gave way to darkness as the car plunged through woodland.

She had to ask at a pub for directions to Rebecca Rycroft's house, which was down yet another narrow road, lined with beech trees. The Forge was a red-brick house; beside it stood a single-storey building, roofed in corrugated iron. Freddie parked and climbed out of the car. She was about to knock on the front door of the house when a woman came out of the single-storey building, wiping her hands on a cloth.

Rebecca Rycroft was wearing pale grey cotton trousers and a white linen shirt. Her black hair was swept up beneath a green headscarf. Her face was suntanned, her mouth wide and generous. Her most remarkable feature was her eyes, which were a deep and vivid green.

'Mrs Coryton.' She held out her hand to Freddie. 'How was your drive? You must be tired. I find I have to concentrate so on those little roads.'

A man, tall, with curly greying hair, looked out of the workshop. 'Mrs Coryton has arrived, Connor,' said Mrs Rycroft. 'Mrs Coryton, this is Connor Byrne.'

Freddie shook Connor Byrne's hand, then he kissed Mrs Rycroft's cheek and went back inside the long, low building.

Mrs Rycroft said, 'I thought we'd talk in the sitting room.'

As she followed Mrs Rycroft into the house, Freddie said, 'Your husband, Milo . . .'

'Milo and I divorced many years ago. He lives in America now – he has remarried and has two daughters. Connor and I live as husband and wife. Connor is a sculptor – we share the studio. We can't marry, because Connor has a wife in Ireland and she's a Roman Catholic and so won't consider divorce. I don't know that I'd marry again anyway. I love Connor very much, but I can't help feeling that one husband was enough.'

Freddie was shown into a sitting room at the front of the house. One armchair was covered in a floral fabric and the other with stripes. An entire wall was shelved with books. On a low dresser were dozens of glass objects, bowls and plates and figurines.

'Sit down, please, Mrs Coryton.' Freddie sat on the floral chair. Mrs Rycroft said, 'Would you like some tea?'

'Mrs Rycroft . . .'

'Rebecca, please.'

Freddie did not offer the same intimacy in return. Rebecca left the room. As with the sculptures in the gallery, Freddie found herself drawn to the objects on the dresser. She reached out and touched with her fingertip the smooth bubbles of glass, the waves and peaks.

'Glass is so pleasingly tactile, isn't it?' Rebecca put down a tray of tea things on a low table. 'Of course, I can't shape glass in the way that Connor shapes stone, but then you can't liquefy stone, you can't heat it and mould it.'

She handed a cup of tea to Freddie. 'But you didn't come down here to talk about glass. You came to talk to me about your sister, Tessa.'

'Yes.' Freddie looked straight at Rebecca. 'Your piece, in the gallery, the glass Tessa. It was a sculpture of her, wasn't it?'

'I never met her, but Milo had told me that she was very beautiful. And she was, wasn't she? I found images of her in libraries, in magazines and books. And I went to an exhibition of photographs.'

'Max,' she said. 'Max's photographs.'

'Yes, Max Fischer. I could see why the camera loved her. Her face had such openness and fragility. And yet there was mystery there, too. I suppose there's always a mystery to beauty. We can't quite understand why it draws us so.' She looked across the room to Freddie. 'I was sorry to hear that she had died.'

'Were you?' she said. 'I would have thought you would have hated her.'

Rebecca did not flinch. 'I did, for a while,' she said. 'My sculpture was in part a message. I thought that if you saw it, then you could decide yourself whether you wanted to know. People don't always want to know the truth, do they? Often, they hide from it. Confession can liberate the teller and destroy the recipient. I thought that this way, you could make up your own mind. And you have, haven't you, Mrs Coryton? Otherwise you wouldn't be here.'

'I think that your ex-husband, Milo, was the father of Tessa's baby.'

'Yes, he was.'

'And you knew?'

'Oh yes. For such a long time.'

'You see,' Freddie said, and her voice shook a little, 'he did such harm.'

'Yes. And so did I.'

'You?'

'I'm afraid so. Would you like me to tell you what happened?'

A silence. Then, mutely, she nodded.

'I loved Milo very much.' Rebecca sat down in the striped chair. 'I was always afraid he did not love me equally. When I found out that he was having an affair with your sister, I was enraged. There is no other word. He'd had affairs before, but this was worse, because of the child. So I telephoned your sister and told her that Milo was seeing someone else. I wanted to make her think that he didn't love her any more, that he didn't care for her or the child.' Rebecca looked directly at Freddie. 'She was upset, of course. That was why she was driving to Oxford that afternoon. She was going to see Milo. She was going to see Milo so that she could find out whether I had told her the truth.'

Freddie whispered, 'You're certain of this?'

'I can never be completely sure, but yes, I believe so.'

'And you knew — then?'

'Yes. I had hoped, when I spoke to you at the child's funeral, that I would discover that your sister had been on the Oxford road that afternoon for some other reason. But that didn't happen.'

'But you didn't tell me!'

'No.' Rebecca frowned. 'At the time, I was relieved. I suppose I thought I'd got away with it. And later, I couldn't see what good it would do. I knew that the baby had died and your sister had survived. Nothing I did would change that.'

I thought I'd got away with it. Freddie remembered the long, dreadful months that had followed Tessa's accident. She remembered Tessa's grief, Tessa's pain.

She said, 'So you just . . . you just went on as if nothing had happened?'

'No. I left Milo and tried to make a life on my own. But I couldn't, not at all. Not until I broke myself into pieces and started again from scratch.'

'It was Tessa who was broken into pieces, not you!' Freddie could no longer hold back her anger. 'And the poor little baby!'

'Yes.' That same straight, unflinching gaze. 'Of course, that's true.'

And yet Rebecca Rycroft, too, had suffered. Freddie remembered how she had felt towards Marcelle Scott after Lewis had left her. How she had brooded on her hatred, and how it had occupied her thoughts, day and night. Hadn't she, too, been broken into pieces by the destruction of her marriage? If she had seen an opportunity to make Marcelle suffer, wouldn't she have taken it?'

'I'm sorry,' she said stiffly. 'I shouldn't have shouted at you.' She took a mouthful of tea. 'You said you had to start again from scratch. How did you do that?'

'First of all, I had an encounter with an angel.'

'An angel?'

'Yes. You may think I'm mad if you wish. Perhaps I was. Oh, there were no feathered wings or haloes – he wore a cloth cap and carried a knapsack. But I believed then and I believe now that something extraordinary happened that day. Anyway, he told me to step outside. That was his advice to me, to step outside. So I did. I stepped outside my own life.'

Freddie had felt the same impulse recently. It had come to her, making up her face in the morning or hurrying down the escalator to the tube, a longing to escape from her own life. Mostly she had brushed the treacherous thoughts aside, but now and then she had found herself following them, as if down a long passageway.

She said, 'What did you do? Where did you go?'

'I went to live on a farm in Sussex. That was where I met Connor. I stayed there throughout most of the war, until my mother fell ill. It was hard, at first. I'd led a very comfortable life before, in some ways, though now, when I look back, it seems rather empty. It's strange how we can fall so easily into lives that aren't right for us. And I'm not sure it's good for us, to live only from the heart. I think we need to use our minds and our hands as well. I worked on the farm and then, eventually, I began to work with glass. It was as if I'd found a missing piece of my life. So that's my story. If there had been a way of changing the past, I would have taken it. But there wasn't, and I could talk to you about regret for the rest of my days, Mrs Coryton, and it wouldn't change a thing. Some events are like a crack in glass. They run on and on, never stopping. And all you can do in the end is to accept the past and move on.'

Freddie looked out of the window. She thought of all the terrible consequences of Rebecca's phone call. She thought of the accident and Angelo's death and Tessa's injury and disfigurement. If Angelo had not died, then Tessa would not have returned to Italy. And if Tessa had not returned to Italy, then she would not have died there. Rebecca Rycroft, Milo Rycroft – they both deserved that people should know the truth. Why should their reputations remain unblemished?

But if Tessa had not gone back to Italy, then who would have looked after the children during the war? Who would have taken food and clothing to the Allied soldiers – soldiers like Jack – in the depths of a Tuscan winter? Who would have helped lead the children to safety? *She was a hero*, Faustina had written. *She was strong and loyal and courageous and we shall always remember her and always miss her*. And Desmond

Fitzgerald: *She was a wonderful woman, Freddie, one of the best, and you should be proud of her.*

If Tessa had not gone to Italy, a multitude of lives would have been poorer. She herself would never have met Jack Ransome. She would not have known love, even though she had allowed that love to slip through her hands.

She knew that Rebecca was waiting for her to speak. If Rebecca had sent out the glass Tessa as a message to her, then what did she want from her in return? Forgiveness, she supposed. Could she? Forgiveness was not, perhaps, one of her talents. Her inability to forgive had driven Lewis away. *Patronizing*, he had called her. *You don't mean to be, but you are.*

To forgive would be a way of drawing a line. It would allow her, perhaps, to step outside.

She rose, gathering her handbag and gloves. 'I think I'll go now,' she said. 'Thank you for telling me this, Rebecca. It can't have been easy.' She looked up at Rebecca. 'Tessa never meant to hurt, but I'm afraid she did sometimes.'

'The glass figure of your sister is yours, of course, if you want it.'

'Thank you.'

Rebecca showed her to the front door. Freddie offered her hand. Then she stepped outside, into the sun. She looked back at Rebecca.

'You mustn't blame yourself, you really mustn't. Things happen, don't they, and no one's really to blame. And, you see, Tessa was always a lousy driver.'

Two things happened.

A month after her conversation with Rebecca Rycroft,

Renate Mayer died, leaving Freddie her collection of Bernard Leach pottery and a legacy of a thousand pounds. A few weeks later, Mr de Courcy threatened to dock her pay after she returned from her lunch hour three minutes late, so she gave in her notice.

The pots were transported up to London by Pickfords. They sat in Freddie's sitting room, earth-coloured and serene, a reminder of the importance of beauty.

Max came to see the pots. Freddie told him about the money Renate Mayer had left her.

'What are you going to do with it?' he asked.

'I'm going to Italy,' she said.

'Are you?' His eyes twinkled. 'Good for you, Freddie.'

Before she left London, she went to Hatchards to buy copies of Jack Ransome's books. She read them on the succession of long train journeys from London to Florence. The first book related Jack's experiences in Italy before and during the war. His second described his life in post-war Italy and a voyage around the Mediterranean.

On her first day in Florence, Freddie wandered round the city, reacquainting herself with the streets and squares. The next day, she explored the shops and bought postcards and a leather bag. She ate breakfast in the mornings at a small café on the Piazza del Duomo and returned to the same place for coffee at eleven o'clock. Sometimes she went to an art gallery or a museum, but more and more she just roamed round the city, aimless and content.

After a week, she stopped planning. Something had slipped away from her, some tension or driving force that she had become so accustomed to, she had only noticed

it when it left her. The warmth of the sun and the friend-
liness of the people were enough for her. She took pleasure
in the history and spectacle that greeted her round every
street corner and the familiar sights that reminded her that
a part of her belonged to this city. Sitting one afternoon
in the Piazza della Signoria, she recalled that this was where
her parents had first met. Her mother had told her that her
father had been working at his easel, which he had set up
in the shadow of the Palazzo Vecchio. He had been painting
the statues on the Loggia dei Lanzei. He had approached
her mother, who was travelling round Italy in the company
of an aunt, and had offered to paint her portrait. Their love
affair had been conducted in silence, because a chaperone
had always been present during the painting of the portrait.
But through look and gesture, love had been declared, and
an assignation made. After the portrait was finished, Gerald
and Christina had run away together. They had married
three weeks later in the English church in Rome.

The sun seemed to sink into her skin. Freddie was content
to sit for hours on the terrace of the café, watching the
people in the square, her gaze drifting now and then to
the candy-striped Duomo. Sometimes she lay for an entire
day on the parched grass in the Boboli Gardens, reading a
book. Or she sat on a bench, the book tucked away in her
bag, watching the Oceanus fountain. She caught a bus to
Fiesole and discovered that someone had bought the Villa
Millefiore. The crumbling frontage had been plastered and
painted, and to the side of the villa, a workman was shovel-
ling sand into a cement mixer. She remembered how, when
they had first come to live with Mrs Hamilton, she and

Tessa had been frightened of the villa's creaks and shadows. She remembered swimming in the pool and the way the soft, lacy pondweed had drifted against her limbs. She had felt so free.

Then, one morning, three weeks after she had arrived in Florence, she woke with a headache. Pulling back the curtains, she saw that the sky had clouded over. Iron grey, it hung heavy and metallic over the hot, humid city. She couldn't face breakfast; today, her aimlessness had a dispiriting quality. She felt disconnected from the city and all the rushing lives that surrounded her. This place had its darker side, the beggars crouched in the doorways, palms outstretched, and the fanaticism and cruelty that had blackened its history.

The sky cleared and the sun burned down once more as she walked to the Galleria dell'Accademia. Inside, tourists crowded in front of the works of art. Freddie tilted her head to look up at the paintings. Contorted figures writhed on the Cross and blood gouted from the slits in the flesh of Christ's white, waxy torso. A man jostled against her; dizzy and overwhelmed, she rushed out into the street.

She walked on, towards the Piazza di San Marco. She found a quiet café, where she sat down and drank a glass of water and a coffee. She knew that it was not Florence that was failing her, but her own courage. Had she got it wrong all along? What if, in the aftermath of Tessa's accident, she had set herself on avoiding adventure? And what if, in doing so, she had also avoided love? What if she had fled to safety – a safety that had turned out in the end to be illusory?

She had denied herself beauty, and she had denied herself love. She had been afraid of their transformational power – but did she intend to spend the rest of her life in flight?

Take a chance. Take a risk. Have an *adventure*.

Her headache was easing off. She left the café and walked across the square to the monastery of San Marco. Inside, the high walls kept out the heat of the sun and only a handful of people browsed the exhibits in the Museo. Slowly, she moved from one exhibit to another, and then she paused. On a painted wooden cabinet, an angel knelt before Mary. This angel had yellow hair and wore a pinkish-brown robe. His wings were gorgeous and multicoloured, decorated with stripes of yellow and cobalt blue and black and red, with a single blue eye, as on a peacock's feather, on one unfurled wing. Rebecca Rycroft's angel, with his cloth cap and knapsack, had been a very English angel. This one, thought Freddie, with his multicoloured wings and golden curls, was Italian.

Leaving the monastery, she made her way to the post office and booked an international call. In the afternoon, she returned to place the call. She stood in the booth as the operator put her through to an international exchange, who then connected her to the exchange in London. The London operator put through her call to Lewis and Marcelle's house in Chelsea. Marcelle answered the phone; after a few frozen pleasantries, Freddie asked her for Jack's address and phone number in Rome. There was a brief silence, as if Marcelle was actually considering refusing her, but then she said, 'Yes, of course,' and read out the information to her.

Freddie thanked her and cut the connection. Then she placed a second call, to the number in Rome.

Freddie sat on the terrace of the café.

On the piazza, half a dozen priests, dressed in black, headed towards the Duomo. A couple, the girl leaning her head against her boyfriend's arm, moved through the crowds. A child broke into a run, chasing a red balloon, and a dozen pigeons took off into the air. A tourist angled his camera to the Baptistry and clicked the shutter.

She saw him then, some distance away, small against the monumental edifice of the Duomo. Pale-coloured jacket and trousers, dark blue shirt, and the sunlight on his fair hair. Was it him? She could not at first be sure. She stood up, craning her neck. It *was* him – surely it was him – and her heart rose like a bird taking flight.

Jack had seen her now; he raised a hand in greeting.

She walked across the square to meet him.

JUDITH LENNOX

The Heart of the Night

Alone in Nazi Berlin, a young girl's
nightmare journey has only just begun.

In the spring of 1936 Kay Garland embraces an exciting
new life of glamour when she becomes paid companion
to Miranda Denisov.

The two girls soon become firm friends, and when
Miranda falls in love with a young Parisian, Olivier, Kay
helps her keep the relationship secret. But Miranda's
father learns of the affair and promptly dismisses Kay,
leaving her penniless and stranded in Nazi Berlin. By
chance she meets Tom Blacklock, who pays for her ticket
home, and is destined to play an important part in her
life. As for Miranda, she makes a decision that will put
her in the path of disaster.

With the outbreak of war come death and destruction
and, for both women, consuming passion, along with the
fear of losing all that they hold dear. After Hitler's defeat,
there are new dangers – and opportunities to find love
where least expected.

Acclaim for Judith Lennox's novels:

'A gripping and intelligent romance' *Good Book Guide*

'Completely unputdownable' *New Books* magazine

'A beautifully turned, compassionate novel. Judith
Lennox's writing is so keenly honest it could sever
heartstrings' *Daily Mail*

978 0 7553 4486 4

headline
review

JUDITH LENNOX

Before the Storm

A wild autumn day in 1909: Richard Finborough catches sight of twenty-year-old Isabel Zeale at the harbour at Lynmouth and is captivated by her beauty. Scarred by her past, Isabel has no intention of letting anyone get close. But Richard pursues her, and his persistence and ardour win her heart.

The couple marry and have three children, Philip, Theo and Sara. A fourth is added when Ruby, the daughter of Richard's old friend, comes to stay with them after her father mysteriously disappears. The Finboroughs' lives seem enviably perfect.

Then, in the 1930s, the reappearance of an old acquaintance turns Isabel's world upside down, while Ruby uncovers a series of dark truths about her father that lead her to a terrible conclusion. As conflicts simmer in Europe, it seems that love, war and secrets are set to tear the family apart . . .

Judith's Lennox's novels have been highly acclaimed:

'A beautifully turned, compassionate novel. Judith Lennox's writing is so keenly honest it could sever heartstrings' *Daily Mail*

'Great, old-fashioned storytelling in the best sense' *Daily Express*

978 0 7553 3134 5

headline
review

JUDITH LENNOX

A Step In the Dark

Simla, India, 1914.

Married at eighteen to the dashing Jack, beautiful Elizabeth Ravenhart is devastated when her marriage is cut tragically short.

Left penniless, Bess is persuaded by her domineering mother-in-law Cora to return to England, leaving her infant son Frazer behind until she can afford to send for him. But Cora has no intention of parting with the child, and Bess's desperate attempts to track him down come to a shattering conclusion.

Twenty years later, a knock on Bess's Edinburgh door sets in motion a chain of events that no one could have foreseen. For Frazer has come to claim his family – and his birthright, the majestic Ravenhart House. None of their lives will ever be the same again . . .

A breathtaking journey from colonial India through wartime London to the remote wilds of Scotland, Judith Lennox's stunning new novel is an unforgettable story of love and loss, greed and desire, and the secrets that can bind a family – or ultimately destroy one . . .

Judith Lennox's novels have been highly acclaimed:

'A fast-moving, complex story' *The Times*

'A beautifully turned, compassionate novel, Judith Lennox's writing is so keenly honest it could sever heartstrings' *Daily Mail*

'Great, old-fashioned storytelling in the best sense' *Daily Express*

978 0 7553 3132 1

headline
review

Now you can buy any of these other bestselling
books from your bookshop
or direct from the publisher.

FREE P&P AND UK DELIVERY
(Overseas and Ireland £3.50 per book)

The Heart of the Night	Judith Lennox	£7.99
Before the Storm	Judith Lennox	£7.99
A Step In The Dark	Judith Lennox	£7.99
The Long Song	Andrea Levy	£7.99
The Return	Victoria Hislop	£7.99
To The Moon and Back	Jill Mansell	£7.99
Stand By Me	Sheila O'Flanagan	£7.99
The Birthday	Julie Highmore	£7.99
The Only Way Is Up	Carole Matthews	£7.99
A Woman of Secrets	Amelia Carr	£7.99
The Life You Want	Emily Barr	£7.99
The Saffron Gate	Linda Holeman	£7.99
Good Things I Wish You	Manette Ansay	£7.99
The Hand That First Held Mine	Maggie O'Farrell	£7.99

TO ORDER SIMPLY CALL THIS NUMBER

01235 400 414

or visit our website: www.headline.co.uk

Prices and availability subject to change without notice.